Beloved

Jenna K. Lawson

To all the underdog men in this world and the wild, ferocious women who adore them.

Acknowledgements

I want to thank my mom for helping me bring this book to life. She was the only person I shared this project with. Not only did she dedicate her time to reading the manuscript multiple times before publication, but she challenged me to slow down my writing process in order to flesh out the plot and characters.

I love you, mom.

Author's Note

I am a huge fan of the Hades and Persephone myth, and I've always dreamt of writing my own version. When I began writing this book, I was determined to make it happen but like most of my books, the story went in a completely different direction. I derived inspiration from Sarah Ruhl's playful, wacky stage production, *Eurydice*, which I was lucky enough to see as a teenager. *Eurydice* is a retelling of the Orpheus and Eurydice myth, in which Death (the equivalent of Hades) is intent on making Eurydice his bride. While in the Underworld, Eurydice reunites with her dead father, and the theme of memory is heavily explored.

Like the play, *Beloved* doesn't follow a traditional Greek mythological retelling but seeks to build its own world, mythos, and rules. For example, the dead resemble the living, but they exist in a contained world that prevents them from indulging in worldly pleasures. *Beloved* was one of the most enjoyable books I've ever worked on because I wrote it at a very dark point in my life. The story is about rebirth, and I found the same theme cropping up in my own life.

Beloved was also the first fantasy novel I've written, a dream I've had for over ten years. The fantasy aspect of this story was very escapist for me, and I plan on building a series around this book. My hope is that every character will have a shot at their own story.

Thank you so much for showing interest in my book, and I hope you enjoy it!

Childhood Friends

Seven-year-old Theodore Kershaw panted as he wriggled underneath the sweltering playground slide, which baked in the hot late-summer sun. Conrad and his gang of fourth-grade cronies scoured the area, gravel crunching beneath their sneakers. The gravel embedded itself into Theodore's scraped knees, his single front tooth clamping down on his bottom lip as his green eyes watered. Something tugged in his chest as he sought shelter from the cruelties of recess, unaware that he was *this* close to his destination.

Whatever that was.

Even though bullies like Conrad and his gang made him feel small and helpless, Theodore *knew* he possessed a higher purpose. Even as early as two, his parents and older brothers had chased him down the street because that strange pull in his chest had urged him to look for something.

No, *someone*.

Recently, the sensation had only intensified, like he needed to use the bathroom but couldn't. Theodore's parents had taken him to the local psychiatrist, a kindly doctor who diagnosed him with severe anxiety, which explained his unrelenting stammer.

"We know you're under there, little toad," Conrad mimicked the croaking of a frog as he snapped something in half. "Why don't you croak for us?"

Tears pricked little Theodore's eyes as he drew his scuffed knees to his chest, feeling helpless, alone, and unable to defend himself. The crunch of gravel signaled Conrad's approach, his shadow bleeding through the baking plastic, except… the silhouette didn't belong to Conrad.

"Leave him *alone*!" A girl shouted fiercely. Theodore's jaw slackened as the girl planted both hands on her narrow hips. No one ever dared cross paths with Conrad Slater. "Why don't you pick on someone your own size?"

The group of boys "oohed" in unison before breaking out into mocking laughter.

"Look what we have here, boys," the ringleader shouted. "Fresh meat. I've never seen you on the playground before. Word of advice? Steer clear of pond scum like Theodore Kershaw."

The faceless silhouette assumed a fighting stance, despite her small stature. Theodore's pride felt a little bruised, some part of him wanting to shout that he didn't need some stupid girl's help. But that strange humming in his chest, like the flapping of a hummingbird's wings against his sternum, intensified with her nearness, like a physical alarm that told him he was close to finding the 'X' on the treasure map. Now he needed to dig, unless the treasure turned into something like *Jumanji*. In that case, no thank you.

Conrad and his gang laughed out loud. "Do you seriously think a pipsqueak like you could fight any one of us?"

"Try me," she challenged.

Theodore had no clue what happened next. A rush of wind, a flurry of leaves, and a cacophony of startled screams. He pressed his ear to the underbelly of the warm red slide to listen more closely, but he quickly shifted backward as something small with a mop of wild, dark hair squeezed into his already claustrophobic space. Theodore watched as the girl pushed back her mane of hair to reveal a round face with large hazel eyes, a small nose, and a wide mouth. Upon seeing his startled expression, she flashed her piranha teeth.

Several were missing, though that didn't lessen the impact of her smile. The flap of hummingbird wings in his chest softened into a low purr as he stared.

And stared.

And stared some more.

"What's the matter?" She gave him a bemused look. "Are you scared of my shark teeth?"

Theodore slowly shook his head, his gaze soft and unblinking.

"N-no," he stammered worse than ever. "You're... you're..."

Beautiful, he finished in his mind. *Exactly how I imagined you.*

Suddenly, Theodore's mind flooded with images from... *before*. Memories that made his young heart ache and rejoice in equal measures. His heart overflowed all the more because he had finally discovered his purpose.

"My name's Koreyna, but I hate being called that," she stuck out her tongue. "I prefer Korey. What's your name?"

"Theodore," he managed shyly, heat creeping up his neck.

He wanted to stroke her untamed hair because it looked so soft and voluminous, but he restrained the urge because seven-year-olds didn't act like that for one and, secondly, the nature of his memories warned him against doing so.

She may not belong to you, a voice whispered inside his head, but the warning made him want to touch her all the more.

These memories and emotions were too heady for someone his age to manage, but he had done it before.

"Theodore?" She scrunched up her nose. "Can I call you Teddy instead?"

"As l-long as you don't c-call me Teddy Bear," he glowered.

Korey laughed raucously and slapped his knee. "Boy, I like you. I think we're going to be the best of friends."

"Even with the w-way I t-talk?" Teddy rounded his shoulders with a sheepish grimace.

His stammer had never bothered her in the past, but he hated the thought of his slow manner of speech grating on her nerves. This wasn't the first time Teddy had asked, for once upon a time, life for them had been quite different.

"I don't have a problem with the way you talk," she shook her head. "If anyone tries to mess with you, they'll have to go through me first."

Teddy fell a little deeper and harder than before, rendering him immobile and speechless as his green eyes memorized her face. Like always, Korey was oblivious.

"Come on," she grabbed his wrist, jerking him out of his trance. "There's an army of pirates and robots who need our help!"

The fact that he nearly stumbled over his own feet trying to keep up with her didn't bother him at all because that's how their relationship had always been. Korey protected him in the light of day, while he guarded her from the shadows. Their childhood was filled with blistering sunburns, scraped knees, chlorine from the swimming pool, and cold Popsicles in the evening shade. After Korey stuck out her purple tongue, he showed off his orange one.

In the winter, they rolled around in the snow to trick the neighbors into believing they had been out in the cold all day so they would make them hot chocolate with extra marshmallows. They were joined at the hip upon discovering that a fence separated their backyards with a trench deep enough for either to slip through. Korey ran screaming from his house one lazy afternoon after he'd forced her to watch *Mars Attacks!* Teddy had been inconsolable, convinced that he had lost her forever, until she showed up on his front doorstep the next morning, ready to conquer her fears.

Over the years, their friendship deepened as they plucked slivers from each other's fingers, played in the mud as they pretended to build the pyramids of Giza (something Korey had read in one of her books), and scouted the banks of their favorite river for frogs and tadpoles. Korey read aloud from books as they watched the sun dip below the horizon, and sometimes they spread out a quilt on her roof to stare up at the sky. As they shopped for used books and old records as teenagers, Teddy imagined they were *more* than friends, something that was an option if he was willing to take the risk. The only question that remained was whether or not she was interested in him.

Growing up, he wasn't the only boy that noticed her. In the sixth grade, she befriended another boy who tried stealing her holographic Pokémon cards. Or, at least, that's how Teddy framed him. Naturally, he found something wrong with every teenage boy or dreamy celebrity. Like any teenage girl, she plastered posters of Legolas and Edward Cullen on her bedroom walls, and he wanted nothing more than to take a Sharpie to their faces.

Teddy hadn't encountered these obstacles before. The same distractions were available to him - perhaps more so. While the bitter ache of loneliness made those distractions tempting, he resisted in the name of love. Besides, Korey had blossomed into a full-figured beauty that made every other woman pale in comparison . There were thousands of dreams, memories, fantasies, hopes, and desires crammed into one body and, at some point, he no longer resisted inhaling the rosy scent of her hair or watching her profile as the fiery sun bathed her face in a radiant glow.

Teddy's heart ached with every pulse. Sleep evaded him. Food lost its taste. Seventeen years after that fateful meeting on the playground, he was no longer content with playing her sidekick. Enough was enough.

And so he approached Korey's family-owned flower shop with more than a century's worth of doubt. The state of the world had warned that *he* was coming, and Teddy could no longer pretend that he would stand by and watch a sinister entity embrace the woman he loved with *everything* he had. Inhaling a deep breath that failed to calm his jangling nerves, his sweaty palms slicked on the door handle as he flung it open, eager to change his destiny.

Once Upon A Time

Once upon a time, far below the earth's surface, beyond the realm of lush forests and exotic gardens, existed a place of fire, smoke, and ash. An obsidian castle hewn from the Underworld itself sat at the center of this strange universe, the residence of the dreaded ruler, Hades. Flanked by an army of shades, Hades wielded his sword against the terrors that roamed his kingdom. In battle, he proved harsh and merciless, his features hewn from the very rock that built his fortress.

He returned from these excursions spattered in blood and gore. He didn't mind the violence. It distracted him from the void that gnawed at him on those long days he sat upon his cold, hard throne, or those long, lonely nights he lay in bed, his pale skin and onyx hair bathed in rippling blue light, his arm draped across the empty space beside him. When his solitude threatened to devour him, he peered at his reflection in a hazy pool of green water beside his dead garden. Slowly, his features transformed. He watched in awe as the scene before him exploded with life and color.

Unbeknownst to him, a goddess from above, one on the cusp of womanhood, generated this life, this eternal state of spring. This young, innocent, headstrong goddess, one who loved her mother very much, was ill-prepared for the changes that were bound to disrupt her world.

And that is where our story begins...

- Beloved

How are legends born?

There's a fine line between fiction and reality that's too blurry for my taste. I was named after Persephone, the Greek goddess of spring, you know. Well, more like Persephone's lesser-known appellation, Kore. My mother discovered my curious ability to foster the growth of fruits, vegetables, and plants when I was no more than two years old. In other words, some higher power had blessed me with a magical green thumb.

As a child, I'd wanted everyone to know that I had special powers, like Matilda or Hermione Granger, but my mother naturally wanted to keep my abilities a secret for fear of how others would react. Not just our small community, but the *entire* world. Would people hunt me down with overzealous bloodhounds and pitchforks? Would government leads seek to use my power for their own selfish motives?

Doom and gloom aside, I still waited for my invitation to Hogwarts with a lightning bolt squiggle on my forehead. Spoiler alert: the damn letter never came. Since I was forced to keep secrets, I lurked on the fringes of social groups throughout my childhood and adolescence. Except for Teddy, of course. My best friend since the second grade had been a scrawny youth who hadn't liked to talk because of his relentless stammer, so he was the perfect friend for me. He kept my secrets in exchange for my protection against bullies.

During recess, Teddy and I used to race into the forest and sprawl out next to the river while I entertained him with my tricks. That was the first time I had ever heard

him laugh. When I was eighteen, a deadly contagion swept the globe that created food shortages in my community, forcing me to take action. Now that I was legally an adult, I had to accept whatever consequences that may follow. And so with everyone's watchful eyes on me, I touched the ground and allowed my magic to flow through my fingers, producing every kind of fruit and vegetable imaginable.

From that point on, everyone gathered around me as though I were a saint. My gift allowed parents to feed their starving children, especially poor families. When the pandemic ended, we celebrated with flowers exploding overhead like crackling fireworks. We danced. We drank far too much wine. Teddy tucked a flower behind my ear and watched my beaming face with shy, expectant eyes.

For the Fall Harvest Festival, I made pumpkins grow five times their normal size, until they were like the tiny homes that were popular among my generation. Everyone gathered around the massive pumpkins and gutted them so that children could float down the river that snaked through my hometown, Pebble's Creek. After the triumphant pumpkin race, people churned out hundreds of pumpkin pies. The enormous seeds were roasted in salt and butter. Women used the remnants for pumpkin spice facials that became a staple of their beauty regimens.

Even though most people in their early twenties wanted to get the hell out of our small, isolated town, I stayed behind and earned my degree online in business; my mother's flower shop was more important than big cities and fast cars. Also, people depended on me, like Miss Kitty, who needed help tending her garden. I didn't belong in a city with no connection to the earth. Where else could I experience the cool sensation of digging up fragrant soil? Where else could I bury my toes in the sand while reading saucy romance novels on the banks of the river? Where else could I ride on the front of Teddy's bicycle as we ventured into the forest for some nighttime tree-climbing?

That's right. Nowhere.

Speaking of Teddy… as though my thoughts had triggered his spidey sense, he passed the store window and pushed open the front door, the cluster of bells jingling overhead. Teddy was tall, sinewy, and lithe, his wavy, shoulder-length brown hair framing a rather striking face. The moment his jade eyes found me watering plants in the greenhouse, he vaulted over the counter and raked a nervous hand through his gold-streaked curls. Leaning against a heavy, wooden post some distance away, he quietly observed the way I serenaded the flowers and plants as I nourished them with my favorite brand of practical magic. Today, the soundtrack from *Sweet Charity* played in my head, something Teddy undoubtedly appreciated since it was the only musical he tolerated. Much to my dismay, since *Moulin Rouge!* was my all-time favorite movie. It wasn't as though I hadn't tried to indoctrinate him from an early age, but gritty crime dramas like *Taxi Driver* and *The Silence of the Lambs* were more to his liking.

No thank you.

"Hey, big spender..." I sang with an extra dose of sass on Teddy's behalf. The flowers stretched toward me as

though my breathy voice was the sun. "Spend a little time with me..."

Three days ago, I noticed more than a handful of wilted plants and flowers in the greenhouse, as though some dark force had overturned my jurisdiction. Either that, or I was losing my touch, something that... perplexed me.

Not terrified. Dismayed? Certainly.

But nothing as strong as fear.

Not yet.

Even as I struggled to reassure myself, I couldn't shake the ominous, sinking feeling in the pit of my stomach that the normally pleasant spring winds carried something dark and treacherous. I could worry about that later. Right now... well, I was embarrassed to admit that Teddy's sweet, comforting presence distracted me. It might sound strange, but I could almost see his aura, or at least sense its vibration whenever I closed my eyes or accidentally brushed his hand, something that was happening a lot more frequently lately.

Three nights ago, his warm, calloused hand had brushed mine as we gazed up at the smattering of constellations on my slanted roof, a homemade quilt spread out beneath us. Normally, he froze, turned beet red, and stammered an apology whenever he accidentally touched me, but not this time. Instead, his eyes had sought permission to do... *something*. And then his long fingers had caressed the inside of my palm, carefully tracing every line

and crease. My eyelids had fluttered closed so I could concentrate on the sensation of him touching me.

We hadn't moved for hours, not until a cold spring rain had chased us down the ladder. I had ignored the way he'd closely watched me, as though seeking a particular reaction, his dark hair plastered to his face, equal measures of longing, hope, and fear in his eyes. I couldn't bring myself to acknowledge his actions... especially now that several days had passed. Hell, I'd noticed the way he'd watched me over the years, even when he thought I was oblivious. Men of all ages had given me yearning looks since I was a teenager, especially after my magic had been exposed, but even now I was forced to turn interested suitors away because my overprotective, albeit loving mother expected nothing less.

Twenty-four years into my existence, and I still couldn't date or flirt. I hadn't even been kissed, save for the ones my grandmother peppered all over my face while squeezing my cheeks. Even though I seemed like a happy-go-lucky young woman on the surface, sometimes the deep longing for something more drove me crazy, so I channeled my frustration into my magic, creating otherworldly flowers and creeping vines no one was able to identify. Teddy's shy touch had been my first taste of sexually charged intimacy, something I didn't take lightly. So, one could imagine that I was quietly losing my shit.

"Why h-haven't you stopped by the s-shop?" Teddy asked quietly, the accusation heavy in his voice.

I glanced over my shoulder with a small huff. "Have you seen these plants? They're dying. I've been wracking my brain for days, but I can't figure out why my magic isn't working. Do you think I'm losing my touch?"

The diversion was sincere, yet effective. Teddy pushed off from the wood post and towered over me as he neared. He surveyed the wilting flowers for a long moment, humming low in his throat.

"Patrick c-came by my dad's shop t-today and said four of his c-cows were found dead on the outer l-limits of his p-property," he informed me slowly, making my eyes widen in horror.

"What happened?" My hand covered my mouth. "Do you think a wolf attacked his cows?"

"The cows w-were untouched," he stammered, the softness of his brilliant eyes making my stomach flutter uncontrollably, even in light of the tragic news.

"Do you think they'll cancel the spring festival?" I asked worriedly.

Teddy gave me a pointed look, though he couldn't resist flashing me a wry half-smile.

"I t-think the town has b-bigger fish to fry, don't you?" He arched a brow, his tone reprimanding.

"Sorry," I shook my head as though hoping to unscramble my brain. "The town is our priority, especially after everything the community has been through."

Nearly six years ago, a vicious contagion that earned the nickname The Red Death had swept the world into a maelstrom of death, uncertainty, and instability. Even as crops the world over withered and decayed, my magic alone had sustained the remote mountain town of Pebble's Creek. The tales of the Bubonic plague had become legend over the centuries, but nature had turned legend on its believers as though indulging in some private joke.

"Why h-have you been avoiding m-me?" Teddy called my bluff.

My hazel eyes widened, shocked by his uncharacteristic bluntness.

"I haven't been avoiding you," I wiped my hands on my floral apron and brushed past him.

"Like you're d-doing now?" He followed in hot pursuit.

I whirled on my heel and planted my hands on both hips, ready to snap that my mother would skin him alive if she caught him following me like a lost puppy... but his normally pale face was splotchy, his breathing slightly ragged, his hair tousled, and his green eyes tender. He took a step closer.

"Korey," he murmured, eyes blazing. "I d-don't care if we get in t-trouble. I c-can't wait anymore. Korey..." He took another step closer. "I'm... I'm in l-love with you."

At that precise moment, the world disappeared, except for Teddy and I. On some level, I had known this for

years, had even hoped for it, but what could I do with this information?

"What?" Hot tears rimmed my eyes.

"You k-know what I said," he shook his head slowly. "You've k-known for a l-long time, haven't you?"

I couldn't deny the truth of his words. Our relationship had always felt more special than a friendship, even in childhood. And I had loved him as my friend, confidante, and forbidden fancy. But even now at twenty-four, would my mother allow it? What if I rejected him in favor of my family? Would he eventually fall in love with someone else?

The thought plunged through me like a hot dagger. What if I disobeyed my mother? It wouldn't be the first time. What if Teddy and I kept our relationship a secret? Images of clandestine meetings flooded my mind, and I brightened with the possibility. I had an idea.

"Meet me by the river tomorrow morning," I grabbed one large, pale hand and kissed his knuckles. The gesture filled me with a delicious warmth. "Our usual place."

Teddy's brow furrowed in confusion, but he nodded as his eyes searched my face for a better answer.

"Tomorrow," I promised and since showtunes were on the brain from earlier, combined with the fact that I was a certified dick, I burst into song, waving my arms overhead as though tracing a rainbow. "Tomorrow! Tomorrow! I love ya, tomorrow!" Teddy groaned as I grabbed a broom and used the handle as a microphone. "You're only a day away!" ~

I spent the rest of the afternoon breathing new life into the wilted plants and riding my bicycle throughout town to deliver flowers for the spring festival. Everywhere I looked, fresh tulips and daisies shuddered from the lingering winter chill. Even though the wind nipped and the brisk air teased goosebumps to life on my bare arms, I wore a jade floral sundress with flouncy sleeves and wildflowers woven through my hair. My soles were black from walking barefoot, a habit Teddy found endearing.

Teddy...

The memory of his stammered words plucked some long-buried chord deep within me that radiated through my fingers and toes. Oh God, what would my mother think when she found out? Unlike other young men around my age, she trusted him implicitly. Sure, she forced me to keep my bedroom door open when we hung out. When we were children, Teddy once removed his shirt in the July heat and chased me around the neighborhood. At ten years of age, I was already keenly aware of my mother's stance on members of the opposite sex. So when Teddy leaned against the hood of her car and adopted the smug air of Casanova, the only thing I'd managed to do was drag him away before my mother could see him.

That had been the first - and for many years - only sign that he'd liked me as more than a friend. Every other

attempt on his part had left me second-guessing myself. Had that lingering stare been real or imagined? Growing up, everyone thought we were meant for each other because of how close we were. Plus, we complemented each other well.

I was the brash, outspoken one, whereas he possessed his own quiet brand of strength with his wry comments and dry wit. The gossip had made both of us consider each other in that shy, timid way young lovers often do when first taking notice of each other. I thought of all the times other girls had shown interest in him - and how he'd ignored them as if they hadn't existed. I remembered when Teddy and I had gone to our senior prom as friends, how he'd edged closer to me as we watched our classmates dance... until Rex, the blonde, chiseled star quarterback of the football team had asked me for a slow turn on the dance floor. When I'd accepted, Teddy hadn't spoken to me for weeks like I had somehow betrayed him.

Come to think of it, there were times I caught him staring at me in a way that suggested he knew something I didn't, and I was desperate to know his secret. That didn't resolve the issue of my mother's protestations, however. By the time I got home, my stomach was a tangled, writhing mess of nerves. My mother and I lived in a spacious two-story house on the outskirts of town with the Kershaw household adjacent to ours . The edge of our garden met the fringe of dark, lush forest Teddy and I so often explored - sometimes with long sticks we used to duel with. I won most of the time, or at least he *let* me win.

"I'm home!" I wiped my dirty feet on the welcome mat as the screen door collided with my back.

The living room was furnished with exotic, tasseled cushions and statues of elephants. The rich, spicy scent of sandalwood burned in the air. My mother was basically the town's resident hippie, which was quite an anomaly in a place filled with truckers and farmers. The dream catcher hanging on the front door had at first been misconstrued as a pentagram upon our arrival, but then my mother had started teaching yoga classes downtown that slowly morphed into crystal bowl meditations. The Kershaw family inviting us over for dinner sealed the deal in terms of the community accepting us, but still…

Aside from Teddy, my mother and I had always been the best of friends. Us against the world, she would always say. Our living room was a testament to that. Framed photographs decorated every surface. Memories from our trips to Alaska and South America. A picture of my four-year-old self dressed as a cow for Halloween nestled in her protective embrace. A picture of my ninth birthday party at the dinosaur park.

These memories were small reminders of every moment she had loved and protected me. And now Teddy was challenging me to step outside of the safety net she had created for me the day I was born.

"Dinner is ready!" She hollered from the kitchen. "Vegetarian chili and cornbread, your favorite."

Now that she mentioned it, I inhaled a delicious combination of warm butter and a variety of tangy spices that made my mouth water. I rounded the corner to find her ladling chili into a purple ceramic bowl, one she had made herself, from the crock pot.

"Not that I'm complaining, but isn't vegetarian chili and cornbread our Thanksgiving tradition?" I asked while sniffing the air.

She continued stirring the chili.

"It's nice and chilly outside," she winked in response. "How about a bowl of chili for a chilly night? Get it?"

"Oh my God," I groaned. "That was possibly your worst pun ever."

"Teddy would've loved it," she traced an imaginary tear down her cheek. "If he were here right now, I wouldn't have to suffer your abuse."

My nerve-endings prickled at the mention of my best friend, though I said nothing. My mother cautioned me as she handed over a scalding bowl of chili topped with grated cheese and sour cream. We sat at the round table that overlooked the garden. The table itself was Moroccan with an overlay of colorful mosaics - all rich cobalt blue, saffron gold, and ruby red. I tasted my first bite of chili and an explosion of flavor played on my tongue. Cumin, cayenne pepper, juicy tomatoes, chickpeas, onions, and black beans. A ribbon of melted cheese dangled from my mouth in a very lady-like fashion.

"So how was your day?" My mother tackled her own bowl of chili with a prim sort of refinement that I had always lacked.

My stomach dropped. Was this my moment to reveal the truth?

"Good," I dabbed my mouth with a napkin, which gave me an excuse to avoid eye contact.

A pregnant pause.

"Did anything special happen today?" She pressed.

This wasn't an uncommon question for her to ask, but I had a sneaking suspicion she was baiting me on purpose. I was a terrible liar. I was all surface with no hidden depth. Who was I kidding? She would eventually find out.

"Actually, yes," I sat a little straighter. I met my mother's curious gaze. "A man visited the shop today and we... talked. For a long time. He said... Well, he said he'd like to see me again and... I want to see him, too." My mother froze. Words began tumbling from my mouth. "I'm twenty-four-years-old. I've never been on a date or kissed a man. I don't understand why you're so insistent that I remain alone forever, but I'm tired of waiting! I'm tired of watching my friends travel, get married, and have babies. Not that I want kids, but I'd like to feel as though I have the option."

The blood drained from my mother's face

"Um," she tucked a lock of pale blonde hair, the color of wheat, behind her ear.

Her eyes, a bright sky blue, made me think of freedom. That was precisely what I craved. I had a good life. A *great* one, in fact. But life could be a little sweeter if I was allowed to experience life outside of a romance novel. I watched my mother gather her bearings, silent and hopeful.

"Was this man a stranger? Have you met him before?"

A million conflicting thoughts scrambled my brain, but ultimately I chose a lie. I didn't want my mother to discourage my friendship with Teddy if she disapproved. I had to test the waters first.

I licked my lips. "He was a stranger." I searched my brain for an adequate physical description, landing on one from my favorite retelling of the Hades and Persephone myth, one I had read hundreds of times over. For many years, the man described on the page had haunted my dreams. Teddy was the boy-next-door who made my stomach flutter, whereas the other promised something dark and forbidden. "He was tall and strong with broad shoulders and a thick head of near shoulder-length black hair. He almost looked Spanish or Portuguese with his dark, glossy hair and pale, pale skin." The image in my mind was clearer than crystal. "He had a sharp, jutting nose, high cheekbones, and a full, pink mouth. Have you ever seen a man like that before?"

My mother stared at me with shock written all over her face, but her eyes… they were filled with the deepest sorrow that immediately speared me with guilt for having lost myself in a description that wasn't Teddy. At the same time, the presence of this fantasy didn't negate my longing for him. How often had I noticed the way he towered over me with that strong, lithe body of his? How often had I longed to play with his overlong hair or graze the stubble on his jaw when he forgot to shave?

My mother closed her mouth with a steely edge. "Yes, as a matter of fact, I know him quite well, and I forbid you from speaking to him. Do you understand? In fact, I'll drop by the shop tomorrow to make sure he doesn't come sniffing around. Let me handle him."

Tears glistened in my eyes.

"That's what you always say," I gestured helplessly. "Are you ever going to treat me like an adult?"

She reached across the table and grabbed my hand.

"I know I seem unreasonable," she whispered, squeezing my fingers for reassurance, "but you need to trust me. I know sometimes you feel like you're never going to have a life outside of me, but there's so much I'm not allowed to tell you. Trust me," she said emphatically, squeezing my hand harder, "and I promise you'll have everything you've ever dreamed of. Okay?"

A lone tear cascaded down my cheek. "Okay," I murmured as a plan solidified in my mind. "Do you mind opening the shop for me tomorrow morning? I have a few errands to run."

My mother opened her mouth as if to protest, but promptly closed it.

"Of course," she smiled weakly. "What errands?"

My spoon scraped the bottom of my bowl as I languidly stirred.

"Teddy and I are going to deliver some flowers," I stirred faster. "It might take a few hours."

A relieved smile graced her mouth. My mother loved and trusted Teddy like the son she'd never had. With any luck, she wouldn't suspect a thing.

Acid Rain

Early the next morning, I journeyed to our usual spot, a patch of grass between two large oaks that overlooked the gurgling river. I was keenly aware of the birds chattering overheard as I spread a patchwork quilt on the ground. I placed the picnic basket and two empty wine glasses on the blanket, my nerves fluttering pleasurably. I mean, he told me he was in love with me, so what did I have to lose?

I'd kept him at arm's length for years because of my mother's strictures, but our bond had been rife with emotion from the beginning, something that was difficult to explain. Last night I'd created a playlist of his favorite music and gathered a variety of fruits we could sample to help us transition from friends to something more. I waited before my simple offering, my eyes scanning the early morning fog that shrouded the clearing in mystery. I anxiously wrung my hands as I waited.

And waited.

And waited some more.

My eyes widened and mouth stretched into a broad grin as Teddy emerged from the mist, his expression unreadable as he steadily approached with long, purposeful strides. The ragged breath he sucked in betrayed the nerves hiding behind the seriousness of that expression, one I had seen countless times over the years whenever he faced something larger than himself. The moment his jade eyes clapped on mine, something tugged deep inside of me, as though dislodging a compressor that had contained every racing heartbeat, every wave of goosebumps, and the overwhelming knowledge that the man before me was someone I could trust with my life. Even as years of repressed longing rushed to the surface, I knew only peace.

When he noticed the spread on the quilt, he brightened like the dawning of a new day, positively luminous. We enveloped each other in a tight embrace as his hard body collided with mine. I had hugged him thousands of times, but now our hands roamed each other's bodies. My hands smoothed a path up his lean back while he tangled his hands in my long, dark hair. Teddy smelled faintly of musk and salt, his forehead glistening with a sheen of sweet as I pulled away from him.

The scent was… pleasant. Arousing, even. Heat pooled in my lower belly as I deeply inhaled his masculine musk. Never before had I smelled anything like it. His chest rapidly rose and fell, a tremor coursing through his body as his eyes memorized every detail of my face. His lips parted slightly as though he wished to speak, and the way the corners of his wide mouth clung together shattered my patience. Tangling my fingers in his golden brown curls, I drew him close and kissed him with the tenderness and innocence of two best friends discovering each other for the first time. Teddy kissed me with a tremor of uncertainty, and I noticed he kept his eyes open as though hardly believing what was happening to him. I detached my lips from his to kiss every inch of his face, savoring the taste of salt on my tongue.

"God, I l-love you," he breathed as I tasted his neck.

"I'm fairly certain I've been in love with you for years," I panted as I tugged on his clothing.

Teddy caught my wandering hands before they could venture too far. "Pretty sure?"

I stared up at him.

"What do you expect?" I shrugged. "My mom is protective of me. I've never rebelled against her before, but I wouldn't change anything."

His expression relaxed a fraction of an inch.

"I've n-never kissed a girl b-before," he confessed breathlessly.

My jaw slackened. "Never?"

"I've been w-waiting for you," his eyes gleamed with an emotion I couldn't place, his half-smile modest yet barely contained.

I couldn't believe he'd waited patiently for so many years to share this experience with me. I had always assumed that he never flirted or dated because he was painfully shy. To think he had denied himself the pleasure of a woman's touch on my behalf moved me beyond words.

"Why don't we sit down?" I gestured to the blanket as we sank to our knees.

I opened the picnic basket and withdrew a cluster of purple grapes.

"Lie down," I whispered.

Teddy sprawled out on the quilt, one trembling hand resting on his stomach, and I twined my body around his as the grapes dangled above his mouth. To be honest, I felt a little cheesy and stupid for replicating something I had only ever seen in movies, but I quickly forgave my lack of experience, and instead drew upon every erotic short story and grand, sweeping romance I had ever read. As I lowered the cluster of grapes, I stroked the opposite side of his face and neck with my free hand.

"Eat," I beckoned as I ran my fingers through his rumpled hair.

His teeth flashed white as he plucked each grape from its stem. I snagged his malleable earlobe with my own, something I had always fantasized about, and his soft, erotic whimper surpassed my expectations. Once he finished, I rose on my elbows and tasted the sweet juice on his lips, tracing the seam of his mouth with my tongue. Teddy moved quickly and rolled over on top of me, pinning me beneath his comforting weight, and our eyes locked the moment we both realized he was hard.

I wrapped my legs around Teddy's waist as he fished inside the picnic basket for a peach, one I had grown myself using my magic. Teddy's jade eyes were adoring as he grazed the fuzzy, sweet-smelling fruit along my cheek and jawline. As though reading each other's minds, we each took a lusty bite from the peach at the same time. Juice squirted everywhere as we devoured the fruit, the taste sweeter than

any ordinary peach. The fruit had an almost aphrodisiac-like effect as our wet, open-mouthed kisses filled the otherwise peaceful morning.

My breasts ached strangely as he kissed my throat and collarbone, and I couldn't resist slipping the spaghetti strap of my sundress down one shoulder in a silent invitation for him to devour me as hedonistically as the peach. God, why hadn't Teddy shown me this hidden part of himself earlier? The moment I bared my breast, he froze, suddenly unsure.

"Are we r-really doing this?" He stammered, even as the heat of his gaze traced my pink areola. "Korey," he sighed wistfully, "you have n-no idea what I've imagined d-doing to you."

I squirmed beneath him, making him wince in the sweetest combination of pleasure and pain.

"Show me," I challenged and arched my back. "Please."

Teddy's eyes widened and, for a moment, I recognized the waif-like boy I had found hiding on the playground and remembered the way he'd stared up at me as though I were an angel rescuing him. That look of awe had never faded, but the expression had transformed from one of child-like innocence to testosterone-fueled hunger. Clearly unwilling to waste one more second on doubting where he stood with me, Teddy peppered my face with frantic kisses as he massaged my breast, edging closer with every brush of his lips and tongue, until his hot mouth

engulfed my nipple. I tossed back my head in rapture at the sensation of hot, slick wetness tugging on my breast.

Tugging on my other spaghetti strap, he practically inhaled my other nipple, sucking and licking with surprisingly competent kisses that made every touch seem more raw and genuine. I adored the way his hair tumbled into his eyes. I adored the way he panted and gasped for breath as he ground his hips into mine. Where had he been hiding all my life? Why the hell had he waited so long?

Teddy reached between our bodies and hiked up my dress so that his fingers could trace… *down there*.

Down there?

To think I had been an avid romance reader since I was twelve. His pink, kiss-swollen lips curved in a disarmingly lopsided smile that betrayed his immense satisfaction.

"You're s-so wet," he breathed. "I've always w-wanted to m-make you wet."

I shuddered as his fingers pushed deeper and explored my oversensitive cleft, the touch shocking and embarrassing, but also incredibly arousing. Teddy withdrew his fingers and admired the way the streams of pale light slanting through the branches overhead made them glisten. And then he sucked my juices off his fingers, making me gasp in shock. Sure, I had read about devilish rogues getting hanky panky in the bushes with innocent virgins before, but to witness my best friend tasting something so intimate and

personal made me want to scream. God, I needed a life outside of plants and magic.

"What's w-wrong?" He gave me a bemused look, my wetness making his parted lips shine. "You asked m-me what I d-dream about."

This was true.

"What else do you dream about?" I asked with a note of eager apprehension. "So we're on the same page."

Teddy shrugged and pushed the mop of hair back from his eyes, shy and guarded once more.

"I w-want to... you know," he gestured helplessly as his face reddened like a tomato. "Lick you." His voice dropped as his eyes bore a hole in my lap. "Down t-there."

Ah, so he was just as bad at dirty talk as me. Good to know we had one more thing in common. A range of conflicting emotions surged through me. Shock that my childhood best friend often fantasized about licking Miss Kitty. I couldn't fathom why a man would find that part of a woman's body appealing, but Teddy's plaintive voice convinced me that he really, really wanted to taste my lady parts, which strangely made me burn. The thought made me scoot forward and slip off his unbuttoned flannel shirt before tugging his ratty t-shirt over his head.

Teddy wasn't a male model by any stretch of the imagination, but I found his pale body strangely appealing. He sucked in a breath each time my fingers grazed his abdomen, as though painfully aware of my touch. Impatient,

I unbuttoned his jeans and eased them down his hips, his massive erection testing the elasticity of his white boxer-briefs. I gripped him through the fabric and pumped several times as though I were a professional.

"What else do you dream about?" I gazed up at him innocently, the gentle breeze tousling my loose curls.

Teddy covered my hand with his own and slowly eased the front of his boxer-briefs down, until we were skin-on-skin. I had trouble making eye contact with his prodigious length (God, I've read too many Kathleen E. Woodiwiss novels), but I also couldn't tear myself away from the dusky, pulsing rigidity of him gripped tightly in my hand.

"Do you dream about me touching you like this?" I asked innocently.

I hated myself for asking questions that would force Teddy to give detailed explanations, especially since I knew he hated stammering through a conversation that was important to him. He nodded mutely, tightening his grip on my hand.

"Does this feel good?" I asked gently.

He bobbed his head, his jade eyes narrowed to slits as he watched me through a haze of pleasure.

"Can I m-make love to you?" He stammered nervously.

I pushed my dress down the length of my body, until my hair lapped at my naked back, every feminine curve on display. I stretched out on the blanket before him and propped my legs open the way a femme fatale would, a front I used to hide the shy, vulnerable, inexperienced young woman about to make love to her best friend on the same riverbank they had captured frogs, fish, and tadpoles. Teddy pushed down his boxer-briefs and slowly crawled up my body, trailing sweet kisses along my torso until his hips were aligned with mine. Our harsh, panting breaths intensified as the head of his *cock* dipped inside my wet heat.

Slowly, carefully, he eased inside of me, and I cried out as something tore, easing the transition in spite of the pain. I spread my legs wider as Teddy stretched my tight opening, the discomfort almost unbearable. Instinctively, I contracted my walls and Teddy shuddered violently, though he remained utterly still as he kissed my face and stroked my hair. I would never forget the way he patiently waited until I was ready for more, placing my needs above his own, while showering me with affection. An uncharted world lived within my newfound lover, and I wanted to know *everything*.

As my body relaxed and my whimpers became soft moans from the sheer power of our joined bodies, Teddy slowly withdrew, his mouth hot on mine as he thrust deep inside once more. My eyes fluttered closed as he kissed one side of my face while stroking the other, the slick sensation of our bodies moving harmoniously tearing soft cries from

my throat. Over the years, I had imagined what sex might feel like, but nothing came close to the almost transcendental pleasure that bathed me in a white, incandescent light. As the rate of his hips accelerated, they began to roll against mine in a sensual rhythm that took my breath away. That peculiar ache between my thighs intensified with every stroke, until the tension in my lower belly unfurled, my body soaring through ecstasy as I convulsed around him. My eyes fluttered closed as my breasts trembled. I writhed on the quilt and, when I opened my eyes, Teddy watched me with such love and tenderness that it broke my heart.

"I love you, Teddy," I reached up and caressed his cheek.

The words were barely out of my mouth before his insatiable lips were on mine. I poured my heart and soul into the kiss, until he trembled violently with the delectable taste of his high-kenning cry on my tongue. He collapsed on top of me as his arms gave way, and I wrapped my legs around him to prevent him from withdrawing because I never wanted to exist without him.

"Damn, Teddy," I stretched my arms overhead while he regained his composure. "For someone claiming inexperience, you sure know what you're doing. What other tricks do you have up your sleeve?"

Laughter exploded from him and vibrated through my body.

"My only s-secret is that I l-love you," he murmured. "And t-that I don't w-want you dancing with anyone else at the spring f-festival. Only m-me."

"You're adorable when you're possessive," I teased and kissed his sweaty forehead, but he only hummed a response as he drifted off to sleep.

~

The deep rumble of thunder overhead roused us from our slumber, and we scrambled for our clothes as fat raindrops splashed from the black storm clouds choking the once beautiful sky. The sweet mountain rain of Pebble's Creek was normally cool and refreshing, but this downpour made my skin burn like acid. Teddy shucked his worn flannel shirt and draped the clinging fabric around my shoulders as our heavy footfalls splashed through muddy puddles.

"My grandma's quilt," I reached for our picnic spread as he tugged on my arm. "What about the picnic basket?"

"We'll g-grab everything l-later," Teddy reassured through chattering teeth. "Come on."

Before I turned my back on the happy memories we had created beneath the canopy of trees, I gasped as more than a dozen rotting fish bobbed along the river's current. The hairs on the back of my neck prickled.

Something dark lurks on the horizon, my brain warned.

~

Teddy captured my burning lips on the outskirts of the forest, and I watched the way his lean, sinewy body vaulted over the rotting fence after giving me one final, soulful look. I removed my sandals and covered my head with the flannel shirt as I powered my legs through the long, wispy grass. A dense forest surrounded the small town of Pebble's Creek, the swift, unforgiving river carving a path through main street. I could see my family's flower shop with the large greenhouse in the back. That was my destination.

I should've returned two hours ago, but I'd been too busy smooching Teddy to notice the time. I imagined the way his sly mouth curled in that familiar half-smile, his jade eyes bright with intelligence and secrecy. I remembered the tangle of our limbs as we slept naked in the shadow of our favorite trees. I shook my head as I wiped acid raindrops from my eyes, the slow burn making my vision blur. I could dwell on those moments later. Right now I needed to open the shop and figure out what the hell was going on.

The moment I found coverage, I sighed in relief and crouched to retrieve the small brass key from underneath the welcome mat. Suddenly, the pressure in the air changed. A low hum vibrated through my core, as though I had sensed the strum of guitar strings through my body. My skin prickled with a sort of unease that wasn't wholly unpleasant.

"I understand that's the oldest trick in the book," a low, smooth voice mused from behind, making the guitar strings strum harder.

I straightened and whirled around to face the epitome of tall, dark, and handsome. The man's oddly striking face was a collection of sharp and soft features, his wide mouth irresistibly full and pink, his nose large and hawkish, and a cascade of tousled black waves framing a sharp, unearthly pale face.

The face of the man that had haunted my dreams for years.

The black suit and dress shirt he wore were impeccable, the silver tie and black Oxfords creating a strange combination of gloomy, sophisticated, and sexy. He towered over me with his broad shoulders, a black umbrella shielding him from the acidic gale. I shifted uncomfortably beneath the weight of his gaze, powerfully aware that my hippie dress clung to my body. More than that, I hated myself for finding this man incredibly attractive, even as my thighs were slick with Teddy's release.

"I would make polite conversation and ask if you're from around here, but the fact that I've never seen you before says otherwise," I wrapped Teddy's flannel shirt around me for protection from this intruder. "Are you lost?"

"Hardly," he eyed the worn flannel shirt with disdain, though his expression softened once his amber eyes returned to my face. "Actually, I've been looking for *you*."

"Oh?" I maintained a neutral tone and expression.

"I recognize you from the newspaper," he nodded encouragingly. "The beautiful young woman from a backwater town who single-handedly sparked the world's imagination."

"More like appetite," I corrected with a forced smile.

One corner of his mouth quirked upward in faint acknowledgement of my corny joke. I couldn't stop making eye contact with him. The man's irises were the exact shade of sunlight slanting through a glass bottle of root beer. God, did sex make a woman hyper-aware of every remotely attractive male? I struggled to remember the euphoria that had coursed through my veins mere seconds ago,mmy head was more whipped than a bowl of mashed potatoes.

Even though I'd only enjoyed my first taste of sex that morning, I briefly wondered what this man's ripe lips tasted like. As though reading my thoughts, his amber eyes twinkled knowingly. Horrified, I whipped my thoughts back into shape, reminding myself that I couldn't throw away my lifelong friendship with Teddy for a fine piece of ass. Friendship? Fine piece of ass? Right then I wanted to smack myself in the head with a hammer.

"I appreciate your open admiration, but I'm actually seeing someone," I chewed my bottom lip as I gauged his reaction. "He may not seem like the jealous, possessive type, but he wouldn't appreciate your flattery."

There. I had successfully asserted a boundary. The strange man's eyes glittered malevolently; his wide mouth curved in a deep frown. My back collided with the purple door of the flower shop as he grabbed the flannel shirt and tossed the well-loved garment aside, as though my boundaries were meaningless to him. I watched Teddy's token of love flutter to the ground. I lunged for my security blanket, but the man steered me in the opposite direction.

"Why not introduce me to the finest coffee shop Pebble's Creek has to offer?" His velvety voice was equal measures of bitter and sweet, sort of like dark chocolate, as he ushered me under his umbrella. "I'm *dying* to know more about you, Koreyna Sakis."

Great. Of course he knew my full name. Damn publicity.

"What do I call you?" My eyes focused on memorizing his face so the police could later create a composite sketch based on his likeness.

"I'm a tax collector by trade," he shrugged elegantly, "so you might as well call me Death."

Monster

Everyone on main street stopped and gawked at the man holding me captive.

"Is that young Korey Sakis with a dark, brooding stranger? Where's that stammering Kershaw boy who usually trails after her?" I could practically hear the flurry of questions in my mind, my perception of their thoughts tainted by things I'd overheard in the past, and the small-town gossip swirling below the surface made my cheeks burn.

Hyper-aware that our arms were linked, I shrugged him off and created much-needed space, my cold reception earning a sidelong glance from my companion. On the bright side, Death the Tax Collector was less likely to murder me because everyone in town had seen me strolling through the historic downtown with him. As we approached The Bluebird, I caught a glimpse of our reflection and paled. My cobalt blue dress with the plunging neckline was practically glued to my skin, exaggerating my large bust and the swell of my hips. My hair was a tangled, sex-rumpled mess from my excursion with Teddy, my large eyes overbright, and my skin practically glowing.

My lover's touch had awakened something in me that had lain dormant for years, and the sight of Teddy's handiwork had the power to make me dissolve into a puddle, if not for the dark presence that loomed behind me. The stranger's amber eyes were also fixed on our reflection, the twist of his lips making the air crackle between us. I turned away from the glass window and stared up at his pale face, and I was met with a look of absolute starvation.

"Here we are!" I gestured brightly to the front door, ignoring the heat that crept up my neck. "The Bluebird is famous for their sweets and baked goods. I recommend ordering a cinnamon roll along with your coffee if you have a sweet tooth like me." I checked my wrist, momentarily forgetting that I wasn't wearing a watch. "Well, look at the time. My mom will be furious with me when she realizes that I didn't open the shop."

The stranger arched one inky black brow, challenging me to stay.

"Didn't you agree to coffee and conversation with a curious spectator?" His sultry voice was as smooth and sweet as a milk chocolate truffle. To be honest, I preferred dark chocolate with flecks of sea salt. Or, at least, that's what I told myself as I crossed my arms in defiance. "Surely you can spare thirty minutes of your time? After all, I've traveled all this way to meet you. It would be rude of you to decline my offer, and I know you well enough to predict that you won't."

Despite the honeyed sweetness of his tone, something dark and forbidden lurked beneath the surface of his veneer that made me tremble, giving me no choice but to accept. I didn't protest when he placed a large hand on the small of my back and guided me inside the diner, my spine tingling from both fear and excitement. I had to keep my wits about me, though. It didn't matter if he was the most striking man I had ever seen; he could be a psychopath for all I knew. A psychopath I had agreed to share coffee and conversation with.

The Bluebird was a small-town diner that was the real deal, not some diner with a jukebox that strove for a 1950s retro vibe. No, The Bluebird reminded me of a quaint bed and breakfast with floral wallpaper and delicate china. The Bluebird made me feel warm and comforted, like being invited to Teddy's house for a hot meal. I watched my companion survey the diner with a detached sort of curiosity that piqued my own interest. Death the Tax Collector, for lack of a better name, peered inside the glass display case near the front counter that housed apple pie, peach cobbler, cookies dipped in mint chocolate, turtle brownies, and other baked delights.

"What do your kind call these?" He jabbed a finger, smudging the glass like an oblivious child.

"My kind?" I echoed with a frown. "I don't know about you, but that sounds mildly insulting. Like you think you're better than everyone else because you leapt off the pages of a billionaire romance novel."

My companion's head whipped around to fix me with a bemused look, the corners of his mouth twitching as though he fought hard not to smile.

"Billionaire romance novel?" He scoffed. "Does such a thing exist?"

"Where exactly are you from?" I cocked my head. "Have you lived underground your whole life or something?"

"Something like that," he murmured vaguely, his attention once more on the spread inside the display case. "To be honest, I don't know what any of these are, so I'm going to order one of everything."

The waitress who eyed him from behind the counter as though he were a mouth-watering steak and not a human being nearly swooned.

"Right away, sir!" I could almost imagine her saluting him as she leapt into action.

"One of everything?" My eyebrows shot up my forehead. "You're going to have a major sugar crash, you know."

"Impossible," he scoffed and turned his aristocratic nose up at me with a regal, dignified air, clearly not used to being challenged. "I'm not affected the same way as your kind." He leaned over the counter and slipped several gold coins, a currency I had never seen in my life, to the waitress piling one of everything onto a massive platter. "One black coffee for me. A chamomile tea for the lovely young woman standing beside me."

I gripped his shoulder and forced him to turn around. "Who the hell are you? How do you come by your information?"

"I've already told you," he shrugged elegantly, the ghost of a smile teasing his lush mouth. "I'm more commonly known as Death, but you may call me Decadence."

~

Decadence, if that was his real name, perfectly embodied the meaning of that word. Everything about him exuded indulgence, from the way his voluminous black hair framed his face in loose waves, to his sharp, aristocratic profile. Even the way he slowly devoured each pastry was luxuriant, as though he savored the taste of every morsel. The way he drew his fat bottom lip glazed with honey into his mouth made me squirm a little as I struggled to keep my thoughts pure.

Leaning back in his chair with a glazed bear claw poised in one hand, he beckoned with an easy, roguish smile, "Tell me about yourself."

I sipped my piping hot chamomile tea, the soothing aroma calming my frayed nerves. "What do you want to know?"

Decadence took a large bite of his pastry, managing to look elegant with his mouth full as he spoke. "Interests and favorite pastimes, likes and dislikes, past lovers - ."

"I'm going to stop you right there," I interrupted, "because this sounds more like first date territory than mere curiosity. I have a boyfriend, remember?"

Teddy and I hadn't discussed the status of our relationship, but I assumed he wouldn't object if I made it official. Decadence frowned deeply, and I could almost see his black aura pulse angrily.

"I thought you were bluffing," he said flatly.

"No, his name is Teddy and we've been best friends since childhood," I straightened in my seat, eager to share my newfound happiness with a complete stranger, especially one who needed to learn a thing or two about boundaries.

"Teddy?" He mused as he sucked his fingers clean. "You don't say."

There was a sarcastic edge to his voice, the displeasure rolling off him in waves, making me babble like an idiot.

"Yeah, Theodore Kershaw, otherwise known as Teddy," I gestured wildly as I spoke, unable to contain my excitement. "He works at his dad's auto shop as a mechanic with his three older brothers. Teddy is the complete opposite of his family, though. Shy and quiet with a gift for music. Ask him to play any song on his guitar, and he'll have the notes memorized by heart within an hour." The intensity of my companion's gaze made me smother a self-conscious giggle. "I know I'm gushing about him, but I can't help myself. I've been in love with him for years, my one and only."

My companion's mouth twisted, as though he had tasted something sour. I sipped more of my tea, hyper-aware of his scrutiny. After a long moment of charged silence, he reached across the table and brushed my bare forearm with his long fingers. The physical contact made me shiver, for his touch was pleasantly cool, and I was immediately reminded of winter blooming into spring in the delicate balance of life and death. Uncomfortable, I moved my arm out of reach.

"Are you certain that you truly love him?" His rich, chocolatey voice blanketed my senses. "After all, you've never been in love before. Perhaps you're mistaking infatuation for love."

I recoiled from him.

"Excuse me?" I spluttered. "You've known me for a grand total of thirty minutes and think you're qualified to analyze my love life? Boy, do you have some nerve."

Decadence flashed me a toe-curling smile and chuckled lightly.

"And you're as fiery and free-spirited as I remember," he countered. "I suspect you're going to storm out at any moment, so I'll make my words brief. You're a young, vibrant woman who has lived in the same backwater town since birth. You've never known love outside of your childhood best friend." Decadence leaned across the table, his face no more than two inches from mine, and whispered, "I know you often lose yourself in fantasy. Your mother keeps you on a short leash, but I sense the longing that burns a hole in your heart. I know you want more. More than Pebble's Creek. More than empty promises of romantic tales that keep you awake at night. *More than Teddy."*

I tried jerking away from him, but he tangled his hand in my hair to keep me in place, though his touch was gentle. Why hadn't anyone come to my rescue? Couldn't they see I was being accosted? My eyes shifted in their sockets to catch someone's eye, but time had slowed as though my companion and I existed in another dimension. Shadowed figures loomed in the darkness, save for one standing in the bright window, his jade eyes trained on me. My heart leapt into my throat, and I jerked away from Decadence, leaving him bereft.

"Teddy!" I waved enthusiastically.

My best friend didn't seem the least bit confused as he gazed at me through the window, only… disappointed. This reaction bewildered me more than ever. The Bluebird was bright and cheerful once more, the sounds of clattering dishes and sizzling bacon clouding the air. The back of my neck felt singed, as though Decadence had branded me with his cool touch.

Teddy disappeared from the window. A moment later, he opened the door and pushed his way through the crowd looking ill-tempered. My heart sank as I realized he was angry with *me*, as though he accused me of betraying him with a man who called himself Death! My gaze dropped to the worn flannel shirt Decadence had discarded earlier that was now clutched in Teddy's hand, and I suddenly understood why he was upset. He'd come looking for me and found the token of his love crumpled on the ground like a piece of garbage, all because I had allowed a stranger to hypnotize me.

"I've b-been looking everywhere f-for you," Teddy snapped before I could explain. "I had thirty m-minutes to spare, so I d-dropped by to pay you a visit and f-found this," he lifted the flannel shirt. "On the g-ground. Do you know how worried I've b-been? C-come to find that you were s-seen walking arm-in-arm with a c-complete stranger."

"Teddy," I hopped up from the table and cupped his face, "there's nothing to worry about. This man approached me outside the flower shop and asked if I could show him where to find a good cup of coffee. That's all, I swear."

His temper cooled as I stroked his face and kissed his brow. A shadow fell over us and I turned, realizing that Decadence had stretched to his full height as he slipped on his suit jacket. He watched us with an unreadable expression, though the temperature in the diner had dropped several degrees.

"Without trust, there is no love," he cast the unnecessary barb, staring directly at Teddy as he edged around the table.

Teddy wedged himself between the dark stranger and I to shield me from view.

"I hope to see you soon, Koreyna," Decadence completely ignored Teddy as he offered me a small, knowing wink. "Think about what I said."

With the promise of our next meeting seasoning the air, Decadence disappeared as strangely as he had arrived.

~

"What s-secret conversation d-did you two have?" Teddy demanded for the tenth time since leaving The Bluebird. "Why w-won't you t-tell me?"

"Give up the chase," I said exasperatedly as I pushed through the screen door on my front porch. "Decadence, or whoever the hell he was, more or less had a few choice words about my love life, which I would rather forget."

"Don't you t-think I would w-want to know if those c-choice words were about me?" He trailed after me through the small kitchen. "Or us?"

I ignored him, though the thump of his boots vibrated through my legs as we ascended the rickety staircase that led to my bedroom. I wanted to forget about the way my chest had ached with longing to experience something other than what I had always known. The problem was, I had never dreamt about anything particularly realistic.

When I was twelve, my dream had involved being draped onto a swan bed by none other than Gerard Butler wearing a mask and black leather gloves. Not exactly realistic. But Teddy had used white tape to create a mask for Halloween, completing the ensemble with a cape, to match my own lacy costume. Later, I'd discovered that Teddy had been snooping through my diary and read my list on the "Top 20 Ways I Want To Be Touched By The Phantom." In hindsight, my best friend had been a good sport about my obsession and, even from an early age, had tried to fulfill the qualities I wanted in a man, realistic or otherwise.

That's why Death's claims stung, because longing for more experience made me feel ungrateful. I pushed open my bedroom door and gazed upon the fairy lights strung around my bed. My canopy was sheer and lacy, complementing my crushed velvet bedspread. The fairy lights added an ethereal glow that fueled my obsession with all things romantic and decadent.

Oh God, not that word.

Teddy followed me inside my bedroom as I snatched a comb from my dresser and began attacking the snarls in my hair. Without a single word, Teddy plucked the comb from my grasp, the mattress dipping as he perched on the edge of my bed.

"I've always wanted to b-brush your hair," he stammered. "Even when you r-refuse to s-share information about me."

Nerves fluttered in my stomach as he passed the comb through my hair, seizing the opportunity to trail his fingers through my locks.

"Were you attracted to h-him?" He sighed luxuriantly, despite the tension in his voice, obviously enjoying this small act of intimacy.

My scalp tingled as the comb tugged through my hair, and I was enjoying the experience as much as him, though I wished he would drop the damn subject.

"Why would you ask me something like that?" I scoffed, not wanting to answer the question. "I never pegged you as the jealous type."

"M-maybe I am," he replied solemnly. "At l-least where you are c-concerned. Does that b-bother you?"

"No," I shrugged after a moment. "I think it's kind of sweet. I know for certain that I would whip another girl around by her pigtails if I caught her flirting with you."

A surprised laugh exploded from Teddy, and I couldn't resist a small grin because I loved that laugh more than anything. He seemed so shy and quiet on the surface that his laughing fits were always unexpected. Making him laugh made me feel proud of myself, as though I had accomplished something life-changing. My hair was completely brushed out, but Teddy continued to play with my strands, as though indulging in some long-held fantasy.

"I'm so in love with you," I whispered.

Teddy ceased running his fingers through my hair the moment the words left my mouth, and I squeaked in protest as he tugged back my head using my hair and passionately devoured my mouth.

"I will n-never get used to h-hearing you say t-that," he murmured between kisses, turning me around so that he could push me back onto my bed.

My stomach bottomed out as he slowly crawled up my body, leaving a trail of kisses in his wake. As he settled his weight on top of me, he stammered, "You have n-no idea how jealous and w-worried I was when I s-saw you with that other m-man, because he s-seemed like everything you've always w-wanted. How c-could I compete?"

Those jade eyes stared down at me with such hope, fear, and vulnerability that I couldn't cope. Regardless of whether or not I'd found Decadence attractive, Teddy deserved to know how much I wanted him. My face brightened as an idea popped into my head.

"You know what?" I snapped my fingers. "I have a surprise for you. Wait here, I'll be right back."

I wriggled out from under Teddy's weight, until he reluctantly rolled off of me, though his eyes glimmered with curiosity. Thankfully, my walk-in closet was attached to my bathroom, so he didn't see the red floral dress I slipped off the hanger or the black lingerie I'd been saving for more than a year. One of my close friends, Victoria, owned a lingerie boutique downtown, one of the more hip places in a town dedicated to hunting, fishing, and basically anything outdoorsy.

After I slipped on the lingerie, I left the bottom row of buttons on the dress unbuttoned to show off my legs as I sauntered back into my bedroom. Teddy reclined on his elbows, his eyes widening in interest as I wrapped my bare leg around the doorframe and tossed my head back, allowing my hair to ripple down my spine.

"Oh m-my God," he murmured as I traced circles on the floor with my toes, every step bringing me closer to the bed, my smile coy and flirtatious with a hint of bashfulness.

Teddy's unnaturally bright gaze was fixed on my breasts, my deep cleavage exaggerated by the black balconette bra.

"Don't think I haven't noticed the way you look at me," I purred, feeling embarrassed and strangely powerful all at once, "especially when I wear this particular dress."

Teddy nodded dumbly. "Yes."

"Tell me what you imagine doing to me in this dress," I demanded as I tugged his body further down the bed, dislodging his elbows as I straddled his hips. "I want to hear your voice. I want to know all the filthy things you want to do to me."

Hey, some of my romance novels were starting to pay off! I was dirty talking my way through this exchange like a child riding a bicycle without training wheels for the first time. Teddy sat up in bed and ran his calloused hands down my arms as his eyes moved in a circle around my face and breasts. Tentatively, he reached for my dress and tugged the bodice down several inches, until my breasts overflowed from the exposed satin bra. Something fierce and wild flashed in his eyes as they devoured the sight. Teddy groaned low in his throat as he tightly squeezed my breasts, exaggerating their fullness until I thought they might explode.

"I have one f-fantasy," his tongue plunged between my breasts as he reached around to squeeze my ass, all while rocking his hips beneath me. "I imagine you w-wearing this dress with a l-long braid. We're s-stretched out beside the r-river and, all of a sudden, you j-jump up from the grass and run. I chase you through the f-forest and I'm b-breathless, but I can hear your l-laughter."

"Teddy," I pressed a finger to his lips. "Why don't you show me?"

Without a single warning, I leapt off my bed, making him bounce on the mattress, and raced into the deep, dark forest that framed our neighborhood, where absolutely anything was possible.

~

I squealed and giggled in delight as Teddy's panting breath echoed in the vast forest close behind me. Blood red flowers and twisting vines sprouted up in my wake, blocking his path. I wove through the trees like a prancing gazelle determined to outwit its pursuer, but he powered his legs fast and hard, until he caught the hem of my fluttering dress. I released a high-pitched scream as several buttons on my dress popped open, exposing my thighs and belly button. I could see why Teddy favored this fantasy.

My bare feet pounded on a bed of moss and soggy leaves, my soles occasionally slipping on a slimy rock. My hair trailed behind me like a beacon, as wild and untamed as the forest. My frantic breaths scorched my throat as I emerged into our favorite clearing, the river a silver thread on the horizon. I caught my breath a moment too late, for Teddy wrapped his arms around my waist and hauled me over his shoulder like a prized conquest. I knew my best friend was competitive from years of playing video games and cards, but hot damn. Blood rushed to my head as I bounced on his shoulder with every step. Once we reached the banks of the river, he spread me out on the gras near my grandmother's quilt.

- -

"What now?" I asked breathlessly as he sat back on his haunches.

Crickets chirped in the distance as the sun arced across the sky. The clouds on the horizon were suffused with bright gold and peach. I frowned as I remembered the dead fish floating in the river below, but Teddy smoothed his hands up my bare legs, until my bottom half was completely bare. Without uttering a single word, he slowly unbuttoned my dress until the cool mountain air made me shiver. Teddy's normally bright eyes were dark with desire and an all-consuming thirst as he trailed the petals of a fallen flower down my body, replacing the soft caress with his short fingernails that rasped against my skin. I stretched my arms overhead and arched my back as he repeated the alternating sensations of soft and rough over and over again, until I was wet, throbbing, and aching like mad.

"Do you t-trust me?" He stammered as he eased the black thong over my hips and spread my legs wide.

"I couldn't possibly trust anyone more," I writhed on the ground in a desperate plea for his touch.

My heart palpitated as Teddy lowered his face between my thighs, a protest ready on my lips… until his tongue licked open my cleft, the touch so raw and intimate that I was unable to contain the whimper that resounded from deep within my soul. I'd read about this in books, but words were unable to convey the trust involved in allowing a man to lick my pussy.

Yep, that's right. No more silly euphemisms. No more dancing around the reality that my body had awakened to something more powerful than itself.

Teddy suckled and licked the tight, sensitive bud at the crest of my sex I often massaged when pleasuring myself, but the rumble of his groans and the wild, animalistic way he devoured my pussy made the experience incomparable. My fingers tangled in his hair as the climb gradually became steeper, until a bright light unfurled from the center of my body, filling every square inch of my trembling limbs with a euphoric weightlessness. Teddy kissed up my body, and I could taste my salty musk on his lips as he lovingly stroked my hair.

"You have n-no idea how l-long I've wanted to do that." he flashed me a crooked grin, his voice hoarse and breathless. His eyes were strangely hard and fierce as they searched my face and, after a long moment, he whispered, "Korey, will you m-marry me?"

"What?" I breathed in shock, though my heart fluttered with pleasure.

Teddy suddenly looked abashed and averted his gaze.

"I w-want to elope," he confessed. "Your mom likes me well enough, b-but she would never let me m-marry you." His grip on me tightened. "I'm terrified of l-losing you, Korey. Something w-weird is going on, and I think w-we should just run away t-together."

He gave me a desperately hopeful look, and I couldn't resist throwing my arms around his neck. He was right. My mother would never agree to this. We needed to seize control of our future.

"Yes!" I exclaimed. "Of course I'll marry you, but we should wait until after the spring festival. We could leave that night while everyone else is celebrating."

"The n-night of the spring f-festival," he declared with determination. "We'll leave t-then."

After nodding my consent, he kissed me deeply, the relief sharp and fresh on his tongue. "I'm s-so in l-love with you. Nothing c-could k-keep me from you. Nothing."

Let Me Follow

"Were you ever going to tell me about your little coffee date?" My mother leaned against the doorframe of my bedroom.

I lay on my stomach on my bed, idly flipping through my illustrated copy of *Beloved*. Death the Tax Collector's uncanny resemblance to Hades still rattled me. The Hades and Persephone myth was a coming-of-age story about sexual awakening and, while I felt drawn to the mysterious stranger I'd met today, Teddy was exceptional at making me feel things I never knew possible. Didn't that also count? Bad boys didn't have a monopoly on good sex.

"He cornered me as I was struggling to unlock the front door," I said, which wasn't a lie. "I told him to leave me alone, but he…"

My mother crept inside my bedroom and perched on the edge of my bed.

"Cast a spell over you?" She offered.

I froze.

"Something like that," I blushed furiously, "but that's not possible." Reflecting on my earlier exchange with him, I confessed, "I almost felt like he was compelling me against my will. Strangely, he didn't know what half of the pastries were at The Bluebird, so he ordered one of everything and ate voraciously, despite his muscular build. Somehow he knew I like chamomile tea and claimed he'd read about me in the newspaper. What I don't understand is why he's come knocking four years after the pandemic. It doesn't make any sense."

There was a brief silence.

"Perhaps he was making preparations," my mother shrugged elegantly. "Once he knew where you were, perhaps he spent years collecting information until he knew you like the back of his hand."

Something about her words chilled me. I made no response.

"Are you attracted to him?" She asked softly.

"I thought he was strange, but I won't deny that he possessed a certain magnetism," I admitted, my cheeks flushed with shame. "Thankfully, Teddy found us and dragged me away from him."

Her face immediately brightened.

"I wonder how Teddy must've felt seeing you with another man," my mother stroked my long, wild curls.

My heart skipped a beat. This was the first time she'd ever acknowledged that Teddy might view me as more than a friend.

"Haven't you seen the way he looks at you?" She continued stroking my hair. "Every time he catches sight of you, his entire face lights up as if you are the sun, the moon, the stars, and everything in between. Men are unwieldy creatures, but I would *love* to see you with someone like him."

My eyes widened with shock. After all these years of keeping me from dating and an entire day of sneaking around with Teddy, *now* she was casting her vote? I should've jumped up from the bed and wrapped my arms around her. I should've confessed everything about where I'd truly been that morning, but my relationship with Teddy was too raw and precious to share. Not just with my mother, but *everyone*. I wanted to sneak around and experience the thrill of danger with someone I felt unquestionably safe with.

"Huh," I flipped a page of my book, the sound of crisp paper like music to my ears, "I've never thought of him that way before."

~

The next afternoon, I closed the shop for lunch and walked the three blocks to the auto shop where Teddy worked. The shop reeked of oil, exhaust, and mechanical parts. It was a distinctly masculine smell, and I remembered all those times Teddy had reeked so wonderfully after a long day's work. What he hadn't known was my secret fantasy of burying my face in the crook of his neck and inhaling until my lungs were fit to bursting.

For as shy and soft-spoken as he could be, he possessed an undeniably raw, potent brand of masculinity that was entirely his own. I found Teddy changing Mr. Carpenter's oil with dark smudges on his cheeks. The moment he caught sight of me in a pristine white sundress with a knitted halter top and gauzy, semi-sheer skirt, a dull flush mounted his cheeks. The memory of our lovemaking passed between us, and I found myself grinning like an idiot.

"You're g-good to go," Teddy gave Mr. Carpenter a small wave as the old man slowly maneuvered his way onto main street.

The moment the shop was empty, Teddy rushed forward, realizing two seconds before he touched me that his hands were filthy. He stared down at his blackened hands, frowning in quiet discontent.

"You wore t-that white dress on p-purpose, didn't you?" He accused hotly.

"Maybe," I reached up on tiptoe and buried my nose in the crook of his neck, like I had always wanted to do.

Sweat, grease, and a potent, masculine musk.

My breath released as a shuddering exhale. "I thought you might want to mark me now that I'm yours."

I pulled back and Teddy grinned crookedly. "That's p-probably the cheesiest t-thing I've ever h-heard you say, but I've been w-waiting to hear it my entire l-life."

He raised two fingers and streaked my unblemished cheek with black grease. His gaze was both tender and hot as he marked me, and I stepped back long enough to show him the brown paper bag I'd been hiding. Teddy looked confused.

"I packed us lunch," I announced. "My mom is taking over the shop for the afternoon, so I thought we could make some deliveries before driving into the country to find a quiet spot."

Teddy's face brightened, making me think of what my mother had shared the previous night - that I was the sun, the moon, the stars, and everything in between to him.

"Wait r-right here," he pointed at the ground. "I'll go tell m-my dad."

That was one great thing about the Kershaw family. Even though Teddy worked for his parents, they were flexible with his schedule to make room for the guitar lessons he offered at the recreational center and to help make deliveries for my mother's business. By the time he returned, I was already waiting in his pick-up truck, an old clunker that had taken us on thousands of adventures. Teddy and I drove to the flower shop and loaded up the bed with plants and flower arrangements. During excursions like this, we always listened to old rock bands like Queen.

Or more like blasted the music from the speakers as we sang at the top of our lungs. "Don't Stop Me Now" and "Fat-Bottomed Girls" were among our favorites. The best part about making deliveries was how happy everyone was to see me, especially when Teddy was there. Roses, lilies, tulips, daisies, and pink carnations.

Once we finished, we drove deeper into the countryside to a clearing in the woods that granted us much-needed privacy. As we drove, I caught Teddy stealing glances at me over a dozen times, and my heart raced a little faster with each rapt look. Teddy parked in the center of the clearing and turned down the music as I spread out our goat cheese and honey sandwiches. Instead of taking a bite, he simply stared at me with fear and hope warring in his eyes.

"Did you only r-realize that you l-loved me when I confessed my feelings, or h-have you loved m-me for a long time?" He asked waveringly.

Teddy's constant need for reassurance surprised me, because he always seemed so resolute. Other women might have grown impatient, but his deep need for love only made me ache for him.

"I've loved you from the beginning," I said shyly, "as my friend, confidante, playmate, and wise advisor."

Teddy frowned glumly.

"Not as a l-lover?" His eyes desperately searched my face.

"I've had a crush on you for a long time," I said patiently, "but I never thought we were a possibility. I only realized how much I've always loved you when I dared to take the risk. Does that make sense?"

Teddy's frown deepened, as though he was bitterly disappointed with my answer. I reached for him and stroked his jaw. I loved the way his stubble rasped against my fingers.

"It doesn't matter how long I was aware of my love for you," I reassured. "All that matters is our history and how every step has brought me closer to you. How long have you known?"

"Forever," he said with surprising clarity and, no matter how hard I pressed him, he refused to elaborate on the specific time and day.

"Was it hard keeping your love for me a secret?" I asked as I nibbled the crust of my sandwich.

Teddy took a large bite, his hands smeared with grease. "It was the h-hardest thing I've ever d-done," he confessed, "especially when you were attracted to other m-men. All those times w-where you openly g-gushed about celebrities or that f-football player you d-danced with at our senior p-prom drove me insane w-with jealousy."

I touched his sleeve, my heart heavy with guilt and sorrow. "I'm sorry I made you feel that way. It was never my intention to hurt you. If it's any consolation, I've gotten jealous, too."

That piece of information caught his attention. "R-really?"

"Yes!" I exclaimed with a laugh. "Whenever we watched movies where there was a sexy woman on screen, I wanted to cover your eyes."

For the first time, one corner of his mouth curled upward. That alone communicated that he was incredibly pleased, not to mention the way his eyes glittered as they met mine. At that moment, "She's Got You High" began to play, and I cranked up the volume before hopping out of the truck. Teddy watched through the dirty windshield as I twirled barefoot in the tall grass, my white cotton dress fanning out as I spun on tiptoe. Teddy climbed out of the driver's seat and marched toward me.

For one, heart-stopping moment, my smile faltered until he swept me into his arms, his dirty hands marking my dress as they roamed everywhere.

"This is f-for all the t-times I wanted to a-ask you to d-dance but c-couldn't," he declared haltingly as he twirled me under his arm. "And t-this is f-for all the times I w-wanted to touch and k-kiss you," he buried his face in the crook of my neck and pressed a smoldering kiss there, his stubble tickling my tender flesh in the most delightful, spine-tingling way.

I tangled my fingers in his thick hair and forced his head back. "And this is for all the times I should have kissed you senseless instead of fawned over some stupid celebrity like a rabid fangirl," I breathed against his lips before devouring him in a fiercely passionate kiss.

I was the one to light the match, but Teddy poured gasoline on the fire by grabbing me and lowering my body onto the bed of grass amidst gold and cobalt wildflowers. The birds twittered as he made love to me on the rich soil that had served as the playground of our youth.

Teddy and I lay sprawled naked in the grass afterward. He kissed and nuzzled me, his limbs tangled with my own. Handprints were smudged all over my thighs, my stomach... my breasts. I was completely and thoroughly marked in the gentlest, most tender way possible. When the crickets began to chirp, we dressed and climbed back inside his truck.

On the way home, he played Tracy Chapman's "The Promise". The lyrics told the story of a powerful love that distance couldn'tovershadow. The words washed over me in the bluish gloom of the semi-darkness. Teddy had played this song hundreds of times on the guitar for me, and I knew instinctively that he'd been expressing his love for me in his shy, sneaky way. I reached for the hand not gripping the steering wheel and brought his knuckles to my lips. After he parked in front of my house, he walked me hand-in-hand to the porch. When we reached the front door, he shrugged out of his flannel shirt.

"Here," he wrapped the garment around my shoulders.

Lifting a brow, I challenged, "Don't you think my mom will notice me wearing your favorite shirt?"

"Don't you t-think your m-mom will notice grease marks all over your b-breasts if you go inside w-without it?" He fired back with an equally snarky, albeit playful look.

"Good thinking," I knocked on his head several times. "I love you, Teddy."

A barely perceptible look flashed across his face, as though he hardly dared to believe my words. He kissed me furiously, passion setting his jade irises ablaze.

"God, I t-think I l-love you too much," he smiled weakly, almost deliriously. Wetting his lips, he stepped closer and whispered, "Do you t-think your mother w-will ever accept our l-love?"

"Actually," I hugged his threadbare shirt around me more tightly, "she confessed that she would rather see me with you than any other man."

Teddy's gaze searched my face, confusion maring his brow. "Why are we s-sneaking around, then?"

"I don't know," I shrugged self-consciously. "I don't want other people invading our space. Besides," I walked two fingers up his chest, "isn't sneaking around kind of sexy?"

Teddy opened his mouth and sucked in a breath, but whatever he'd planned to say slowly bled from him until he was completely deflated. My expression fell.

"What's wrong?" I nudged him.

"S-sneaking around can b-be fun," he agreed rather begrudgingly, "but I'd rather everyone know we're t-together."

I hoped he wasn't doubting me again. Damn that encounter with Decadence! His presence had planted too many seeds in my lover's brain.

"The spring festival is on Saturday," I combed my fingers through his soft hair. "Why don't we break the news to everyone then before we elope? Imagine us swaying under the strands of colorful lights with flowers blooming everywhere. It would be *so* romantic! That gives us three more days of sneaking around. How does that sound?"

Teddy's half-smile was a tad more enthusiastic. "I would d-do anything f-for you, Korey."

"And I would do the same for you," I massaged the base of his skull, making his eyes flutter closed in quiet bliss.

Teddy and I exchanged one final kiss before he sprinted through the front yard to his idling pick-up truck. The moment he drove away, I was plunged into darkness.

But I wasn't alone.

"You certainly could aim higher than *that*," a deep, rich, sultry voice said from behind me.

I whirled around, nearly colliding with Death the Tax Collector's broad, solid chest. He wore a black turtleneck underneath a matching velvet blazer, his pale skin almost iridescent.

"What the hell are you doing here?" I demanded, horrified, as my heart nearly pounded out of my chest. "How did you find out where I live?"

Decadence clucked his tongue and arched a black-winged brow. "Are you this polite to all of your guests?"

"Only when they jump out from the shadows like an axe-murderer," I retorted hotly. "By the way, nice turtleneck. Are you an undercover modeling agent for L.L. Bean?"

Decadence gave his outfit a not-so-discreet once-over. "Is this not considered fashionable where you come from?"

"Maybe in a big city where money is of no consequence," I shrugged, "but around here you're going to find a lot of plaid, flannel, and denim overalls for men and women alike. So you better catch that flight to New York City where that platinum-blonde is waiting for you at some snazzy coffee shop."

His full, pink mouth twisted wryly. "I'm honored that you've thought long and hard about the type of woman I might like, but I'm afraid you're wrong on multiple accounts."

"Oh?" I folded my arms over my chest. "Enlighten me."

I shouldn't have entertained him, but I begrudgingly found that I was curious. Decadence's eyes traveled up my body, as though he could see where Teddy had marked me. Those marks burned like the proverbial scarlet letter.

"As tempting as a platinum-blonde might seem," his heavy footfalls brought him several steps closer, "I much prefer wild, untamed beauties who roam barefoot with light shining through their gowns, outlining their shapely legs. The garland of flowers wound in her long hair speaks of innocence, but the tantalizing curves of her body tells a remarkably different story."

A strange ache weighed in my breasts. Obviously he was describing me. And while I was alarmed, was it so wrong to admit that I was also flattered? After a long, pregnant pause, I exhaled and stepped away from him, craving space.

"I think you should go before I call the police," I warned and moved to step around him.

He blocked the path to my front door with an outstretched arm.

"Do you realize how long I've desired you?" His warm breath stirred the delicate curls framing my face, sending my blood rushing through my veins. "You might make the usual protestations, but I know some small part of you is curious about me. If only you knew that I could give you so much more than a pathetic boy with a stammer that betrays his weakness."

Something deep inside of me snapped.

"It doesn't matter how long you've waited or how much you can offer," I seethed, mere inches from his face. "All that matters is who I choose to love and, frankly, that will never be you."

Decadence spun around when I ducked beneath his arm.

"I *will* have you, Koreyna," he vowed. "One way or another."

~

It rained the entire week leading up to the spring festival - and not just any rain. *Acid* rain. No one could make sense of it. More livestock were found dead without any trace of the cause. The greenhouse protected my plants from the onslaught, thankfully, so there were no plans to cancel the spring festival as of yet.

As the mayor often said: "The show must go on."

The phrase always made me wonder if she'd seen *Moulin Rouge!* Or, like Teddy and I, was a fan of Queen. The possibilities were endless.

Rumors quickly spread about a tall, imposing man dressed all in black. I didn't need to hear the rumors because I saw him *everywhere*, which was rather annoying. And flattering. And creepy in a stalkerish sort of way.

One night Teddy treated me to a movie at the local theater. As we emerged from the auditorium after the credits rolled, Decadence was waiting for us in the lobby. He didn't make any effort to approach us, but simply followed me with his eyes. Teddy's grip tightened on my waist and he refused to let go until I was safely home. Something about the raven-haired man unsettled him.

The way he reacted was born out of insecurity, and I had never known Teddy to harbor such a quality. I sensed his irritation in the way he clenched his jaw or how his eyes narrowed. Sometimes I caught the flare of his nostrils. There was anger, but also fear, and I couldn't make sense of it, other than to assume he somehow knew about my adolescent obsession with the pale, dark-haired god in my prized illustrated tale.

In my youth, I couldn't have imagined loving anyone but the figment of my imaginings, and it was more than a little disconcerting to be confronted with my girlhood fantasy, only to realize that he was as gorgeous as he was entitled. But nothing could stop the dreams. The moment I laid my head on my pillow, I felt a dark, strangely enticing presence pulsing all around me. The shadowy corner morphed into a pale, shirtless man whose shoulders and chest were carved from marble. The man's hair was softer than a kitten's fur, his full lips feather-light and on my skin.

In these unwanted dreams, I was eager and willing, as though I'd never tasted a man before. And when I awoke the next morning, I was wracked with a terrible guilt. How could I be in love with Teddy and yearn for another man's touch? I loved my mother and was grateful for the life she'd given me, but I couldn't help blaming her for how sheltered I was. If only she'd allowed me to experience more, I wouldn't be feeling pulled in two different directions.

The morning before the spring festival, I rode my bicycle to the small bed and breakfast a close friend of mine owned. I ascended the front steps with a bouquet of yellow roses cradled in my arms like a baby and wiped my feet on the welcome mat. The two-story house was painted a beautiful rose pink with a white porch that stretched around the front. Rocking chairs flanked the front door and dragonfly windchimes tinkled in the breeze.

The dining area and living room featured floral wallpaper and curio cabinets with collectible figurines on display. A man wearing a black Henley sat at the long dining table with his back facing me, though his thick, wavy hair and broad, rounded shoulders were unmistakable. If I hadn't guessed his identity, the five or so plates huddled around him, each bearing something different, would have clued me in. As if sensing my presence, the chair creaked under his weight as he glanced over his shoulder.

"You," I narrowed my eyes.

He chewed slowly before swallowing, and I couldn't resist admiring the way his throat worked. "Me."

"What are you doing here?" I demanded rather ungraciously.

His face twitched.

"I sleep and eat here," he dead-panned. "Even though I don't have much use for either. May I assume that you're here to see me?"

At that moment, a slender young woman with long, straight, dark brown hair and a gap-toothed smile pushed through the kitchen door clutching a pan of freshly-baked brownies in two mittened hands. Avery, a close friend from high school, was basic in every sense of the word, but exceptionally beautiful in her simplicity. Avery knew how to chop wood, build fires, and manage a business when her mother was out of town. In other words, she was capable and headstrong with the most resolute will of anyone I had ever met. She rounded the table and placed the pan of brownies in front of Decadence.

"I'll be back with the chocolate sauce," a few long hairs straggled in her flushed face as she raced back to the kitchen.

"Well, I can see you've turned this place upside-down," I remarked dryly. "Now that you've been fed and watered, can I have a word with your hostess?"

Decadence pointed at the pan of brownies. "There's enough to share between us. I could feed you one tantalizing bite at a time."

My heart skipped a beat.

"No, but thank you for the offer," I smiled tightly. "I'm beginning to understand why your name is Decadence."

Avery hustled back to the dining room with a pot and used a wooden spoon to ladle a waterfall of chocolate sauce onto the untouched brownies. The torturously slow process only made the bouquet of roses weigh more heavily in my arms.

"Avery, where would you like me to place your order?" I asked, struggling to conceal my impatience.

"Oh, I'm so sorry!" She handed the spoon to her guest. "Here, you can lick that," she offered as though he were a child.

Flustered, Avery snatched the bouquet from my arms and placed them in a crystal vase in the center of the dining table.

Watching as the man devoured the pan of brownies, I jerked my head toward the door. "Hey, Avery, can I talk to you for a second?"

"Sure," Avery wiped her sweaty forehead on her sleeve and collapsed in a high-backed chair beside the crackling fire. "What's up?"

I lowered myself onto the armchair opposite from her. "What's the deal with your new guest? He seems to be running you ragged."

Avery blew a stray lock of hair out of her face. "I don't really have a choice," she shrugged. "He paid me in gold, so I'll be rich by the time he leaves. Other than that, he's nice to look at. My heart nearly pounds out of my chest whenever he looks at me. Don't you feel the same?"

I glanced over my shoulder at the man in question and found him eyeing us, as though he were eavesdropping on our conversation.

Lowering my voice to a half-whisper, I hissed, "He might be attractive, but he's so smug and arrogant that I mostly want to punch him in the face."

Avery's dark eyebrows rose. "Korey!" She exclaimed.

"You would be doing me a favor by sleeping with him because, from the moment I met him, he hasn't left me alone," I confided, "and I have more than myself to consider now that Teddy and I are together."

Avery's blue eyes widened and she smiled rapturously. "Really? Oh God, that poor boy has loved you for ages. The town has been placing bets on when you would finally take notice for years. Tell me everything," she scooted to the edge of her chair. "Did he break first?"

I nodded, my cheeks flushing with pleasure. "One night we were staring up at the stars from my rooftop. Sometimes he accidentally brushes my hand, but this time he traced the inside of my palm and wrist, as though he were memorizing every detail. It was so romantic. Being the coward that I am, I avoided him until he barged into the flower shop and declared his love for me."

"What did you say?" Avery leaned in a little closer.

For once, I actually wanted the eavesdropping bastard to hear, so I recounted more loudly, "I told him to meet me by the river the next morning. He had no clue what I was up to, until I tackled him and made love to him right there on the grass!"

Avery squealed with laughter. "I have never known anyone as shameless as you, Korey," she grinned mischievously, "but please, please, please don't break Teddy's heart. I was his only confidante throughout high school, and it was very hard for him to keep his feelings a secret. There's nothing he's more terrified of than losing you, because he feels that he somehow doesn't measure up. It's like a complex."

I recoiled from her, as if she had struck me. I didn't like the thought that someone else possibly knew him better than I did. "Why would I ever hurt him? He's my best friend. We know everything about each other."

"Well," Avery made a show of choosing her words carefully, "I've known you since elementary school. You've always longed for something bigger and better, and I think Teddy sometimes feels like he doesn't fit the bill. That eventually you'll crave more."

Guilt twinged in my chest, and I could no longer make eye contact with my friend. Lately, everyone had been telling me that I wanted more than Teddy and my life in Pebble's Creek. Even though I had sometimes lost myself in dreams, I'd always been content… until Decadence had come to collect his due. Would I fail Teddy through my restlessness? The thought alone made me want to burst into tears because I loved him as if he were a part of me.

I desperately needed someone to confide in, but I didn't want the Dark Overlord to know that I found him tempting, like a delicious apple that promised only bad things. Obviously, Teddy knew his heart, but did I know mine?

~

That night Teddy and I played pool at the local bar, The White Owl. The hazy bar was thick with smoke, and I sat at the counter in my black wrap dress (the only blatantly sexy item of clothing I owned) and nursed my glass of red wine as Teddy played with a group of wagering men. They were in for a rude awakening because Teddy was a pool champion. Every now and then, I caught him watching me from across the bar like a stranger eyeing a pretty lady. I could tell from the way he held his pole and leaned against the pool table that he was showing off, something that endeared me to him until I thought my heart might burst.

When we were together, nothing else mattered... but I couldn't stop thinking about my earlier conversation with Avery. I couldn't help imagining the times he'd confided in her about the struggle of unrequited love while I openly lusted after other men and, just like that, I became the villain of my own story. I struggled to put these thoughts to rest and focus on the Southern twang of "Black Velvet" blaring through the speakers. Once Teddy realized my gaze had turned inward, he abandoned the game and shouldered his way through the crowd.

He touched my bare shoulder and peered at me closely. "Are y-you okay?"

I shrugged noncommittally, not wanting to express what was going through my head. Teddy glanced around the bar to make sure no one was spying on us before he cupped my cheek and skimmed my tender flesh with his thumb. Those jade eyes bore into my soul, comforting in their familiarity yet probing in their intensity.

"Please tell m-me," he quietly beseeched. "Are you u-unhappy?

I shot him a glare and removed his hand from my face. "How could you even ask me that?"

Teddy's brow wrinkled.

"You've b-been quiet all n-night," he pointed out. Well, he wasn't wrong. "And I h-heard that people s-saw you with that m-man in front of your h-house and at the b-bed and breakfast earlier t-today."

I blinked and drew back from him. Had Avery said something?

"He showed up unannounced one night," I quickly explained. "I didn't invite him. This morning I made a delivery to Avery, and he happened to be there." My cheeks burned. "I hardly talked to him and told him to leave me alone more than once."

Teddy stared at me for a long moment, his eyes searching, as though he knew something I didn't. The thought unnerved me. We were supposed to know everything about each other, right?

"Are you afraid that you're not good enough for me?" I asked bluntly, making him flinch.

"Sometimes I just w-wish I had m-more control than I really d-do," he said quietly after a moment. "I already know that I l-love you more t-than you love m-me. I've known t-that for a long, long t-time, but I d-don't think I've ever m-made peace with it. Not fully, if I'm b-being honest with myself."

His words doused me with ice-cold water.

"How can you even say that?" I pushed away from him. "How can you be so sure that you love me more than I love you? Obviously you don't know my mind and heart at all."

The only problem was, I feared he was right. I hopped off the stool and shouldered my way through the crowd to the exit, running away from myself more than I was from him.

"Korey!" He shouted over the music, but I ignored him.

Outside, he caught up to me.

"Korey, p-please wait!" He stammered. "I didn't m-mean to offend you. I was simply s-stating a fact. If you knew h-half of what I know, you w-would understand."

Again, more secrets.

"What are you talking about?" I cried, flinging my arms wide. "What don't I know?"

Teddy stepped closer, invading my personal space. "Do you w-want him, Korey? I know you're attracted t-to him. You d-don't have to l-lie to me, but w-would you rather b-be with someone l-like him? Someone who's experienced and d-dangerous and alpha m-male?"

Angry tears rimmed my eyes as I balled my fists, positively furious. He was sabotaging our relationship on purpose.

"Wanting someone and loving them are two different things," I gritted my teeth. "Do you love porn stars more than me or the lingerie models from Victoria's Secret?"

Cold, hard fury flashed across his face.

"I w-wouldn't know because I d-don't look at that shit," his cheeks flushed a dark, mottled red. I'd royally pissed him off. "And I d-disagree. Want often l-leads to love. I b-both want and l-love you. Are you s-saying that you l-love me but w-want him?"

"That's *not* what I'm saying, so don't twist my words," I retorted. "And I refuse to answer your question because I'm not going to cater to your insecurity."

Okay, so now I was basically gas-lighting him. Good job, Korey.

Sure, he was insecure, but perhaps he sensed more than I was willing to share. I knew I'd said the absolute worst thing the second Teddy's body stiffened, as though I'd struck him.

"Maybe we're not m-meant to be more than f-friends," he said hoarsely, unshed tears making his eyes red. "Go on, I r-release you! Now you're free to chase the r-real man of your d-dreams. Sorry for w-wasting your time."

Instead of returning to the bar, he stalked down the street with his head ducked and his hands stuffed inside his pockets. As for me… I was too shocked to speak. I remained immobile long after he had disappeared.

The Promise

I cried myself to sleep that night. Actually, I didn't sleep at all because I was too busy wrestling with my guilt and conflicting emotions. Tears spattered old photographs of Teddy and I like raindrops, the sight of his smiling face making my heart clench painfully. At the same time, I wondered: did I even know what I wanted? I blamed myself for confessing my love prematurely, but the emotions behind the words were true.

Everything boiled down to bad timing. If my girlhood fantasy had arrived before Teddy's declaration of love, would I have chosen differently? I wasn't in love with Decadence, but I was intrigued by what he represented.

The freedom to explore.

But at what cost?

When the early rays of dawn filtered through my bedroom window, I slipped out of bed and padded downstairs wearing my favorite pink bathrobe and matching nightgown. Upon entering the kitchen, I found my mother seated at the round table beside the window. She didn't immediately acknowledge my presence. I watched her stare through the window at a spider spinning its web, beads of dew glistening on the thread-like strands. Steam rose from the cup of tea warming her hands.

After a long moment, I cleared my throat.

"Good morning," I croaked.

My mother whipped her blonde head around to face me. The moment she drank in my bedraggled appearance, she clutched her chest with worry, making crow's feet appear at the outer corners of her eyes.

"Korey!" She gasped. "You look terrible."

I shuffled into the kitchen like a zombie.

"Thank you for that vote of confidence," I pumped my fist like the bad boy from *The Breakfast Club*.

"Did you sleep at all last night?" She asked.

I braced the edge of the kitchen counter and slumped. "Nope."

"Here," she stood, "come sit down. I'll make you a cup of tea."

Compliant as ever, I collapsed on a rickety chair decorated with acrylic sunflowers and watched her place the tea kettle on a burner. The water boiled quickly, and she poured the scalding liquid into my favorite Japanese teacup with its matching saucer, steeped the Egyptian licorice flavored tea bag, and settled the fragrant brew directly under my nose. The sweet scent was instantly calming. My mother sat across from me and closely studied my face.

"Are you going to tell me what's wrong?" She prodded gently.

I stared down at my reflection rippling in the teacup, not liking what I saw.

"Should desire for one person negate your love for another?" I stared at the tea bag bobbing in dark liquid. Nerves fluttered in my stomach. "Hypothetically, if I'm courted by two men - one I've known for a lifetime and one who's a mystery to me - should someone as inexperienced as myself explore at the risk of destroying a priceless relationship?"

My mother reached across the table and squeezed my hand with her own refreshingly cool ones.

"Korey, there's a difference between love and lust," she said carefully, her voice low and soothing. "Some might say the choice is simple because lust is so commonplace, whereas finding true love is the equivalent to lightning striking the same person twice. I've known for a long time that you were destined for a journey beyond my control. The time has finally come for you to make your choice - but once you've made that choice, never waver from it. That's the difference between love and lust: lust is an impulse, whereas love is a choice. If you choose lust in favor of love, you must own your decision, as well as any consequences that may follow. Do you understand?"

Love was a commitment. Loving someone should come easily, but dedication is required to stay the course.

That's exactly how I'd explained my devotion to Teddy the night before, but my answer hadn't been good enough for him. He interpreted my choice as settling for something less than what I desired.

I nodded my understanding and brought the teacup to my lips, my eyelids at a contemplative half-mast.

My mother and I were expected to deliver and arrange the flowers and produce at noon, so I braided my hair and slipped on the red floral dress I had worn the night Teddy had chased me through the forest. My heart constricted at the memory. It felt like a lifetime ago. I hadn't called or texted him since our parting the night before, mainly because I was uncertain of how to proceed. Decadence was an attractive, mysterious presence that made me feel wanted by a powerful, sexy man, but my attraction was less about him and more about my own lack of experience.

Despite presenting myself as strong and confident, deep down I barely knew who I was - but I *did* know I was terrified of losing Teddy. Was Decadence right in assuming that I couldn't walk away from my childhood? That I was choosing the safer option? The moment the thought entered my brain, it clanged heavily in my stomach.

Teddy had agreed weeks ago to help transport the flowers and produce to the small park shaded by a canopy of tall, thick oaks.

I sat at the top of the stairs like a coward as the doorbell rang and inhaled a shaky breath as I watched my best friend step inside the living room. I noticed the way he wiped trembling hands on his jeans and exhaled sharply as he stammered through a short conversation with my mother. The moment she turned away, he craned his neck,

looking this way and that, until his jade eyes found my hiding spot. Knowing I could no longer hide from him, I sprung to my feet and descended the staircase. My skin prickled as he watched me, making my nipples prick inside my bra.

My knees trembled as I neared him. When I reached his level, I found myself looking up, and up, and up a little more - until our eyes finally met, and I realized at that precise moment, I realized my childhood friend was no longer a boy. Or, at least, I'd noticed but never been so aware. He wore the same t-shirt and open flannel shirt as the night he'd chased me through the forest, as though he was capable of reading my mind. His eyes bore into mine with an intensity that made me falter, as if he were challenging me to speak while dreading what might come out of my mouth.

"Hey, Teddy," was all I could muster.

His tense expression hardened.

"H-hey," his voice cracked. Clearing his throat, he tried again. "Hey."

We said nothing as we waited for my mother, though our eyes bounced back and forth between us like a game of ping pong. One moment I glanced up at him and looked away, the next my skin burned from the heat of his gaze. The silence stretched on for an eternity, even as we loaded the flowers and produce into the back of his truck.

Once we were finished, my mother asked, "Are you riding with Teddy or me?"

Teddy eyed me sidelong as he stalked to the driver's side, a hopeful, yet wary gleam in his eyes.

Again, like a coward, I rushed in the opposite direction of what my heart told me to do. "I'll ride with you."

On our way into town, I wrung my hands as nervous butterflies invaded my stomach. It was like I was only capable of making bad choices today.

All you need to do is be open with him, I gave myself a silent pep talk. *He's your best friend. Nothing can change that.*

But, apparently, I was wrong.

Whatever hope Teddy might have felt was gone by the time we reached the park, instead replaced by a sour, taciturn mood. He barely looked at me as we unloaded the flower arrangements. In fact, he seemed determined to avoid me. We placed the flower arrangements on a raised platform where the mayor would speak later that evening, while a small group wound colored lights in the branches overhead.

As the residents of Pebble's Creek began to arrive, I allowed a small child to weave flowers through my braid, as if I were a maiden from a classic fairy-tale. Farmers displayed fruit, cheese meat, and wine in their booths. Older women handed me samples of bath salts and homemade soaps. At one point, I found Teddy leaning against a tree

with his arms folded, his expression bored and rather forbidding.

"Why aren't you with Teddy?" Avery elbowed me as I eyed him from across the sea of faceless people.

I glanced down at my bare toes. "We sort of had a fight. I don't really want to talk about it." Before she could respond, I quickly changed the subject. "How's your guest? Baked any more goods for him?"

Avery rolled her eyes. "I've blazed through a whole bag of sugar since he's been under my roof," she said in mock outrage. I had a feeling she enjoyed his presence more than she allowed herself to admit. "I'm surprised he's not a diabetic, but I've seen him in nothing but a towel and there isn't an ounce of fat on him. I think I can die a happy woman now that I've seen his well-defined pecs."

The thought of Decadence semi-nude turned my stomach. Once upon a time, I would have clamored for the opportunity to see a man like him naked, being the rabid romance junkie that I was, but now I was starting to realize that someone understated like Teddy was all I ever wanted. I lost him in the throng as the mayor gave her speech, but I spotted Decadence in a black turtleneck and blazer in the shadows on the fringe of the gathering.

I nudged Avery. "You should ask him to dance," I whispered.

She eyed him hopefully. "I doubt he would go for someone like me."

"Don't be ridiculous!" I softly exclaimed. "You're a total babe. I'd buy that sexy calendar of you chopping wood."

Avery rolled her eyes but flashed me a gap-toothed smile.

The mayor summoned me to the stage, and, before a sea of spectators, I channeled magic through my fingertips, aiming at the sky. Everyone gasped as flowers shot from my fingers and exploded like fireworks. Children danced in the petals that rained from the sky. The view from the platform was breathtaking. The setting sun painted the sky shades of gold, rosy pink, and indigo with colored lights strung overhead. The falling petals were an added touch.

"Let the party begin!" The mayor proclaimed.

The moment I stepped off the platform, Rex, the blonde quarterback who'd asked me to dance at my senior prom, asked me for yet another turn on the dance floor. He was smooth and polite with a rich, husky voice and broad shoulders. Sure, he was handsome, but my eyes continued to scan the crowd for Teddy, to no avail. Had he gone home already? A tall, gangly man with a dark mullet and matching beard named Bart asked for the second dance and lingered for the third, but his sweaty palms and furry upper lip did nothing for me.

When the theme from *Footloose* ended, Bart was ready to ask for a third dance when a tall, imposing figure overshadowed him. "May I steal her for a dance?" A rich, smooth, impossibly deep voice sliced through the din like a hot knife through butter.

Bart paled at the sight of Decadence, and the blood drained from my body. Those impenetrable amber eyes watched me like a hawk. I was caught between a rock and a hard place, wanting to escape Bart's clutches while also avoiding Death the Tax Collector, but eventually I placed my warm hand in his cool one, allowing him to whisk me away. The crowd gawked as he swept me to the center of the dance floor, if grass could ever qualify as such. My eyes were level with his chest, which forced me to crane my neck in order to make eye contact.

The expression of pure, unadulterated hunger on his face was sobering, forcing me to quickly look away.

- -

"You look exceptionally beautiful tonight, Koreyna," one corner of his snarky mouth curled, "but isn't that always the case?"

I shifted uncomfortably in his embrace. We were standing much too close.

"I mean no disrespect," I began, "but I only accepted your offer out of sheer politeness."

Decadence snorted derisively, a reaction that caught my attention. "We both know you're in my arms because you want to be. If that young man truly wanted you, he would fight on your behalf, don't you think? Where is he now? I don't see him."

Decadence turned and, at that precise moment, I found Teddy watching me from the sidelines, his red, mottled face a patchwork of jealousy, longing, bitter disappointment, and crippling despair. His lips trembled in quiet mutiny; his hands balled into tight fists as he hovered on the verge of action. He looked positively livid in his helplessness, and I could almost *feel* every emotion that flowed through him as if it were my own.

"There you are," I breathed.

Without even a second thought, I broke away from Decadence and weaved through the crowd until Teddy's warm, limp hands were encased in my own as I guided him onto the dance floor. "Every Breath You Take" by The Police morphed into "The Night We Met", as if God had placed the track there himself, and my fingers tangled with his as we swayed beneath the colored lights. Starbursts of yellow, blue, and pink played across his handsome face, and whatever angst that had once pummeled his heart bled into a sense of wonder that took my breath away. Slowly, I brought our joined hands to my lips and kissed his knuckles.

"I'm sorry for what happened last night," I murmured against skin and bone. "It doesn't matter whether I find anyone else attractive, because I choose you." When Teddy opened his mouth, I silenced him with a finger. "I choose you because I love you. I'm dedicated to you because I'm not happy unless I'm with you. And I'll choose you every day of my life because we belong together, you and I. I don't ever want to be parted from you."

Teddy firmly grasped my head and dragged open-mouthed kisses over every inch of my face, his breath hot and erratic on my skin. I didn't care if the residents of Pebble's Creek, who had watched us grow up together, stared and gawked. I didn't care if my mother was shocked. I didn't care if Decadence had been cock-blocked. All that mattered was Teddy and I.

"Let's get out of here," I whispered in his ear.

Teddy grabbed my hand with a renewed will to live, unaware that something dark and malevolent watched from the shadows, and stammered, "Where t-to, my l-lady?"

~

Teddy sat with his back against the tree overlooking the river with me nestled between his legs. I sighed contentedly as he wrapped both arms around me and squeezed.

"I'm the l-luckiest man in the w-world," he whispered against my neck, his prominent nose buried in my hair.

"We're both lucky," I corrected and snuggled against his chest. "I only wish we had done this sooner. Why did you wait so long to declare your love for me?"

Teddy laughed weakly, though he seemed forlorn, as though he carefully guarded a secret that was bubbling up his throat.

"I n-never knew where I s-stood with you," he shrugged self-consciously. "I've always w-waited until I

knew for s-sure. In this case, I c-couldn't wait any l-longer because I knew w-we were out of t-time."

"Running out of time?" I echoed. "What do you mean? We have all the time in the world."

I turned in his embrace and found him watching me with an uncertainty that made me pause.

"What's wrong?" I asked.

Teddy swallowed hard.

"There's something I n-need to tell you," he began haltingly. "Something I n-need to explain to you b-before it's too l-late, but I think w-we should go b-back to your house so we can t-talk without being interrupted."

My brow furrowed as trepidation drowned out our shared bliss.

"Okay," my panic rose as every worst-case scenario flooded my mind. "Are you a father? Are you in love with someone else? Do you have a life-threatening disease?"

"No," Teddy laughed. "I'll explain everything t-to you over a c-cup of chamomile t-tea." He caressed my cheek. "You l-look exhausted."

I swallowed my influx of questions and allowed him to pull me to my feet. The whisper of voices grew louder as we approached the forest. The sun's rays streaked the darkening sky, as though clinging to the present day. Even so, the fading light cast the dense forest in an ominous shadow and, for one heart-stopping moment, I thought I

saw a man silhouetted against a backdrop of eerily pale tree trunks. The rustle of leaves drowned out the sound of the man's breathing, but I knew he was there.

Watching.

Waiting.

A strangely protective instinct overwhelmed me, and I stopped dead in my tracks, flinging out an arm to prevent my best friend and lover from taking one more step.

"What's w-wrong?" He whispered, freezing like an animal that sensed a predator.

"We're being watched," I shivered as my skin prickled with dread. The pounding of my heart rattled my bones. My mind raced at a frenetic pace. "What should we do?"

Teddy whirled to face me, his jade eyes overbright.

"We s-shoulg go back to the r-river," he said breathlessly, taking my small hands in his warm ones. "We'll exchange our vows in the only p-place that has ever m-mattered to us. That w-way no one can s-stop us. N-not even death."

I frowned deeply at his choice of words. Death? Who said anything about dearth? If an axe murderer waited for us in the forest, surely he would follow us if we ran away. That's not how I wanted to spend my final moments with Teddy.

"We need to run," I reasoned through mounting panic. "We need to - ."

"Trust m-me," he urged calmly with beseeching eyes.

I began to suspect that he knew more than he openly revealed, so I followed him in the glittering semi-darkness back to the one place that had ever truly mattered. We raced hand-in-hand to the banks of the endlessly flowing river, and I conjured two flower crowns for us to wear. Wet sand squished between my bare toes as we faced each other and clasped hands. Thornless vines sprouting velvety leaves immediately twined around our wrists, joining us together as we gazed into each other's eyes. His shimmered with emotion, as though memorizing my face for the last time, and the finality of his expression made me choke back a sob. Why was he looking at me that way?

"I promise I will always p-protect and guide you in life and d-death," he stammered. "I will always p-place your needs above m-my own, whether in this l-life or the next."

I thought of how Decadence had once tempted me with vague promises of pleasure and grandeur. My vow flowed freely from my lips, my heart already knowing exactly what to say.

"I vow to always remain faithful in this life and the next," I swore as my eyes bore into his. "I will never falter or betray you. You are my first and only choice, forever and always."

Our joined hands glowed with a radiant light as the vines twined around our arms and waists, binding us together. The phenomenon should have made us panic and struggle against one another, but the vines were a symbol for the bond we already shared. Teddy pressed his forehead to mine as we listened to the trickle of water and the faint rustle of leaves, and then he lightly brushed my lips in the sweetest, most tender kiss I had ever known. I tasted the purity of his love for me, even as something dark pulsed around us, struggling to penetrate the bond we had forged. The moment Teddy and I pulled away from each other, someone a short distance away clapped mockingly with a low, soft chuckle.

Our heads snapped in the direction of that voice, my heart plummeting as my eyes locked on Decadence. Instead of the black turtleneck and velvet blazer, he now donned form-fitting black with a layer of silver armor beautifully engraved with vines and roses. A crimson cloak fluttered behind him, making him look regal, commanding, and decadent all at once.

"I applaud you, Theodore Kershaw," Decadence smirked humorlessly as he clapped slowly. "Few mortals have the stomach to cheat Death. Did you know that I was rooting for you? You've done exactly as you were expected to do for thousands of years, yet you decide to rebel now? What happened?" He spread his arms wide as he stepped closer, making me shiver.

"What are you talking about?" I demanded harshly, not wanting to spare what few emotions Decadence possessed.

But my abrasive words had the opposite effect. Decadence tilted his head and peered at me with a glimmer of admiration.

"You're not afraid of me, are you?" His lush mouth crooked in a half-smile that looked far gentler than the mocking one he reserved for Teddy. "That hasn't changed about you."

I turned back to my lover, who'd remained oddly silent throughout this exchange, and I found him watching me carefully, as though gauging my reaction.

"What is he talking about?" I whispered.

"Don't give in to h-him," he shook his head as frustrated tears welled in his eyes. "No m-matter what h-happens, I'll come for you. I love you, Korey."

"Yes," Decadence mocked once more. "Say your good-byes before I give him the swift, honor-less death he deserves."

The vines binding us withered and fell away and, before I could wrap Teddy in my arms, Decadence blasted him off his feet. I screamed as I watched Teddy soar through the air, landing head-first on a jagged rock before splashing into the river.

"NO!" I screamed, until my throat was raw.

I was beside myself with grief as I tore at my hair, unaware of the presence that loomed inches behind me. Decadence stroked my hair as though trying to comfort me, and I fiercely slapped his hand away. He placed a large hand on my shoulder and turned me to face him, but I beat his armor with my fists and, once I realized they were no match for his protective gear, I slapped his beautiful face and pulled his hair. I wanted to hurt him because of how much he had hurt me. I wanted to make him suffer, but the fight slowly drained from my body as he cradled me against his chest.

"Would you like to see him?" He whispered soothingly. "If you come with me, you can be with him for all eternity." He touched the tears on my face as though fascinated by them and crooned, "Don't you want to see him again?"

Remember Teddy's warning, I told myself. I realized that my lover had expected to die. Teddy had insisted on exchanging our vows by the river because he'd sensed his approaching death. Knowing this broke my heart, but we had bound ourselves with magic. *My* magic.

If I followed Decadence, could I save Teddy? Could I use my magic to cheat Death? Another sobering realization hit me.

"Are you…?" My question trailed off, my mind incapable of fathoming the possibility.

"Death?" Those strange amber eyes softened, and his mouth twisted in a wry smile. "Yes, but I would prefer that you call me Decadence. It's part of my rebranding, you see."

I was speechless. My best friend had just died before my eyes and the man who killed him had the gall to crack jokes?

"Please take me to him," I pleaded, crossing my fingers in the hope that I hadn't made the wrong decision. Decadence offered his large hand. What other choice did I have? Death had proven himself capable of overpowering me, so my only option was to thwart him at his own game under the guise of compliance.

I hated the way he stared at me as I tentatively placed my hand in his, as though he'd dreamt of this moment for ages. I hated the way his breath hitched as our palms touched. More than anything, I hated the way a deep, fathomless chasm opened the ground, separating the cluster of trees that had sheltered hundreds of picnics, conversations, inside jokes, and sweet kisses. The chasm was symbolic of Death tearing our world apart, as though our destinies were beyond our control. I wanted to believe I had a choice, that my decisions carried some weight in the grand scheme of things, but right now the only way forward was descending the steep, crumbling staircase that spiraled into darkness.

You Don't Own Me

Death guided me down the endless flight of stone steps that spiraled further into inky blackness. I stumbled behind my captor, forced to match his relentless pace. Flower petals withered and fell from the crown perched on my head, creating a silky breadcrumb trail as my bare feet scuffed on the ancient stone. The setting reminded me of *The Phantom of the Opera* when the Phantom guides Christine through his labyrinthine world, except my surroundings were neither magical or welcoming. There were no animated sparkly gold arms holding elaborate candelabras. Only cobwebs and ominous statues that flanked every passageway.

Nothing prepared me for the wide river that glowed an eerie, translucent green with silver threads lurking beneath the surface like jellyfish. I was reminded of what I'd learned about the Styx from Greek mythology, and I was startled to realize that those myths contained a grain of truth. Death watched me carefully as he lowered me into the elaborately carved gondola and, like the Hades and Persepone myth, he used a long pole that curled in a decorative spiral to steer us. Skeletal hands emerged from the hazy depths as I leaned over the edge to peer into the water, making me gasp in horror.

"Don't touch the water!" Death's deep, forbidding voice commanded from behind. "These souls are bound for eternal suffering, and I am powerless to stop them if they drag you below the surface."

With silent tears choking me, I wanted to argue that he sounded melodramatic, but what the hell did I know? Did I really want to risk finding out for myself? I needed to save Teddy. That was my mission. And after I saved him, I would demand that he divulge every secret.

I had so many questions, but the ethereal glow of the water hypnotized me, providing only temporary relief from my distress.

"Will I find Teddy in the river?" I asked, noticing how Death clenched his jaw.

"He resides with the souls waiting to drink from the river," he patiently explained, despite his obvious frustration. "The spirits drink from the river to wipe their memories, for death is often too painful for them."

Oh no.

What if Teddy succumbed to this? Despite his cold exterior, Death had the decency to show some sympathy from their plight.

"Do you think Teddy will drink from the river?" I probed, my heart aching in my chest as I wrung my hands.

Death snorted with a careless shrug. "It would lessen my headache if he did."

I shot him a hateful glare before wrapping my arms around my legs and resting my chin on my knees. On the horizon, figures swathed in white carried iridescent lanterns, souls trailing after them as they guided the dead through the maze of passageways. Everywhere I looked, I was surrounded by death. I shivered.

A massive black gate that looked like something out of *Lord of the Rings* loomed ahead. As a ferry approached, the massive black gate opened and revealed a beastly silhouette that emerged from the ominous haze. As our gondola slipped through the open gate, my eyes focused on four massive black paws. Thick fur covered a massive beast with three heads, their liquid eyes glittering malevolently. My jaw slackened and eyes widened as the gondola bobbed past the rock that accommodated such an animal. I swallowed hard as I imagined Teddy traveling through what I assumed was the Underworld from myths and legends.

Lost and alone.

The moment I set foot on solid ground, I needed to save him from this wretched place. Death used his pole to scratch the massive creature's underbelly, and I watched as the dog's outwardly fearsome guard dissolved. I only wept harder. When we reached the heart of the Underworld, I gasped as a velvety blanket of stars shimmered over a diverse landscape. The boiling sun arced over the horizon, suffusing the cobalt sky with threads of forest green, dusky rose, and saffron.

Vast, rolling hills of pale, translucent flowers and trees faded into a grassy basin where the river converged, the banks dotted with thousands of souls. The grassy fields gave way to barren desert and, finally, to volcanic, all-consuming flame. An almost Gothic palace overlooked the landscape, a small village at its base. I loathed admitting defeat, but the Underworld was the most breathtaking sight I had ever beheld. If only this were a ride at Universal Studios with Teddy wedged beside me.

The palace itself was carved from the rock wall with its soaring spires, turrets, and covered walkways. Hundreds of mullioned windows twinkled, as though dozens of candles flickered from within. The gondola bobbed as Death (I refused to call him by his chosen name), leapt onto a grimy dock and offered me one large hand. I accepted his help, momentarily dazed as I absorbed my surroundings. The second my big toe touched the dock, my dress partially fell open, baring one leg, and he swept me into his powerful arms before I toppled into the soul-sucking river.

Our noses were inches apart, mainly because his own was enormous, but I didn't pull away like I should have, the sulfuric fumes overwhelming my senses.

My nose wrinkled, mostly because I wanted to fuck with him for taking my best friend's life. "Did you break wind?"

He looked appalled.

Score one for me, zero for Death.

"Careful," he warned. "I have the power to change my mind at any time. Either that, or I can toss you into the river so that the feckless souls may have a chance at you."

I swallowed my tongue and allowed Death to carry me through the front gate of his palace. As we approached, a looming statue of his likeness with the hood of his cloak drawn over his carved face stood at the center of nightmarish hedges. As if making their dramatic entrance, large bat-like creatures flapped overhead, their shrill cries reverberating through the pungent night air. Death kicked the heavy doors of his palace open, and I gasped as I caught my first glimpse of the interior. Glittering chandeliers hovered close to the gleaming black-and-white checkered floor. Two rows of ornate pillars flanked the Entrance Hall, swirling designs carved into the swirling marble.

The low light cast an amber glow over the scene, though the ivory and gold interior bled into a cobalt ceiling that reflected the starry sky outside. I expected him to place me on my feet, since I was fully capable of walking, but he strode briskly down the center of the Entrance Hall, ascending a winding marble staircase two steps at a time.

"Where are we going?" I asked as his crimson cloak fluttered behind him. I squirmed in his embrace as I struggled to free myself. "You said we were going to find Teddy!"

Death's grip on me tightened as I flailed.

"Hush. You're going to wait in your chambers while I search for him."

"You're a liar!" I snarled as I tugged on his hair and cloak.

"Silence!" He thundered as he kicked open another door and deposited me on a comfortable bed.

The chamber was furnished with red and gold tapestries. In fact, the entire room was bedecked with red curtains fringed with gold tassels, a changing screen, and ornate gold walls dominated by an enormous mirror. The bed was lush and sumptuous with a gauzy canopy. A water basin sat upon a small table in the corner with fresh towels.

Death knelt before me as tears rolled down my cheeks, too absorbed in my misery to appreciate my decadent surroundings.

"What do you want from me?" I shook my head helplessly.

"Koreyna," he reached for me with a sigh.

"Stop calling me that!" I shouted, my shrill voice echoing off the walls. "My name is Korey, but you haven't earned the right to call me anything because you murdered my best friend. Why the fuck am I even here if you won't take me to him?"

Death sighed heavily, and I caught the glimmer of a jewel-encrusted dagger sheathed in his belt as his cloak billowed around him from a spine-tingling draft. He gave me an entreating look as his amber eyes searched my face.

"You're here because I've searched for thousands of years to find you. We knew each other long ago, but you were torn from me. I've plagued the world with sickness, hoping I might lure you out of hiding. The use of your magic drew me like a moth to a flame, and I was powerless to resist claiming you as my own." Death's mouth twisted, as though he tasted something foul. "Your little friend, however, complicated things. I disposed of him because I knew he wouldn't be able to touch you in the Underworld as a dead man. While the dead inhabit corporeal bodies, it is forbidden to experience worldly pleasures with the living. That sorry excuse of a mortal could torture himself for an eternity over a woman that ws never destined to be his for all I care."

The callousness of his words hardened my heart towards him. How could I have ever coveted him?

"So you killed the man I love to manipulate me," I concluded.

Death's face turned a mottled red.

"You're a child!" He seethed through clenched teeth. "What do you know about love?"

"Obviously more than you," I countered. "Decadence is a suitable name for a man who conceals the meaninglessness of his existence with a sumptuous cloak and hollow smile."

Death flinched with slightly parted lips, his eyes wounded and sad, but I suppressed whatever twinge of sympathy I experienced on his behalf and acted quickly.

Plunging my hand inside his cloak, I retrieved the jeweled dagger and slashed the blade diagonally across his face. Blood gushed between his fingers as he clutched his ruined face, stumbling as I shoved past him and raced for the door, my dress and hair streaming behind me like a banner.

"STOP!" Death bellowed as I struggled to wrench open the door.

The damn thing was locked. Son of a bitch.

I whirled around and poised the dagger over my wrist.

"Take one step closer and I'll slit my wrists," I threatened as I edged closer to a set of double doors that opened to a balcony. I didn't want to take my own life, but I wanted him to think I had the upper-hand. Death clutched his wounded face, blood coursing down his armoured sleeve and dripping onto the marble floor. "I don't care how long you've searched for me. I won't allow you to steal my choice after killing the man I love. What good am I if I'm dead?"

He reigned supreme over this realm and , therefore, could do anything he wished, so I was probably fighting a losing battle. But I wouldn't give up. I needed to escape the palace so I could search the river basin for Teddy.

"You're a fool if you think suicide will solve your problems," he stepped closer and offered one hand, palm-up, "but I commend you fot your strength and conviction."

In response, I brandished a sword hanging on the nearby wall, my feet skidding on the marble floor as I raced for the open double doors.

"I bet you do," I gave him a withering look as I slammed the double doors behind me and barricaded them using the sword.

Breathless, I collapsed against the door, sweaty, aching, friendless, and alone. Death had an imposing, muscular body. Surely, he could break down these doors after he bandaged his face. Wounding that pretty face of his had been a small victory on my part, but nothing mattered if I couldn't figure out a way to escape and save Teddy.

Marked For Death

The balcony was bathed in blue light, the twisted balustrade threaded with silver and shimmering cobalt. Ashen vines thicker than my torso crept up the wall beside the balcony, and I flung my leg over the balustrade and gripped the enormous leaves to shimmy down the snake-like vine. The moment my bare feet touched the courtyard's cool flagstones, I felt instant relief from the dry, simmering heat of the Underworld. Greco-Roman pillars flanked a deep, rectangular pool. Several ornate faucets lined the perimeter, like the prefect's sudsy bath from *The Goblet of Fire.* More creeping vines slithered up the courtyard's crumbling walls, and I immediately knew this to be my escape route.

Part of me hesitated because I didn't know what dangers lay beyond the wall, but I was no safer waiting for Death to retaliate. The courtyard was cold and lifeless, the statues of Death weathered and gloomy. This wasn't my home. I climbed the vines, a more difficult task than I expected, and perched on top of the wall like a stray cat, the slashing beams of the blood orange sun illuminating a narrow, uneven passageway that disappeared through a tunnel. The vines extended to the other side of the wall, so I carefully lowered my weight until my feet found purchase on cold stone.

The moment I entered the tunnel, panic spiked as a curling tendril extended from the vaulted ceiling to caress my face. I choked back a scream and tore through the

darkness, until I stumbled down a crooked staircase and fell flat on my face, several layers of dust billowing like a cloud from the collision. Groaning, I clambered to my feet and dusted myself off. Rosy-orange sunlight slanted through the stained-glass windows, creating a kaleidoscope of color on the mosaic floor. Rich tapestries hung between each window, the crimson velvet a stark contrast to the murky floor. I studied the mosaic beneath my feet, remembering Emperor Justinian and his consort, Theodora, ones I had studied in my college textbooks.

The Underworld was a strange catalogue of time, as though each layer of history lived and breathed in this realm. The mosaic floor depicted the cycle of life, death, and rebirth that portrayed Death as both a cruel and merciful part of existence. But which interpretation was the correct one? Based on the short time I had known him, I could easily guess.

The flap of wings and the clacking of sharp nails drew my attention to the vaulted ceiling, where hundreds of dark, leathery creatures swarmed. One landed on my shoulder, and I screamed as I knocked the damn thing onto the floor, its sharp nails tearing the sleeve of my dress as it clung for dear life. More bat-like iguanas descended, and I tore through the chamber until I managed to slam a door that acted as a shield. The creatures' nails scraped on the other side of the heavy dore, and I wiped off the sweat pearling on my brow as my chest rose and fell. A gust of hot air stirred my hair, and I whipped around to find myself on another balcony that overlooked the entirety of the Underworld.

My jaw slackened as I drank in the sight of the radiant sky dissolving from blood orange to velvety blue to smoky ash, as though representing the balance between good and evil, life and death. Lightning crackled far beyond the planes of existence, and the purple clouds that raged on the horizon tugged on something deep within me. Knowing I had nowhere else to escape for the time being, I curled up on the mosaic floor - the distant rumble of the volcano on the far side of the Underworld, the wind that whistled through the palace, and the faint hum of souls lulling me to sleep.

In the midst of my dreams, I was vaguely aware of a man kneeling beside my aching body and scooping me into his powerful arms. Wings flapped overhead as he carried me through the tower, but the cloaked figure's presence held the bat-like iguanas at bay. Dark, magnetic energy pulsed through his veins, and I knew somewhere in the back of my mind that Death cradled me in his arms like the misunderstood hero of a grand, sweeping Gothic romance. Somewhere along the way, the dream had turned into a nightmare.

~

"Teddy!" I surged forward on a soft, comfortable bed, a lifetime's worth of memories flooding me.

Someone shushed me, though not rudely, and caressed my hair as I eased back onto the heavenly nest of pillows. I slipped back into a world of my own, where only Teddy and I existed. That same dark energy hovered on the fringes of my dreams as though the images themselves were tinged with darkness, and I found myself resisting him even in sleep. My body sank deeper into plush softness, the decadent textures of velvet and silk refreshingly cool, as though infused with the same darkness that swaddled me like a baby.

The moment my bleary eyes fluttered open, the first thing I noticed was Death crouched in the shadows beside my bed.

Not creepy at all.

He wore a short-sleeved black tunic and matching black toga-like robe cinched at the waist by a thick black belt. Two slits ran up the length of each leg, exposing the unearthly pallor of his skin. The robe pooled around his gladiator-esque sandals; his gold embroidered crimson cloak the only pop of color. A crown of gold leaves rested on his tousled waves, a deep, jagged wound carved diagonally across his face.

Despite the wound, he seemed... calm.

Watchful.

The moment I stirred, something flared to life in the depths of his amber eyes, yet he remained stoic and remote, as though he wasn't sure how to react. How long had he watched me sleep?

"Not *you* again," I made a frustrated growl as I collapsed back onto my pillows.

Thank God I still wore my red dress and not my birthday suit. I would have completely flipped my shit if I

had woken up naked. The idea would have panned out well for a romance novel. As for real life? Not so much. Okay, maybe I would have been somewhat flattered if Death, Decadence, or whatever the fuck he called himself hadn't cracked Teddy's head like a walnut, but that was a conversation for a completely different story.

Death's pink mouth crooked in a half-smile, completely nonplussed by my reaction. "Are you comfortable?"

"My comfort doesn't matter," I snapped. "Where's Teddy?"

Death's body stiffened as he sucked in an impatient breath. The way his cuffed forearms rested on his knees spoke of power and control, and I was convinced this man, for lack of a better description, possessed layers of hidden depths.

"I searched everywhere for him," he said, "but I found nothing. Either he survived the fall and is safely home bandaging his wounds, or his soul hasn't yet passed through the sorting process. The next time I search for him, I will bring you with me."

The explanation seemed rehearsed, as though he'd practiced it thousands of times before delivering it now. But I realized with a sinking heart that I had no means to search the fields myself. Every part of me hoped Teddy was safely home with a bruised head, but I knew he wouldn't rest until he had released me from Death's clutches. The thought both thrilled and terrified me. Death rose from his crouched

position, and I realized that his long toga-like robe contained shades of silver, black, and red, as though the garment were a living, breathing thing. Begrudgingly, I admitted that Death had style.

"Your maidservant is waiting outside with hot water and a copper tub," he informed me with a regal sweep of his arm. "I would like you to bathe and dress so we may share breakfast together in the Great Hall. You *are* my guest, after all."

I gave him a thumbs-up, which conveyed my silent agreement on the surface while secretly meaning, "Up yours."

Death frowned slightly, puzzled, so I flashed him a sweet smile to cover my tracks. He strode through the open doorway as a woman in ashen blue robes that matched her skin poured a steaming bucket of water into a copper tub at the foot of my bed. The maidservant's braided hair was arranged into intricate loops on top of her head, the strands threaded with silver, blue, and gold. I clutched the crimson silk sheet to my breast as I watched her in silent fascination, waiting for the moment I could catch a glimpse of her face.

"Hello." My voice sounded small and shy compared to how I had earlier spoken to Death.

The young woman whipped around, startled, and I sucked in a breath as the ornate mask covering her face came into view. The mask itself was a light ashen blue, several shades lighter than her skin, the likeness of her face delicate and feminine. The porcelain mask was decorated with gold

spirals that reminded me of a a masquerade ball. To my surprise, the young woman bobbed an enthusiastic curtsy.

"I'm delighted to see you again, my lady," she clapped her hands. "Lord Death has awaited your arrival for centuries now. I'll help you undress so that you may soak in the tub before the water cools."

Her sweet, chipper nature softened my guard, though her words baffled me.

"Have I been here before?" I asked, the question ridiculous even to my own ears.

"Lord Death will explain everything in due time." The young woman rounded the massive bed and offered one delicate hand. "Don't be afraid. I have a fresh gown waiting for you."

"No!" I clutched my dirty, torn dress. "May I wear this one? My best friend, Teddy, might be on his way, and I want to wear his favorite dress when he arrives."

"Teddy?" I imagined her nose wrinkling as she clucked her tongue. "I knew that young man was nothing but trouble the day he arrived at the palace. He's always had a sparkle in his eye for you, but can I really blame him?" She covered her porcelain mouth and laughed. "Lord Death would likely feed me to the beasts that roam the Forbidden Lands if he heard me speak so freely."

What?! My mind buzzed with a flurry of activity.

I grabbed her delicate shoulders. "Teddy's been here before?"

The strange young woman locked her porcelain mouth and tossed away the imaginary key.

"I completely understand," I nodded and released her. "I'll save my tricky questions for Death."

"*Lord* Death," she corrected primly and splayed a hand on her chest. "I'm Cordelia. Of course we've already met, but I know we're going to make fast friends."

Cordelia offered to help me undress, but I insisted on hiding behind the screen while I disrobed, emerging moments later with a soft towel wrapped around my naked body.

"You're not hiding anything I haven't seen before," Cordelia's laugh tinkled like delicate crystal, making my face burn.

I slipped inside the copper tub with my hands clamped over my privates, some of which had to be compromised because I only had two for the job. Once I was safely inside the tub, Cordelia immediately grabbed a bar of soap and scrubbed my body, despite the small splashes I made in the water out of dignified protest.

"Relax," Cordelia breathed as she worked the tension from my shoulders.

Begrudgingly, I sank deeper into the water, enjoying the way the rosemary-infused soap tickled my nostrils and how the small ripples lapped at my breasts. Cordelia doused my tangled hair with a pitcher of hot water, and I couldn't resist moaning from the way my dirty scalp tingled. The water was infused with peppermint, which made my flushed skin feel strangely cool, despite the water's heat. The maidservant massaged lavish mixtures into my hair and used a sharp-toothed comb with a wooden handle to untangle my thick, dark locks. By the time Corelia asked me to rise from the copper tub, I was like putty in her hands.

My skin no longer crawled with grime and filth, and I sighed luxuriantly as Cordelia rubbed oils into my skin. Something about the tantalizing aromas made me forget everything. My identity outside of Death. My life before coming to the Underworld. My eyes bore sightlessly into my reflection as the maidservant dressed me in something Padme Amidala would have worn.

Who the hell was Padme Amidala?

The memory of a slight woman with brown hair and a pixie-ish face swam to the forefront of my mind, but I couldn't make sense of who she was. Pale yellow silk fluttered down my otherwise naked body, held by a solid gold choker circling my neck. The yellow dye faded into purple. A matching sash looped around my waist, emphasizing my curvaceous figure. Matching trains of fabric trailed from gold cuffs around my upper arms. Cordelia piled my dark curls on top of my head and allowed wisps to frame my heart-shaped face. I stared at my reflection, utterly speechless and… lost.

"You're ready," Cordelia whispered, the porcelain mask reducing her voice to a snake-like hiss.

"Ready for what?" I asked blankly, making her burst into peals of delicate laughter.

~

Death's crimson cloak spilled down his back onto the obsidian floor, his pale arms and face reflected perfectly on its polished surface. The roaring flames in the massive hearth bathed his sharp profile in tones of burnt orange and pale gold. He watched the flames with a grim expression, his hands clasped behind his back as though he was waiting for something.

Or someone.

I was incapable of tearing my eyes away from the regal, solitary lord who now faced me with eyes that flashed as brilliantly as the leaping flames. I floated across the Great Hall in my diaphanous gown without knowing my purpose. I couldn't remember why I was here. Wasn't I waiting for someone? Did that even matter?

Death offered his large hand, and I accepted it without question.

Something inside of me protested as he drew me closer, but I couldn't resist the way he pressed a kiss to the inside of my wrist, his touch refreshingly cool on my flushed skin.

"I see you're finally back to your old self," his lush mouth crooked in a half-smile. He kissed the inside of my forearm this time "My queen."

My inner thighs were slick with arousal as his kisses grew hotter and wetter. I tangled my fingers in his gleaming black hair, dislodging his gold-leafed crown, and sucked in a breath before devouring his gaping mouth. His lips were both hot and cold as he cradled the base of my skull with one powerful hand, drawing me closer to his hard body with the other. His full lips were incredibly soft, more so than I had imagined, and I couldn't resist a low, primal moan as I sucked on his bottom lip.

"I assume you're no longer angry with me," he commented wryly between kisses as his fingers trailed down my back. "God, how I've missed you."

My head dipped back as his mouth moved over my chin and down my throat.

"Teddy," I breathed.

That name triggered a lifetime's worth of memories that rushed through me like a pounding waterfall. Teddy's windswept hair as he rode his bicycle. Tedy's wry mouth curving into a secretive smile as he peered at me from across a crowded room with those intelligent eyes. Teddy gazing down at me, his face flushed with need, as he thrust deep inside of me.

These treasured moments coursed through me like electricity, striking Death by way of our connection. He

froze, though he didn't immediately retreat. Instead, that same electricity crackled around him, the manifestation of pure energy. He towered over me as though I were a nasty insect he wanted to grind into the floor with his heel.

"Is it true?" He asked softly, the warm play of firelight warring with the shadows on his glowering expression. "Has he touched you?"

Had he not overheard my conversation with Avery?

"That's none of your business," I lifted my chin, though my voice quavered. "No matter what you think, you don't own me."

Death grinned slyly, though his expression lacked warmth and humor. Beneath the cold, unadulterated fury, I saw flickers of soul-crushing pain and grief.

"Brave words," he applauded mockingly. "Who do you think you're speaking to? I could drain your body of life within seconds and leave that poor wretch to grieve over your lifeless body. After all, he would deserve such a fate," the words wrenched from him bitterly.

"What has he ever done to you?" I demanded, surging after him as he turned his back on me with a snap of his cloak. "I don't understand."

Death whirled on me, a cold, bloodthirsty glint in his feverish eyes.

"*Everything!*" He snarled, furious tears glimmering in the firelight. Several heavy footsteps brought him closer,

until he loomed over me "Why don't I tell you a story?" He hissed malevolently. "Once upon a time, Death stumbled upon a mortal toiling in her garden who, unlike others, wasn't afraid of him, so he whisked her off to the Underworld. They were in love. But one of Death's shades, a mortal sentenced to an eternity of servitude for taking his own life, envied their love. He coveted Death's bride for himself, seizing every opportunity to play music for her and make her laugh. Death sought to punish the shade, but the young mortal pleaded for mercy because she had come to see the shade as a close friend. Against Death's better judgement, he granted her request, only to have that weasel conspire with the celestial beings that rule the heavens, as well as his bride's irksome mother, to steal her from the Underworld. The shade's life was restored as a reward for his bravery and was ordered to protect her from Death's clutches. Her so-called friend poisoned her against Death so he could have her for himself. The celestial beings promised that if Death discovered her hiding place and claimed her virginity, the consummation of their love would bind them forever, making escape impossible."

My head throbbed in its effort to process the influx of information that left me with so many unanswered questions. Had Teddy once belonged to the Underworld? Was Cordelia a shade? Had Teddy worn an ornate porcelain mask like her? How could we have remained tethered to one another for thousands of years? One thing remained clear, however. While the moment didn't call for sass, I crossed my arms and fixed him with a contemptuous glare. If my hackles weren't already raised, if I hadn't perceived Death

as a potential threat for drugging me into forced consummation, I might have infused my response with compassion.

I recognized the emotional depth of his kiss, which made it clear that he truly had waited for centuries but throwing a tantrum and pointing fingers wasn't the way.

"How unbelievably sexist you are for bartering a woman's virginity, like I'm somehow going to sign the contract of our union with my magical clitoris? Um, no thank you. Even if I was in love with you once upon a time, my heart has changed, and I wish you would honor my choices."

My snark only enraged him further, though his voice grew softer in contrast to his hardening expression. I shivered as his eyes bore into mine, promising only retribution.

"Theodoros *is* alive," he breathed the revelation, making my heart leap. "I've been tracking his movements. Predictably, he's infiltrated the Underworld in search of *you*. And you know what? I'm feeling rather generous today. I'll allow your short-lived reunion and hasty escape... but, mark my words, I'll hunt that traitor down like the pathetic excuse of a mortal that he is. I expect you to run fast and hard once you leave the palace, because I'm coming for him. As for you?" I jerked away as he traced the curve of my cheek. "I will make you my bride, regardless of your virginity. Or lack thereof."~

I wore a hole in the marble floor as I restlessly paced my chambers, the train of my silk gown fluttering behind me with every brisk turn. Upon entering my lavish room, I glimpsed the copper tub filled with tepid water. I inhaled the scent of peppermint before rummaging through the various bottles Cordelia had used. The moment I inhaled the scent of pomegranates, my thoughts blurred on the edges. Despite the fuzziness, something clicked in my brain. That was it. Cordelia had most likely drugged me using the pomegranate-infused body oil upon Death's orders.

He disliked my cold fury and allegiance to another man, so he resorted to drugging me to recapture something he had lost ages ago. Well, two could play that game. Raising my arm, I smashed the bottle on the marble floor and, sure enough, tendrils of smoke curled from the thick ooze to form a wispy heart. From that moment onward, I vowed to bathe myself. At least until I escaped the Underworld with Teddy. The memory of Death's threat made my stomach clench painfully, the anticipation of Teddy's impending arrival skewering my heart. It was impossible to track the passage of time in the Underworld because the blanket of stars overhead never brightened, despite the boiling sun arcing low on the distant horizon.

Even though Death had promised a head start, glass crunched beneath my slippers as I heaved the sword, I had used to barricade the door off the wall. The knowledge that he hadn't removed any weapons from my chambers, the only person I was capable of harming being myself, made

me shiver with unease. There was no defeating him because there was no life to snuff out. Teddy had outwitted Death more than once, but he was no physical match for the unearthly god. If Teddy and I were going to escape the Underworld, we needed to agree on our strategy. I crouched behind the silk screen to collect my discarded red dress, but I snapped to attention when I heard a rustle outside.

A choked sob tore from my throat when I saw a flannel arm hook through the balustrade. My gown billowed as I raced to the balcony and reached for his guitar so that he could swing one leg over. Teddy looked *horrible*. Blood trickled from a nasty gash on his forehead. His torn clothing reeked of smoke. One flannel sleeve was missing. Ash streaked his sweaty, blood-stained face.

Teddy's bloodshot eyes hungrily searched my face and, despite looking the worse for wear, I had never seen a more beautiful sight.

"Teddy," I breathed as I wrapped my arms around his neck, drawing him close as his arms encircled my waist. After a moment, I pulled away from him and delicately touched his face, loathe to add more salt to his wounds. "I can't believe you're here."

Teddy's brow wrinkled as his sly mouth curved in a wry half-smile. "Where else w-would I b-be?" He croaked.

"Have you lost your voice?" I stroked his hair back from his face in concern. "Did you inhale too much smoke?"

"N-no," he shrugged bashfully. "I l-lost my voice from s-singing."

"Singing?" I echoed. "Do you mean to tell me that you toured the Underworld like a rock star before coming to rescue me?"

My eyes searched his face. I couldn't believe he was actually here.

"Not exactly," he laughed self-consciously, his unblinking gaze roaming my face and hair. "The m-moment I regained c-consciousness, I ran h-home and grabbed my g-guitar because I knew m-music was my only t-ticket into the Underworld." Teddy's shy, albeit heated green gaze dragged up my body. "After all, t-that's how we escaped b-before, you and I. Thousands of years ago, I s-sang of my l-love for you and my d-desire for a new l-life. This t-time I sang of our j-journey through the ages, how I've p-protected you and earned your love through p-patience and t-trust."

"So the rumors are true?" I asked softly, my lips tingling with a strange sort of urgency.

"Depends on w-what rumors you've h-heard," he eyed me warily, though his attention was drawn back to my mouth.

Wordlessly, I swept across the chamber to the water basin and soaked a white towel. I used the towel to clean the dried blood off of his face, my loving touch making his eyes flutter closed.

"That you committed suicide in a former life and was forced to serve as some kind of servant in the Underworld," I recounted. "That you cheated Death of his bride."

Death's version of events sounded more like a book I would've read on the banks of the river while Teddy scouted for tadpoles, but the possibility that I'd experienced this first-hand without any memories to rely on made me feel strangely duped.

"More or less," he watched me carefully as I cleaned his jagged wound, "but I'll s-share my m-memories with you once we f-find shelter. We n-need to hurry."

I had a million questions. How could he share memories with me? Was that a hidden superpower he'd failed to mention? I felt like I was deliberately being kept in the dark.

"I have a sword and a change of clothes," I jabbed a thumb over my shoulder. "I know that killing Death is impossible, but we need all the protection available to us. He made it clear that, while he's agreed to give us a head-start, there's a bounty on your head."

"Wait," his grip on my waist tightened as I moved to pull away.

My eyes widened, though my body shivered in delight, as his nose tickled the shell of my ear while his calloused hands roamed my bare back. Our cheeks nuzzled as we inhaled each other's scent. My fresh, clean one rubbed off on him as his sweat and musk marked me as his. Our

soft, erotic moans flavored the air as we exchanged our first open-mouthed kiss. Kissing Teddy made me feel awake and energized, as though someone had dipped me in cool water that invigorated my senses. I wanted more, but we needed to leave as soon as possible, so I wrenched myself away from him and savored his salty taste on my lips.

I grabbed my dress and the sword. I would stick out like a sore thumb in the ethereal gown I now wore, but I had no time to change. The gold bands around my upper arms and neck were tight, and I'd already struggled to remove them.

Brandishing the sword, I raised a proud chin. "Lead the way, since you're apparently the expert on the Underworld."

~

Teddy and I pillaged the velvet and silk bed sheets to cloak ourselves once we stepped foot outside of the palace. We escaped using the rotting vines that snaked up the crumbling walls. The sword clanged loudly on the other side as Teddy balanced his weight on top of the wall. He swung his legs over, dropping to the ground with the stealth of a cat.

"That way leads to a dead end," I gestured to the tunnel that housed the bat-like iguanas, barely suppressing a shiver of dread.

"The Den of Beasts," he whispered dramatically. "I used to p-play my lyre for you every d-day while the g-gargoyles flew c-circles around you."

"Gargoyles?" I scrunched up my nose and stuck out my tongue, making his eyes shine. "I don't believe that."

The temptation to kiss me was written all over his face, but instead he pressed a finger to his pink mouth.

"This way," he beckoned as he headed in the opposite direction down a long, winding staircase, and it impressed me that he seemed to have the palace grounds memorized by heart.

Teddy clutched the sword in one hand, his guitar slung across his back, as we traversed a hall of mirrors that reflected our creeping figures a thousand times over, opening to a circular room with a domed ceiling. A statue of a nude woman pouring water into a trickling fountain dominated the intricate mosaic floor, which depicted the everyday life of ancient civilizations.

"This used to b-be one of your f-favorite spots," Teddy's low voice echoed in the cavernous space. Momentarily distracted from our mission, as though Death's threats of retribution hadn't frightened him in the least, he propped the sword against the fountain and reached for me. "Here, l-let me show you."

The moment my hand touched his, a warm current of electricity flowed through my fingertips, as though he transferred some of his energy to me. My mind overflowed with foreign memories.

His memories.

Theodoros crooked a half-smile behind the porcelain mask that bore his likeness as he observed the beautiful mortal splashing like a child in the fountain wearing one of her finest silk gowns. He lurked in the shadows behind a pillar, far too lightheaded and breathless for a shade. The dread of Lord Death catching him in the act of admiring his bride was unthinkable, but he couldn't resist her laughter and high-spirited nature. She wasn't afraid of Lord Death like he was after decades of torture, a rather contagious attitude that emboldened him in his helpless state.

Something about her fire teased the shy, meek Theodoros into misbehaving and dwelling on thoughts he shouldn't. For the first time in decades, he remembered what life had meant before taking his own. Despite owning a corporeal body, he had forgotten the taste of food and wine, the comfort of human touch, and the sweet perfume of flowers. The young mortal with eyes larger than a doe's and rich, lustrous curls that spilled down her back filled the palace with her earthy fragrance that reminded him of dried herbs and the comforting sensation of burying his hands in partially sunbaked earth.

Theodoros had watched her from afar for several weeks with his lyre ready to entertain her with music, but the thought of approaching her made his dead, useless heart nearly pound out of his chest. They were too different, he told himself. No one that beautiful would ever want a shade with ashen blue skin and dead eyes. Lord Death was her equal in beauty, and she was far better off

with an unearthly being that spoiled her with every luxury. She was bound to become queen of the Underworld, whereas he would serve her for all eternity, always watching but never touching.

The mortal broke his miserable train of thought as she ducked beneath the water's surface and emerged a moment later with her small hands splayed on the marble. He sucked in a breath at the sight of her silk gown outlining her luscious figure in sharp detail, his furtive gaze trained on the fabric that clung to her taut nipples, lighting a fire in his soul that begged for more. The swell of her breasts and the feminine curve of her stomach called to him, though her sleek, dark hair made her look completely oblivious to her charms.

He had never known the touch of a woman in his short-lived existence and, for the first time in one-hundred-and-fifty years, he experienced an unquenchable thirst. A low, breathless moan escaped his throat, and he froze as the mortal's eyes clapped on him, though she didn't utter a sound.

"Please forgive me," he nearly stumbled over his own feet in his attempt to flee, too consumed with self-loathing to hear her cry out, "Wait!"

I staggered as my brain soaked up the memory in the span of a single heartbeat.

"I never took you for an exhibitionist," I teased as I slowly opened my eyes, though my heart ached from the sheer intensity of his emotions.

Teddy shrugged his angular shoulders and bit the inside of his cheek to prevent himself from smiling. "I was the v-voyeur. *You* w-were the exhibitionist." Unable to resist, his mouth curled in a slow smile. "Even back t-then you l-loved my eyes on you. Not m-much has changed."

The heat in his gaze made my lower belly simmer with need, despite our life-threatening circumstances. Teddy rubbed the back of his neck, looking chagrined.

"Death was r-right about me," he murmured. "I d-didn't save you for the right r-reasons. You were in l-love with m-me, and I stole you for m-myself because I c-couln't live without you." His green eyes welled with tears. "I c-couldn't endure an eternity of w-watching you with *him*. I n-never thought the celestial b-beings would bargain with Death, as though they s-sensed my selfishness. Do you c-condemn me for that?"

I sobered instantly. "Did you really take your own life before we met in the Underworld?"

Teddy screwed his eyes shut as tears streamed down his face and nodded. At that moment, I felt as though I no longer knew my best friend, or I at least needed to learn about his unspoken past, because he'd obviously suffered more than I could've imagined. We had shared hundreds of lifetimes together, and I wanted to know everything about our past lives so I could remember, too.

"Why?" I asked, unable to comprehend what had been worth taking his life over.

"I married a g-girl from my village," Teddy leaned into my touch as I wiped away his tears, "and she r-ran away with my b-best friend on our wedding n-night. I was

young, f-foolish, and had no c-concept of love. She m-means nothing to me," he reassured me as he stroked my hair, "but I'm s-scarred because of her actions. I am j-jealous, paranoid, and d-distrustful." He clasped my hands and brought them to his lips. "You're the only p-person I've ever t-trusted, but I'm terrified of Death t-taking you away from me. Even worse, I was afraid the embers of your p-past desire were rekindled w-when I found you at the d-diner with him."

"Teddy," I pressed a finger to his lips, "I slashed Death's face with one of his own blades because I hate him for what he's done to us. You could've drowned in the river, and I would have never forgiven him." I paused as something occurred to me. "On second thought, how did you survive that fall?"

"Water n-nymphs," he shrugged as though the existence of gorgeous faced women explained everything.

Now I was imagining a bevy of naked women huddled around Teddy as they breathed new life into his lungs.

"How did they save you exactly?" I asked as a ferocious tiger clawed the inside of my chest. "Did they kiss you? Did they give you mouth-to-mouth like the mermaids in *Hook*?"

"No!" Laughter exploded from him. "Are you j-jealous?"

"No," I sniffed. "You're the jealous one in this relationship. Not me."

"Relationship?" He arched his brow.

I rolled my eyes, growing tired of his monosyllabic answers.

"Do you regret agreeing to protect me from Death?" I probed, giving voice to a fear that triggered my own insecurity. "Do you wish you could have spent your lifetime with a wife and children of your own?"

Teddy's humorous expression grew fierce as he shook his head.

"I c-could never live w-without you," he vowed. "My l-love for you is a blessing and a c-cure that brings me comfort, joy, and p-pain. If I c-could reverse time, I w-would choose you all o-over again." His mouth curved in a wistful smile. "Don't assume I always b-behaved because I h-have no regard for the rules w-where you are concerned."

East of Eden

The palace was deathly quiet.

No pun intended.

We escaped through the servant's quarters, which were cramped compared to everything else. The shades slept peacefully in their bunks, and I peered through the darkness to scrutinize their bare faces, but the shadows were too thick. Teddy noticed my craning neck and nudged me forward.

"Why do the shades wear masks?" I whispered as I struggled to match his long stride.

"They don't c-choose to wear them, if that's w-what you're asking," Teddy scowled. "Death s-strips away our identities by giving us the semblance of d-demons, forcing us to conceal our f-faces with our former l-likeness. Consider it p-punishment for our misdeeds in a p-previous life."

"That's terrible," I shivered. "Is that why you were afraid to approach me in the memory? Because you were ashamed of your face?"

Teddy nodded stiffly.

"Did I ever see your face from... before?" I ventured shyly. "Did you ever show me?"

Teddy's expression grew shuttered as he turned away from me, apparently choosing to ignore that particular question. His reaction puzzled me. Wasn't I his best friend? Why was he hiding our past from me?   Relying on everyone else for answers made me feel helpless, like I had no control over this twisted situation. I followed Teddy in silence as we skirted the edge of the palace and avoided the front gate altogether by slipping into a copse of trees that moaned as they swayed in the hot, dry breeze. The temperature dropped as the branches overhead created a tunnel, the mossy path absorbing our heavy footfalls. The further we ventured into the depths of the forest, the taller and thicker the trees grew, the trunks as fat as one might find in the Redwood Forest. Perhaps even bigger. Silver light streamed overhead, and I pointed heavenward like a curious child.

"What's that?" I breathed. "Does it pose a threat to us?"

I was more than a little anxious about encountering strange creatures on our trek.

"Hardly," Teddy laughed and shook his head. "The Land of Eternal Spring, formerly k-known as Elysian, is h-home to every forest c-creature that has completed a life c-cyle."

Sure enough, a silver doe, like a Patronus from *Harry Potter*, darted through the trees, wispy threads of silver trailing in its wake. Birds chirped overhead and squirrels foraged in the bushes. A scream tore from my throat when a massive bear with glowing eyes burst from the trees.

"Don't w-worry," he squeezed my hand reassuringly. "He won't h-hurt us. We have p-plenty to worry about once we l-leave the forest."

The sigh of relief lodged itself in my throat. The deeper we ventured into the forest, bridges intersected overhead, and bark steps spiraled up the massive tree trunks. At this point, Teddy draped the crimson velvet around my shoulders and drew the hem over my face like a hood. He draped the silk sheet over himself. The memory of Death's warning flooded my mind.

"What's the point of disguising ourselves if Death is able to track our whereabouts?" I asked.

"Death is o-only able to track who enters or leaves his r-realm," Teddy explained. "If he t-told you anything different, he's f-full of shit." I smothered my laughter as he concealed the sword beneath his makeshift cloak. He paused, deep in thought, as he considered our disguises. "This isn't g-going to work," he huffed and dropped the sword on a bed of moss. The rich velvet slipped off my shoulders. "Everyone will k-know we're from the p-palace if we traipse around in t-these. We'll stick out l-like sore thumbs. Do you have that r-red dress?"

I handed him the floral dress. He shook out the wrinkled fabric and nodded his approval.

"This will w-work," he said. "We'll blend in m-more if we're dressed from the s-same time period. Now we n-need to figure out h-how to get that d-dress off of you."

I shivered as his fingers skimmed my bare shoulders. He reached for the gold collar around my neck. Teddy bared his teeth as he twisted the collar back and forth, until the

hinges snapped and the pale yellow silk slithered down my torso.

My nipples hardened in response to the flare of his nostrils, but he simply clenched his jaw and broke the bands around my upper-arms. I crouched and gathered the red dress he'd spread out, seizing the opportunity to quickly dress with his back turned.

"Need to stay f-focused," I overheard him reprimand himself as he scrubbed his face with the heel of his palm.

The moment I reached for the gold threads in my hair, he smacked my hands away and quietly unbound my hair, watching with a hot, yearning look as my curls spilled around my shoulders.

"You're still too b-beautiful," he swore as he tousled my hair in a clear attempt to make me look homeless.

"Hey!" I swatted him as he smeared red, clay-like soil on my face. "I don't see anyone else walking around looking like Oliver Twist."

Teddy's brow furrowed as he concentrated on the task of painting my face.

"The dirt is more for m-my benefit, so I won't t-touch you," he admitted, "but I'm shit out of l-luck because, even with mud c-caked on your face, I still t-think you're too distracting."

I accepted the small ego boost as he threw up his hands and stormed down the path with me hot on his heels, my mouth twisting in spite of myself.

~

Roses of every shade overwhelmed the emerald, green moss that hung from every massive branch. Thorny vines wound around the swirling trees that defied logic and shape. The air was hazy and thick with perfume. I outstretched one arm as I traipsed along the deep, rutted path and allowed my fingertips to graze the silky petals with their velvety leaves and suede-like stems. The long, winding stems twitched with awareness the moment I caressed them, responding to my touch with the sensitivity of a human.

Teddy glanced over his shoulder, his eyes narrowing and mouth twitching, as I plucked a flaming peach rose and gasped as another immediately bloomed in its place. The blossom in my palm disintegrated into layers of petals that I tossed overhead and danced in their slow, fluttering descent.

"This place is amazing!" I exclaimed breathlessly; my cheeks flushed from the sheer vibrancy of this part of the Underworld.

I was in my natural habitat among the trees, flowers, and vegetation.

Teddy crooked his finger with a subtle arch of his brow. "If you t-think this is amazing, wait until you see w-what's ahead."

I slipped my hand in his as he brushed leaves and branches aside to reveal a clearing of flowers that towered as high as four-story buildings. I craned my neck to admire the way sunlight slanted through jade green that faded into neon yellow, midnight purples with lightning bolts of fuchsia, and alternating petals of black and white with streaks of red. I immediately nicknamed the latter Cruella.

"I feel like Alice happily lost in Wonderland," I laughed out loud in disbelief.

"Come on," Teddy guided me to the thick stem of a sunflower. "Follow m-me."

I watched as he wrapped his arms and legs around the stem and shimmied upward, the sword clutched in one hand, the guitar slung on his back making his progress slow. I knotted the velvet coverlet around my neck like a superhero's cape and followed suit, the green stem fuzzy beneath my touch. I placed my feet in the juncture of each leaf as though climbing a rock wall, which Teddy and I often enjoyed doing back home. Silver birds chirped as they glided on the breeze, their song more delicate than fine gossamer.

Teddy offered his hand as I reached the top, panting and gasping for breath. Climbing a giant flower like Mount Everest in a dress without any underwear was worse than climbing the rope in middle school while on my period. What was the word?

Embarrassing.

"I never realized how out of shape I was until now," I collapsed inside the sunflower with its saffron petals and fuzzy center.

Teddy rolled his eyes and waved a dismissive hand, though not unkindly. He scooped two dew drops from the petals and offered one to me.

"Drink," he urged, controlling his stammer through monosyllabic commands.

I greedily slurped from his hand, until the dew drop was reduced to the size of a pea. The water tasted sweet and refreshing, chasing away the fog that had crept around the edges of my mind.

"We should stay h-here for tonight," Teddy lovingly caressed my face before shaking the pea-sized droplet from his hand. "The p-principle of traveling by n-night in a world of p-perpetual dusk is useless."

Teddy's mouth twisted in a sour expression as he stared off into the distance. Even though he was clearly in a somber mood, I couldn't resist admiring the way the wind stirred his loose brown curls. My gaze focused on the small freckle on his jaw, and I touched his knee as I lay among the bed of petals.

"Teddy," I murmured. His head snapped in my direction, as though the gentle caress of his name on my lips had sounded more like a whimper of pain. "I know you're determined to stay focused, but I'm right *here*." I grabbed his large hand and pressed it to my beating heart to emphasize

my point. "I want to escape from this place as much as you do, but there is no guarantee that Death won't make life difficult for us above ground. Remember the dead cattle? The acid rain? He could destroy everything if he wanted to, so why not enjoy our journey together? You might know everything there is to know about me, but I only recently discovered a side of you I never knew existed. Now that I think about it, you've always been so guarded. Don't you realize that you no longer shoulder that burden alone?"

"But..." He gazed over his shoulder at the dark, ominous palace that loomed in the distance.

I unbuttoned the first three buttons of my dress and slipped his hand inside. His eyes widened, his head snapping back in my direction. Teddy's shyness didn't fool me. We'd only had sex a few times, which felt like a lifetime ago.

"I'm right here," I repeated. "Remember? We need to make the most of every moment because our future isn't guaranteed."

Teddy collapsed beside me as he bared my breast to watch his fingers play with my nipple.

"I will n-never get used to t-touching you," he whispered and leaned forward so that his lips ghosted over my swollen areola.

I arched my back, a small moan escaping my lips, the tender eroticism of his mouth driving me wild. The moment I touched his shoulder blade, that strange electricity licked

through my arm, transporting me to a different time and place. Thousands of muddled thoughts and emotions flooded my mind, and I somehow knew Teddy shared this experience.

Theodoros knew only darkness in the wake of his death. Darkness, pain, and memory. Memory was always tinged with pain. Even the happiest of moments were tainted with bitterness. Bitterness for having lost the innocence of his youth. To think he'd ever once believed that he was loved, only for the promise of a brighter future to stab him in the back.

The last moments of his life were burned in his mind upon waking to eternal darkness. The way he'd filled the pockets of his robe with heavy rocks and slowly approached the lake. How the water had crept up his body, until his head was submerged. All he had ever wanted was to find his one and only. Bianca's betrayal was unthinkable. She had made a fool of him in front of the entire community.

Theodoros resigned himself to his fate in Outer Darkness, until Lord Death himself plucked him from the wall of bodies - pale, naked, and shivering. Lord Death added him to the pile of bodies waiting in his grand chariot. As they soared overhead, Theodoros beheld the endless expanse of the most desolate part of the Underworld. The condemned were organized into blocks of writhing limbs, a maze of dark rows connecting like a spider's web. Theodoros barely comprehended what was happening to him; he rolled over and stared at the changing sky, his parched lips struggling to form a single word: "Why?"

Theodoros craned his neck and watched the massive, dark-haired figure clad entirely in red. As a boy, his father had shared legends about Death around the campfire on hunting trips, but Theodoros was unable to deny the creature's regal bearing. Why had he been saved?

A palace rose up like a nightmarish, black-winged crow on the horizon. As the chariot drew near, a portcullis opened to reveal a wide, yawning mouth. If only Theodoros had foreseen the humiliation and degradation that awaited him in that dark, treacherous tunnel, but he was blinded by the promise of a second chance. If only he'd known that this supposed 'second chance' meant a half-life of servitude, one subject to beatings, lashings, and occasionally torture.

The condemned stood naked before Lord Death's scrutiny and, one by one, they were sentenced to their fate. Theodoros watched as the women's necks, wrists, and ankles were shackled and dragged away, their cries of protest echoing through the tunnel. These women were destined to become Lord Death's concubines. A man was sentenced as his personal guard. Not that Death looked like he needed protection. When the specter came to stand before Theodoros, Lord Death's mouth curled in a derisive smile.

"I see you're the only one tall enough to make direct eye contact with me," he lifted an imperious chin, both hands clasped behind his back.

Theodoros merely stared at those strange amber eyes, his throat working as he swallowed hard. What cruel torture awaited him?

Lord Death's eyes narrowed. "I am of the opinion that you were once the greatest swordsman in the region. Being the son of a blacksmith, I assume he taught you well."

Well, this was unexpected. Was that respect Theodoros heard in his deep, commanding voice?

"Yes," he managed, his heart hammering in his chest. "I've never lost a fight."

Lord Death crossed his powerful arms over his broad chest and stroked his chin. "I could place you in the armory," he mused aloud, "but you might also prove useful as a member of my guard."

Hopeful that Lord Death might spare him the humiliations others before him had suffered, he dared to step forward.

"I can also sing and play the lyre," Theodoros blurted.

For some intangible reason, it seemed important to impress this man.

A man...

When had anyone thought of Death as a man, much less a lord?

Lord Death stepped closer, invading his personal space. The respect Theodoros had sensed teetered on the edge of a blade as the lord commanded, "Sing."

Theodoros froze.

Never had he performed in such a vulnerable state, but Lord Death watched him like a hawk, the razor-sharp bridge of his

nose haughty and aristocratic. Somehow, he knew his fate depended on this demonstration, so he opened his mouth and allowed his voice to swell in his throat. Lord Death's nostrils flared as he cocked a fist and punched him in the gut. Theodoros doubled over and choked on the bile that crept up the back of his throat.

"Did I command you to stop singing?" Lord Death snarled. "Sing!"

Trembling, Theodoros straightened and began to sing once more, though his voice was hoarse from the blow. This time Lord Death's fist collided with his nose. Bright red blood spattered his bare chest and flooded his mouth with its metallic tang. How could he still bleed? Apparently, pain and suffering was only the beginning in the afterlife.

Rage bloomed in his chest, his fists clenching on thin air, but he never stopped singing. The ritual continued. With every blow, his voice wavered. The more he resisted, the harder Lord Death pummeled him. Eventually, when he was sprawled on the ground, the pale, dark-haired man straightened and clapped mockingly.

"Ah, so you're a man of many talents," Lord Death arched one black-winged brow.

Theodoros gasped for breath.

"Some might say that," he panted, beaten into submission.

Almost.

"The condemned rarely speak to me with such familiarity," Lord Death's eyes narrowed. "Some might call that admirable -

courageous, even. But all I see in your behavior is insolence. I command that you serve in the armory, as well as entertain my guests with your musical talents, though I forbid you from speaking to them. The curse that will be placed upon you strips the condemned of the ability to experience worldly pleasure. Do you understand?"

Afraid to question him, Theodoros nodded. Lord Death placed one hand on the crown of his head and muttered an incantation in some foreign, exotic language. Theodoros watched, panicked, as his pale, naked flesh darkened to an ashen blue, and he felt his eyes sink deeper into his skull. Touching his face, he felt papery, wrinkled skin and hollowed cheeks. The blood cooled in his veins as his senses dulled. The only emotion left was a dull, hollow ache in his chest that begged for relief but received none.

Lord Death offered him a white, sleeveless tunic, a belt, sandals, and a sumptuous red cloak with gold embroidery. Despite its richness, his fingers barely discerned the velvety texture.

"Here," Death offered an ornate mask to him. "This bears the likeness of your human face. Only remove it in private. You are forbidden from showing your face to anyone, do you understand?"

The blood that streamed down his face was cooling, though still warm.

"Am I not human?" Theodoros eyed the mask warily.

The corners of Lord Death's mouth tilted upward in a faintly cruel smile. "Not anymore."

"Oh, Teddy," I cradled his head to my breast and stroked his hair. Tears stung my eyes. "I never knew... I never knew..."

Theodoros slept on a hard bed in tight sleeping quarters with four other shades. He was expected to train new recruits for Death's army that barely had any flesh to cover their bones. Lord Death watched from the shadows as Theodoros slashed and parried with expert precision, defeating all in his path. Despite being skilled with a blade, he was exceptionally kind and patient, much to Lord Death's contempt. Theodoros often sensed his master's eyes on him, and he couldn't decide what he thought of his contributions until his master commanded that his tunic be torn from his body. Lord Death forced him to kneel with his back facing him and whipped the shade for making polite conversation. In the aftermath, a female servant tended to his wounds.

"No one here is your friend," she advised him, "so keep your head down and don't create waves."

Theodoros spent long hours in the armory forging beautiful swords, shields, and armor that matched Lord Death's gilded lifestyle. The palace was sumptuous and many feasts were held where Theodoros was expected to perform. The women were exceptionally beautiful in their sheer gowns that teased glimpses of their legs and breasts. They wore coin anklets, bracelets, and glittering jewels on their fingers. Their faces were often shrouded by a veil or heavy ornamentation, leaving only their kohl eyes visible. The sight alone could tempt any man, but not Theodoros.

While his eyes wandered in a vain attempt to reclaim his manhood, he felt absolutely nothing for these women. Sometimes

he stared on purpose, hoping to force himself into feeling lust, desire - anything - but he was a dead man in possession of a physical body.

Even though his voice filled the palace, no one paid him any mind. It was difficult to accept that he was both dead and invisible. His body might require food, but even the savoriest of meals had no taste. When Theodoros asked why a dead body required food and sleep, Cordelia, and Viola, two female shades that treated him like an irksome younger brother, explained that it was part of the curse that bound them to Lord Death.

"It's part of our punishment," Cordelia huffed impatiently. "Eating without taste and sleeping without dreams is torturous, but we have no other choice."

Theodoros learned to live in perfect compliance for more than one-hundred-and-fifty years, but not without struggle. Theodoros was often strung up for a good lashing simply for glancing at a member of his master's court. Over time, though, he learned to be obedient and, more importantly, inconspicuous. He was a shade, after all, nothing more than a shadow. Until Lord Death's bride arrived, that is.

It all began with a change within Lord Death himself. Or perhaps nothing had changed within the man, other than his desire for substance. All Theodoros knew, based on the rumors circulating among the shades, was that his master had left the Underworld to walk among the living one ordinary day and returned with a haunted look in his amber eyes, as though he had become aware of his own half-life. Theodoros vaguely remembered

his life from before and wondered if his master had experienced something that made him realize how he hadn't lived at all.

While he wasn't dead, he certainly wasn't alive.

Lord Death disappeared a handful of times, only to reappear more electrified than before. Theodoros watched from the shadows. He might've found Lord Death's lifestyle gluttonous and reprehensible, but he was determined to serve for his own survival. One day, Lord Death ordered that new armor be made.

"What's the occasion?" Theodoros dared to ask, only because his master appeared to be in good spirits.

Lord Death's eyes softened as his attention turned inward. "At long last, I have found my queen," his voice rumbled deep in his chest. "I want to look my best for her when she arrives."

This was the softest he had ever seen Lord Death. The shades welcomed the presence of his bride if it meant influencing their master for the better. If his fate could be changed, would that trickle down to those who served him?

Sweat poured from behind Theodoros' mask as he forged the new armor, his hands blistered and aching, despite his determination to please the man he served if it meant his own absolution. To his immense relief, Lord Death was extremely pleased with his handiwork.

The silver armor was etched with swirls resembling thorny vines and blooming roses, imbuing Lord Death with a grand, sweeping romanticism that Theodoros envied, an emotion that was alien to him where his master was concerned. There was nothing

Lord Death possessed that he longed for. Not until the day Lord Death's bride arrived.

The shades waited on the palace's front steps, looking to the horizon for Lord Death and his future bride. Theodoros watched, his hands clasped behind his back, as his master stepped from a gondola wearing his special armor. A red cape billowed behind him as he offered his hand to a much smaller figure inside the bobbing craft. Lord Death's massive body blocked the young mortal from view, which only heightened the suspense. Everyone craned their necks for a better look.

The moment he stepped aside, the rays of the artificial sun that arced above the distant horizon silhouetted his bride, creatingan ethereal, golden halo. The gold shimmered around her as she emerged from the haze, and the sight of her slammed into Theodoros, that first glimpse provoking a long-buried voice to scream at the top of its lungs until the primordial sound penetrated the marrow of his bones. She was unlike any of the women Lord Death often entertained with her large, unassuming eyes and heavy braid that slowly unraveled into a thick shawl before his eyes. Light exploded from his chest with the force of an ancient voice from him like the same golden rays that bathed her form.

She possessed an aura of femininity that made every muscle in his body tense with awareness as she drew closer to him. Only when his master wrapped an arm around her shoulders did he remember why she was there.

"My bride," he caressed her cheek. "May I introduce you to your maidservant, Cordelia," he gestured to the female shade who curtsied primly. "And this is Viola."

Another female shade bobbed. Theodoros sucked in a shuddering breath as Lord Death fixed him with a stern look. The young mortal's gaze followed, making his dead heart twitch. Something in his gaze must have betrayed his interest, for Lord Death's upper lip curled.

"This one's not important."

That didn't stop the young woman from staring at him, however, and Theodoros prayed she saw a man and not a creature.

"Oh, Teddy," I wrapped tight arms around him.

I could almost feel the way his soul had reawakened. To see myself through his eyes was the complete opposite of how I saw myself. There was nothing mysterious about me. I was a normal person with human struggles, and I wished Teddy could have seen that from the beginning.

As if reading my thoughts, he whispered, "T-this is only the b-beginning."

On the endless night of her arrival, a feast was held to welcome the young mortal. Theodoros studied her from the shadows as she ate and drank beside a preening Lord Death, her flushed cheeks and tangle of dark curls the very picture of health. She wore a gauzy, white gown with two slits up each leg that exposed her beautifully sandaled feet and up her bronzed legs. Coins dangled from her earlobes, drawing attention to her neck and collarbone. The plunging neckline of her gown barely disguised her full breasts and deep cleavage. From the innocence reflected in those large eyes, he knew she possessed the soul of a young, carefree girl and the body of a woman. And, oh, how

Theodoros burned for her. Not only physically, but deep within his soul.

Under the present circumstances, he couldn't decide if he was intoxicated or dismayed by her presence. If she became Lord Death's queen, he would be forced to live in agony for the rest of eternity knowing that he could never be with her. But at least he could be near her and that admiring her from afar reclaimed some small part of his humanity.

Not that he could touch her face, taste her lips, or inhale her scent. Even with food, the spread before him was a promise of endless torture, another reminder that he was less-than… only the idea of not being a whole man was sharper now that he'd laid eyes upon the mortal. Long after the food had been cleared, the wine flowed freely. His voice rang clear and true in the Great Hall as he played the lyre before Lord Death and his bride. The dark lord's eyes never left her face as she watched Theodoros play with the utmost delight.

Jealousy flared in his breast as Lord Death trailed kisses from her knuckles up her arm, and he both loved and hated the way the young mortal's eyelashes fluttered closed from sheer bliss. Not only was Lord Death intent on reducing him to a mere speck of dust, but he was free to kiss and touch the one woman who had rekindled Theodoros' will to live. Even if all he could lay claim to were her eyes on him, he must be content with that.

But, of course, he was deprived of even that small pleasure.

Once he was finished, a group of chained, scantily clad shades entered the chamber and danced seductively while the males sitting cross-legged on an extravagant rug played heavy, rhythmic drums that stirred something primal in the soul. The dancer's skirts were sheer, teasing glimpses of their shapely legs, and the scarves tied around their waists jingled with gold coins stamped with Lord Death's sharp profile. Theodoros found no joy in the spectacle, for the female shades were forced to dance against their will. They were slaves who had gone to bed with the men of Lord Death's court, but the worst part was how they weren't capable of experiencing pleasure, making the physical union painful.

Theodoros was expected to watch, but his gaze drifted to the beautiful mortal and noticed her shift uncomfortably. Lord Death crooned something in her ear, making her smile weakly. Sensing his gaze, Lord Death's malevolent eyes flickered to the insolent Theodoros, prompting the dark lord to rise from his throne.

"STOP!" He thundered with alarming ferocity.

The dancers faltered as the music came to an abrupt halt. Lord Death's billowing robes swirled around his sandaled feet as he strode across the chamber to where Theodoros stood, his trembling fingers clutching the lyre to his chest.

"Why do I find your gaze upon my bride instead of the dancers?" He seethed. "Are they not good enough for you? Do you find them distasteful enough to cast longing glances at my bride-to-be instead?"

The shade cowered before his master.

"N-no, my lord," Theodoros stammered.

Lord Death towered over him.

"This marks the second time I've caught you staring at my bride," he made no effort to lower his voice, allowing everyone to enjoy the spectacle. "If I catch you looking at her for a third time, I will banish you to the Forbidden Lands to be ravaged by the wolves. Do you understand?"

Theodoros hunched his shoulders. "Yes, my lord."

Lord Death stared down his long, sharp nose at his servant for a prolonged moment before sweeping his robes aside.

Clapping his hands, he announced, "The dancing shall commence!"

With Lord Death's back turned on him, Theodoros stole a furtive glance at the young mortal and found her returning his stare, sympathy reflected in the depths of her eyes.

I hated Death for how he had tortured and humiliated Teddy, especially in front of me. What had he been hoping to gain by ruling with an iron fist?

"I'm sorry if I was the reason for your torment," I whispered as my smooth cheek slid against Teddy's rough one.

Teddy buried his hands in my hair. "You h-have always been w-worth the pain," he rasped.

Theodoros saw Lord Death with the young mortal all over the palace, but he kept his distance out of fear. Sometimes he played the lyre for them in the throne room or while they ate meals, their overt displays of affection nauseating and soul-crippling. Theodoros hadn't felt such powerful emotions in over one-

hundred-and-fifty years, and his body's reawakening after so many years of numbness made such emotions overpowering. Each time he caught sight of her in a new gown or with her dark, lustrous curls arranged in a tempting display, he engulfed her with his eyes, knowing that was all he could afford. But the devouring looks weren't enough, so he avoided her to protect his fragile heart.

No matter how often he struggled, he couldn't erase the transcendent experience of a bright, golden light beaming from his chest. The feeling reawakened every time he saw her. Surprisingly, the dark lord's threats didn't seem to dissuade her.

One day, she stopped him in passing. His heart simultaneously soared with joy and plummeted with dread, though he bowed his head out of respect and made sure to avoid eye contact.

"Wait," she grabbed his wrist, making his nerve-endings burst to life. "That night the feast was held... were you upset by the dancers, too? Is that why you were staring at me instead?"

Her blunt question startled Theodoros. Her fresh, clean scent washing over him only made things worse because, for the first time after a long winter, he could once again bask in a woman's scent. Inhaling deeply, he filled his lungs beyond capacity, unable to drink in enough of that floral, earthy scent.

The scent of life.

"Yes," he slowly pulled his arm from her grip, despite his body's loud protests. "Even if my lord doesn't consider them human, I don't think anyone, dead or alive, deserves to be forced against their will." He didn't wait for her response. Instead, he stalked down the corridor with an air of stiffness, leaving her to stare after him.

Or so he hoped.

"Our first conversation," I breathed reverently.

"You were s-so much more beautiful up c-close," Teddy cradled me against him. "Your c-concern for the shades sealed m-my fate."

He lay in bed that night, unable to think of anything else but her. The way she had touched him… the way she had appealed to his humanity. He could still feel her touch imprinted on his ashen blue skin like a brand. And her scent…

In the darkness of his room, his tongue darted out and wet his lips. He wondered what she tasted like.

Now that he knew they were both morally opposed to the enslavement of the dancers, he wondered what else they had in common. Fragments of his past were clicking together. Would he have fallen in love with her rather than Bianca if she had lived during his lifetime? The answer was a resounding yes, but something puzzled him.

What drew her to him?

Pity?

The thought alone made him sick. Was she truly in love with Lord Death or was she blinded by infatuation? If he pursued her, the stakes couldn't be higher, but he was desperate to understand why she evoked such emotion in him.

He needed more.

He needed to know her. To breathe in her scent and touch her. To hold her.

And so he began spying on her around the palace at great risk to himself. Theodoros learned that she was warm and kind to the shades. She treated Cordelia like an equal and openly shared stories about her life in the hopes of rekindling a taste of what it meant to live in those who had forgotten. He learned how she'd lived on the outskirts of a small village with her mother. She loved working in her garden and dancing at festivals.

He could imagine her wandering through her village barefoot with a basket dangling from one arm and flowers woven through her dark hair. It was clear that she loved a simple, tranquil life, which placed her at odds with Lord Death.

Curious.

Very, very curious.

Theodoros wasn't able to follow her everywhere, so he pestered the female shades for information. Begrudgingly, they revealed her efforts to tackle the long-dead garden in her courtyard, for she believed the palace needed a touch of spring to make it feel like home. The one subject Cordelia refused to discuss was her relationship with Lord Death, though it was clear to everyone that she was able to put the dark lord in his place, a quality Theodoros admired for his own lack of bravery. He only scolded himself for spying on her when she swam in the fountain, for her wet, clinging gowns made her wildly indecent. He wanted to join her and undress her, an act that was forbidden. It was one act of rebellion to admire her from afar, but to actually touch her?

Here, the flashback from earlier replayed in my mind, stitching the tale to completion. The weight of his longing made my breasts ache with a heavy quality that only eased when I rubbed them against his chest. Teddy was right. I *did* like the thought of him watching me from afar.

In the aftermath of getting caught, Theodoros avoided the young mortal for fear his reckless behavior would provoke the wrath of Lord Death, but one day her silhouette appeared at the mouth of the armory as he dipped blades into fire. His traitorous heart nearly hammered through the wall of his chest upon catching sight of the white lilies dappling her hair like mournful stars. The flowers themselves represented death, but her bronzed skin shimmered with life. The temptation to reach out and touch her overwhelmed him, so instead he studied the way her midnight blue cloak pooled around her feet, blinding him with the purity of the flowing white gown beneath. The gauzy material was slightly transparent, and his eyes traced the outline of her body, his blackened hands itching to mark her flawless form.

If Theodoros knew for certain if Lord Death had claimed his bride, perhaps it wouldn't torture him when his master openly fondled her breasts and traced the column of her throat with his parted lips. The thought made Theodoros clench his fist around the sword hilt in a white-knuckled grip. How long would he be forced to endure this suffering?

"Why were you spying on me the other day?" The young mortal swept forward, startling him from his tortured thoughts.

She carried herself like a regal queen, on top of already playing the part so well.

Cordelia had warned him that she was blunt and commanding, something he hadn't prepared himself for.

"I wasn't spying," he mumbled sheepishly, twitching uncomfortably beneath the weight of her expectant gaze.

"Oh, you were definitely spying," she tilted her head to one side.

He forced himself to drop his gaze, which was a colossal mistake because her nipples were partially visible through the sheer material of her gown. He imagined the white fabric slithering down her naked torso, exposing the fullness of her large breasts. He shivered with fever.

"Don't be ashamed. I admire you from afar in the throne room all the time," she eyed him expectantly. "I love the sound of your voice."

"Oh?" *He moved around his worktable to create distance, but she followed him.*

His aloof guard didn't fool her. The forbidden nature of their encounter only intensified his need to taste her lips and bury his hands in her hair, the way he had been denied in his former life.

"Do shades not know how to take compliments?" *The young mortal edged closer.*

Was she actually teasing him?

"Not exactly," he grimaced behind the mask, "but I can only speak for myself."

Her dark hair spilled around her shoulders like a dark shawl, so close that he could gulp lungsful of her perfume.

"Should I seek to flatter you, despite your aversion?" She tapped her foot, and it took every ounce of control not to unlace her sandals and devour her toes.

"I don't follow." He resisted the urge to preen as she watched him hammer the flaming metal into submission, a faint glimmer in her eyes as she admired the flex of his bicep.

A palpable sexual tension flickered to life between them, but Theodoros couldn't conceive of anything other than a one-sided attraction. How could she ever possibly want him?

"I'm curious about you," she toyed with the sash around her waist, suddenly shy. "I would like to request your presence for entertainment purposes. This might come as a surprise, but I am rather lonely without my family and friends."

Theodoros ceased the merciless pounding and stared, hardly daring to believe his ears.

"You were the first p-person who truly saw m-me," Teddy whispered in my ear as he toyed with my overly-sensitive nipple. "From that m-moment on, I would have f-followed you anywhere."

"Have you always had such filthy thoughts about me?" I teased, breathless as he pinched and rolled my flesh.

"Always," he nuzzled my neck. "I h-hope you don't m-mind."

"Of course not," I shook my head. "I want more."

My head tilted back as his mouth hovered above my own, the brush of our lips both tender and sensual, as his hand skimmed up my inner thigh. Another memory ensnared me as my body fell victim to his touch.

Koreyna.

The young mortal's name.

Theodoros whispered her name in his mind as he played the lyre on the balcony overlooking her courtyard or in the garden as she tore brambles from the dead flowerbeds. His heart pulsed her name with every heartbeat as she sprawled in the tall grasses of the river basin and shared strange tales from her own village.

He whispered her name like a mantra in the isolation of his room, the light of her apparition bathing his body in a radiant light. Her fingers crept up his bare chest in the darkness, making him shiver in delight as his back arched. The dreams were difficult to shake, especially in her presence. Theodoros learned over months of careful maneuvering that Koreyna was a dichotomy of personal qualities that fascinated him.

Cheeky, mischievous, outspoken, and charming, while also sweet, shy, and incredibly kind-hearted.

The more time he spent with her, his physical desire evolved into a fever-pitch maelstrom of deep-seated yearning for her entire being. It was almost like a woman had been created from his hopes and dreams.

Theodoros expected her to ask about Lord Death, but instead she asked about him. Where was he from? Did he miss his family? What was it like to be a shade? He wrestled with himself as

he answered her endless barrage of questions. Practically bursting at the seams with his need for human connection, he didn't want to stoke the flames of his unrequited love, for it wasn't possible to imagine Koreyna loving him in return. It didn't matter that he'd memorized every detail of her lovely, heart-shaped face. Theodoros remained a servant, therefore not her equal.

Whenever her warm, cheerful demeanor lulled him into a false sense of security, he remembered Bianca, the one who had condemned him to his fate.

"You don't talk much," Koreyna hugged her knees as she perched on the lip of the fountain, the same one he had watched her bathe in once upon a time. "I think pulling out my own teeth would be easier than convincing you to share your secrets, which is a shame because I like the sound of your voice."

Theodoros remained utterly still, unsure of how to respond. Thus far he had been a stoic companion.

She sighed heavily. "Why won't you tell me your name?"

"My name doesn't matter," he lightly strummed his lyre, producing a melodious sound that echoed in the vast chamber. "I'm a servant, therefore my identity is irrelevant."

"You're wrong," her nostrils flared with vehemence, though her stern voice softened quickly. "Your identity matters to me. Shouldn't that be reason enough? We're friends, aren't we?"

Theodoros flinched. He'd never considered himself to be her friend because he'd always silently begged for more.

"Theodoros," he offered with a potent spike of adrenaline.

She rolled the syllables of his name around on her tongue, making him shiver like a wilted plant that had received a much-needed dose of sunshine.

Koreyna flashed him a cheeky grin. "Now that wasn't so hard." She extended a hand and traced the grooves of his porcelain mask with curious fingers. Theodoros froze, hardly daring to breathe, though her skin never brushed his. "I always wonder what you're hiding behind the mask, for your likeness paints a rather handsome picture." His heart pounded in his chest as her fingers raked through his loose curls and skimmed the length of his arms. He ached to reciprocate her curious exploration, but he simply couldn't. "You're so soft and warm," she breathed as she sandwiched one of his large hands between her own. "I honestly don't know what I expected. You're so beautiful with your blue skin and ashen curls. I often dream of caressing your porcelain lips with my own. Sometimes I watch you train Death's army, and I'm hypnotized by the strength of your elegant body."

Theodoros briefly closed his eyes as he savored the tantalizing warmth of her body, made irresistible by her words. Was this a dream?

"Why are you touching me and not…?" He trailed off in a quavering voice, hoping against all odds for something that was never meant to be.

Koreyna withdrew her touch and hugged her knees to her chest, looking more like a frightened child than a young, vivacious woman. She peered up at him with those large eyes that always reduced him to a puddle.

"If I share one of my secrets, one I haven't told anyone, will you show me your face?" She tentatively asked.

"I don't want to frighten you," he reached to cup her face, surprising them both. "The mask represents what I looked like before I was punished for taking my own life. Those who commit suicide are sent to Outer Darkness, but only a handful are selected to serve Lord Death. The shades live with their scorched visage to remind themselves of how they compromised their identity when they took their own lives."

His words stunned Koreyna into a momentary silence.

"Did you know that I fought to have you as my companion?" She blurted. "Death had a fit when he learned how I had requested *your company. I'm not supposed to be around you, but I don't care. You're the only person in this world I can relate to. What Death doesn't know won't hurt him."*

Laughter exploded from Theodoros; the sound rusty from disuse. He couldn't help but admire Koreyna for her daring.

"Even though it may seem like I'm attracted to Death," she went on, "I miss my friends and family. I only ran away with him because I thought I could escape my mother. Embracing my death and coming to the Underworld were my two acts of rebellion. I wanted to prove to my mother that I was capable of making my own decisions, but now I'm not so sure of what I've done. Now I may never see her again. I can only imagine how helpless and terrified she must feel with me gone, and it makes me hate Death for seducing me into a decision I wasn't prepared to make. In other ways, I can't hate him at all because I wouldn't have met you otherwise."

Theodoros only had one takeaway from her impassioned speech.

"You're a member of the undead?" He blinked in surprise. "But I thought..."

"Doesn't everyone know?" *She shrugged with a humorless smile.* "I stepped on a snake in my garden, which had been planted there to orchestrate my death."

A lone tear rolled down her cheek, tempting him to smear the glistening droplet with his thumb. Instead, he gripped the edges of his mask with trembling fingers and removed the protective shield from his face. Koreyna's lips parted as she drank in the sight of him. Humiliation immediately swept through him, and he quickly moved to replace the mask, but she stopped him. Cupping his sunken cheeks in both hands, she swept her thumbs across his ashen blue complexion.

Slowly, ever so slowly, her fingers traced his pronounced cheekbones and sunken eye sockets. Theodoros shivered as she traced his thin, wide mouth, the one feature that remained somewhat normal. Unable to restrain himself, he swooped in and captured her warm, soft lips in a quick, chaste kiss.

The moment his lips touched mine, something sparked between us, past and present.

Koreyna's lips were unbelievably soft, his own mouth creating the most delicious sound as he pulled away. He stared at her, wide-eyed in shock as she touched her lips, as though his mouth had branded her. At that moment, he didn't care if he had

overstepped his boundaries. All he knew was that he could no longer hide from her.

"We can't do this," Koreyna shook her head wildly, though her cheeks were red. "Death would kill us if he found out."

"May I point something out to you?" Theodoros posed. "We're already dead. Well, you're at a higher level than I am, but..."

"There's no escaping him," she paced the mosaic floor and wrung her hands.

"What if we weren't dead?" Theodoros rose and took one hopeful step closer. "Could you love me if I looked like an ordinary man?"

"Love?" She whipped around to face him. "Not even Death loves me. He doesn't know how."

"That's what I want from you," he breathed as he caressed her exposed collarbone. "I want to know what it means to live in your presence. I want to feel the warmth of the sun on my back with you in my arms. I want to court you like a mortal man with garlands of flowers in your hair. I want to fill every space in your heart like you do mine."

Koreyna took a faltering step backward.

"But you hardly know me!" She exclaimed, though he noticed her pulse fluttering beneath her skin.

"Time is irrelevant," he peeled back another layer of her excuses. "I want to devote the rest of eternity to learning everything there is to know about you." Koreyna opened her mouth and drew in a breath.

"Do you love Lord Death more than you could ever love me?" Theodoros interjected, his nostrils flaring with jealousy.

She recoiled in shock.

"I think the answer to that question should be obvious," she threw him an accusing look before storming from the chamber.

Watching her flee carved out his heart and innards, spilling them onto the mosaic floor, leaving him hollower and more bereft than death ever had.

Self-reproach mingled with intense emotional pain as the image of my past self-leaving a slumped, listless Theodoros tattooed itself into my brain. I could taste the jealousy and fierce possessiveness on my tongue as I saw my body curled around Death's in his mind's eye. Death sat on his throne, my lips grazing his neck, and my fingers tangled in his thick hair. A crash resounded in my head as Theodoros trampled his lyre and angrily stalked from the throne room. God, had I been that kind of teasing bitch? Had I truly once dangled myself in front of Teddy, only to spurn him the moment he acted on his desires? No wonder fate had bound us for generations. We had a lot of shit to figure out.

"Don't be so h-hard on y-yourself," Teddy traced the shell of my ear, reading my thoughts. "You were c-confused and helpless."

Knowing words weren't enough to reassure me, more images flooded our connection.

The moment Theodoros trampled his lyre in a fit of jealousy and despair, Lord Death dragged him by the hair to the courtyard and savagely whipped him until the shade was bruised, bleeding, and immobile. The last thing he saw before losing consciousness was Koreyna's stricken face, her eyes wide with horror. Theodoros awoke on his bed. Koreyna hummed a song he'd played for her a thousand times over as she washed his lacerated back, the melody punctuated by her sniffling.

"I'm so sorry," she whispered. "This was all my fault. Look at these scars..."

The scene faded to black, but my guilt remained.

Theodoros avoided Koreyna for weeks, until one day he couldn't resist meeting her by the fountain.

"I never meant to hurt you," Koreyna whispered with tears sparkling on her cheeks like precious gems. "I shouldn't have run away. The truth is, each day I've spent in your presence has brought me one step closer to falling in love with you. I requested your company because I was drawn to you, and I've dedicated the past six months to inventing excuses to be closer to you."

Theodoros remained stoic as Koreyna removed his mask with trembling fingers. Heat flooded his body as those impossibly large eyes bore into his. Her fingers slid into his hair as she reached up on tiptoe and sealed his mouth with a kiss. The sweet warmth of her mouth flooded his own as he drowned in the contact, the salty tears leaking through the seam of his lips being the only thing tethering him to reality.

"I'm so in love with you," Theodoros moaned as he devoured her tears with hot, open-mouthed kisses. The dam holding back his wild longing was broken. "I'm not supposed to want you, but I can't help myself."

Koreyna moaned as he teased her jawline and earlobe with the gentle scrape of his teeth. She pulled away abruptly, detaching her mouth from his with a wet, lewd sound that made her blush. Thodoros half-expected her to run back into Death's embrace, but instead she unclasped the brooches holding her plum gown together.

The rich silk slithered down her body, his jaw slackening as his eyes devoured the sight of her dewy nipples, the feminine slope of her belly guiding him to the juncture of her thighs. Koreyna stepped backward into the trickling fountain, her gaze never once faltering, and he frantically tore at his dark red cloak and long, sleeveless tunic as she submerged her lush body in the cool water with a suggestively crooked finger. Theodoros splashed into the fountain with decidedly less grace, but the flailing of his long, lean limbs as he collapsed on top of her made Koreyna throw her head back with laughter. The twinkling of her mirth morphed into a wide-eyed, anxious desire as his cock brushed her lower belly.

The smile faded from her lips as she watched his lanky, powerfully corded body hover above hers, his gaze intense and mouth unsmiling as he gently rocked against her. Koreyna looked away, apparently overcome.

"I love the way you look at me," she whispered as her slick hands glided over his tight chest and stomach. "I've never lain with a man before, you know."

He froze. "Not even Death?"

Koreyna slowly shook her head, that familiar gleam returning to her eyes. "My mother's greatest fear was that I'd leave her in *favor of a husband, so she spent a lot of time chasing suitors away. In many ways, I'm grateful because I've never wanted to share my body with a man until now."*

A man...

"With me?" He spluttered.

A fierce look overcame her as she shoved him backward into the water so that the trickling stream splashed on them as she straddled his hips. Theodoros screwed his eyes shut as his cock burrowed inside of her, a sharp cry tearing from her lips as he tore through some unknown barrier. The incredibly tight grip on his cock made him swallow a high, kenning cry, a feat that was made impossible once he opened his eyes and beheld the sight of water sluicing down Koreyna's naked body, her taut, rosy nipples begging for his mouth. Pure instinct drove him as he cradled their joined bodies. He sat up to wrap his arms around her and bathed her breasts with plundering strokes of his tongue, instinctively rocking his hips against hers at the same time. Koreyna gasped and clung to the fountain overhead as water poured down his back, hair plastered to their faces as he plunged his tongue inside the warm, wet cavern of her mouth.

Admittedly, he had no idea what he was doing, only what provoked incredible sensations that ripped through his body. Theodoros memorized every sound and expression Koreyna betrayed, the sensuality of their parted lips brushing with each thrust driving him wild.

When her eyelashes fluttered closed and her body convulsed around him, he shuddered and found his own release at the thought of giving her pleasure. Koreyna grabbed fistfuls of his dripping hair before he had time to breathe, kissing him beneath the splash of cool water with a ferocity that made him ache. A small, delighted squeal escaped her when his arms wrapped around her waist and squeezed her tight. The lovers kissed tenderly in the fountain for what seemed like hours. The other shades might consider him greedy, but now Theodoros craved all of her - mind, body, and soul.

The memories became a blur of happiness as a rush of images filled my mind. Theodoros laughing softly as the bat-like iguanas - excuse me, *gargoyles* - trailed after me as I squealed in fear and delight. Us making love on the balcony overlooking Death's kingdom. Us making love in the armory with my backside perched on his work table as I lavished his well-muscled chest in kisses. Us quietly discussing our former dreams, hopes, and aspirations. Our fondest childhood memories. The family members we missed the most. My face swimming in his line of vision as I mouthed, "I want to go home." The overwhelming determination that swelled in his chest as he whispered, "Let me go with you."

"I want to see the moment your life was restored," I begged as I tugged on his threadbare t-shirt, baring his lean back and shoulders.

Overcome with desire from the visceral images of our lovemaking, I pushed him backward and straddled his hips the same way I'd done thousands of years ago, except Teddy and I had upgraded to a giant sunflower since we apparently liked to keep our sex life interesting. Teddy gazed up at me with such awe and longing, the thought of him loving me for an eternity making me overflow with emotion for him. My dress fell away as he finished unbuttoning the front.

"Don't you r-remember?" His jade eyes shone hopefully as he interlaced our fingers.

Awareness flickered in my mind. I squeezed my eyes shut and concentrated on that small spark of recognition, until the scene illuminated like a movie screen. I wrung my hands in anticipation as a bright light consumed Theodoros. The bluish-gray waves I had once known transformed into rich brown locks that made my fingers itch with the desire to run my fingers through them.

The light touched every part of him, like reanimating a human that had been turned to stone. The lanky Theodoros I had known with the broad shoulders and narrow hips remained unchanged, though his gloomy pallor blossomed into pale skin with light pink undertones. The long fingers that reminded me of pale spiders unfurled as he studied his palms, and it was clear that he couldn't quite believe his eyes.

"Theodoros?" My tentative voice echoed somewhere in my mind.

The young man in question slowly turned, and I sucked in a breath as the most beautiful eyes stared back at me. The high, smooth planes of his cheekbones created faint hollows beneath that made him look chiseled in a boyish sort of way. His protruding nose jutted above his pink slash of a mouth, the sensual curve of his lips soft and inviting. Those impossibly green eyes softened as I explored his face, as though we were meeting for the first time. Theodoros avidly gauged my reaction, his eyes intensely searching.

"Are you disappointed?" He flashed a shy, crooked smile that displayed his prominent canine teeth, which I instantly adored.

"No," I shook my head, completely dazed. "I'm in love."

Those jade eyes sparkled as his grin widened, though his expression faltered when a cool, toneless voice interrupted our first proper meeting.

"We have made a deal with Death, brave Theodoros," the omnipresent voice filled every space with excruciating light. "We are trusting you to protect her with your life. We've agreed that if he discovers her, she will remain bound to him in the Underworld upon sealing their physical union. While she will remember nothing, you will remember everything. If you love her as much as you claim, you will need to convince her that she belongs to you. Death is bound to take her from this world one way or another, but it is entirely up to you to either save or relinquish her. Are you ready for the journey that lies ahead?"

Theodoros swallowed hard, a blinding light searing me from the inside out. When I no longer thought I could handle the pain, my entire world faded to black.

Past Lives

I awoke hours later beneath the heavy velvet coverlet, my cheek pressed flat against Teddy's bare chest as he dripped beads of dew on my forehead. My head pounded from the influx of memories. Unlike before, now I remembered *everything*. I was no longer out of the loop, but the information dump was so large that only disjointed fragments pieced together to form a somewhat cohesive whole. As the sleep-induced fog cleared from my brain, a tidal wave of emotion, past and present, crashed over me, as though a gaping wound had been ripped open.

The image of two orphaned children on the cold, unforgiving streets of Paris flickered to life in my mind. Several lifetimes ago, Teddy and I had raced through the crooked streets like the hellions that we were, two street urchins with a special talent for mischief. We rarely starved between pickpocketing and my magic. We gorged ourselves on the fruit I spun out of thin air, too greedy to share with anyone else. We sold flowers in the streets, rare specimens from exotic lands, or so we claimed.

I often found myself drawn to the fresh baguettes in the bakery's display window. Teddy always reached inside his coat pocket and offered a few of his own francs, unable to resist spoiling me.

"I'll always t-take care of you," he whispered in the darkness of our makeshift tent of stolen laundry as he gazed upon my prone form clutching a ragged porcelain doll to my chest.

One Christmas Eve, the unthinkable happened.

We were separated.

A distinguished bourgeois gentleman and his young wife caught me with my hand in his coat pocket. Instead of rapping my knuckles with his cane like others had done in the past, they gathered me in their arms and swaddled me in blankets as the carriage bobbed along the rutted path to their chateau. I was beside myself with panic, convinced I had lost Teddy forever, and I refused the bowls of steaming broth they spoon-fed me in an effort to warm my fingers and toes. Against all odds, Teddy found me in the walled garden and convinced me to escape with him, but the young, pretty wife caught us in the act. Upon discovery, the couple I would come to know as maman and papa embraced him as their son.

Being forced to call himself my brother infuriated Teddy, but that didn't stop him from claiming a few desperate kisses in the walled garden as it became clear that our adopted parents were bound and determined to separate us as we grew older.

"Do you remember kissing me in the garden?" I murmured as Teddy quietly stroked my hair. "Remember the creeping vines and the roses that bloomed even in winter? And the blue butterflies? How could I have forgotten?"

Teddy's hand froze mid-stroke, his long fingers tangled in my hair.

"I r-remember chasing all of your suitors a-away out of sheer desperation to k-keep you," he murmured. "I h-hated being called your brother because I wanted s-so much more."

"What happened to us?" I laced our fingers and gazed up at him dreamily. "My brain is struggling to keep up."

Teddy's expression darkened and, for a moment, I regretted asking.

"They c-caught me in your bedchamber one n-night." His grip on me tightened. The memory of my fingers skating up his flat abdomen as the soft candlelight silhouetted his lean body through his white linen shirt made me flush. I remembered grasping his pert backside through his breeches as he writhed above me.

"They tried separating us by arranging for me to marry someone else," I said, the memory clearer than crystal, "but you fought for me." The warm glow in my chest quickly faded. I shuddered and pulled away from him. "You killed him."

Teddy's brow wrinkled as he raked a frustrated hand through his wavy hair. "He challenged me to f-fight for your h-hand, Korey. One of us was g-going to die. Would you rather it have been m-me?"

Ignoring him, I demanded, "If losing my virginity was such a big deal to Death, why fight so hard to protect it? I'm starting to resent the fact that all these men treat my body like it's a prize to be won."

"You're *not* a prize to be w-won," he countered fiercely. "The thought of another m-man touching you makes me d-die inside. Wouldn't you f-feel the same about me t-touching another woman? I *earned* the right to t-touch you every chance I was g-given, unlike Death."

Earned? What the hell was that supposed to mean?

"But you still manipulated the outcome by eliminating my choices," I argued.

Teddy's spine stiffened. "What are you s-saying?"

"My entire life has been controlled by other people," I huffed. "My mother never allowed me to date. Death kidnapped me and held me captive. Even you have sheltered me, the one person I trust above all others. It would be nice to experience the freedom of choice for once."

The blood drained from Teddy's face, as though I had kicked him in the stomach.

"I've never regretted that my only c-choice has been you," he managed hoarsely. "I t-thought you would have felt the s-same. I guess I was w-wrong."

"Teddy, that's not what I meant," I reached for him, but he avoided my touch as he tugged on his t-shirt.

"We n-need to leave," he said flatly. "You m-might resent me for giving you so few c-choices, but Death can have you over my d-dead body."

~

Teddy avoided eye contact with me all morning, or at least what I thought was morning. The corners of his grim mouth were weighed down as we leapt from one flower to the next. Our feet kicked up clouds of pollen, making us sneeze until our eyes watered. Despite his muttered, "Bless you," he stubbornly looked away from me and, boy, was he stubborn as fuck. I slid down the fuzzy green stem that resembled a massive fireman's pole, his hands instinctively catching my waist when my bare feet touched solid ground.

My heart fluttered with relief, but his hands were gone as quickly as their warmth branded my skin. Frankly, his petulant mood pissed me off a little because I felt like he'd deliberately misunderstood my words. Teddy and I rarely fought, so the tension between us made my stomach churn. Why couldn't he empathize with me for two seconds? Did he not recognize that I was at everyone else's mercy? Instead of having the freedom to choose a lover for myself, my virginity was up for grabs.

The truth was, I would have chosen Teddy every time, but what bothered me was his lack of faith that I would've chosen him at all. To know he couldn't fathom the thought of another man touching me was flattering because I, too, was possessive, but I was afraid that our romance sat on a kernel of doubt that would poison its potential for growth. I smacked my forehead, coming to a realization as I trailed after him through the lush greenery. Teddy's heart had been destroyed by his first love and best friend's betrayal, enough that he'd lined his pockets with rocks and

drowned himself over it. The moment he'd glimpsed a future with me, some dickhead god had treated us both like pawns in some twisted game. No wonder he fought so hard for me.

"Teddy," I grabbed his sleeve, forcing him to stop.

Even now his eyes were fixed on the ground until I said, "I want you to know that I've loved you from the beginning. It breaks my heart that you think you need to fight so hard for my love when I freely give myself to you."

Teddy's step faltered, though he remained unmoved.

"But you w-want more than me." The accusation was tinged with despair. "I'm not enough for you a-anymore. You say you're c-content with our life b-back home, but you make vision b-boards of far off p-places."

"Those are adventures I imagine sharing with *you*," I countered desperately, wanting nothing more than for him to recognize how much I loved him.

Nothing would sway his mind, however.

Teddy shook his head forlornly. "I s-saw the way you l-loked at him, Korey. I'm not s-stupid. It's been eating at m-me for days." He smacked his forehead over and over again, frustrated with himself. I grabbed his fist and cradled it to my breast. Sighing heavily, he managed, "The celestial beings said l-long ago that Death was p-prophesied to welcome a queen into his k-kingdom, and they thought it m-might be you."

"The answer to that question is obvious," I scoffed, working extra hard for one of those sly grins. "I rejected him in favor of you, remember?"

Teddy's frown only deepened, as though key details were conveniently missing from the story that only he knew.

"According to them, you flocked to m-me because you were afraid of t-the intense emotions Death inspired in you. They s-said there would c-come a time when Death would tempt you, and you would either s-sucumb or remember your l-love for me. One more g-good reason for me to fight for your l-love, so you would remember everything we've s-shared when the time c-came. I refuse to let you g-go, though I'm terrified of fighting a l-losing battle."

I watched, speechless, as Teddy slipped his warm hand from my grasp with silent tears streaming down his face. Part of what he said worried me because Death *had* tempted me more than once, and I feared that what he said might come true.

~

A tension I'd never experienced with Teddy settled between us as the landscape shifted with jarring immediacy. I almost crashed into my travel buddy when he halted on the fringe of greenery separating the Land of Eternal Spring from an entirely new battleground. Peering around him, I gaped at the endless stretch of desert ahead of us. The desert vaguely resembled the Sahara, though the blanket of stars

overhead would hopefully provide some relief from the heat. But where the hell would we sleep?

Teddy's knuckles turned white as his grip on the sword hilt tightened. "When I w-was a shade, I heard r-rumors of a tunnel at the far end of the Crimson Desert that l-leads to the Forbidden Lands, our d-destination. There's an exiled witch in the Forbidden Lands that m-may help us escape."

I eyed the fine grains of sand that swept the barren land like a gorgeous, sparkling haze.

"Why do they call it the Crimson Desert?" I shivered.

"Many battles were f-fought here," Teddy explained, his eyes scanning the horizon rather than meet my probing gaze. I suspected that he seized the opportunity to avoid looking at me, a decision on his part that cut deep. "The legends c-claim that Death spilled so much b-blood here, the sand was p-permantently stained red. While that doesn't s-seem to be the case now, I know for a f-fact that dangerous c-creatures and fallen soldiers lurk b-beneath the sand."

I swallowed hard. "Are you sure there isn't another way out of the Underworld?"

For the first time, Teddy's uncertain gaze found mine. Tentatively, he clasped my chin between his thumb and forefinger.

"You're s-safe with me," his mouth crooked in a weak half-smile. "I earned a r-reputation in the Underworld as a better s-swordsman than Death h-himself."

I rewarded the proud swell of his chest with a flirtatious smile. "I never knew you were so competitive, Teddy."

A look of determination flashed across his face. "You have n-no idea."

~

Despite the Crimson Desert's reputation, the endless sea of shimmering dunes bathed in midnight purple shadows captured my imagination. The desert's serene quality made it impossible to believe that dangerous, blood-thirsty creatures lurked beneath the surface. In fact, the desert filled me with nostalgia for the days Teddy and I had splashed around muddy construction sites pretending to build the pyramids of Giza. My brain was still sorting through my new memories, but Teddy and I had undoubtedly embarked on more than one adventure - our trek through the Underworld being our latest one. And to think he worried over not being included in my vision board?

"Remember when you forced me to watch *The Mummy*?" I panted as we mounted a sloping dune.

We had walked for several hours in silence, entirely focused on our surroundings for signs of danger.

"Yeah," Teddy sheepishly rubbed the back of his neck with his free hand. "I remember you c-checked your food for scarab beetles for two years after that. S-sorry."

"I know you don't regret a thing because I insisted on sharing a bed with you, since I was too scared to sleep on the floor," I teased, laughing loudly. "Do you know that I almost kissed you while you were asleep next to me?"

Teddy's head whipped in my direction, those beautiful jade eyes bright with hope. "Seriously?"

"What can I say?" I shrugged. "I always had a crush on you."

Teddy watched me expectantly for a long moment, clearly hoping for more. "Why didn't you s-say anything?"

"I didn't want to ruin our friendship if you didn't feel the same way," I mumbled, feeling my face grow hot. Before he could drill me with more questions, I quickly changed the subject. "How were you always able to find me?"

Teddy pressed a flat palm to his chest. "Our souls were b-bound so we wouldn't stray far f-from each other, but there's an anxious f-feeling in my chest that always g-guides me to you. That's why I s-stammer where I didn't b-before. The sense of urgency causes anxiety that c-can only be soothed with music and your p-presence."

"But you always stammer around me," I pointed out, though hardly wanting to make him self-conscious.

"Believe it or n-not, I stammer more when I'm not around you," he revealed. "The further away I am f-from you, the worse I feel. When I'm around you, t-though... it's more like a loud p-purring that vibrates my entire c-chest."

Without warning, he dropped the sword, grabbed my hand, and pressed my palm flat to his chest. "See?"

Sure enough, the cavity that protected his steadily pounding heart vibrated intensely like a trapped hummingbird. In fact, I'd compared his fluttering pulse using that visual more than once. Slowly, the vibration traveled through the ground and up my legs and, for a moment, I was ecstatic, until Teddy's green eyes widened in horror.

"We have c-company," he brandished the sword as he pushed me behind him in a protective stance.

The fine grains of sand shifted beneath our feet as the vibration intensified, and I gasped as something black crested the surface, like a fin slicing through gold waves.

"I know w-what these creatures are," Teddy said ominously. "The m-moment it strikes, run as f-fast as you can."

"What about you?" I panicked as the black fin made a beeline for us.

As the fin drew near, something black and amorphous exploded from the sand, the creature's mouth peeling back like a banana to reveal rows of serrated teeth. I screamed as the creature lunged forward like a catapult, frozen in place as the blade sliced through the air. Black ink sprayed everywhere as the sword decapitated the creature's sightless head. Now that I had a chance to gaze upon its broken, hissing body, it looked like a cross between a shark

and a lamprey, something decidedly worse than a scarab beetle.

"Run!" Teddy grabbed my hand and dragged me away from the dead creature, only dimly aware that our fronts were soaked with inky blood.

More fins appeared as we raced down the slope of one dune and up another. I screamed and covered my head like a coward as the lampreys exploded from the sand and gracefully arced in a crescent moon before raining down upon us like missiles. Teddy perfectly aimed each blow as he hacked at the air, spraying blood everywhere as he protected my body with his own.

We ran, faster and harder, completely out of breath. The dunes eventually evened out to hard, flat ground, though the vibration never ceased. Another creature exploded from the sand as we neared safe territory. Teddy whimpered, dropping the sword as the beast sank its teeth into his leg and dragged him backward. The blood staining our hands made his fingers slip easily through my grasp.

"Teddy!" I screamed in horror as the creature dragged him across the sand.

"Korey!" He shouted with a pained helplessness; misery etched into every line of his face.

Cold fury flared to life in my breast as I picked up the fallen sword and bound after him, powering my legs as hard and fast as possible. I swung the blade overhead and hacked off the lamprey's head with multiple strokes, since my arms weren't as powerful as Teddy's. The lamprey writhed without its head, but I pried its jaws open, eliciting a sharp cry from Teddy as the serrated teeth slipped from his calf muscle. My stomach churned as the metallic tang of human blood infiltrated my nose, and I struggled not to stare at Teddy's blood-soaked leg. I surveyed his body for other wounds, noticing how glazed his eyes were.

"I'm going to help you stand," I murmured softly as I draped his arm around my neck, squeezing his fingers for comfort. "Can you do that for me, my love?"

Teddy's breath hissed through clenched teeth as he balanced his weight on his uninjured leg. Hauling him to his feet was excruciating and painstakingly slow, but that didn't stop me from whispering soft words of love and encouragement in his ear as we moved across the remaining expanse of Sahara-like desert.

"Show me how strong you are, Teddy."

"I'm not going to let anything happen to you."

"I'm here."

Teddy collapsed on the hard, flat ground and spread out, as though fully planning on taking a nap. Knowing he might never wake up, I slapped his cheeks to keep him awake. On the verge of hyperventilating, I tore open his pant leg, nearly gagging at the sight of his mangled flesh.

My eyes swept the barren landscape searching for help, only to realize we were in the middle of nowhere with Death himself on our heels. I choked back tears as I watched

the light fade from his eyes, as though the laprey had injected his body with poison. Acting on pure instinct, I wrapped my hands around his wound and closed my eyes as I channeled my life-giving energy through him. I hadn't used my magic since entering the Underworld because I hadn't wanted Death to track our whereabouts, but Teddy was not going to die on my watch.

"Please give him life," I whispered. "Please give him some of *my* life."

A flash of sharp pain awakened in my forehead, and I was dimly aware that something warm dripped from my upper lip. I pushed through the pain and channeled more energy through him. Slowly, ever so slowly, the mangled flesh beneath my touch healed, whole and smooth once more.

"Korey?" A familiar voice echoed in my head.

Teddy's stricken face swam into view and, despite the black ink on his face, I captured his mouth in a hazy kiss. His fierce determination to protect me made me fall a little harder and deeper with each passing second. Teddy returned my kiss with heat and enthusiasm, but my lips dragged down his chin as I slumped onto his lap, exhausted and in desperate need of a nap.

Warm Bodies

I awoke hours later with a splitting headache. The inside of my eyelids were painted a flaming peach that made sense upon cracking open one eye. Teddy's face flickered in and out of shadow on the other side of a crackling fire, his face and shirtfront splattered with the lamprey creature's inky blood, which had long since dried. Despite the sorry state of his appearance, he seemed focused and serene as he lightly strummed on his guitar with eyes closed.

The melody soothed my headache, and I watched him for a long moment as my heart constricted. Teddy sang in that strangely multi-faceted voice that touched on something deep inside of me. He sang of longing to experience lost love in the early days when the world seemed perfect. The sheer mourning of his soul made my eyes prick with tears. He expressed our bittersweet history with a level of emotion that wrung his vocal chords like a dishtowel.

Closing my eyes, I allowed the song to play as a backdrop for the memories from past lives that were slowly piecing together in my mind. After Teddy mortally wounded that man who sought my hand in marriage, we eloped to the Northern shore to avoid scandal. Within the span of a single lifetime, we had gone from pickpockets to bourgeois and, finally, to recluses in a small cottage on the jagged outcrop of rock that overlooked the beach. We lived in complete isolation and spent our days wandering the sandy shore, the muted tones of beige and gray somehow comforting amidst the salty breeze.

One evening, I burned my hands on the bubbling stew over the fire and Teddy wrapped my hands in bandages torn from his linen shirt. Despite the cramped cottage, he insisted that I remain in bed while he tended to my wounds, sleeping with his arms wrapped protectively around me at night. When the burns faded to a healthy pink, he stripped off his linen shirt and breeches and whisked me out of bed to splash in the waves, the salty gale tangling our hair as he spun me around in circles. Eventually, Teddy collapsed in a fit of breathless laughter on the shore, though desire overcame his mirth when his eyes settled on my soaked chemise. He rolled over and smoothed both hands up my thighs, pushing up the sheer fabric, until - .

"Korey?"

My heart seized when his pale hand touched my shoulder. My eyes snapped open as I bolted upright.

"Don't sneak up on me like that!" I smacked him, though his attentive expression never wavered.

"How long have you b-been awake?" Teddy stroked my hair.

"A while," I shrugged, feeling sheepish. "I didn't want to disturb you, but I… lapsed into our memories and realized we, uh, once had sex on a beach. Do we have a kink for public places or something? I'm noticing a trend."

Teddy quickly ducked his head, clearly not accustomed to sharing these memories. My smile faded as his hands fumbled, obviously not knowing what to do with them. After a long, uncertain moment, he glanced up with tears rimming his bloodshot eyes, which only made his jade irises pop.

"Are you in p-pain?" He coughed to mask the waver in his voice.

"I woke up with a headache, but your voice drove away the pain," I touched his face. "Why are you crying?"

He stared at me for a long moment.

"I can't believe you s-saved my life," he turned beet red as tears spilled down his cheeks. "I expected you to r-run and save yourself. I didn't think…" A sob wracked his body. "I n-never believed I meant that m-much to you, but your s-small sacrifice made me love you that much m-more." He wrapped his arms around my shoulders and hugged me tightly. "Now I refuse to g-give up."

"Don't ever give up," I cradled his head against my chest and stroked his hair. "We're partners in crime, after all. What would I do without you?"

After a moment, Teddy lifted his head slightly and traced my exposed collarbone with his lips.

"I want you," he declared with surprising clarity, his entire body trembling with need. Before I could point out that we were covered in some bizarre creature's blood, he dragged me to my feet. "Come on. We're going s-swimming."

"Swimming?" I echoed.

For the first time, my eyes drank in our surroundings. We were in a cave of sorts with walls made of amethysts or the Underworld equivalent that shone like frosted lavender. The crystals illuminated the spacious cavern, the ground covered in crystallized fragments that crunched beneath our feet. The fire's sunny disposition contrasted with the cave's cool, unearthly tones.

Teddy guided me down a spiral staircase that opened to a much wider space filled with steam. A natural hot spring radiated warmth from the center of the cave, and we both gravitated to its lavender depths. Teddy wrapped his arms around my waist and pulled me flush to his body, my blush intensifying with the realization that he was aroused. The memory of our bodies tangled on the beach and sand coating his backside like a second skin made my pulse quicken, but nothing compared to the excitement of him plucking my dress open one button at a time.

It dawned on me that Teddy was aroused because saving his life had made him feel loved. The thought made me tremble with anticipation as he peeled back my dress, the brush of his fingertips on my bare skin reducing my bones to jelly. I had read hundreds of romance novels since I was thirteen, and the reality of having sex was so different from the printed word. Deep, soulful, and exhilarating with the charged air of blistering exploration. When I had first given myself to him by the river, I had done so on the basis of our friendship, but now I possessed a wealth of memories that proved our timeless love, making me feel safe, cherished, and protected.

The filthy, ragged dress fluttered down my body and pooled around my feet, leaving me breathless as Teddy openly gawked at me. He had probably seen my naked body more than a thousand times and committed every detail to memory for those stretches of time he had to win my love all over again, but his eyes still widened as though seeing me for the first time. His reactions made me feel powerful and feminine. A strange heaviness pooled in my breasts as my inner thighs grew slick. Teddy cupped my tender breasts and savored their weight as he rolled my nipples with his thumbs.

Eager to return his caresses, I unbuttoned his jeans and drew the zipper down over his erection, my tongue dragging across my lower lip as I fondled him through his briefs. Teddy released a low, breathless moan as he rolled his hips in that same thrusting motion he used on me, sending a lightning bolt that seared through my core. More than a little aggressive, I yanked his flannel shirt down his lanky arms and tugged his t-shirt over his head.

"Easy there, t-tiger," Teddy laughed nervously, though the exuberant glow of his boyish face betrayed his pleasure.

I scraped my fingernails over his pebbled nipples in response, his shy laughter quickly dissolving as I licked his bare chest. I wet my lips and hummed as I tasted the sweat that had earlier poured down his back and chest, the scent musky and painfully masculine. I had never inhaled a man's natural scent before, or at least not in this lifetime, but my body recognized him on a deeply primal level. He

stammered something incoherent as I yanked down his jeans and urged him to slip his feet through the leg holes until he was entirely at my mercy.

Taking control of our lovemaking and exploring his body made me feel empowered, as though I'd finally come into my own. No more living vicariously through fictional characters, creating vision boards, and dreaming about the future. At long last, the future was knocking on my door, and I was more than eager to dive into this journey. A strange fire coursed through my veins as I kissed and licked every inch of his body. I lavished his chest and abdomen with hot, open-mouthed kisses before dropping to my knees.

The tantalizing lines that marked his pelvis fascinated me, and I relished his soft, plaintive groan as I traced them with my tongue. My unexpected surge of confidence waned somewhat the moment I considered his length, its dusky shade and weeping tip making my heart race with fear. My eyes wandered the length of his body and found him watching me with a feverish hope.

"I've never done this before," I murmured shyly.

He arched a skeptical brow. "Are you s-sure about that?"

An image flashed in my mind from one of my past lives, one who had sought sanctuary in a cathedral after being accused of witchcraft by the common folk. Teddy, a priest, had taught me how to read and write, given me spiritual guidance, and protected me from those who sought to harm me. One night a tentative knock had sounded on my

door. It was Teddy. Unlike his usual white and gold robes, he wore a linen nightshirt, his eyes blazing as he devoured the sight of my white, billowing nightgown. We both knew he shouldn't have sought me out in the middle of the night, but he was in love and after months of internal conflict, he was willing to turn away from his chosen path to be with me. I saw myself sucking hard on him as we lay sprawled in my bed, my head bobbing as I massaged his sac. His fingers were tangled in my hair as he moaned softly. He'd come fast and hard.

The memory was sudden and fierce, as though Teddy had placed it there as a reminder that I knew exactly how to pleasure him.

"Man, I used to be kind of a slut!" I exclaimed, making unexpected laughter explode from the latest incarnation of my lover.

God, I loved his laugh. I loved the way his eyes danced with amusement, like he truly believed I was the best thing known to mankind. At that moment, I wanted nothing more than to bring him to his knees.

Teddy cupped my cheek with a tenderness that broke my heart. "Korey, you don't h-have to - ."

The fact that he even thought to give me a choice sealed his fate. Before he could finish his sentence, I licked the glistening head of his cock (look at me using big words), the salty taste not altogether unpleasant. Teddy made a strangled sound in his throat as I slowly eased the fat head into my mouth.

Accommodating his entire length was difficult without scraping his tender flesh with my teeth, so I tapped into my memory bank to draw upon past experience, learning that I could stroke his shaft and suck on his head at the same time.

Still, I felt clumsy and inexperienced, but Teddy whimpered and sucked in one strangled breath after another as he clutched fistfuls of my hair, making me feel more like a wanton sex gooddess than a complete novice. The way he tugged on my hair stimulated my scalp, and I couldn't resist stroking him harder and faster. A naughty idea floated innocently to the forefront of my mind, one that piqued my curiosity. Teddy already made me feel incredibly irresistible, so how could I solidify that idea in his mind? My mouth released the head of his cock, and I cushioned his length between my breasts.

I gazed up at him as I rubbed his shaft between them, eliciting a groan the moment our eyes met. His cock flushed a deeper plum as a fresh surge of arousal pulsed through him.

"Sometimes it hurts how ridiculously p-perfect you are," he gasped between pants as he began to unravel before my eyes. "The way you s-stare up at me w-with those huge eyes, so innocent and p-pure, as if you have no c-clue what your touch d-does to me. It m-makes me want to…"

Teddy screwed his eyes shut and bared his teeth as a seemingly endless series of hot spurts erupted on my chest and face. The pulsing of his cock between my breasts and the

look of absolute rapture on his face made me burn with a keen awareness of the hollowness between my thighs. Knowing I had brought him pleasure satisfied me completely. I didn't expect any more from him, but Teddy gathered me in his arms as soon as he recovered and jumped into the hot spring with a thunderous splash, the water scalding in the most pleasurable way. When I resurfaced, coughing and gasping for breath, I noticed the inky black lamprey blood swirling on the surface as the dried splatters trickled down my neck. I ducked under the water's surface once more and scrubbed my face, eager to feel clean and refreshed.

A pair of lean arms wound around my waist and hauled my upper body from the water. Now that we were somewhat clean, Teddy immediately devoured my mouth, his kisses erotic, demanding, and all-consuming. My head tilted back on a breathless moan as he kissed and licked my throat and glistening breasts, his mouth swallowing one nipple while kneading the other.

"You s-saved me," he murmured as his lips ghosted over my wet skin. "Korey."

"Teddy," I breathed in response because that was the only word I wanted on my lips.

Lifting his head, he glided up my body, those beautiful jade eyes flashing in the faint lavender glow. A powerful emotion welled deep inside of me as our eyes exchanged a thousand unspoken words. A lump formed in my throat as tears pricked my eyes, making his brow wrinkle in concern. Cupping my face, he captured every tear, and I hoped he could taste the depth of my love on his tongue.

How could loving someone so fiercely cause such beauty and pain?

We embraced each other with our foreheads pressed together as we basked in the heat of the hot spring, the deepening of our union transcending the physical realm. I wrapped my legs around Teddy's waist as we drifted in circles around the hot spring, a slow dance that solidified some intangible emotion between us.

Our lips brushed in the faintest suggestion of a kiss as he weaved through the water, the steam rising from the spring to dampen our skin and curl our hair as it dried. Everything seemed magnified in those moments. The parting of his lips. The hitch of my breath. The slick heat of our bodies beneath the water's surface. With my legs hooked around his waist, he carried me back to our cave and the crackling fire.

The crystallized fragments clung to our bodies as he slowly sank into me, pausing for several moments to savor the way my walls expanded to accommodate his length. Straddling him, I rolled my hips experimentally, feeling it necessary to capture every sensation. After all, our future wasn't guaranteed.

"I love you," I breathed in the stillness of the cave as his hips lifted off the ground to move with mine.

Teddy sat up, his back covered in fragments, and wrapped his arms around me. Our joined bodies found a slow, sensual rhythm that made me explode in a shower of fiery sparks. The air thickened, charged with electricity, making it difficult to breathe, but nothing could stop me from rolling on the ground beneath him as he thrust into me with vigor. The delicious friction massaged something deep inside of me that had remained out of reach until now, and I clung to his lean frame as pleasure coiled in my lower belly. The coil wound tighter and tighter, until one final, deep thrust made that tight ball unravel in a tangled mess.

The sweetest euphoria I had ever known blossomed in my lower belly like the birth of a new sun, heat spreading through my limbs like wildfire. A play of light and shadow captured the revenant gleam in Teddy's eyes as he watched me fall to pieces in his arms, that untested power fuelling his hips as he ground out his release. Those adoring eyes remained open and unblinking as his body convulsed, the strained cords of his neck making him look wild and untamed, especially with his mop of tangled, unruly hair. After what seemed like an eternity, he collapsed on top of me, comfortably squishing my body beneath his weight. I tenderly kissed his forehead as he trembled all over, his sweat-slicked skin glistening in the firelight.

"I l-love you s-so much," he stammered. "No m-mater what happens, p-please protect my heart."

"I promise," I vowed as I cradled his head to my breast, kissing the untamed crown for emphasis.

Teddy's lack of faith irked me, especially after sharing my body in such a loving, soulful way. No matter how often I redirected my mind as we stared into the flames, I had a terrible feeling in my gut that Teddy was keeping something from me. He behaved as though he expected our plans to fall apart. The longer we traveled, the more desperate he seemed, as though torn between savoring every moment of our time together and quietly mourning.

I knew Teddy wouldn't go down without a fight, but I was beginning to suspect that my coming-of-age had more to do with fulfilling my promise of devotion than living out some romantic fantasy from my youth.

Begin Again

We lost track of time as we languished in our cave, exploring the nuances of each other's bodies. Teddy knew exactly what I liked. He sucked on my toes, kissed the hollow of my ankle, and licked the back of my knee, making me writhe in unexpected bliss. I knew he'd discovered these hidden delights before, but I ignored my rather insistent past that often flooded my mind with helpful suggestions, but I wanted to explore Teddy's body for myself this time. I quickly learned that his hands were extremely sensitive, so I bit the fleshy mound of his palm and slowly drew each finger into my mouth. The small whimpers that escaped his throat as he watched me through slitted eyes made my stomach flutter with satisfaction.

No longer concerned about my use of magic, I rotated my wrist and produced fruit from behind his ear after making love in the hot spring, my own small contribution to stage magicians the world over. We feasted on pears, mangos, kiwis, dragon fruit, and peaches. Sweet juice gushed from every bite that dribbled down my forearm in a silent invitation for his mouth to follow its track. We hadn't packed soap for the journey, but the hot spring was surprisingly cleansing. We seized the opportunity to bathe often, sometimes more than once a day. We even soaked our filthy clothes in the water and watched the blood and grime coil on the water's lavender surface.

It was impossible to keep track of time in this subterranean world, but Teddy often played his guitar before curling up on the hard ground beside me, his light, raspy tenor layered over my rich alto. On the fourth day, I studied the play of light and shadow on his shuttered expression as his fingers plucked delicate notes from the strings.

"We're not escaping the Underworld, are we?" I questioned flatly. "You're simply stalling before Death finds our hiding place. You want to steal as much time from him as possible."

He ceased strumming, as though every ounce of energy had drained from his body, and he neither spoke nor met my gaze. The silent confirmation of my suspicions made my eyes burn with hot, angry tears. I couldn't believe he hadn't shared this plan with me, but my heart ached with a bittersweet longing imagining him evading Death simply to spend more time in my embrace.

"The fragments have slowly pieced together over the past few days, and I don't remember traveling this route the last time we escaped the Underworld. Why didn't you tell me our game of cat-and-mouse only had one outcome?"

Teddy swallowed hard as he tentatively met my gaze.

"We still have a c-chance," he stammered determinately. "The w-witch of the wild is rumored to live in this n-network of caves. Based on the l-legends, the witch once s-served Death in his royal c-court before he exiled h-her to The Forbidden Lands. She roams the salt f-flats with her bloodthirsty w-wolves. I'm convinced she can help us escape because she h-hates Death."

Well, this was news to me.

"How are we supposed to find her, though?" I spread my hands in a helpless gesture. "We're completely isolated in these caves."

"There's a narrow p-passageway that leads to a series of c-catacombs that almost looks like a p-place of worship." Teddy rubbed his chin thoughtfully. "She garnered a c-cult following after being exiled. They worshipped her like a g-goddess. I've ventured below once or twice as you s-slept, but I didn't linger b-because I didn't want Death to find you while I was g-gone."

"I still don't understand how we're supposed to find her," I shook my head.

"The legends say to call out for h-her where she most often d-dwells," he explained with an excited gleam in his eyes, like a World of Warcraft fanboy with a new friend. "I remember other shades s-swapping stories about the witch who t-transformed into a white owl to escape Death after he s-spurned her love. Once we r-reach the salt flats, we can summon her."

My mouth curved in a half-smile every time Teddy lapsed into a flowery way of speech, like he no longer had to use modern slang to disguise his true origins.

"Why have we been hiding here if you knew where to find her?" I asked.

Teddy sheepishly rubbed the back of his neck, like a scolded child. "I needed s-somewhere to heal my leg b-because you fainted before you c-completely healed me. Also, I thought we c-could find her in these caves, but my attempt to s-summon her didn't work. As for w-why we've remained here so long…" He trailed off. "I w-wanted to give you the adventure you've always d-dreamt of. And I could n-no longer c-contain my n-need to touch you."

I blushed fiercely, though our eyes remained locked.

"Now that our clothes are dry, I think we should leave as soon as possible," I said. "I'll admit that I feel a little betrayed that you kept so much from me, especially since your life hangs in the balance. Not mine."

"Korey," he reached across the fire, his tone pleading.

I rose and donned my wrinkled dress while struggling to ignore Teddy's wounded expression. He'd never meant to withhold information from me (or perhaps he had) but he hadn't done so to hurt me. I understood that much, but I remained skeptical about seeking help from an exiled witch who sometimes prowled the salt flats as an owl. Teddy's knowledge was based on legend, but I supposed I had to demonstrate the same faith in him that I asked for in return.

Once Teddy and I were dressed, he doused the fire, slung his guitar over his back, and grabbed the sword propped against the rock wall. My gaze swept over our cozy cave and the hot spring where we'd laughed, wrestled each other, and made love, taking one last look before moving on.

The network of caves seemed endless as we journeyed through semi-darkness, the amethyst ceiling

glowing with a faint, shimmering light. Teddy often glanced over his shoulder to make sure I remained close to him, though his melancholic gaze suggested that he ached from our earlier conversation and sought relief. I merely stroked the spot between his shoulder blades and kissed the nape of his neck, making him relax somewhat. As for me, my body tensed with every step that further plummeted us into darkness.

The narrow passageway opened to a cathedral-like cavern with vaulted ceilings. Our eyes widened from a mingled sense of awe and wonder, and I imagined the scrape of stone as leathery hands carved ornate designs into the walls. A statue of a cloaked woman with large eyes and hair that fell beyond her waist stood where an altar might have been. Her expression looked calm and serene, but something about those large eyes unnerved me as the pupils followed my every movement. I had never traveled to Europe (or at least not in this lifetime) but tourists often commented on feeling the layers of history through the architecture and, considering my story was woven into the tapestry of time, the abandoned place of worship transported me back to antiquity.

Two statuesque wolves with elongated snouts and porcupine-like hackles flanked the immobile witch. Now that I actually knew what she looked like, something pricked my subconscious like a thorn drawing blood. I wandered closer, unable to tear my eyes away from her face.

"I know her," I breathed as a rush of memories flooded my mind. "My village worshiped her before I was

lured into the Underworld and met you. I know exactly what to do."

"Korey," Teddy protested lightly, though he quietly observed me from afar as I knelt at the statue's bare feet peeking from beneath a pool of fabric, pressed my forehead to the ground, and prayed.

Long, leafy vines erupted from my palms and curled around the statue before blossoming into pink and white chrysanthemums, a flower that represented grief and loss. How else could I describe her tragic story? Hundreds of years before I had come into existence, a young boy had stumbled upon a creature that was capable of shedding its skin to adopt a human form. The creature assumed a child's form that evolved as the boy grew into adulthood, and they had splashed in the pond beneath the willow tree, the best of childhood friends. One day, the young man announced to

Esme, the ethereal beauty with a tangle of white hair that made her luminescent skin glow brighter, that he was arranged to marry a girl from his village.

Desperate to keep him, Esme shed her animal hyde and abandoned the wild in favor of a mortal life. The young man brought his new bride home wearing nothing more than gossamer threads. Needless to say, his parents and the village at large were shocked. The young man, too weak to counter their disapproval, spurned Esme in favor of the woman he was arranged to marry, disregarding her sacrifice in destroying her animal hyde so that she could remain in the mortal realm forever.

The young man visited Esme for trysts, until he grew too old to make the journey. As he neared the end of his life, his children scattered, shouldering Esme with the responsibility of caring for the man she loved. When Death knocked on his door, she pleaded with the pale, morose god to take her with him. Seeing how painfully beautiful she was, he agreed, imbuing her with magical properties that would enable her to survive the harsh conditions of the Underworld, and eventually became her lover. No one understood why Death cast her from the palace and banished her to The Forbidden Lands, but some claimed she'd turned to stone the day her lover tricked a young mortal into dying to make the young fool his bride - that young fool being... me.

The goddess had forsaken immortality for legend because her heart could not endure another rejection.

I channeled my compassion, empathy, and remorse into my prayer as the flowers bloomed all around her lovely face and, slowly, the stone began to crack and crumble. Teddy dragged me away from the falling debris as a flesh-and-blood woman emerged from the statue, her delicate feet touching the stone floor as she brushed stray bits from her wild tangle of hair. The witch goddess wore a plum cloak over a lavender gown that complemented her large green eyes, the color paler than Teddy's. A tangle of white curls spilled around her shoulders, the brightness of her unearthly skin and hair almost blinding.

Teddy shielded his eyes as the witch goddess clapped her hands and, a moment later, the wolverine creatures leapt into existence, stone crumbling around their large paws as they shook out their spiky fur, which tinkled like plum, fuchsia, and white crystals. The witch goddess' serene expression turned feral the moment her eyes landed on me.

"I recognize you," she pointed with a long, pale finger, her tone derisive. "You're the one that stole my place in Death's bed."

"No," I shook my head resolutely as she circled us like a vulture. "I fell in love with another man and escaped Death's clutches."

Her pale green eyes fell upon Teddy.

"You mean *this* cherub?" The witch raked her fingers through his semi-long hair, making my heart plummet. To his credit, he jerked away and hugged me closer to his chest. The witch sobered instantly, the cruel twist of her lips softening into acute longing as melancholy filled her heavy-lidded eyes. "Now you know what it feels like to have another woman touch your man."

"We're not here to torture you," I frantically pleaded, choosing my words carefully.

"Why *are* you here?" The witch demanded regally.

Man, Death and this royal pain-in-the-ass were meant to be. A sudden idea popped into my head.

"Death has been searching for you," I lied smoothly with my customary bright-eyed delivery. Teddy stiffened beside me. I squeezed his bicep, urging him not to blow our cover. "Since I've been nothing but trouble, scarring his pretty face and such, he's reconsidering your exile."

The witch goddess' expression twitched. Meanwhile, Teddy kicked me and I returned the favor.

"Really?" Those pale green eyes gleamed with hope. "After everything that happened between us? I had hoped for so long that we would reconcile our differences… until *you* arrived." Her nose wrinkled as she looked me up and down. "What does he even see in you?"

Teddy opened his mouth in my defense, but I clapped a hand over it. I understood that she nursed a broken heart, but my guilt shrivelled in my chest every time she opened her pretty mouth. The name of the game was survival.

"Death hasn't made up his mind," I shook my head. "Look, I don't know what happened between you two, but he only abducted me because he was lonely and in terrible pain. I think he understands you better now that I've fallen in love with another man. I'm sure you know how Death can be," I rolled my eyes as though talking to a close friend. "Sometimes he needs a little perspective."

For the first time, the witch goddess cracked a smile, though her soft expression quickly morphed into one of suspicion. "Why should I help you escape the Underworld?"

I sucked in a deep breath. This was our moment.

"Death sent us on a quest to find you." The lie escaped my mouth before my brain could process its absurdity, though she seemed more convinced by the

second. "He wants you to come to his palace as soon as you send us on our merry way."

The witch goddess narrowed her eyes. "That doesn't sound like the Death I know."

Shit.

We needed to leave as soon as possible. My plan wasn't taking flight, on top of two ravenous wolves baring their blood-stained teeth at us, their cloying breath hot on the air.

"Death mentioned you were a stubborn one," I laughed nervously as I backed away from her with my arms circling Teddy's narrow waist. "We'll head back to the palace and let him know you're not coming."

The witch goddess' nostrils flared as she hissed a command in a language I didn't understand, though the meaning of her words became clear the moment the wolves growled ferociously.

"Run!" I screamed.

Teddy pushed me closer to the nearest passageway but, as opposed to bravely wielding his sword, he grabbed the guitar slung on his back and strummed. The moment his fingers touched the chords, the wolves paused and nervously wagged their bushy tails. I watched in complete awe.

When he opened his mouth and began to sing, I understood why he'd brought his guitar to the Underworld.

I didn't recognize the song because he'd never shared it with me before. The song told the tale of a shade that fell deeply in love with a young mortal who offered him a second chance at life. Their love was forbidden and, despite the odds being stacked against them, they managed to escape Death's clutches on the condition that he would prove his love with each passing lifetime. He poured his heart and soul into loving a woman who no longer remembered their history. As small children, she always protected him from bullies. As teenagers, he invented clever schemes to discourage interested suitors to ensure he was the last one standing. No matter how often she declared her love for him, the possibility that Death might come for her one day haunted him. Would their love withstand the test of time?

I realized that Teddy had been allowed into the Underworld because of our story. Not only was he asking for the witch's help, he was empathizing with her heartbreak by sharing his own fear of loss. My first inclination had been to lie, using her pain as a weapon. Teddy's, on the other hand, was to be truthful and sincere. Maybe I wasn't good enough for him - not the other way around, as he feared.

The witch goddess hadn't moved a muscle or batted an eyelash since he began to sing. Even as the words faded, Teddy strummed until the cavern was eerily silent. Unperturbed, he bowd, slung his guitar on his back, and faced me with a solemn look. The witch goddess didn't move or order her wolves to tear us apart. As for Teddy and I, neither of us uttered a word as we climbed back up the

winding passageway to the stretch of salt flats that awaited us.

~

"Why did you l-lie to her about Death w-wanting her back?" Teddy demanded as we traversed the endless maze of passageways. "Why would you dangle s-something like that in front of her?"

The accusation in his voice deeply wounded me, making my step falter as I flashed him a guilty look. His forbidding expression made my shoulders slump in shame and defeat.

"I didn't think about hurting her," I admitted sullenly. "In fact, I hadn't thought of anything other than your survival."

"And yours?" He challenged, arching a heavy, dark brow.

For a long, tense moment, I remained silent.

Quietly, I murmured, "I would lay my life down for you, Teddy." He stared at me, stricken. Before he could protest, I swiftly interjected, "I know we're in this together, but I would do anything to make sure you were alive and happy, even at my own expense."

His stunning eyes searched my face.

"But you *are* my h-happiness," Teddy whispered with downcast eyes. "I've f-fought too hard for your freedom to watch you submit t-to Death. Over my d-dead body."

I opened my mouth to request that he stop using those particular words when a light appeared at the end of the narrow, claustrophobic tunnel. The rock itself had gradually morphed into blown glass that reflected our disheveled appearance. I longed for wide, open spaces and a glimpse of the sky after many days of isolation, but the potent charge in the air as we neared the cave's mouth made me pause. That peculiar charge had enveloped me in Pebble's Creek as acid rain had poured from the sky.

We emerged from the cave, and I gasped as my eyes drank in The Forbidden Lands for the first time. A vast landscape of glimmering salt stretched before us, purple capped mountains looming on the horizon in their crystallized majesty. A fathomless crevasse divided the salt flats like the angry, jagged scar that tore through Death's visage. A bolt of lightning, closely followed by a crash of thunder, illuminated the churning of soft lavender, deep plum, and angry magenta clouds. Acid rain poured from the sky, each raindrop creating a small welt as the droplet burned my skin.

The rain plastered Teddy's brown hair to his face, making him look weak and small compared to the small army charging forward on the other side of the yawning crevasse. A small army of ghoulish skeletons with meat clinging to their bones flanked Death as he perched on the edge of the divide, the fearsome gale whipping his crimson cloak with a majesty that seemed specific to him. Two outcasts from a backwater town versus the fearsome, battle-trained minions of Death. The odds were extremely unfair, to say the least. Death reminded me of schoolyard bullies like Conrad and his cronies, and once again my only protection were the vines that shot like cords from my palms.

"We need to run," I yanked on Teddy's arm out of sheer desperation.

"Only to f-find a place for you to h-hide," he shouted hoarsely over the pounding rain.

I gaped in horror. "Are you seriously going to fight him?"

Teddy raised the sword with a sly half-smile. "My f-father was a blacksmith, remember? As a shade in Death's p-palace, I w-worked in the armory. How d-do you think I beat you at every l-lightsaber battle?"

"I don't appreciate you making light of this situation," I frowned deeply.

He gently grasped my chin between thumb and forefinger and lightly kissed my swollen, burning lips. "And I d-don't appreciate you doubting m-my ability to p-protect you."

"That's fair," I grudgingly conceded. "Well played, Kershaw."

Death glowered as Teddy planted another soft kiss on my lips and grabbed my hand, dragging me in his wake as he ran like the devil. Our pounding feet splashed water everywhere, until Teddy skidded to a halt some distance

away from the divide and forced me inside a dark cave that probably housed any number of wild, dangerous creatures.

"No m-matter what happens to me, s-stay here," he implored with wide, frightened eyes as he stroked my hair with blistered hands. His jade eyes memorized every detail of my face, unable to resist kissing my forehead and eyelids as if this was our last time. "Promise m-me you'll run and n-never look back. Don't let him f-find you, okay?"

I shook my head fiercely as hot tears blurred my vision. "I'm not promising anything. You're going to live, Teddy," I touched his face. "I love you too much."

Teddy gathered me in his arms and kissed me with such bruising strength that I collapsed on my back the moment he released me. I watched him pick up his sword, his brown hair whipped back as he emerged from the cave to face his one true enemy. Death waited for him, a lone figure cloaked in red and silver armor against a backdrop of purple. The rain plastered his shoulder-length black hair to his angular face, the red scar I had given him a distinct slash across his determined features.

Teddy dashed at break-neck speed across the salt flats, his gait quick and light in contrast to Death's heavy, deliberate movements. Lightning streaked overhead as Teddy lunged mid-air and crashed his sword down upon his opponents with a fierce shriek. Even though they were the same height, Teddy's lithe elegance gave him the upper hand as he drove Death backward with unrelenting force, the clang and hiss of their swords renting the air. My fingernails dug into my palm as I watched Teddy swerve and duck before launching an attack of his own, his body moving so gracefully that I wondered how I could have never guessed his secret. Teddy bared his teeth, his face contorted beyond recognition. I had never seen the quiet, mild-mannered boy I had grown up with so angry.

Death looked mutinous as he extended an arm and channeled his power to force my beloved onto his back.

"No!" A loud cry tore from my throat, not heeding Teddy's words as I ran from the cave.

The fall knocked the wind from his lungs, leaving him to cough and splutter on the ground.

I was absolutely furious as I came to his rescue. "Don't you dare touch him!"

Death spared me a lethal glance. "I won't hurt him if you return to the palace with me, or would you prefer that I reveal your indiscretions?"

I blanched. Teddy clambered to his feet and lunged at Death once more.

"Korey would n-never betray me!" He growled as he repeatedly sliced the air with his sword.

Death ducked and evaded each blow.

He was toying with his prey, making cold fury bloom in my chest. Part of me was tempted to reveal the truth before any permanent damage could be done, but I didn't want to distract Teddy. My hands tingled with magic as I imagined disarming him with an unexpected shot of vines, but I remembered the way his mere presence had made my plants wither.

"Take my hand, and I will spare his life!" Death flashed me a lazy smile as Teddy hacked away, his blind hatred robbing him of that easy grace.

I didn't know what to do. If I accepted Death's hand, I would forsake every trial Teddy had suffered to protect me. I couldn't rely on Death's word. Teddy might die either way. I screamed as the larger man gripped my lover's throat and squeezed, until Teddy gasped and choked for breath, his sword clattering on the ground. I lunged for the sword, grabbed the hilt, and stabbed Death beneath the armpit where there was a gap in his armor. Air hissed through his clenched teeth as blood sprayed from the wound, and he released Teddy as he staggered backward.

Teddy quickly jumped to his feet and approached Death with a white-knuckled grip on his sword. Something about this situation didn't feel right. Death was immortal; I didn't believe for one second that his wound had drained him so quickly. Instead of using brute force, Death employed a new tactic, one I hated even more.

"To be honest, I don't know whether to admire or pity your dog-like loyalty to a woman who so clearly pities you," Death's insidious voice made Teddy freeze. "Why do you think she gave her body to you? Don't you think she grew tired of you trailing after her like a lovesick puppy? The moment I stepped back into her life; she didn't care that I brushed your pathetic excuse of a garment off her shoulders. She came with me willingly. Little Korey hadn't been in the Underworld more than a day before she sought me out and kissed me as though her life depended on it."

Teddy faltered as his insecurities rose to the surface. He stared at the ground with listless arms, on the brink of defeat. No, this couldn't happen.

"I wouldn't have kissed you if I hadn't been drugged!" I interrupted, desperate to clarify the situation. "I would have told Teddy, but I didn't want his fears to get the best of him."

That was the moment Teddy glanced over his shoulder, and the sheer disbelief in his eyes shred my heart to pieces. He opened his mouth to speak, but within a single heartbeat, Death impaled my best friend and lover on his sword, using the moment of distraction to his advantage. A scream tore from my throat as Teddy's knees buckled, the blade sliding from his chest as he collapsed into my arms. My tears dappled his pale face as he gulped in quick, shallow breaths.

"No, please don't leave me," I covered his bloody wound with my hand, as though I could heal him if I concentrated hard enough. "I'm so sorry."

I wailed, my heart utterly broken, as his body seized.

"Korey," he murmured before drawing his final breath.

I buried my face in his hair and breathed in his familiar scent as I rocked him back and forth, my head pounding with the force of my tears. After a moment, I peered up at Death through a haze of pain, surprised to find him watching me with traces of sympathy and… remorse? The gorgeously cruel expression had been replaced with a thoughtful one, as though none of this had gone how he'd expected.

"*Why?*" I demanded hotly. "Why did you take him from me?"

Death's full mouth pressed into a grim line, but he didn't utter a single word. My gaze returned to Teddy's face, a fresh wave of agony ripping through me as I closed his sightless eyes. Never again would I see those beautiful, intelligent green eyes sparkle with a soulfulness that was entirely unique to him. Never again would I burrow my face in his fluffy brown hair, or breathe in all the mechanical smells from his father's auto shop. Memories from our last few days together flooded my mind. The lovemaking, the love songs in the dark, the whispered conversations about our future once we escaped the Underworld.

All gone.

After a moment, Death crouched beside me, and I instinctively clung to Teddy's lifeless body a little tighter.

"Korey," he murmured. "There's a walled garden in your courtyard with an ivory bench that overlooks an overgrown flower bed. We can lay him on the bench as his final resting place while you mourn, if you'd like. I know his death comes as a shock."

"No shit, Sherlock," I swiped my runny nose.

Death scowled. "Either that, or we can leave him here for the beasts that roam these wild lands. They won't value his remains the way you do."

I blanched and wiped my eyes. Teddy's death had sealed my fate. I would spend an eternity grieving over the love of my life while Death insisted that I belonged to him. The thought made me feel dead inside.

Eventually, Death convinced me to release Teddy's body, and I hovered close to ensure that he took care of my beloved while we journeyed to a waiting chariot. The trek back to the palace was long, though not nearly as arduous as the one Teddy and I had undertaken, and I followed Death up the endless flights of stairs to my chambers where he spread

Teddy's limp, lifeless body on a marble bench through a cobbled passageway in the courtyard. Teddy's face looked oddly serene as I folded his hands on his abdomen.

Death watched me fuss over my fallen lover's body, until at last he spoke.

"You're not reacting at all the way I expected," he mused in a strange, detached sort of way that made my blood run cold.

For the first time since leaving The Forbidden Lands, I tore my eyes away from Teddy's face and turned a horrified look on Death. "Excuse me?"

Surely, I hadn't heard him correctly.

"I expected the celestial beings to give your friend an advantage over me," he stroked his chin thoughtfully, as though Teddy's death was of no consequence to him. "I thought you would have remembered your love for me the moment I killed him, but I'm beginning to realize that you truly cared for him."

Death's tone was nonchalant, though his face was drawn and pale, as though he were a friend who sympathized with my loss instead of the cold-blooded murderer that he truly was. I didn't know what to say, so I turned my back on him and said nothing at all. When he nudged me from behind, I clenched my teeth.

"Do you realize that I won?" He scoffed. "I did exactly as I promised and now you belong to me. I will give you time to grieve your loss, but I expect you to prepare yourself for a new life."

I brushed away the hand he'd placed on my shoulder as I stood, fixing him with a look of incredulity. "Good Lord, what did I ever see in you?"

"What did you ever see in *him*?" He countered.

"I think the problem has always been *me*," I touched my chest, speaking more to myself than him. "I can imagine myself being swayed by your magnetic presence, but it took me until now to realize what love truly is because I was too immature to understand. And I still am. I allowed you to persuade me that morning in Pebble's Creek, but I doubt you're any different now than when I first met you,."

"I don't know how to do such a thing," he shook his head, forlorn.

"Play the part of a human?" I couldn't resist casting the small barb.

"No," he bowed his head solemnly. "I don't know how to love the way Theodoros loved you. His love for you poured like a river from his soul, and I envy that because there is no evidence that I even have a soul." Death shared this as a fact about himself rather than self-deprecation. "I know desire, pleasure, jealousy, and possessiveness, but I don't know selflessness and compassion, hence the nickname Decadence." He offered a weak smile, though his fingers traced his mouth as though he was unfamiliar with such an act. "I only smile because the gesture makes the dead feel more comfortable in my presence, not because it stems from a place within myself. The closest I have ever come to happiness was almost making you my queen, and I've searched tirelessly for you throughout the ages. Now I'm beginning to realize that I've made a grievous mistake."

His words stirred a painful, blinding hope in my heart.

"Does that mean you have the power to restore Teddy's life?" I brightened.

Death arched a black-winged brow. "While I cannot restore his life, I could reanimate him."

My eyes widened. "What does that mean?"

"He will be able to talk and move, but his body will lack a soul. Over time his body will decay." Teddy would become a zombie? "Or if you'd like, I could slow the decay of his body in its current state so you may visit him as often as you'd like."

I nodded mutely. I had visions of restoring the garden to its former glory to honor him. My future looked bleak, but hope still burned in my heart. I was capable of generating life. What if I could heal him?

"Will his soul pass through the Underworld?" I reached for his cloak as he swept from the garden.

"Yes," he stared at the hand that brushed the hem of his crimson garment. "The sorting process can take several weeks, but I will inform you the moment he has entered my realm. I bid you farewell."

I watched him slither into the darkness, until the sleeping Teddy and I were alone. The moment he disappeared, I collapsed beside the marble bench and sobbed until my heart was wrung dry of tears. As I curled up on the flagstones beside Teddy, unwilling to leave his side, I sensed Death's presence beyond the hedges as I drifted into a restless slumber.

The Young Widow

Over the next three weeks, I poured my blood, sweat, and tears into that garden as I waited for news of Teddy's soul entering the Underworld. The flowerbeds were full of thorny brambles, and I welcomed the pain as they tore apart my hands. In the meantime, the palace's dressmakers fitted me for black silk gowns and replaced my crimson bed sheets, coverlet, and curtains with black velvet, satin, and lace. Black had never suited my lively personality, but a solemn, hollow-eyed woman replaced the vivacious girl I had once been. I swept through the halls of the palace entirely clad in black, a veil concealing my pale, wan face.

The only person I removed the veil for was Teddy, though he could no longer gaze upon me.

Each morning I placed my hands over his wound and channeled my life-generating powers through him and, as the magic flowed through me, black roses, lilies, and smaller flowers that glowed blue and purple in the semi-darkness bloomed around him like an altar.

Cordelia visited my chambers for breakfast, lunch, and dinner and watched me with palpable concern from behind her mask as I sat on the balustrade, my attention focused on the sun's arc above the horizon.

"Lord Death is waiting for you to dine with him this evening, my lady," Cordelia clasped her dusky blue hands with her usual prim disposition.

Ever since bathing me that first time, she hadn't overstepped her boundaries as one of Death's servants.

"I'm not hungry," I rested my chin on one propped knee. I refused to eat anything from the Underworld for fear that I would become a natural, inextricable part of Death's palace. "Tell him I would rather gnaw off my own leg than share a meal with him."

The best part of being Death's captive was roasting him on a regular basis and watching his subordinates squirm in horror as I flouted him at every turn. Cordelia practically choked on her gasp.

"Lord Death is concerned for your well-being," her voice wavered as she stepped closer. "Surely you must be willing to consider his vested interest on your behalf."

"He should've thought about that before he murdered my actual my best friend," I turned away from her.

Cordelia had nothing more to add to the conversation. The moment she left, I produced an apple with a graceful turn of my wrist, something Teddy would have appreciated, the crunch of my first bite echoing through the perpetual night. Since returning to the palace, I had survived on a steady diet of fruit instead of the hot meals Cordelia struggled to force on me. The moment I heard Death's heavy footfalls outside my door, I hurled the half-eaten apple into the courtyard. As expected, the door burst open to accommodate the hulking death god.

He wore a black tunic and leggings with a matching cloak. He'd worn black ever since returning from The Forbidden Lands, though not because he mourned Teddy's death like me. I had a sneaking suspicion he wanted our outfits to match, which I would have found weirdly sweet under any other circumstance. In light of recent events, his desire for us to look like a couple merely repulsed me. I imagined how our upcoming interaction would play out, like a scene from *Beauty and the Beast*.

"I thought I told you to come down to dinner," I heard his rich, petulant voice in my mind.

"I'm not hungry," I crossed my arms and turned away from him.

"Fine, then go ahead and STARVE!" I imagined Death's hackles raising like that of the Beast's.

Except there were no womanizing candlesticks there to coach him through a normal human interaction. There was no promise of a slow-burn romance as I came to see beyond my misunderstood captor's front, only dread and resentment.

The scene that ultimately played out was vastly different from the one that echoed in my head. Instead of screaming demands in my general direction, he lumbered forward like a Gothic prince from a Stephanie Meyers novel and perched beside me on the balustrade. Death's large hand hovered above my knee, but I shrank away from his touch.

"I know you're surviving on a steady diet of fruit," he said knowingly, his nostrils flaring as though he struggled to control his temper. His thumb lightly caressed my cheek. "I'm worried about your health. Unlike your usual exuberant self, you look pale and wan. Come dine with me and replenish your strength. If not for me, then do so for your young man."

I wracked my brain for a way to change the subject.

"What happened between you and Esme?" I blurted, hoping to delay his coercion.

Death's frown slowly spread into a smug smile. "Jealous?"

"No," I shook my head, annoyed that he would even ask. The presence of that half-smile reminded me of our conversation where he'd explained that such an act was unnatural to him. The grin he wore now seemed genuine enough, but the uncertainty of its sincerity made my skin crawl. "Why did you banish her after embracing her as a lover? She still loves you, even after your rather cruel punishment. I find it hard to believe that you never reciprocated her feelings."

Death scoffed. "Love? I am not capable of such an emotion."

"The fact that you exiled her to The Forbidden Lands demonstrates the depth of your emotion," I argued. "Anger is a secondary emotion, you know."

Death withdrew his touch as his spine stiffened. "I banished her because she couldn't accept that our physical union possessed no greater depth. She was more than welcome to take others to her bed, but she refused. A water nymph once stoked my lust, but Esme turned the creature into a bean sprout and stomped on her. Then she tore through my kingdom, destroying everything in her path in the hopes that I would acknowledge her as my one true love. Esme is nothing more than a nuisance, the quintessential thorn in my side."

Death's cruel words made me recoil from him in shock and outrage. I wanted to defend the poor woman who had once been reduced to chaos in order to validate her existence.

Instead, I asked, "Then why are you so intent on keeping me here? There are more beautiful women in the world that would satisfy your loneliness. What makes me so different?"

Death looked thoughtful for a moment before vaulting over the balcony and landing with a grunt on the square tiles below, his boots kicking up clouds of dust that made me cough. He extended a hand to me, but I opted for the thick vine that crept up the wall, shimmying down its length until my feet landed on solid ground. I followed him as he edged closer to the eerie green pool that dominated the courtyard. My skin prickled with the intensity of his gaze as he crouched beside the pool and gestured for me to come closer. With a note of apprehension humming in my chest, I knelt beside him and watched his fingers swirl the green

depths into a small whirlpool that gradually evened into a distant memory, one that was conveniently missing from my latest collection.

As I peered into the pool's depths, the other half of the story unfolded before my eyes.

~

Every young man in the village had noticed that Koreyna was no longer a child; she had practically blossomed overnight. They cast her longing looks as she wandered the dirt path with a basket dangling from her arm and flowers in her hair. No one dared approach the young woman, however, because her mother closely guarded their relationship. Despite her best efforts, the mother struggled to protect her daughter's innocence, for a shadow lurked in the forest who stirred Koreyna like no other.

One morning, the breeze dislodged the garland of flowers from her hair, giving her a breathless, windswept appearance. Koreyna froze, for she sensed him before noticing the large figure move through the trees. A murky shadow fell upon the vegetation she had coaxed to life, a sense of foreboding welling in her stomach. A crimson cloak trimmed with gold slithered among the twigs and fallen leaves. A pair of strong legs and sandaled feet flashed as the cloaked figure strode through the lush forest.

    Others claimed the black leather of his sandals was stained from the blood of mortals. Her eyes widened as she drank in her first glimpse of Lord Death. He was massive, far bigger than she had ever imagined.... but his presence posed a problem, for he mindlessly traipsed through her carefully cultivated garden, crushing vegetables and fruit beneath his powerful feet. Infuriated, she plucked a fallen apple from the ground and hurled it at his head. The apple bounced off his helmet, prompting him to turn and stare at the offending fruit.

    Slowly, two amber eyes found her and simmered with an intensity that took her breath away. He reached up and removed the helmet that obscured his face, the iron disguise making him more monster than man. Thick, shoulder-length black hair tumbled around his sharp, angular face. His full, pink lips and amber eyes contrasted beautifully with his pale skin. He plucked the apple from the ground and squeezed the fruit until it exploded. The primal act was darkly sexual. Koreyna shivered in delight.

    The destruction of the ripe fruit allowed her first taste of arousal, one that stirred her curiosity..

    Lord Death had spied on the young mortal around the bonfire one hot summer night. He watched from the line of trees, transfixed, as her long, thick braid unravelled in a perfect silhouette against the roaring fire, her head tossed back in laughter. *Take her,* an insidious voice whispered. *She's the one you have been waiting for.* Lord Death had never removed his helmet for a mortal, but something about her youthful innocence and fiery spirit broke him, making him do the unthinkable.

And so he watched and waited as the scaly, black snake coiled around her ankle and sank its fangs into her unblemished skin. He searched his realm for many weeks until, finally, the lifeless bodies parted to reveal *her*. He'd known the moment he'd encountered her in the garden that she belonged to him and, as he strode forward with purposeful steps, she watched him with fascination and awe. Scooping her into his arms, he carried her back to his palace where she would become his bride.

In the beginning, they exchanged smoldering kisses and she allowed him to explore parts of her untouched body. But Koreyna quickly found him lacking. Lord Death's cruelty, selfishness, and inability to love made her grow distant. No matter how often he showered her with jewels and sumptuous fabrics, she wanted *more*. His physical beauty wasn't enough. His companionship wasn't enough.

The prophecy had described him as temptation itself, yet temptation manifested in the unlikely form of a shade with a pair of wandering eyes...

~

I jerked away from the pool, speechless. The transfer of memory hadn't required physical touch like with Teddy, the experience of which had been warm and comforting, but the swirling combination of my thoughts intermixed with Death's filled the previously missing gaps of my story. The black snake coiled around my leg, the searing pain of its fangs piercing my flesh, and the sound of my mother's screams as I crumpled like a rag doll in the hazy garden. As I lay dying with poison flowing through my veins, a fragile butterfly landed on my face and, beyond its gently flapping wings, I saw my spirit leave my body. Death had been waiting. I hesitated before placing my hand in his, but my acceptance sealed my fate as we evaporated in a swirl of shadow.

    The opulent luxury of Death's world astonished me and, for the first time in my humble existence, I was free. Free from my mother's control. Free from duty and obligation on those lonely nights I dreamt of being swept away. Ghostly flower petals wilted from my hair as the powerfully irresistible and mysterious Death carried me over the threshold of his bedchamber, eager to claim me as his own. He knelt before me as I perched on the edge of his massive bed, one long finger tracing the outline of my cheek as the gold flecks in his eyes shimmered in the low light.

    The twisting candelabras cast a golden hue to our surroundings, heightening the romance and magic of the moment. Refusing to break eye contact, his pale face inched closer to mine until our lips brushed in a sensual caress. The cool, feather-light touch ignited my body, and I surged forward, tangling my fingers in his soft black hair as I ravaged his mouth with unpracticed kisses.

I jolted from the memory, nearly toppling into the pool as I gasped for breath. The light from the pool cast Death's sharp face in deep shadows and pale green ripples.

"Are you still intent on ignoring the powerful draw between us?"

The memory of Death's kiss had been powerful… but Teddy's presence in my heart loomed even larger.

"I don't see the point of denying my initial attraction to you," One corner of my mouth crooked humorlessly. "I remember nicknaming you Decadence as an insult to your opulent lifestyle compared to the suffering of your subordinates. Time in the Underworld is slowed to a snail's pace to prolong the agony of the dead. Those you have plucked from Outer Darkness who serve as shades in your palace shrink in your presence, on top of the former lovers you have sentenced to exile for craving more than a meaningless affair." The line of his mouth hardened, but his obvious displeasure spurred me onward. "Even after all these years, I don't see that you've changed. You're beautiful to look at, but what is your outer shell costing you? If you were not selfish, Teddy would still be alive."

Death frowned deeply. "Do you not feel empathy for my plight? For my inability to love, despite my best efforts? For my desire to belong, despite my curse to endure eternal solitude? Do you not understand what drives me to selfishness, lust, and apathy?"

"Honestly," I shrugged, "I'm not capable of feeling sorry for you right now, as harsh as that might sound."

Death watched as I clambered to my feet, dusted off my backside, and swept across the courtyard to where the thick vines awaited me. Teddy had once said Death meant to tempt me, and I could feel his magnetic pull. He wanted me to feel sorry for him. He wanted me to excuse his despicable behavior, and, in light of Teddy's death, I simply couldn't.

"What if I told you there's another way to bring back your young man?" A warm, dry breeze carried Death's low voice across the courtyard.

I froze and slowly glanced over my shoulder.

My eyes narrowed. "Are you fucking with me?"

Death rose and clasped his hands behind his back.

"Theodoros was easy to defeat because I used his weakness against him," he began, pausing for dramatic effect.

"What are you talking about?" My hands clenched into fists.

"While his love for you is undoubtedly his strength," Death explained with a smirk, "surely his lack of faith in believing he is properly loved is his weakness. Sowing the seeds of doubt was my only chance of winning the fight because, as you may have already noticed, he was the superior swordsman."

My eyes filled with hot, angry tears. "You truly are a monster," I hurled the barb.

"Ah, ah, ah," he clucked his tongue and waved a finger. "You haven't heard my offer. As we speak, your lover is pacing the banks of the river, stewing over your indiscretion. The fact that you haven't come for him in nearly a week only heightens his agony. Even now he considers drinking from the river and erasing his memories of you. If you are able to convince me that true love prevails by convincing him of your unwavering love, I will set both of you free."

I stalked across the courtyard.

"Teddy is here in the Underworld?" I tightly gripped the front of his tunic and restrained the urge to shake him. "Why didn't you tell me sooner? Take me to him right now!"

Death's mouth curled in a slow smile. "As you wish."

Is Your Love Strong Enough?

Just as Death had described, Teddy frantically paced the tall grasses of the river basin wearing a scowl. The dead milled around him like patients in a psychiatric unit - hopelessly bored and waiting for a discharge that would never come. Teddy wore his ratty t-shirt with a blood stain on the front where the sword had pierced him, the familiar flannel shirt, and his Converse sneakers. The only real difference in his appearance were the dark shadows beneath his eyes that contrasted with his pale skin. The moment I saw him, I dashed after him in my black mourning garb. Death lingered some distance away.

Teddy's eyes widened as I flung my arms around his neck.

"Oh my God, Teddy!" I sobbed in relief as I clung to a surprisingly solid form.

I didn't know what I'd expected to find. An actual ghost, perhaps? A man covered in a white sheet? The shades were solid, so why had I expected anything less? My arms wrapped around his neck, my body flush with his, but I stumbled as Teddy jerked away from my embrace and stormed off. I caught Death's smirk when I glanced over my shoulder.

Bastard.

He wanted me to fail at something so deceptively simple. Part of me wondered if he'd planned this all along.

"Teddy!" I shouted as he disappeared behind an untamed hedge weighed down by pink hibiscus flowers.

"Go away," he responded flatly.

I rounded the hedge and caught him digging a hole in the ground to escape inside the hedge itself. I grabbed his ankle and tugged.

"Looking for Narnia?" I quipped in a lame attempt to soften his resolve. "Why are you hiding?"

I wanted to prove Death's assumption that Teddy had no faith in my love for him wrong, but his attempts to escape into the hedge weren't helping my case. I grabbed both ankles and dragged him across the soft grass, making his t-shirt ride up.

"Hey, let me go!" Teddy squirmed in my grasp.

The scene would've been comical, if not for the obvious reasons of Teddy being dead and me being held captive by a gorgeous, entitled asshole. And then something dawned on me. I dropped his legs and he struggled to his feet wearing a disgruntled expression.

"Teddy," I stared at him, wide-eyed, "what happened to your stammer?"

"I'm dead now, thanks for asking," he retorted sarcastically. "I'm sure you'll be relieved to know that we're no longer bound. Now you're free to run off into the sunset with Death."

My heart plummeted as I realized that Death was right; Teddy had no faith in my love for him whatsoever.

"I only kissed Death because I'd been drugged," I reached for him, only for Teddy to flinch away. "The moment I remembered our vow, I broke the embrace."

Teddy's expression drooped with heartache, as though unable to stop torturing himself over the mental image.

"The elixir is more of an aphrodisiac than a drug," his eyebrows drew together in yet another scowl. "I know that you wouldn't have touched him if some secret part of you hadn't wanted to."

It was strange hearing words pour so effortlessly from his mouth; it was like meeting him for the first time. The thought was exciting, but the hard quality of his words filled me with dread and an overwhelming sense of helplessness.

"I don't know what you expect me to say," I shrugged. "I don't care if you know more about elixirs than I do. I didn't kiss him of my own free will. That's not how consent works."

Teddy's expression twisted into one of pure torture, even as his eyes gleamed with a tentative hope. That hope quickly faded as he raked both hands through his semi-long hair.

"I'm completely helpless now," he paced back and forth through the tall grass. "Everything is out of my control. I can no longer save you and, though I'm already dead, the thought of you alone with him absolutely *kills* me inside."

"Teddy, slow your roll," I urged, bracing his shoulders. "Death has agreed to free us on the condition that you're able to forgive me and move on. It breaks my heart that you don't have more faith in me."

Teddy arched a skeptical brow. "Do you honestly think we can trust him?"

"He claims your weakness is having no faith in my love for you. Come on," I grabbed his bitingly cold hand, "let's prove him wrong."

To my utter relief, he squeezed my fingers in return.

~

I sensed Teddy stiffen beside me.

"Let me get this straight," he made a time-out gesture. "Korey and I are simply going to leave with you watching from the sidelines like some benign presence?"

"More or less," Death's eyes narrowed as he tilted his head to one side. "You're simplifying matters by missing a few key details, however."

Teddy crossed his arms, though he was sandwiched between Death and I, making it difficult to match an expression with his wary, hostile tone.

"How so?"

Death looked quite pleased with himself as he explained, "I'm dismayed by the lack of faith you have demonstrated in young Korey, so I am inclined to challenge you. Poor little lamb," his voice caressed my eardrums as he peered around Teddy to flash me a disarming smile. "How gut-wrenching your skepticism and distrust must feel for the woman who has known you since childhood. Come to think of it, far longer than that. Are you sure she even *wants* to leave here with you?"

"Don't listen to him," I whispered against Teddy's nape. Stepping out from behind my childhood friend and lover, I asked, "Why are you goading him?"

"Ah, lovely Korey, the girl of his dreams who has spent more time filling the gaps of his halting words than recognizing the man he has become," Death's eyes glittered strangely. "What an interesting dynamic the two of you share."

"Tell me what I have to do," Teddy's murmur sliced through the contentious exchange. "Please, I'll do anything."

My lover's groveling surprised me, though his words also brought tears to my eyes. The depth of his love made me feel incredibly lucky, but I wished he could recognize the strength of my own. Death looked pleased.

"If you want her as badly as you claim," he began smoothly, "I expect you to walk ahead without any acknowledgement of her presence. That means no whispering her name, no glancing over your shoulder to make sure she's behind you. There will be no indication that she is following you. Faith in her love and willingness to be with you will carry you to the other side. If you reach Pebble's Creek without violating my conditions, then your life will be restored. If you are unable to complete the task, you will find yourself back in the Underworld with a fearsome god whose patience has been tested. Understand?"

Without once acknowledging my presence, Teddy nodded tersely and began his trek across the fields with the fragile hope that I would follow.

~

The journey through the Underworld was treacherous. My heart pounded as I maintained a safe distance from Teddy, who didn't once check to make sure I was behind him. The wide expanse of rolling hills gave way to jagged, unrelenting rock. My bare feet protested, but I hardly dared utter a sound as we followed the river's winding path. The ground disappeared as we traveled and, having no gondola or other means of traversing the water, we clung to the rock wall that I barely managed compared to Teddy's sure-footedness.

Obviously, he had made this journey before.

And so had I, once upon a time, but my memory was foggy. We crept along at a snail's pace, his progress faster than mine. Sweat poured down my face and back, making my grip slick. Climbing in a long, flowing gown was ridiculous, and I cursed Death for not allowing me to change into something more practical. It was clear that he'd wanted to make this trek as difficult as possible.

My bare toes occasionally snagged on the silky fabric as I rooted for a secure foothold. I swallowed my screams, though Teddy froze as a few loose rocks splashed into the churning river. We passed the sleeping three-headed guard and sat motionless as we waited for the front gate to crack open, ushering a batch of new souls that had yet to be sorted. Once the gate swung open, Teddy quickly slipped through the opening, while I scrambled to catch up. I barely made it through in time, and I noticed the strain of Teddy's neck as he struggled not to look, his eyes trained on the muddy shore.

This test of faith wasn't a simple one for him, but he poured his heart and soul into our success. Through narrow, dimly-lit passageways with errant roots either hanging in my face or nearly tripping me, Teddy didn't once glance over his shoulder, and I managed to control the whisper of my gown, the hiss of my breath, and the pitter-patter of my bare feet. The tentative hope in my heart began to flare as we emerged from the endless maze of tunnels, and I silently cheered my companion onward. I envisioned the determined set of his jaw and the intent flash of jade green eyes as he guided me home, and as a light appeared at the end of the tunnel, I saw him hover on the edge, sorely tempted. *You can do it!* I mentally encouraged him. *One more step and you're free. Then all you need to do is wait for me.*

As if hearing my thoughts, Teddy squared his shoulders and extended one leg at the exact moment a sharp root pierced the sole of my foot. A wail of agony tore from my lungs as I stooped to examine my foot. The moment I opened my mouth, Teddy whipped around with frantic eyes.

"No!" I cried and waved for him to turn around, even as tears streamed down my face. "Teddy, look away!"

But it was too late.

As if an elastic band were tied around my waist, the invisible tether flung me like a slingshot back through the endless passageways, through the swirling darkness and greenish gloom, through the front gate and along the frothy river, until I lay sprawled in a panting heap at Death's feet. Teddy struggled to his feet some distance away.

"See?" One corner of Death's mouth curled as he stared down at me. "I told you he doesn't have enough faith in your love."

Before I could argue that Teddy had failed out of concern for my well-being, the god looped an arm around my waist and dragged me back to the palace. Unable to resist, I glanced over my shoulder and saw Teddy sprawled on the grass, his mop of dark hair straggling into his desolate eyes. Vaguely, I was aware that my foot no longer ached and, when I returned to my bedchamber, I found that the root shaped hole had disappeared. ~

Even though I knew Teddy had failed because of me, I didn't know what to think or feel. Death's suggestion that my best friend lacked faith in me placed a lead weight on my heart as I arranged a set of elaborate conbs in my hair. When Death, the object of my utter and complete loathing, had first brought me to his sumptuous palace, I had quietly gushed over these combs whose beauty had fulfilled every Disney princess fantasy I'd had since childhood. If Mulan's father had given her a cherry blossom comb when she returned home from war, why couldn't I have one? If Ariel could use dingle-hoppers to brush her hair at the dinner table, why couldn't I?

Based on every version of the Hades and Persephone myth I had read about, especially the modern interpretations of the myth, I was meant to embrace the power of my sexuality through Death and fulfill my destiny. Instead, that one kiss had cost something precious and dear to my heart, leaving me hollow and bereft. Instead, I'd experienced my sexual awakening with Teddy, the simple, sweet boy-next-door. My supposed love affair with Death was eroding the trust that had remained unshakeable between Teddy and I for ages.

I should be with him right now instead of nursing my wounded pride, but I'd kept my distance since the failed mission in order to protect my heart. I couldn't shake the awful feeling that I had betrayed him. If I hadn't kissed Death, drugged or not, there would've been no heart-

breaking distraction. Teddy would still be alive if it weren't for me.

I didn't know if I was meant to be his, but he'd declared his love for me a thousand times over in the hopes of protecting me from Death's clutches. Even without Teddy, I was putting up a good fight, but how long could that last? Death had spun cobwebs around my brain and used that smoky voice to his advantage, lulling me into a muddled state of mind. Was I fulfilling my destiny here in the Underworld? If so, why did the thought suck the life from me?

Teddy had remained the most important person in my life, and I was failing him, despite his love and protection. From what I remembered of our history, he'd received the short end of the stick for thousands of years, a reality that gnawed at my heart until I was on the verge of cursing whatever higher power was responsible for punishing the one man that had remained loyal to me every step of the way. Like the coward I was, I couldn't bring myself to face him. I avoided the river basin where he roamed. I could almost imagine him pacing in the tall grasses, his presence no more than a whisper as he agonized over my absence. Agitated and alone.

No, that would be giving myself too much credit. My heart squeezed at the thought, a fresh surge of tears smudging my kohl eyes. Blindly, I searched for a handkerchief and dabbed my eyes.

Once my vision had cleared, I noticed something move in my vanity mirror. I jerked sharply, startled, as I whirled around on my cushioned stool.

"Teddy!" I exclaimed in shock and delight, the pleasure of seeing him climb over my balcony like a forbidden lover clashing with intense self-loathing.

He still wore the ratty t-shirt stained with blood, the worn flannel shirt rolled up to one elbow, the jeans riddled with holes that flashed glimpses of bare skin, and the muddy Converse sneakers. Teddy's green gaze bore into mine, his expression unreadable.

"Where have you been?" He demanded, unable to hide his exasperation, his brow deeply furrowed, and hands balled into fists. I winced, the sting of his displeasure like a whip across my face. "I've been waiting for you."

I cleared my throat in my struggle to remain poised. "It's only been a few days."

"Weeks, actually," he corrected sharply.

"Oh," I ducked my head, horrified that so much time had slipped through my fingers, despite Teddy knowing how impossible tracking time in the Underworld was, at least for a beginner like me.

Sensing my distress, he strode across my chamber and knelt before my stool, the all-too real sensation of his touch on my cheek. Even after practically abandoning him, his first instinct was to comfort me, as though serving as my guardian had become entangled with his desire to play the lover. Funny, I had always thought of myself as *his* protector against those who mocked his stammer and sensitive soul, only belatedly realizing his strength.

"If you only knew how often I've dreamt of you over the last few weeks," he breathed as his touch traveled up my cheek and disappeared into my hairline, like he wished to dislodge the combs from my hair so that I looked natural the way he preferred. "It's already been established that I'm jealous, but I *hate* seeing you dressed up for him, especially knowing that he's kissed you," he swallowed hard, his eyes bloodshot. "I know you enjoyed it. The last few weeks have been agony because I can't stop picturing him caressing your breasts and tasting your lips. I resigned myself to my fate a long time ago, but each subsequent lifetime has emboldened me." His touch prickled down my bare arm, the memory of him exploring my body and whispering soft words in my ear making me shiver. "My love for you compounds itself, fueling the rebellious streak that I should claim you as my own." Teddy's voice quavered as he gazed upon me with beseeching eyes, clearly edging around the question that burned in his throat. "Now that I'm stuck here without a body that you're allowed to touch, I find myself praying to whoever might be listening that you'll choose me over him, that we will slowly grow old together and enjoy a simple life in a backwater town no one would've heard of if it wasn't for you." His mouth curved in a wry half-smile, though his mirth quickly faded. "The fact that you haven't sought my company in weeks has made me lose faith, so I'm here because I need you to put me out of my misery. What are you thinking, Korey?" Sucking in a trembling breath, I forced myself to look at him. He at least deserved that courtesy.

"I've been avoiding you because I have something to tell you," I began tremulously. He froze. "You're my best friend and my soulmate, but I don't know what else to do." He frowned as tears spilled down my cheeks. "It's obvious that you don't have faith in me. There wasn't a competition between you and Death before, but now we have no other choice. If I kill myself to be with you, I'll be sent to Outer Darkness and we'll never see each other again. I've channeled my magic through your body hoping to restore your life, but I've never come close to succeeding. The only choice I have left is tolerate Death until I can join you." Teddy opened his mouth to protest, but I powered through my confession. "The thought of living in such close quarters with Death terrifies me. What if I learn that he's an array of dichotomies? Merciless and merciful. Just and unjust. Apathetic and kind. Bleak, while also full of possibilities. What if the prophecy is true? What if I discover my role in the balance of life and death? I want nothing more than to be with you, but what if I have no other choice?"

Teddy's expression faltered, the flat line of his mouth drooping slightly.

"Is sharing a simple life with me not as important in the grand scheme of things?" He asked hollowly.

"That's not what I said," I reached for him, but he pulled away from me. "Please don't second-guess me, Teddy. You know how important - ."

"Did you enjoy kissing him?" He interrupted sharply. "Did he make you feel *alive*, Korey?" He mocked, his tone bitter and harsh. "Are you falling in *love* with poor, lonely Death? Give me an honest answer. Don't feed me some bullshit story about you giving up on our love because you have no other choice."

"Please don't talk to me that way," I reprimanded, his uncharacteristic behavior unsettling me. "I'm trying to have an open, honest conversation with you."

"Answer the damn question!" He shouted.

Something inside of me snapped.

"Yes!" I exclaimed, my eyes wild with rage. "I loved every minute of touching him. Is that what you want to hear? Do you want to hear all the juicy details of our kiss? I was attracted to him from the moment I first saw him. Are you happy now?"

Teddy's eyes widened in surprise. For a moment, he looked disoriented as he absently scratched his head. He dragged a hand over his face, smearing wet tears on his cheeks as a sob tore from his chest. Tears filled my own eyes as I realized he hadn't fully prepared himself for the truth of my answer. It was clear that he'd hoped I would alleviate his fear, and I had not been in the right state of mind to do so, but now the loss of our relationship was inevitable, something neither of us would ever be ready for.

I swiped the tears from my cheeks. "Teddy, please let me explain."

Teddy hugged himself with tears streaming down his face as he struggled to his feet.

"I don't know what I expected to hear," he whimpered, "but it definitely wasn't that."

"Teddy," I pleaded as I trailed after him, but he moved out of reach until he stood on the balcony overlooking the small courtyard.

"This has been *so* hard," he wept. "But no matter how hard this has been, I've pushed through because I t-thought you were on the other side... but now you're n-not. I h-have never felt more dead than at this m-moment." I covered my mouth and sobbed as I watched him fight for control. Fixing me with his bleary, unfocused gaze, as though pausing to commit me to memory in spite of himself, he rasped, "Good-bye, Korey."

"No!" I screamed as he dove head-first over the balcony and disappeared from sight.

The moment Teddy disappeared, I flung open the heavy doors of my chamber and ran from Death's palace, not caring if the tucks and folds of my silk gown came undone, or if the sulfuric air ripped through my hair. I couldn't live without my best friend. I couldn't live with myself knowing that I had hurt him, though I could barely comprehend the depth of his agony. I wandered the banks of the river, the panic in my chest rising as my eyes scanned a vacant landscape. Or, at least, vacant of the only soul I yearned for.

That didn't stop me from searching harder. I approached other souls and asked if they had seen a tall, lanky young man with shoulder-length brown hair, intelligent green eyes, and a sly mouth. Sensing that I was from Death's palace, they shrank from me and flitted away. An hour later, I returned to Death's fortress a disheveled mess, but my unkempt appearance didn't keep me from prowling the vast corridors like a regal queen in search of the dark god. I pushed open the carved doors of his throne room and found Death sprawled lazily on his throne, his expression one of painful boredom.

He wore the flowing black robes, crimson cloak, and black gladiator sandals that were his custom. His bored expression brightened the moment I entered the throne room, one corner of his full mouth curling in silent acknowledgement of my presence. Death rose from his throne, inky black silk swirling around the pale expanse of his powerful legs as he descended on me.

"I've been waiting for you," he sa greeted. "I asked Cordelia to find you, but she heard shouting coming from your chambers."

Death traced an imaginary tear track down my cheek as he studied my face. I hated the way his cool touch glided down my face. I hated the way he stroked my tangled, windswept hair. I hated the way he looked at me as though I were his entire world. I couldn't stay. Everything that Death offered was ash compared to the pain of losing Teddy.

I had to make things right before Teddy was forever beyond my reach.

"Teddy snuck into my chambers," I struggled to maintain eye contact with the imposing, willful god. "The fact that I hadn't sought his company in weeks concerned him."

He arched an inky black brow. "Oh?"

I swallowed thickly and nodded. "He wanted to know my plan because he could no longer endure the torture."

"And what did you say?" He languidly stroked my bare arm, the low, simmering quality of his voice warning danger. "Did you fill his head with the visceral details of our passionate love affair? How you wandered into the dining hall and wrapped your arms around my neck? How you devoured my mouth and raked your hands over my body as though you could no longer resist the temptation?"

The velvety texture of his voice spun that familiar web that clouded my thoughts and judgement, but the ache of my heart tore through the gossamer like a sword. I shook my head violently.

"Stop doing that!" I snapped, barely registering his startled expression before plowing forward with surprising vehemence. "I freely expressed that I enjoyed your touch, though your company is lacking. I openly acknowledged how the thought of ruling beside you is enticing… but I also couldn't deny wanting to spend my remaining lifetimes with him. Once I knew how the fear of losing me tears him apart, the way forward was clear. Death," I sucked in a shaky

breath, steeling my resolve, "The time has come for us to part ways."

Death considered me for a long moment, as though incredibly amused.

Slowly tilting his head to one side, he mocked dryly, "Are you breaking up with me?"

I lifted my chin, summoning a regal air that demanded his respect. "There was never anything to break. I demand that you restore Teddy's life and release us from captivity."

Death stalked forward, forcing me several steps back, until my body collided with the wall.

"Do you honestly think I will honor such a request?" He seethed, hovering so close that his aristocratic nose brushed mine. I could practically hear him grinding his teeth. "If your little friend thinks he understands heartache and misery, he is sorely mistaken. You barely have the slightest comprehension of the unrelenting melancholy that clings to me like a second skin. Do you know how long I've waited for you? Do you know how drastically your mere presence in my realm has invigorated me?"

"And what about my freedom to choose?" I pleaded. "I'm on the verge of sacrificing the most important relationship in my life because of you."

"I'm not going to change my mind," his mouth curved, his amber eyes hungrily roaming my face. For the briefest moment, desire flickered to life in my lower belly, but I crushed the unwanted emotion like a cockroach. "And you know why? Because you're as guilty of wrecking that darling childhood friendship as me. You're the one that kissed me. You're the one that surrendered to me. You're the one that sought my company and made me feel special before throwing yourself at a love-starved shade like a common whore. You're the one that drank coffee with me after losing your virginity that morning to another man. And you honestly think I'm going to let you toy with my emotions now that you've annihilated that mere speck of dust you call a friend? Maybe you're the problem, Korey. Maybe you're the cruel, heartless one."

I swallowed hard.

"Stop!" I wailed as I raked my fingers down my tear-stained face. "I never meant to hurt anyone. I want him back. That's all I want."

"What makes you think he wants to leave with you?" Death whispered cruelly.

I stopped crying long enough to stare up at him in mute horror. "What do you mean?"

Death backed away from the wall. He spread his hands wide. "Why don't you see for yourself?"

I followed the sweep of his crimson cloak to the circular pool of mercurial water I had glimpsed once or twice upon visiting the throne room. Death stood beside me with his hands clasped behind his back as I approached the floating basin of water. My reflection rippled on the surface, but that wasn't at all what I had come to see.

"Show me Teddy Kershaw," I commanded in a quavering voice.

The mercurial pool rippled; the image of Teddy crouched beside the fast-flowing river appearing on its surface. One knee was bent as he reclined one one arm, the very picture of tranquility. This struck me as odd, based on our last interaction, but I soon noticed how his fingers worked against the current of memories. Teddy idly cupped the water and allowed the white threads to stream between his fingers, as though carefully weighing an important decision. I heard his internal dialogue in my head, as though his thoughts were my own, and I squeezed my eyes shut as several blinding flashes of light flooded my mind.

The flashes were no more than a second long, but I recognized the little girl extending a helpful hand to a poor, shivering boy hiding beneath the playground slide. I saw my long hair spill through his fingers like the thread-like memories now clinging to him, and his intense love for me burned in his chest, nearly overwhelming him as he kissed my nape. I remembered that night, how I'd mustered the nerve to confess how I'd shared coffee with another man in the wake of our lovemaking, and I cringed as I heard the lies pour from my lips. I experienced Teddy's heart-stopping dread and disappointment because even then he knew I was lying. Not his words exactly, but a flurry of emotions coursed through him as he grappled with the realization that Dead had finally come for me. But how could he say good-bye?

Was his fate the same as that of Tantalus from the Greek myths? To spend an eternity having the love of his life dangled in front of him for someone else's pleasure?

"ENOUGH!" He wanted to scream, but instead he convinced me to elope with him.

I captured every emotion, every gesture, and every thought in the span of one heartbeat.

I saw Teddy following the path to the Underworld with a guitar slung on his back and, every now and then, he encountered a figure that threatened to end his journey, but he calmly weaved our story through a melody, one so powerful that every menacing shadow was moved to tears. Tears dripped down my face as I ground the heel of my palms into my eyes, feeling Teddy's desperation pound through me as he climbed the creeping vine over my balcony, like Romeo searching for his lovely Juliet. The utter joy upon finding me was quickly replaced by an overwhelming sense of frustrated helplessness that only compounded on itself, until he lost everything, making him wonder if the struggle had ever been worth it.

As though playing a cruel joke, his mind conjured the memory of my dark curls spread out on the quilt like a blanket, every inch of my bronze skin on display. I looked so young, innocent, and radiant as he tasted my breasts, unable to tear himself away.

"I love you, Teddy," I whispered against the shell of his ear and, even though I couldn't see his face, I knew he closed his eyes and savored those four life-changing words. So, after all these years, had she been worth the struggle? And immediately the resounding answer was, "YES!"

I choked back a sob as every moment flashed before my eyes, starting from the beginning. I experienced the moment he saw me from across the Great Hall, my braid coming undone as I danced with carefree steps. I saw him chasing me through The Land of Eternal Spring as I giggled and shrieked, unaware that Death lurked in the shadows. His fingernails dragged down the length of my torso as I lay sprawled in the grass, eager for his touch. I knew his bitter disappointment and outrage when he was chosen as my eternal protector because of his pure, selfless love.

Even though my memory was gone, we discovered our love for each other before death claimed us, only for us to find our way back to one another in the next life. Mine always ended with him cradling me in his arms and, as I slipped into oblivion, he whispered, "I love you." Watching me die over and over again was more painful than the prospect of losing me, a revelation that surprised and moved me. What I found even more surprising was that his favorite lifetime was our current one. Not because I forced him to watch *Grease* and *Chicago* an ungodly number of times.

No, he loved this particular lifetime more than any other because I had the nerve to cover his eyes during the

"Cell Block Tango" scene, like he was with an Alzheimer's patient who was beginning to remember that she had once loved him. I played with his soft, fluffy hair more frequently as we grew older. Teddy would never forget the time I'd

lured him into a frog hunt on the banks of the river in order to seduce him. The moment we reached our hiding spot, I slowly undressed as we watched each other, until we were both stripped down to our underwear.

    My mother caught us splashing each other in the river, which landed us both in trouble. We'd only been fourteen, but I'd wanted him to notice me as more than the girl who lived on the other side of the fence, not realizing he was already ten steps ahead of me. Keeping his love a secret had become so fucking hard because his feelings only grew deeper and stronger with each life. And Death was going to take that away from him?

    If he lost me, which he suspected was the case, why torture himself with these memories? The thought of Death touching and kissing me the way he couldn't without a proper body killed him inside, even though he was already dead. And so he cupped a handful of the strange water, closed his eyes, and brought the liquid to his lips. The memories bled from his nose and mouth as he drank deeply, the very reason for his existence draining from him. Within seconds, the image of my smiling face was gone, his mind as blank as a new sheet of paper.

The vision in my head slowly faded, his voice no more than a whisper, and the cold bite of the marble floor the only indication I had sunk to my knees. My breathing was labored, and I stubbornly ground my palms into my eye sockets because I didn't want to accept that Teddy had given up. He might've believed that he'd made the ultimate sacrifice for me, but I couldn't help the flare of anger that

insisted he'd quit out of sheer spite and fear. He'd been terrified of losing me to someone else, to feel like the weaker of the two options, so he'd refused to listen to me and decided to completely erase everything we had shared. I wanted to scream, shout, and pound the marble floor with my bare hands, but some rational part of me knew that behaving this way would only temporarily numb the reality that Teddy's fate was entirely my fault.

I couldn't accept that he was gone. There had to be another way. Death crouched beside me and touched my shoulder.

"Why are you crying?" He gently stroked my hair, his voice softer than before. "Don't you realize that he simplified your choices? You're welcome to visit him anytime. Eventually you'll rebuild a friendship with him, one devoid of pain and suffering. Don't you recognize the beauty of this arrangement?"

I uncovered my swollen eyes and fixed him with a glare. Death was more stunning than a figure hewn from marble. The contrast of his smoldering eyes and inky black hair took my breath away even now, but I realized as I studied his aristocratic face that he was no Prince Charming. He wasn't the heroic love interest of a romance novel. He wasn't destined to save me from a life of monotony the same way I didn't exist to save him from his loneliness.

"You're a monster!" I angrily hissed, not for the first time. "Have you learned nothing about love?"

Death frowned, as though my reaction puzzled him in that detached way of his.

"Of course," he shrugged elegantly. "I coaxed you into the Underworld instead of forcing you. I killed your friend in a proper duel and allowed him to sneak inside your bedchamber so he could learn the truth. I carried his body back to the palace and spread him out on the bench in the courtyard so you could visit him as often as you pleased. I allowed you to roam freely, instead of forcing you to spend quality time with me. I know I am sometimes cruel and impatient, but that is my nature. I have exercised a lot of control over my jealous and possessive tendernies, even if it didn't seem like I was trying. I am not a mortal, Koreyna, so the practice of expressing selfless love does not come as easily to me as it does to your friend. That doesn't mean I'm not in love with you, even though you hold me to a higher standard."

Death's argument left me speechless. From the moment I'd first met him, I'd struggled to prevent him from derailing my romantic relationship with Teddy. Part of me yearned to accept Death's offer, but the fate of a soul wandering beyond the palace walls needed to be rectified. I inhaled a shaky breath.

"If I remain with you, will you restore his life and send him home so that he may live a full, happy life?"

Death chuckled darkly, making me frown. He acted as though a naive child had asked the most ridiculous question.

"What's so funny?" I asked.

"The way you weasel your way through these arrangements amuses me," he caressed my cheek with his knuckle, making my blood run cold. "Do you honestly think he would remain in the earthly realm knowing you are down here with me? As long as he remains in my domain without a proper body, I trust him to be around you. Fragments of his memory might return over time, or he may fall in love with you again since that is his tendency, but at least he can't touch you like a proper man. Not the way I can."

I smacked his large hand away from my face. "Do you think death is powerful enough to stop me if I truly want to be with him?"

Death's eyes narrowed as his nostrils flared dangerously. "You're bluffing."

"I'd like to make a bet on those odds," I challenged as I folded my arms. "I'm feeling pretty lucky, so why don't you work on bringing him back to life while I describe the pleasure he's given me ever since I lost my virginity to him on the banks of the river."

Death's face twitched, his amber eyes practically bulging out of his skull, as he paced his throne room like a ferocious tiger. Unexpectedly, he overturned the basin of water, soaking his cloak and the checkered floor. I clutched my pounding heart and edged closer to the door as he wrenched his throne from the dais and screamed. The moment my hand clutched the doorknob, he rounded on me.

"And where do you think you're going?" He seethed.

"To my chambers," I raised my chin. "To contemplate what an eternity spent with a selfish brute like you will look like."

The energy drained from Death's body as he watched me slip from his throne room, his expression of utter defeat never once leaving my mind.

The Sacrifice

Images of Teddy sacrificing everything he had worked for filled my heart. He had remained dedicated to me, even when he could have pursued a life of his own. The knowledge of my betrayal gutted me. I hadn't told him the truth before, and I'd been stupid enough to think that he hadn't known. Of course, he knew. Our emotions were bound as one.

I thought of all the times I'd avoided Death. Remembered the times I'd toyed with his affections, like an adolescent drunk on power. Every step of my journey had led me to this moment. To the decision I mulled over in my mind.

Rising from the bed, I slithered down the thick vine winding up the crumbling stone wall and followed the path to where Teddy lay sprawled on the garden bench. Small, thorny vines had grown around his body, which sprouted hundreds of iridescent flowers that glowed faintly in the semi-darkness. I tore the vines away from his body and knelt beside him with my tearful eyes fixed on his pale face. The pink slash of a mouth that had flashed thousands of shy half-smiles from across a crowded room suddenly looked thin and colorless. A web of blue veins forked underneath his translucent skin. Even in death, Teddy was lovely in a tragic, poetic sort of way.

I breathed deeply as I placed my hand over his wound and stroked his face.

"I'm no longer afraid of death," my voice quavered as I channeled my magic through the hand covering his wound. After all, if Death had the power to take, I had the power to give. "And I'm willing to lay down my life for the man I love if it means restoring his own."

I screwed my eyes shut and breathed deeply as I repeated this mantra over and over again, until a blinding light radiated from my chest, the warmth spilling down my arm and through my palms.

"I am no longer afraid," my breath stirred his hair as I leaned forward. "Restore this man's life. Take me instead."

Energy drained from my body. My vision blurred. My voice lost its strength. But I persisted because I was determined to sacrifice my life for the man who had given me everything. Tears coursed down my face as an iron fist squeezed my brain.

A moment later, a large hand covered my own as Teddy gasped and coughed. A sob tore from my throat, and I placed a hand over his beating heart. Teddy's long eyelashes fluttered open as he gulped lungfuls of deep, shuddering breaths.

"Teddy?" I tentatively stroked his cheek, making him jerk backward. I shushed him softly and brushed a few locks of hair from his face. "You're safe, my love. I'm here. No one's going to hurt you."

Teddy's wild green eyes searched my face for a long moment, like I was familiar and alien all at once. His hands roamed his body and face, his overjoyed expression growing frantic as I collapsed. My spirit tugged from my body as Teddy cradled me to his chest the same way I had seen at the end of every lifetime, and I heard his pleas as I hovered somewhere out of reach. Darkness slithered into my line of vision, and I saw Death clad entirely in black, his hands clasped behind his back.

"She gave her life for you." his voice slithered like a snake across the garden. "Are you happy now?"

I Know Your Face

"Comfortable?" A deep voice asked from the shadows.

I craned my weak neck to the best of my ability, but that familiar presence refused to step forward, as though my death were a game of hide-and-seek.

"Are you angry that I beat you at your own game?" My words slurred.

"Was that your ploy?" He mused. "I thought you sacrificed your life in the spirit of true love. Poor Theodoros will be gravely disappointed when he learns the truth."

Wait a minute... where was I?

"You wouldn't know true love if it bit you on the ass," I retorted scathingly.

"Wouldn't I?" Death snorted mirthlessly. "I could render your sacrifice meaningless; you know. I could take his life with a snap of my fingers and make him suffer eternally for daring to touch you."

I clenched my teeth as I grasped for a sense of my surroundings. "You wouldn't dare."

"You're right," he agreed. "I wouldn't do such a thing because it would mean losing you forever."

I shot up in bed, realizing the shadows were from a cold washcloth draped over my face. Death eased me back onto the pillows and pressed the cold compress to my now throbbing head.

"I intend on keeping you as an… *experiment*… of sorts," he stroked my face with a pleasantly cool touch. "No matter how often Theodoros fails to demonstrate his faith in your love, you are quick to carry his torch. One would think the power of your sacrifice would restore his memory, but it seems that you have swapped places with him for the time being. Imagine how often he persuaded you to love him, aware that he was the only one who knew what had come before. Now it's your turn to persuade *him*."

I squeezed my eyes shut as tears leaked from beneath the washcloth. "He doesn't remember *anything*?"

"No," he replied solemnly.

"What about you?" I sat up in bed again. He pressed on my shoulder to prevent me from doing so. "I thought…"

"I would rather see you in the arms of another man than have you waste your death, your contempt for me making it impossible to touch, kiss, or simply *be* with you.

And so I'm willing to relinquish my possession of your love, for I'm learning more from your example than I ever experienced in your embrace. If you are able to make him remember you and everything that came before, I will release both of you to live happy lives apart from me. On one condition, that is."

I paused for several heartbeats, hardly daring to believe my ears.

"The moment you draw your last breath, I will claim you in a final embrace as I carry your spirit across the sky," he murmured. "I've had visions of your death, yet another reason I tethered your soul to your body like Peter Pan's shadow to his feet."

I couldn't resist a wry, disbelieving smile. "How the hell do you know about Peter Pan when the most basic of pasties remain an unsolved mystery to you?"

"J.M. Barrie is a member of my court as a resident storyteller," Death gave me a perplexed look, as though I had asked a ridiculous question.

"Oh. Right."

My mind pulsed with the endless possibilities of other souls that might reside in his realm. Maybe Teddy and I could embark on a few adventures now that he was alive, if only to make the best of our situation. Except... now that his memory was gone, would he even feel the same way about me?

"Who else is a member of your court?" I asked out of genuine curiosity, needing as much information as possible for my future excursions with Teddy.

"Plato and Aristotle were members of my court for some time, but I banished them after enduring their endless philosophical squabbles," Death sighed wearily. "Susan B. Anthony and her minions signed a petition against Louis Carroll for his preoccupation with underage girls. I replaced them with J.M. Barrie and Dr. Suess because they are the least contentious, but I often find myself speaking in rhyme."

Unexpected laughter bubbled up my throat, and I winced as my head throbbed anew. Death's brow wrinkled in concern, though his mouth curled in a tender half-smile, genuinely pleased with my mirth. Perhaps Death was more complex and multi-layered than I had given him credit for. Part of me desperately hoped his generosity wasn't some kind of trick.

~

After Death swept from my chambers, Cordelia fed me a tonic that made me fall into a peaceful slumber. My dreams were filled with a serene darkness that bathed my aching head in cool, refreshing water. Even in sleep, my throat was dry and parched, my thirst exacerbated by the cold cloth that bathed my forehead. After what seemed like an eternity, I swam back to consciousness, my heavy eyelids cracking open to glimpse threads of saffron light illuminating the black silk curtain drawn over the balcony.

A cool hand cupped my cheek, the other resting on my bare shoulder. "My lady?"

I groaned and shifted under the coverlet, savoring how my nipples brushed against the velvet. "Where am I?"

My voice sounded hoarse, like a frog or a long-time smoker. Or a long-time smoking frog. I stretched languidly in bed and buried my hands in my mop of curls disguised as a rat's nest. Definitely not my finest moment. Oh well, at least I was more or less alone.

A porcelain mask decorated with ornate gold filigree swam into view as the figure hovered above me. I *knew* that face. Behind her stood a blurry figure with a mop of shoulder-length brown hair that fidgeted restlessly. I stared at the blob in an effort to make sense of whoever lurked on the fringes of my awareness. The longer I stared, the more my vision cleared.

An achingly familiar pair of soulful green eyes studied me with equal intensity, confusion wrinkling his brow even as wonder parted his lips. My reaction? I clutched the black coverlet to my naked breast and screamed. Teddy flinched, startled and confused. Cordelia brushed him aside with an irritated huff.

"My lady," she squeezed one hand and smoothed back my tangled hair. "You're safe."

"What's going on?" I blubbered, eyeing the bashful, yet determined young man that hovered over the ashen servant's shoulder. For a heart-stopping moment, I thought

he recognized me. The way he searched my face as though struggling to remember who I was broke my heart. "Why am I naked?"

Teddy quickly ducked his head and moved to the opposite end of the chamber.

"Three days ago, I gave you a tonic designed to induce heavy sleep for recovery," Cordelia explained in a soothing voice as she rubbed my arm. "We removed your dress because it was blood-stained, and you were sweating from fever."

"We?" My eyebrows traveled up my forehead as my attention slid across the room.

Teddy paced in a shadowed corner, casting me surreptitious glances every few steps.

Cordelia grasped my chin and turned my face back to face her.

"Don't worry." Her laughter tinkled like delicate glass. "No men were allowed. Flora, Lord Death's servant, and I undressed you. I would have preferred a peaceful rousing, but *someone* insisted on hovering." Cordelia's tone was uncharacteristically sharp as she eyed my best friend. "You do realize I can't bathe or dress her with you lurking in the corner like that, don't you?"

Teddy seemed utterly lost as Cordelia herded him out of my bedchamber like a stray cat, making my heart twinge with sadness.

"Don't be so hard on him," I reprimanded. "He doesn't remember anything."

A wave of realization pummeled me, and I struggled to remain optimistic in light of my current circumstances.

"I've always treated him like a pesky younger brother," Cordelia waved dismissively. I watched her bustle around the chamber as she poured a variety of concoctions into the copper tub at the foot of my bed. "Even if his memory has been lost, he will know if we treat him differently. I will never forget the way he watched you sleep," she sighed fondly as she guided me into the copper tub. "Those who drink from the river are not often confronted with the source of their pain."

"Do you think he will remember me with time?" My brow creased as I sank into the steaming water.

"The longer he remains in your presence, the more he will remember," she poured water down my back, drenching my hair. "Lord Death believes his memory is contingent on true love, but Theodoros doesn't realize the struggle that will be involved in reclaiming his identity because of the emotional depth he reserves for you alone. Therefore, the true test," she concluded as her fingers worked my scalp into a rich lather, "is whether he will overcome his unshakable doubt. Lord Death will undoubtedly test him, so the only question that remains is how hard Theodoros will fight back."

A shiver of trepidation raced up my spine.

"Hasn't Teddy fought hard enough?" I countered. "Maybe it's my turn for a change."

"Theodoros was a shade," Cordelia stated as though no further explanation was required.

"I don't understand," I confessed, feeling like the world's biggest fool.

"Once Theodoros was plucked from Outer Darkness, he committed himself to eternal servitude," Cordelia explained as she rinsed my hair, water splashing onto the marble floor, "but instead he chose to live out his punishment in the mortal realm. The opportunity of a second chance is rarely given to a shade, though such opportunities are not granted lightly. Theodoros is expected to learn from his past in order to curb jealousy and doubt, his two fatal flaws. Unfortunately, Theodoros seems to mistake his redemption for holding onto you more tightly with each passing lifetime. If he's not careful, he may lose you forever."

"He shared the details of his agreement with the celestial beings before his memory loss," I protested. "They never said anything about redemption, only evading Death."

"Don't you realize that was part of the test?" Cordelia forced me to lean forward so she could scrub my back. "The celestial beings are tricky folk that govern the laws of the universe. Never take anything they say at face value. Also, they are prone to changing their minds. Gods are fickle creatures, my lady. Even Lord Death is not always true to his word."

This revelation, above all others, frightened me the most.

~

When I emerged from my bedchamber, I found Teddy learning against the wall; he visibly perked the moment he saw me. My heart skipped with the realization that he was drawn to me without actually knowing why, making it easier to remain positive in light of his complete memory loss. Instead, I focused on the stretch of lean, sinewy muscle on display.

He wore a short, white, sleeveless tunic that reached mid-thigh, a thin black leather belt cinched around his waist. He wore gladiator sandals similar to Death's and a dark red cloak draped diagonally across his chest, the rich material clasped at his shoulder. He looked exactly how I remembered him from our first meeting, except he was no longer a shade. Our story had come full circle to the beginning.

Teddy's gaze moved over my cobalt blue gown, unable to hide the appreciative gleam in his eyes. A light blue, filmy gauze shrouded the pleated cobalt beneath. The gold leaf pattern matched the long strands of coins that hung from the belt around my waist. The gauzy, billowing sleeves ended in a ruffled frill around each wrist. On paper I would have loved the gown, but I was used to bare arms and free-flowing skirts that allowed me to run and climb trees.

I waited for Teddy to make some crack about my outfit with a knowing twinkle in his eye, but instead he breathed, "Wow."

Teddy swallowed hard. The look of sheer terror on his face shocked me. I couldn't make sense of his reaction, since he'd always seemed so comfortable around me. I decided to play dumb out of curiosity. How would Teddy act around me without his memory to rely on? Would I learn something about him in the process?

"What were you doing inside my room when I awoke this morning?" Pretending I didn't know him felt as natural as writing a college essay in crayon. "Or evening. I can never tell the difference in this place."

Teddy offered a weak half-smile, though his eyes burned bright. That familiar shy streak was alive and well.

"Are you from here?" He perked in sudden interest.

"No, thankfully," I clasped my hands. "I'm from a small mountain town called Pebble's Creek. Where... where are you from?"

It took everything I had to choke out the words. Honestly, though, I was more grateful that he wasn't repulsed by me. *This situation is workable,* I reminded myself. *Patience.*

Teddy's brow furrowed thoughtfully. "That name sounds familiar. Have I been there before?"

Those utterly lost eyes bore into mine, desperate for answers. My heart shattered into a thousand pieces as I froze, unsure of what to do. Should I find a remote corner for us to talk so I could bombard him with information? Or should I gradually expose him to everything he once knew in the hopes of jogging his memory? The latter option sounded more reasonable.

"My purpose here is to help you remember who you are," I offered a small, reassuring smile. "And to be your friend."

Teddy's lips parted slightly as his eyelids grew heavy. "Are you a… a…" He snapped his fingers. "Damn, what is the word I'm looking for? Some kind of special creature or… divine being?"

Heat crept up my neck, though I remained stoic. "What do they look like?"

Teddy raked a frustrated hand through his brown curls. "They're beautiful and ethereal," he halted mid-sentence and backtracked. "Not that I'm saying you're beautiful." His face turned beet red. "I mean, obviously you *are* those things, otherwise I wouldn't have made the comparison." He glanced around at our surroundings. "Is it hot in here to you?"

"Breathe," I gently reminded him, unable to suppress the small, pleased smile that twisted my mouth.

I vacillated between wanting to twine my arms around his neck and bursting into tears. I had never heard

Teddy talk so much, and I *adored* how open and unguarded he was. Watching me intently, he sucked in a deep breath.

"I'm sorry," he shook his head forlornly. "I don't have the words to describe your role in my life, but I'll settle on a beautiful, mysterious stranger who's here to help me discover my life's purpose. Er, or something like that." He quickly looked away and rocked back on his heels.

"Hey, at least you remember how to breathe, sleep, and eat," I laughed, briefly touching his bare forearm.

A flash of electricity sparked between us, our breath hitching in unison. I quickly jerked away, and I noticed him glance down at where I had touched him. When he thought I wasn't looking, he rubbed the spot with a worried expression on his face.

I cleared my throat, unable to meet his gaze. "Would you like to go for a walk?"

~

"I've been meaning to ask you… if you don't have special powers, what are you doing in the Underworld?" He asked as we leisurely strolled the covered walkways that overlooked Death's kingdom.

The phrasing of his question almost made me lose it.

Almost.

Special powers? I was beginning to feel like an otherworldly seductress capable of bedazzling any man. I thought of *O Brother, Where Art Thou?* where George Clooney and his gang were seduced by a trio of women they believe capable of turning them into frogs. Was that Teddy's unbiased opinion of me?

"That's kind of a tricky question," I sighed.

"Why?" He prodded.

"At first, Death brought me here to make me his bride," I explained matter-of-factly, the words sounding ridiculous even to my own ears. "Right now I'm hovering somewhere between a captive and a possible love guru for a god that doesn't know what that special four-letter word means."

"Love?" Teddy echoed with a note of distress. "Do you love him?"

"Hardly," I dead-panned. Lowering my voice to a conspiratorial whisper, I slashed my finger across my face. "Have you seen the scar that runs diagonally across his face? That's my handiwork. I used his own blade against him when he tried to touch me. He hasn't ventured down that path since."

I thought my story would impress Teddy, but he didn't seem convinced.

"You're on a first-name basis with him, though," he shrugged glumly. "I could never imagine addressing him so informally." *Oh, you have no idea what words have poured from that sweet mouth of yours,* I thought. "Are you two close?"

Cordelia's assertion about Teddy's fatal flaw being jealousy was beginning to make sense. Was it wrong for his possessiveness to make me preen with delight? In his mind, he'd only known me for thirty minutes and he was already jealous. Maybe being a shameless tease was my fatal flaw, in which case we were a match made in heaven.

"Not particularly," I shrugged. "I can't really figure him out. Sometimes he seems cold and detached, other times cruel, and occasionally I catch glimpses of slivers of humanity. A lot of the puzzle pieces don't fit together."

"Puzzle pieces?" He scrubbed his forehead with the heel of his palm. "Why does that sound so familiar?"

My heart filled with compassion watching his struggle.

"A puzzle is where you break a picture into tiny pieces that fit together, and the point of the activity is to put them back in their proper place."

"That's what my mind feels like right now," he sighed in resignation. "My memories are jumbled like puzzle pieces, except I don't know where to begin." He glanced at me sidelong. "Do you happen to know anything about my past, or why I'm here?"

I'd dreaded this moment. What was I supposed to say? I couldn't lie to my best friend. I couldn't imagine leaving him with no answers. I slowed as we rounded a corner to face him. The sight of him towering over me with

his broad shoulders and lean waist filled me with the urge to touch every part of him.

"I know everything about you," I murmured as I nervously wrung my hands.

Teddy reeled back in surprise. "Like in a special powers sort of way? Are you like…" He snapped his fingers again. "A person dressed all in white who watches over me?"

A part of me wanted to laugh. Another wanted to cry. An even stranger part wanted to exclaim, "Surprise! Welcome to Arkham State Mental Hospital. I am known as the woman in white."

As tempting as that third option was, I didn't want to confuse him. Or be cruel.

Instead, I said, "For the last time, I don't have special powers! Actually," I touched my head in dawning comprehension, "I kind of do. I'll show you later."

"How can you possibly know everything about me if you don't have special powers?" He frowned.

I pinched the bridge of my nose. This was harder than I'd anticipated.

"How do I explain this without sounding like a fool?" I drummed my fingers together. "Okay, so we've basically known each other for thousands of years. Every time we're reborn, we somehow find each other, except you've always had the upper hand when it comes to remembering everything. We've been best friends for years and, well, we're also, um... *romantically* involved."

Teddy rubbed the back of his neck, looking sheepish.

"I have no memory of us," he winced almost apologetically. At the same time, he seemed wistful, like he wanted something he couldn't name. "In fact, I don't know what it means to be romantically involved."

Openly admitting this took every ounce of courage. I stepped closer and murmured, "Do you not remember sex, kissing, or foreplay?"

Teddy's eyebrows traveled up his forehead, his eyes round with an oblivious sense of wonder. "I literally didn't understand anything you just said."

For some reason, I inwardly rubbed my hands together and cackled. The idea of Teddy being a theoretical virgin with no concept of kissing, caresses, or heavy petting lit a fire deep inside of me.

When he'd taken my virginity on the banks of our favorite river, I hadn't known the things he had. I'd been at his mercy. The thought of Teddy drinking from the river still pained me deeply, but perhaps we had been given an opportunity to explore each other from an innocent perspective. I would need to approach him slowly and prove with my actions rather than words how desirable I found him.

If he saw how I chose him over Death every time, maybe the trauma of his past would heal.

"Why are you laughing?" He asked, narrowing his eyes.

I bridged the gap between us and stroked his hard chest through the white linen, transferring some of my body heat to him.

"It's a secret for now," my mouth curled in a slow, wicked smile, "but I guarantee we're going to have lots of fun."

Touch

Over the course of the following week, Teddy learned that I did, in fact, possess special powers.

One morning he complained about having stomach pangs, so I conjured his favorite, a ripe dragon fruit, in the palm of my hand. His beautiful jade eyes widened as his jaw slackened, and I shrugged modestly as I handed over the spiky fruit, as though living the life of a walking, talking farmer's market was no big deal.

Once I taught him how to slice the faintly sweet fruit into chunks, he devoured its soft flesh as though he had never tasted anything so wonderful.

"Good?" I asked with a small giggle.

Teddy surfaced for air, and the sight of his pink lips drained every last drop of moisture from my mouth. Moments like this tested my willpower. True to my word, though, I didn't fling my arms around his neck and kiss him senseless. There was no need to rush the process. At the risk of sounding heartless, part of me was grateful that Teddy had drunk from the river.

For as close as we had always been, Teddy had remained guarded and watchful, as though preparing himself to have his heart ripped out at any moment. Even throughout our journey to escape the Underworld, he'd acted melancholy, taciturn, paranoid, and desperate, which was the complete opposite of the gentle, sweet man I knew like the back of my hand.

Not anymore.

Now Teddy was open, vulnerable, curious, and hungry for knowledge. Without intending to, he'd given me the opportunity to fall deeper in love with him through our shared experiences. That shy innocence alone made me imagine how I could corrupt his angelic ways.

"How did you do that?" He rotated his own wrist for emphasis, though no fruit appeared.

"It's all in the wrist," I demonstrated again.

Watching me carefully, he swirled his wrist like a magician producing a white rabbit from a top hat, but unfortunately the pesky rabbit missed his cue.

"Here," I braced Teddy's shoulder, my body close enough to soak up the heat radiating from his own.

Aligning my outstretched arm with his, I cupped the back of his hand and channeled my magic through him as we rotated our wrists as one. Instead of a dragon fruit, a peach blossomed in his palm.

"Wow," he breathed with a half-smile as he experimentally rubbed the fuzzy peach against his cheek before inhaling its sweet scent.

"Go on," I encouraged brightly. "Take a bite."

The peach squelched as he devoured the entire fruit in almost a single bite. Juice dribbled down his chin, and I desperately wanted to lick him. God, he was such a tease without even knowing it. Wiping his mouth with the sleeve of his tunic, he asked, "What else haven't I tried?"

We grew bananas, black cherries, mangos, raspberries, blueberries, strawberries, and hybrid fruits that didn't exist in the real world. Teddy feasted until his normally flat stomach grew distended.

"You're incredible," he sighed contentedly, his open expression of awe humbling me.

"They don't call me the Willy Wonka of fruit vendors for nothing," I flashed him a cheeky grin.

"Willy Wonka?" His face screwed up in confusion.

I smacked my forehead, making him flinch. "Oh my God, I can't believe you don't remember *Willy Wonka and the Chocolate Factory* or the iconic Gene Wilder! We spent hours watching his movies growing up, especially *Dr. Frankenstein*."

Teddy slowly shook his head with a deer-in-headlights look. "Translation, please."

"How do I explain?" I tapped my chin thoughtfully. I spread my hands to indicate a movie screen. "Movies tell a story through pictures that move so rapidly that the human eye perceives them as reality. Or, at least, I think that's how it works. Look, you were the film expert, whereas I filled my head with musicals, romance novels, and Disney princess movies."

"Musicals?" His eyes brightened with interest, probably because he recognized the word 'music'. "Were those some of my favorites?"

Teddy's pained groans from before filled my ears as I pictured his sullen expression. No, musicals were not among his favorites, but a little white lie wouldn't hurt him.

"Yes, actually," I tucked a lock of hair behind my ear, noticing the way his eyes followed the motion. "Growing up, you wanted everyone to believe that your favorite films were *Taxi Driver*, *Alien*, and *One Flew Over the Cuckoo's Nest*, but behind closed doors… every day after school you hopped the fence separating our backyards and begged me to watch *Moulin Rouge!* That was your all-time favorite."

Okay, so I was brainwashing him now. So what? Everyone wishes they could change at least one thing about their loved ones. Was it too much to ask that Teddy wouldn't take a scantily-clad Nicole Kidman for granted?

To my relief, he suggested, "Maybe you could act out some of our favorite movies sometime to jog my memory."

Brightening, I exclaimed, "That's a great idea! What would you like to see first?"

"*Moulin Rouge!*" He responded immediately, stirring my suspicions.

"Do you have any idea what it's about?" I blushed fiercely. "Should I explain first?"

"No, I want to be surprised," he insisted. "For some reason, I have a feeling it's really going to get the blood flowing through my brain."

"Or other parts of your anatomy," I disguised my words with a cough.

Teddy's head snapped in my direction. "Are you okay?"

"Yeah," I thumped my chest. "Something was tickling the back of my throat." Realizing how dirty that sounded, I amended, "Or I just swallowed wrong."

Oh my God, my brain was broken. Hyper-aware of his presence, every word that touched my lips sounded positively filthy. Not trusting myself to speak, I pushed away from the wall, noticing the way Teddy's smiling mouth drooped in disappointment.

"Where are you going?" He pushed away from the wall.

My spine tingled with the awareness of him trailing after me. Did he not feel the same tension? Teddy had seemed more than dazzled when we first met, but he'd lapsed into a familiar shy reservation that drove me crazy. Teddy leapt backward when I whirled around to face him, a look of surprise on his face.

"Do you harbor any deeper feelings for me?" I asked, unable to stop myself.

So much for taking things slow. God, how had he managed to preserve his sanity all those years I wasn't able to remember him?

"What do you mean?" Those soulful green eyes bore into mine. "I don't remember anything from before."

"Forget about before," I waved, realizing belatedly how sharp my tone sounded. "From the moment you first saw me, how did you feel? What did you notice about your body? What have your instincts told you?"

Teddy sheepishly rubbed the back of his neck, heat creeping up to color his ears a bright red.

"Overwhelmed," he murmured shyly, "like being flooded with so many different emotions that my only option is to shove them down so I'm no longer on the verge of exploding. I feel like I'm dangling from a thread that continues to fray in your presence, and I'm terrified of what will happen if I lose control."

That was all I needed to know.

Teddy's breathing grew shallow, until it ceased altogether, as I bridged the gap between us and placed one hand on his chest, while the other idly toyed with his brown curls. I watched his pupils dilate until the black engulfed the jade of his irises as I stared up at him with large, inviting eyes. "May I kiss you?"

I watched his Adam's apple bob. "I don't know what that is, let alone how."

"Follow my lead," I whispered against his lips before capturing them in a soft kiss.

Teddy's flat line of a mouth remained unresponsive as I kissed and nipped, wanting to gently ease him into the experience. He trembled against me as my lips whispered over his, my fingers burying themselves in his soft cloud of hair. A low whimper escaped his throat as my tongue traced the seam of his mouth, begging for entrance. Gradually, I coaxed his mouth open, my tongue tentatively slicking against his. My body thrummed impatiently as I moaned into the wet cavern of his mouth, ecstatic to finally touch, kiss, and taste him once more. The moment my tongue touched his, however, he jerked away, breaking the kiss, and planted a hand over his mouth as though wanting to preserve the sensations that lingered there.

"Teddy?" My eyes shone concern as I reached for him, but he turned and fled, rocks crunching under his quick steps.

As I watched his retreating figure, it was tempting to dwell in self-pity, but I remembered how long Teddy had fought for me.

Overwhelmed, Teddy had confessed to feeling. *Like being flooded with so many different emotions that my only option is to shove them down so I'n no longer on the verge of exploding. I feel like I'm dangling from a thread that continues to fray in your presence, and I'm terrified of what will happen if I lose control.*

Teddy had always been forced to exercise control over his emotions and behavior and had most likely resorted to repression because it had proved the most effective way. No wonder he was so guarded. Perhaps I shouldn't have pushed him, but we had to start somewhere. Right?

My skin prickled with awareness. I glanced up and found Death smirking in the shadows of the stone archway that overlooked the dead garden, his muscular shoulder pressed against a weathered pillar. It was the first time I'd seen him since waking from my near-death experience and, as I watched, a pale woman with luminescent skin and hair curled around him possessively. I swallowed my gasp as the woman's plump mouth curled triumphantly as though she'd beat me at some game I hadn't known I'd been playing.

Death's eyes glittered strangely as he embraced Esme, never once tearing his eyes from me.

When I returned to my bedchamber, a note was attached to Teddy's guitar, the one I had left behind in the cave after his death.

I'll scratch your back if you scratch mine, the note read in elaborate cursive.

I clutched the guitar to my chest, somehow knowing exactly who had penned the note and their cryptic meaning.

~

The next morning, I poured my heart and soul into my garden. The black roses and cobalt flowers that glowed in the semi-darkness tangled with spring wildflowers that chased away the unrelenting night, as though the plants I generated sensed the change in me. I no longer mourned Teddy's death, instead filled with hope and optimism for the future. Speaking of Death…

The hairs on the back of my neck stood on end as a charged energy engulfed me like a spell cast on an unsuspecting victim. I remained crouched on the cobblestone path with my hands buried wrist-deep in acrid soil, as Death's cloak slithered among the foliage. I hadn't invited his company, so why was he here? Without uttering a word, he lounged across the stone bench where Teddy's immobile body had once been.

Even though his presence threatened to smother me with its intensity, I clamored to speak first.

"I noticed you spying on me yesterday," I said by way of greeting. "I was surprised to see Esme with you. Have you chosen to embrace her with open arms, after all?"

"Why?" Death's mouth curved in a half-smile, though his glittering eyes betrayed the depth of his amusement. "Are you jealous?"

"No!" I scoffed, though my mother's voice whispered one of her sage bits of wisdom about women protesting too much when they denied coveting a man.

Something along those lines.

Personally, I resented the thought because I had nothing to hide, though it irked me that Death had turned my life upside down for centuries, only to change his mind when I was ready to sacrifice my life for another man. If it hadn't been for his single-minded focus on me, Teddy and I

wouldn't be trapped in the Underworld. If it hadn't been for him drugging me with his elixir, roofie, or whatever magical name best suited its purpose, Teddy wouldn't have suffered a painful death and opted to forget our past.

And Death's response?

He wanted me to jump through more hoops with the expectation that he could slither back into my good graces, while simultaneously banging a lovesick woman on the side.

To say my loud protests were compensating for something was the understatement of a century.

Begrudgingly, I allowed some of my resentment to overflow as I added, "Though I couldn't help wondering why you wanted to claim me for a bajillion years when Esme always remained within reach."

Death feigned boredom as he studied his blunt fingernails. "Why should my motives matter to someone like you?" Those intense amber eyes bore into mine. "Do I look like the sort of man that takes rejection lightly?"

I nearly tripped over my words as I replied, "I only want to understand your game." I self-consciously tucked a lock of hair behind my ear. "I don't exactly trust you. I don't want to believe you're using Esme without caring about how much she loves you. To think she traveled all this way with Teddy's guitar, considering I almost tricked her into a bad situation…"

Death's eyes narrowed, the sharpness of his gaze piercing like a dagger. "*I* was the one who brought his instrument back to my palace after collecting the witch from her humble cave." He tilted his head with a coy look. "Who do you think penned that note?"

I blanched as icy fingers crept up my spine, though I deliberately misunderstood his implication. "Esme?"

Death's gaze further intensified. "No."

I'll scratch your back if you scratch mine.

I shuddered as the note adopted an entirely new meaning. "I thought Esme wanted to help Teddy remember his past after he demonstrated compassion for her plight."

Death tilted his head further as he narrowed curious eyes, his thick hair spilling over his bare shoulder in tousled waves. For the first time, I noticed he wore a toga-like robe with no tunic beneath, one ivory pectoral and pebbled nipple exposed to the dry air. Even as I cursed his existence, I couldn't deny his beauty. Briefly, I imagined my palm smoothing a path across his pale, hairless chest and brushing my thumb along his full bottom lip. I shook my head as Teddy's face surged to the forefront of my mind, impaling me on the same sword that had killed my best friend.

"Don't you think I want him to remember his one true love?" His lip curled slightly.

I arched a skeptical brow. "Personally, I think you have a selfish motive behind every kind gesture."

To my surprise, Death's full, pink lips spread into a broad grin that made line after line crease around his mouth. The liquid gold of his eyes and the fall of dark hair that contrasted so beautifully with his pale skin made him look like a fallen angel, and I found myself briefly hypnotized. I shook my head again, wanting to clear my thoughts of his influence, irritated with myself for my weakness. Sure, I craved adventure and experience, but never at Teddy's expense.

His eyes danced like hot coals as he plucked a red apple from a branch overheard and admitted rather slyly, "Is it wrong to admit that I enjoyed the sight of you teaching young Theodore Kershaw how to properly kiss, even if he seemed to have forgotten how to use his tongue?"

I squawked, mortified, as my cheeks flamed with heat. The air thickened between us as his white teeth broke through the apple's glossy skin with a resounding crunch.

"So pure and innocent," he purred. "If he only knew the delightful things he could do with that tongue."

Heat pooled between my thighs.

"This conversation is over," I moved to stand, but Death's free hand shot forward and quite literally froze me in place. I remembered the way Death had blasted Teddy off his feet on the banks of the river, how a jagged rock had struck his head before he toppled into the water, and I was suddenly terrified of what Death might do in my vulnerable state. I channeled my power through the creeping vines, aiming to bind his arms, but his magic was far more powerful than mine. The vines wriggled like tentacles around an invisible bubble that protected him, leaving me helpless and completely at his mercy.

Death took another bite of his apple as he pondered me with that familiar detached air, as though I were nothing more than a science experiment.

"Humans are interesting creatures," he mused. "The way they desperately seek purpose to validate their existence. I haven't always represented death, you know. I was an unborn soul that the celestial beings randomly plucked from the well for their own selfish purposes, only to be cast down from the heavens when I was no longer needed. I was chosen to build an empire out of darkness." An angry heat flushed his impassive face. The unshed tears that pricked his eyes rendered them glossy and bloodshot. "Without the love and compassion freely given to others, I materialized as a fully-formed being with no concept of human emotion, my only purpose to validate the dead's past lives. But the dead were ungrateful and weak. Their pain was too great, so they drank from the river to forget their lost purpose and, consequently, their memories belonged to me. I gorged myself on an endless stream of memory like the glutton you once christened me. No matter how often I lived through the lives of others, I remained starved. Can you even comprehend how lonely and bereft my existence has been? All I want is a companion to share an eternity with."

Death's story probably only scratched the surface of everything he'd endured, and I realized with a pang of sorrow that he was not the only one who had suffered in this game. I often forgot how ancient he was with his disarming good looks, and I struggled to imagine what it must have been like to exist without parents or siblings. In other words,

no one to rely on, no one to teach him the difference between right and wrong, no one to teach him emotional regulation, or even to comfort him in the dark. My memory was devoid of his backstory, and I was oddly proud of him for sharing his struggles with me. Perhaps things would have been different between us if he had chosen to lead with his vulnerability rather than control and intimidation.

Of course, falling in love with Teddy would have been inevitable, but perhaps I could teach Death how to make himself more accessible to others, so he no longer had to suffer.

Death reached out a tentative hand and caressed my cheek. "When *he* sacrificed his memories, the image of you became a blur as I sifted through them. Arranged marriage had certainly provided plenty of opportunities to bed you, but he was never selfish or impatient - even when you approached him with hope and desire in your eyes. Do you have any idea how fiercely that look made me burn? I've seen that same look when we've met, but that smoldering ember cools the moment you learn how impatient, selfish, and loathsome I truly am. Sometimes I want to punish you for betraying me when you should have been *mine,* though I'm quite certain I will never measure up to your precious lover."

The pure vitriol that dripped from his words made my heart hammer in a desperate fear. I wanted to help him, but this situation teetered on the edge of a blade; one wrong word could send everything crashing. "What do you want from me?" I gasped as I struggled against the invisible bonds that strapped me to the ground. It broke my heart that he didn't trust me not to run away. "I want to help you."

"Why?" He snarled. "What do you hope to gain?"

"Obviously I want to go home," I rolled my eyes, "but I genuinely care about your happiness. What if... what if I coached you?" At his perplexed look, I added, "You know, gave you advice on how to improve your relationship with Esme."

Death's frown deepened. "I no longer desire Esme."

"But you're obviously sleeping with her," I countered shyly.

"I only fuck her because the physical exertion takes the edge off of having you in my palace as a constant temptation," he explained bluntly, making me blush all at once. "And her company temporarily distracts me from what I've promised you and what that means for my future."

Death pleaded with soft eyes as they roamed my face, begging me to change my mind.

"Why me?" I shook my head. "There's an entire world - er, Underworld - out there filled with millions of hopeful bachelorettes to choose from. Getting hung up on one girl is only going to make you miserable. I can, you know," I would have gestured if my hands were not frozen in place, "help you find someone else. I'm a hopeless

romantic, so I have loads of advice I can give you... even if I'm on Esme's shit list for trying to dupe her."

Death stroked his chin thoughtfully, even if he seemed a little crest fallen. But the turning of the cogs in his mind gave me hope.

"I want what you have with the young man," he murmured after a long moment. "Could you truly help me?"

"Of course!" I exclaimed brightly. "Is there someone who belongs to your court that interests you?"

Death shook a solemn head. "I want a mortal woman. Someone with few living relatives and no past lovers. Someone that no one will miss when I take her to my realm."

I wanted to point out that he was starting to sound an awful lot like Buffalo Bill, but I kept my mouth shut because he seemed genuinely excited for the first time since knowing him. We would talk about the whole abducting-a-mortal-woman topic later.

At that moment, Teddy of all people appeared in the garden wearing his clean mortal garb, which matched the red floral dress I reserved for gardening. Teddy's green eyes swept the scene, darting between my immobile crouch on the cobblestones and Death's lazy sprawl on the stone bench.

He shifted uncomfortably, as though unsure of his place. "Hello."

Death relinquished his power over me as he stretched to his full, imposing height, the double slit in his silk robes exposing his powerful legs. I slouched in relief and clambered to my feet on shaky legs. Teddy dove forward to catch me, but Death beat him to the punch.

"Don't expect him to act on impulse, like yours truly," he whispered in my ear. "I've seen his memories. If you wait for him to act first, I guarantee you will remain my captive forever."

I reeled back in shock. Was that friendly love advice from Lord Death? What a strange creature he was. Before I could react, his full lips grazed my cheek. Over one bare shoulder, I saw Teddy's nostrils flare. He glared as Death strode from the garden, leading me to suspect that he'd kissed me simply to make Teddy jealous. Hey, at least my beloved was beginning to remember his defiant attitude toward Death. Now that's what I call progress!

"Hey," I greeted breathlessly as I pushed my tumbling curls back from my face. Death had taken the suffocating blanket of charged energy with him. The memory of our so-called first kiss doused me in refreshingly cool water, leaving me with that hyper-aware crush feeling fluttering in the pit of my stomach. If his fidgeting was any indication, he was experiencing the same. "It's nice to see you back to normal. Not that you didn't look good before."

The high-pitch of my voice made me cringe. Teddy's jade eyes traveled up and down my figure, lingering on the neckline that exposed a glimpse of cleavage.

"I really like your dress." His pale cheeks turned splotchy. "A lot." Mimicking my earlier words, he added, "Not that you weren't beautiful before. Now you're…"

Suddenly, it was very important that I see myself through his eyes.

"What do you see when you look at me?" I asked, surprising myself.

Teddy studied me for a long moment, the heat never leaving his face. He cleared his throat.

"I see loose, tumbling curls escaping a flimsy," he gestured helplessly for the right words, "*arrangement*. Dirt speckles your face, chest, and hands, but it makes you look incredibly, um," he gestured once more, clearly hoping I would fill in the blanks, "instead of dirty."

"Seductive? Charming? Jaw-dropping?" I offered with a coy, flirtatious smile.

"Um," he rubbed the back of his neck. "What are... What are you doing back here? I've been looking for you everywhere. I didn't expect to see *him*."

The question trailed off into an awkward silence. Apparently, neither Death nor Teddy were capable of addressing each other by their actual names.

"I've been gardening all morning," I offered helpfully, smiling warmly as I hopped between clusters of flowers. "My mom and I own a shop in Pebble's Creek that sells flowers and produce. The town is small enough where I can make deliveries on my bicycle, but you've helped me deliver flower arrangements in your pick-up truck thousands of times. As teenagers, we used to blast Queen with the windows rolled down. Those are some of my favorite memories of us growing up."

Hopefully my reminiscing didn't overwhelm him, but I couldn't help myself. Everything sort of spilled out of me whenever he drew near. Teddy paused in interest when he glanced down, and the breath hitched in my throat as he picked up his guitar for the first time since his death. I watched in silent wonder as his palm smoothed across the scuffed wood and lightly traced the strings with his fingers.

"This is incredible," he breathed. "I've never seen anything like this before."

"That guitar belongs to you," I gently revealed. "You're a musician. I've been serenading the flowers all morning to keep them alive, since the sunlight is too weak here. Wanna see?"

Teddy stared up at the sky, as though he couldn't imagine it as anything other than a vast blanket of stars streaked with salmon pink and saffron gold, but he nodded meekly as his gaze fell on me once more.

Clutching his guitar, I began to sing "What A Wonderful World" as I strummed the familiar melody. The roses and other unearthly flowers perked as my rich, husky voice bathed them in a radiant warmth that rivalled that of the sun. Teddy's lips parted as the flowers bobbed their heads, nearly jumping out of his skin when vines slithered

across the cobblestones like baby snakes. The timeless song filled me with joy and nostalgia, until tears wound paths down my cheeks, mostly because I'd never imagined Teddy forgetting something as simple as music. The song ended abruptly as I turned my back on him.

A moment later, his hand tentatively rested on my shoulder, the warmth of his palm searing through my dress. Instead of feeling smothered by his presence, I felt warm, safe, and comforted. I glanced over my shoulder and offered him a tremulous smile.

"Why are you sad?" His wrinkled brow overshadowed a pair of soulful eyes that deeply penetrated my being.

"I'm not sad," I wiped my eyes and sniffled. "That was the first song you taught me on the guitar. We used to sing together all the time. I remember you wrapping your arms around me to position my fingers on the right chords, and I could barely focus because my heart was beating so fast. Long story short, it took forever to learn that song, but I hardly think you minded."

"I obviously taught you well," he grinned boyishly. "Hearing you sing fills me with an indescribable joy, but nothing compares to the first time I laid eyes on you."

The unexpected praise was so sweetly delivered, Teddy reminded me of a bashful child seeking approval.

As opposed to kissing him senseless, I offered, "Would you like me to play more?"   "Only the songs we've played together," he nodded decisively.

Over the next three hours, we sat cross-legged near the flowerbeds while I played everything in my repertoire, from "Lullaby" by The Cure to "Prince Charming" by Adam and the Ants - two relatively simple melodies that were enhanced by quirky, strange lyrics. Teddy especially enjoyed bellowing the introduction of the latter song, and the spunky quality of his delivery revealed glimpses of that secret part of his personality he reserved for me alone. Over the course of an hour, I helped him memorize the male counterpart of

"Shallow" from *A Star is Born*. After at least ten attempts, we nailed the ballad (sort of), but the heady blend of our voices created an intimacy that not even a kiss could match.

"If only I could sing like Lady Gaga," I sighed wistfully as my fingers plucked a random melody.

"Is she a member of Lord Death's court?" Teddy asked with the most earnest expression I had ever seen, and I couldn't resist bursting into laughter.

"What's so funny?" He blinked innocently.

"You're just so damn cute, I want to gobble you up!" I scrunched up my nose and saw the way his boyish half-smile faltered as his dreamy gaze intensified.

For a fleeting moment, I thought I had offended him… until he scoffed with an uncharacteristic huskiness, "Cute? Not handsome, sexy, or mind-blowing?"

The fact that he echoed my earlier teasing as a way of shamelessly flirting with me stoked the flames blazing in my lower belly. Now I understood why he'd changed the subject earlier.

"Here, I'm going to teach you how to play the way you taught me," I crouched behind him as I settled the guitar in his lap.

My loose curls tumbled around his shoulders as I placed my hands over his and guided them exactly where they should be. The truth was, I had no clue how to teach him the proper chords because I knew everything from memory, so I merely touched him and breathed in his scent as my breasts caressed the spot between his shoulder blades.

"All you do is strum," I instructed dumbly as I moved his calloused fingers over the strings. "Eventually, the music flows through you like magic."

Oh, barf.

I was officially the worst music instructor ever, but he proved me wrong as his fingers began slowly picking out a familiar melody, one I recognized from our youth. The hum in his throat vibrated through his back to me as he crept through the dark tunnels of his mind.

"I know this song," he whispered.

On some instinctive cue, he opened his mouth, his back expanding with his deep intake of breath, and sang. My eyes drifted closed as I remembered those summer afternoons I dug my bare toes into hot sand with a Jennifer

Cruisie novel open in my lap as Teddy serenaded me with such calm foreboding. I watched his fingers struggle to regain their confidence, and my voice melded with his rapsy one as I joined him in song, the sound like the caress of a razor blade on soft skin. My hands covered his as our voices faded, heat simmering between every point of contact. Teddy played for a long time, repeating the song over and over like a child who had just learned his first steps, until his voice lulled me into a trance.

My sweaty palms slicked against his skin as he slowly turned and stared directly into my eyes, our noses brushing. I angled my mouth against his and kissed him full on the lips. For the first time since his death, he kissed me back, though his lips were clumsy and unpracticed. I captured his bottom lip and sucked on it, teaching him through example rather than words. Teddy mimicked my actions, devouring me with open-mouthed sweeps of his tongue that betrayed his ragged breathing and the small hitch in his throat as I slicked my own against his. We shuddered violently as our velvety tongues felt the faintly rough texture and strangely sweet taste of our mouths.

The guitar clattered on the ground as he pushed me backward onto the flowerbeds, my view of the velvety sky fringed with spiky petals and creeping vines. Black roses unfurled as the exotic blooms glowed with an ethereal reverence. Teddy's lean body settled over my curvaceous one, his narrow hips absently grinding against my mound in some unconscious display of need as he lapped at my mouth like a starved man. He obviously didn't understand what he

was doing, but was simply following his body's instincts. Our kisses grew frantic and uncoordinated as he tenderly swept the hair away from my face so that he could kiss every upturned feature.

I loved this untapped side of Teddy. Our attraction, our mutual desire - everything confirmed we were meant to be. Never in my life had I felt so close to a person.

"I love you, Teddy," I whispered breathlessly as he tortured my earlobe with his teeth.

My beloved immediately froze. "Love?" He panted against my neck.

"Yes," I tangled my fingers in his loose brown curls. "Don't you love me?"

His body grew rigid.

"I-I don't know how I feel," he stammered, a call-back to the Teddy I had always known.

I heard him swallow hard as I planted my hands on his chest and pushed him away from me.

"I don't understand," I shook my head with a frown. "Even if you don't remember our past, you seem to love me as you always have."

Teddy looked crest fallen. "I-I'm sorry. How can I love you if I don't know anything about you? I don't even know your name."

I reeled back in shock. Teddy's openness to my presence had completely blinded me to the fact that I hadn't bothered with proper introductions.

"Korey!" I exclaimed, wounded beyond measure.

The initial excitement of wooing Teddy was wearing off.

"Korey," he breathed reverently, making my traitorous heart soften.

"Stop doing that!" I lightly shoved him away from me.

"What?" He spread his hands in utter bewilderment. "I didn't do anything."

"You say my name oh-so sweetly, tell me how beautiful I am, and kiss me like your life depends on it, but you have no clue what you feel for me. I'm sorry," I covered my face at the sight of his wounded expression. "I know I'm acting like a prima donna, but you don't have any idea what it's like to have someone you love not remember you in some froeign, unearthly place with a captor that has turned into your sole confidante."

At that precise moment, I felt like the world's biggest asshole because Teddy had, in fact, known what it was like to love someone who couldn't remember him. On top of that, he'd lived with the fear of his life being upended by a god who'd once enslaved him. A god that threatened the most important relationship in his life. Even if Teddy

couldn't remember these dynamics, he sensed them, for they were deeply ingrained in his soul.

My best friend had experienced this struggle over and over again - and without any tantrums. Well, except for that one time he killed my betrothed in a duel.

For the first time, I walked in his shoes and, boy, did it *suck*. My cheeks burned with shame, especially seeing the look of utter heartbreak on his face as I considered our shared state of helplessness. At least Teddy found me attractive and sought my company. With those two ingredients, falling in love was a possibility… but he could also fall in love with someone else. Or, worse, his doubts could overpower any affection he might have for me.

Overcome with panic, I mumbled an excuse and fled, desperate for solitude. I couldn't think properly with those green eyes pleading for something not even he understood.

"Korey!" The gentle breeze carried my name across the courtyard.

Too embarrassed and ashamed to act like an adult, I huddled under my coverlet until I fell into a restless slumber.

Who Is She?

Teddy and I played a seemingly endless game of tag over the following week. This alone turned my world upside down. We had never played games like this before. Our communication had always been straightforward. If there was a misunderstanding, we were quick to clear the air.

Every morning that I placed a basket of fruit near his door in case he got hungry, I felt like a spurned lover desperately struggling to regain my footing in his life. It all began the morning after he rejected my love, or at least told me he didn't know how to feel, a by-product of our situation that was easier to accept in theory than in practice.

One morning I followed Death down an arched corridor that led to a separate tower, one I'd never explored. I gasped the moment he pushed open a set of heavy double doors. Tendrils of ivy and intricate butterflies were carved into the wood, contrasting with the black moths that dominated the palace. The round tower housed a library with thousands of leather-bound books lining the curved walls, their spines barely visible in the weak light that filtered through the stained-glass windows featuring knights rescuing damsels in distress in captivating shades of indigo, crimson, and liquid gold. Fire-breathing dragons patterned the mosaic floor.

My eyes drank in my surroundings, the ever-changing theme of the palatial rooms stunning me into silence. As apprehensive as I was about Death, he was proving to be a wonderful distraction from my aching heart.

"I brought you here because I want to study the classics," Death announced, looking quite romantic himself in a white linen shirt with billowing sleeves, black high-waisted trousers, boots, and a sweeping cloak. "Women are often impressed by a man who is able to quote Jane Austen and Charlotte Bronte, don't you agree?"

"As long as you don't pull a Darcy and insult her family while declaring your love for her," I muttered under my breath, my curious gaze fixed on the towering ladders attached to the shelves, tempting me to ride one of them.

"What was that?" Death's sharp gaze narrowed on me.

"I'm just saying," I spread my hands placatingly. "The fact that you're looking for a new lover while your old one prowls the palace like a jungle cat is concerning. I suggest you find a new home for the feral one before she burns down your home and leaves you permanently disfigured."

I didn't expect him to catch the reference, but he surprised me with a roguish grin.

"Are you always this charming in the morning?" He quipped.

"I don't think you should pursue a mortal woman," I skimmed the shelf for a leather-bound book, my free-flowing gown swishing around my bare legs. I found *Dante's Divine Comedy* and *Notre Dame de Paris* on the shelves. Maybe Death needed to research humanity's perception of

the afterlife and the dangers of obsessive love before diving headlong into another disaster. "Honestly? I think the idea is selfish. Why rob a young woman of her life before it's even begun?"

I wanted to challenge my captor, but he merely smirked as though he didn't care how I perceived him.

"Mortals are strange creatures," his amber eyes glittered as he studied me. "One's life begins the day they are born, yet they are never satisfied, their gaze always trained on the horizon."

"Don't mince words with me," I jabbed his chest, though I begrudgingly admitted that his observation was spot-on. Not that I would stroke his ego by sharing this thought. "We experience multiple stages of life, each one promising different opportunities for growth. Why would a mortal woman choose a life in the Underworld over marriage, children, and falling in love? Or being surrounded by friends and family? Or traveling the world?"

Death flinched, as though I'd struck him, and heat flushed his pale, waxen cheeks. I hadn't meant to insult him, only to present the facts.

"I rarely visit the mortal realm as an ordinary man, hence why I seem so out of touch," he began coldly, "but I understand enough to know that a woman would gladly embrace an eternity with me over a lifetime of financial debts, nagging children, and a complacent spouse. Do you honestly think she would choose a world in which she is surrounded by synthetic examples of what she will never measure up to? Do you think she would prefer a man who makes love to a screen rather than a real woman?" Death arched one black-winged brow. "I pity a mortal man's lack of imagination and skill in the bedroom. Upon entering the Underworld, recent generations act as though their stones will shrivel up and drop off without one more hit of their preferred drug, unable to realize how the generations that came before somehow managed. Mortal men are fickle and easily bored, Korey. Why would you return to a world filled with endless temptation and the ever-present threat of being replaced by a shiny, bouncy new toy?"

Death had slowly advanced on me throughout his monologue, until his boots brushed my bare toes. Didn't he realize that I faced more temptation in his presence than in the safety of my own world? I needed to remember my purpose, as well as everything I knew about Death that drove me to Teddy.

"Life isn't always like that," I lifted my chin, struggling not to dwell on thoughts of Teddy straying in the midst of his confusion.

I remembered every part of our history. He'd never wandered before. Neither had I. We had existed in our own world, not once tearing our eyes away from each other. But now... I told myself that I only spent leisurely mornings with Death because befriending him was necessary for the cause, but I increasingly found myself drawn to him, as though he were wrapped in metallic paper that caught every twinkle of light.

I mulled over Death's words. Maybe his assertions contained a grain of truth. Maybe I was foolish and naive. What if I returned home and the weight of the modern world fractured my relationship with Teddy as we grew older? What if we were safer here in the Underworld?

"Any woman would happily forsake her life in favor of my love, devotion, and loyalty," Death finished in a low voice, his warm breath caressing my upturned face. I could almost hear him add, *"You, in particular."*

"You obviously have a low opinion of mortal women to believe she would sacrifice everything to be adored by you," I said through clenched teeth as I struggled to regain my bearings. Something about his presence intoxicated my senses, as though he'd bathed in the same elixir that had tricked me into kissing him.

My harsh words only buoyed his mood, however, like a hunter coaxing an animal into a trap.

"Do you truly believe your young man would have waited centuries for you with zero contact?" He goaded. "He probably would've sought another woman's company out of sheer boredom. Unlike me."

I wanted to point out that Teddy had, in fact, waited centuries, whereas Death had simply lounged on his throne with a bevy of court ladies ready and willing to fuck him.

"Do you want my help or not?" I snapped fiercely, my hands balled into tight fists, my fingernails digging into the flesh of my palms. "We're wasting precious time."

Death flashed me a gloating smile, which made me burn with anger.

"I've said everything I've needed to," he waved an elegant hand. "What do you have in mind, if not a mortal woman?"

"I think you should invite the members of your court for a private reading of the classics, such as Jane Austen and the Bronte sisters," I suggested while struggling to regulate my breathing. Anger surged through me faster than adrenaline. "That way you can impress the women of your court, and it will also give you an opportunity to socialize with them. Maybe you'll find someone who sparks your interest."

Death frowned deeply.

"That's a terrible idea," he shook his head with a forbidding look, which only deepened my irritation. "Jane Austen and the Bronte sisters don't exactly see eye-to-eye. One author who shall remain nameless has dominated the limelight for decades, leaving very little room for anyone else, which has only caused bitter resentment. Although that particular feud is nothing compared to Michelangelo and Leonardo Da Vinci. The latter still teases poor Michelangelo about looking like a baker after a day of chipping away at a slab of marble."

My irritation ebbed somewhat, replaced by reluctant intrigue. I wasn't an artist myself, but I had enjoyed my art history class in college. I'd always wanted to travel to Italy to see the Sistine Chapel, but the prospect of bumping into the artist himself sounded even more promising.

"What about someone neutral, like… I don't know, William Shakespeare?" The sentence rolled off my tongue as though name-dropping was the most natural thing in the world. "Assuming the greatest playwright of all time is neutral."

My companion's brow rose questioningly.

"The greatest playwright of all time?" Death echoed with a coy smile. "Tell that to Oscar Wilde."

My determination to evade Death temporarily forgotten, we scoured the bookshelves for Shakespeare's most notable works and debated over which plays should be performed. Eventually, we settled on showcasing his most famous scenes, like those episodes of popular TV sitcoms that compile the most side-splitting moments into a single thirty-minute slot. Comparing Shakespeare's works to a sitcom seemed blasphemous, but it was the most logical way of explaining the concept to my companion. I sprawled out on the white rug as he recited passages from *Romeo and Juliet,* and I either gave a thumbs-up or thumbs-down for whether the scene should be included, a process that also seemed blasphemous.

"Ah me!" I recited on his cue, my upper body propped up on one elbow.

"She speaks!" Death exclaimed. "Oh, speak again, bright angel! For thou art as glorious to this night, being o'er my head as is a winged messenger of heaven…"

He performed the role with passion and gusto, comfortable enough with the material to avoid stumbling over his words.

"O Romeo, Romeo! Wherefore art thou Romeo!" I brought the back of my hand to my forehead as I dramatically tossed back my head.

When I opened my eyes, I saw Teddy standing in the doorway, his eyes wide with shock. Even as I sat up with bright-eyed hope reflected in my eyes, his taut expression flinched as though I had struck him. Teddy eyed my flowing purple gown with its jewelled clasps that held the dress together and a deep plum sash tied loosely around my waist, the thin fabric clinging to my breasts and outlining my legs through the skirt. No matter how diligent I was, the sleeves refused to remain upright and constantly slipped down my shoulders. My hair tumbled wildly around my shoulders from having rolled with laughter on the rug from Death's portrayal of *Much Ado About Nothing*. My cheeks were most likely flushed with pleasure, my eyes shining with fading amusement.

The longer his eyes devoured me, the harder his expression grew. The moment Teddy's eyes landed on Death, he whirled on his heel and strode from the library.

"Teddy!" My voice echoed down the corridor as I sprang to my feet. "Teddy, please wait!"

He moved swiftly down the carpeted, arched corridor lined with stained-glass windows, elongating his stride to

further distance himself from me. I bounded after him like an eager puppy, until I was close enough to touch his back.

"What?" He snarled with hackles raised, making me cower from him as I released my hold on his tunic.

For one, fleeting moment, I caught a terrifying glimpse of someone I didn't recognize, someone who had completely hijacked Teddy's personality. Remorse immediately flooded his expression, but the tension in his body remained. My eyes were appraising as they swept over him, if a little hesitant. He wore charcoal gray leggings, tall boots, and a jade green tunic with a thin belt lashed around his narrow waist. He looked dashing, princely, and perhaps the most comfortable I had seen him since inhabiting Death's palace, though I doubted he would accept my compliments.

"Why are you so angry?" I demanded hotly, more defensive now that he'd caught me in a moment of weakness.

"I don't understand your relationship with Lord Death," he ground out, his cheeks suffused with an angry heat. "Are you in love with him, too? You seem to spend an awful lot of time together. Every time I seek out your company, you're with him and I wish he would *go away*."

I stared up at him in open-mouthed shock. I'd never seen Teddy act so openly possessive. Upon meeting Death, I'd learned that my best friend was a jealous lover, but he'd carefully guarded this secret, never betraying the full extent of his emotions. Now that his memories had been erased, he

lacked his former restraint, which encouraged that I raise my guard.

"Why does it matter?" I countered, unwilling to reassure him so easily with him acting like a brute.

To realize he had so little faith in me stung worse than having a lemon squeezed over an open wound.

But you're not as innocent as you'd like to believe, a nasty voice whispered in my mind. *Admit it, you enjoy Death's company. You're beginning to feel compassion for him. You're tempted. Don't kid yourself. You're only defensive because you don't want Teddy to learn the truth. You don't want to give him the satisfaction that he has a right to be jealous.*

Rather than listen to this small, insidious voice, I chose stubbornness in its stead. "It shouldn't matter to you who I spend time with. You have no love for me anyway, remember?"

I cringed to hear the words aloud.

"I never said I had no love for you!" Teddy growled in frustration as he raked a hand through his freshly-washed hair. "I said I didn't know how to feel. If you want me to be more specific, sometimes I feel like my skin isn't able to contain everything inside of me every time I catch a glimpse of you. Other times your touch sets me on fire. Sometimes I feel lightheaded and dizzy in your company. Sometimes I feel unsure of myself, yet somehow hopeful that you'll see me the way I see you. When I see you with Lord Death, on the other hand," his expression grew dark and foreboding,

"everything inside of me goes berserk. When I see you laughing and smiling because of him, I suffer from the deepest pain I've ever known, like I've been betrayed... but I don't know why. How do I quantify that? And why should I?"

A lump formed in my throat. Some part of Teddy thought I had betrayed him, yet I hadn't done anything!

Your inaction speaks for itself, the insidious voice whispered once more.

"What do you mean?" I shook my head.

Teddy's expression darkened. "I see the way he looks at you, as though he's starving," he pointed over my shoulder where Death lurked in the library, "and I see the way you look at him."

The blood drained from my face.

"You're wrong," my voice rose as I slowly advanced on him. "You're only seeing what you want to believe."

Something dangerous flickered to life in the depths of his eyes.

"I don't see you trying to stop him!" Teddy shouted, absolutely beside himself with grief.

"Trust is a choice," I jabbed my finger at his chest. "Either you trust me, or you don't. We were best friends before, but you still didn't believe in my love for you. We've been given a second chance. Is this how you're going to

squander it, by shouting in my face and accusing me of betrayal?"

My censure drained the tension from his body, and he stared at me with lost eyes as he gestured helplessly to where Death waited.

"I don't trust him, so why should I believe you?" He asked with such earnest conviction that it stomped out any hope I might have felt.

Slowly, I curled in on myself, my eyes staring sightlessly over Teddy's shoulder.

After a long moment of tense silence, he nudged me. "Korey?"

My eyes focused on his contrite face. "I only spend time with Death so I can help him find a replacement in the hopes that he'll release us. Before you came to my rescue, it's true that I kissed him because he'd drugged me with an elixir. You once told me that the elixir only opened my eyes to my desire for him, but that's not true. I noticed he was attractive the moment I met him, but I wouldn't have acted on those feelings because I'm devoted to you. I don't love Death, I love *you*!" I choked on a sob, embarrassed that I'd been reduced to tears. Teddy lightly grasped one of my balled fists, but I withdrew from his touch. "Death used the kiss to manipulate and distract you from your sword fight, and my confirmation of the kiss literally killed you. Don't blame Death, blame me because I'm the reason you lost your life. I cursed Death for taking you from me, and then I cursed you for losing faith. I was so overcome with grief when I learned that you had drunk from the river that I sacrificed my life to bring you back. Even if you returned to Pebble's Creek without me, even if you found someone new to love, I wanted you alive and happy. Death spared my life so we could be together, so we could prove the strength of our love. I won't lie to you. There's something intoxicating about Death's presence. Sometimes I enjoy his company more than I should in light of everything that's happened. I wanted the opportunity to explain everything to you, but I was unsure of how much information I should give you. I promise to be as honest and transparent as possible… but if you find that you truly can't trust me, please put me out of my misery because I refuse to be with someone who doesn't believe in me."

Avoiding Teddy's gaze, I brushed past him, my tears blinding my journey down spiraling staircases and crooked passageways. Distantly, I recognized the Entrance Hall as I pushed through the set of double doors and descended the front steps, eager to escape to the familiarity of nature where nothing or no one could harm me.

~

"So what *is* your type?" I asked Death one morning as I toiled in the garden, my tone conversational. Death slowly paced back and force while twirling a dandelion between thumb and forefinger. "Not that I approve of your plan to snatch a mortal woman."

Death smirked as he cast me a sidelong glance. "Voluptuous and sensual with a wild mane of hair and lovely breasts," he said imperiously, though he awaited my reaction expectantly.

I pointedly cleared my throat, ignoring the hot flush that swept over my body. "What about her personality? Don't you think that's more important, considering you'll spend an eternity with her?"

"Of course, I forgot you're the expert on long-term relationships," he quipped before thoughtfully tracing his full mouth. "Vivacious, high-spirited, and courageous enough to sometimes put me in my place. Also unfailingly kind and compassionate," his tone grew wistful as he twirled the flower stem.

I paused to study his profile. It dawned on me how badly he longed for a companion.

"I never realized until now how lonely you must be."

Death hummed noncommittally, perhaps unused to anyone sympathizing with him.

"The loneliness is tolerable most of the time," he shrugged elegantly. "My thirst for companionship grew when I brought Esme to my palace. I couldn't resist her beauty, especially knowing she was from the Otherworld and had suffered greatly at the hands of men. At the time, she possessed a fragility I craved like nothing else."

"Why did you push her away when she wanted more?" I pressed, hoping that he might come to the conclusion that he didn't need to steal a mortal woman to be

happy. "Maybe the woman of your dreams has been under your nose all this time."

Death grunted in obvious displeasure as he crushed the dandelion with a single flex of his powerful hand, making me wince. The subject of Esme and their past obviously touched on a nerve. I doubted that I'd discover what had truly happened between them. It didn't make sense for a man who desperately longed for a companion to turn away from someone so painfully beautiful and willing. The idea of them together fit like a glove, for Esme seemed ferocious enough to keep him in check, but I wasn't stupid enough to voice my thoughts.

"It hasn't escaped my notice that something is amiss between you and the young man," he expertly changed the subject, arching one inky black brow.

I braced my thighs as I crouched in the unearthed bed of soil.

"Why don't you ever call him by his name?" I snapped. "Referring to him as my young man makes you sound like the father I never had."

His upper lip curled. "The last person I want you to associate me with is your father."

I gave him a cheeky thumbs-up. "That's great! Otherwise this situation would be very awkward."

Death regarded me shrewdly for a moment, one corner of his mouth curling in a begrudging smile.

"Very well," he conceded with a huff. "Why has *Teddy* been absent from your company? Does he not recognize your worth?"

Ignoring his barb, I grumbled, "Why do you care?"

"For selfish reasons, of course." His pacing grew more frenzied. "The less time he spends with you, the more likely you'll change your mind about me. At this point, I might send you back regardless of the outcome because I find myself only interested in an untainted lover."

Despite the cold, cruel nature of his words, he glanced over his muscular shoulder, gauging my reaction, and I suspected he cast the barb to reel me in like a trout. Was the whole please-help-me-find-a-replacement-for-you bullshit a ruse to spend more time with me? Or, worse, to make me jealous? And when I failed to respond, did he insult me to make me crawl on my hands and knees before him?

The thought infuriated me, but I had to remember that Death was emotionally constipated.

He enslaved lost souls who had taken their own lives as punishment, for Hell's sake. Of course, he was a generally misunderstood, incredibly manipulative, self-centered asshole. I sat back on my haunches and scowled, making Death halt abruptly and pivot to face me.

"Does it not bother you that I have moved on so quickly?" He demanded, his implied accusation confirming

my suspicions. "That I am ready and willing to replace you like you have me?"

A thought occurred to me.

Could Death be punishing me for spurning him for another lover?

Maybe he *had* loved me in his own selfish way thousands of years ago, but perhaps he'd never moved on because he couldn't allow the one couple who'd cheated him to escape his clutches. It was possible that he exerted his influence over me to create friction between Teddy and I.

"I never *replaced* you," I countered. "That implies I once loved you, which was never the case."

"Exactly," he seethed. "I should have been your only choice, yet you found a new lover as if I were defective. Why not me? I know I'm selfish, cruel, and indulgent. I may not know how to love selflessly, but I'm obviously more than patient because I waited for you without taking any lovers in between. How can you suggest that I don't love you? At least I have my memory," he snarled, anguish making him cruel. "At least I remember that I love you. How could I forget?"

I sprang to my feet and moved to strike him, but he caught my wrist in a powerful grip, his arm slithering around my waist to draw me close.

"Tell me you don't want this," he breathed.

I thought of the failed trek through the Underworld that had resulted in Teddy's death and memory loss, how he'd been unable to resist checking to make sure I was safe when I cried out. He hadn't trusted that I would follow. I remembered the look of shock and horror on his face the moment he saw me climbing over the rocks and, at that moment, I knew we had failed the simplest of tests.

As heartbroken as I had been to learn that he no longer remembered me, I'd thought of his memory loss as a new beginning. If he spent time with me without doubts and insecurities clouding his judgement, he would see me for who I was. Instead, he questioned my relationship with Death and hovered on the outskirts of my company. Not knowing how to justify my existence to someone who should trust me unconditionally, I questioned whether he was the right man for me after all.

As Death had once pointed out, I was young and inexperienced. Maybe I don't know myself as well as I thought.

"Sometimes I do," I quietly admitted with heavy-lidded eyes.

My heart constricted as Death's face split into a wide, boyish grin that completely defied everything I knew about him, and my fingers itched to trace the lines around his mouth. His large, aquiline nose brushed mine as his lips inched closer, his hot breath caressing my tingling flesh. I watched his eyes drift closed and, the moment my own followed, Teddy's bright, soulful eyes flashed in my mind.

The memory of returning to my small village after escaping the Underworld with Theodoros surfaced. I remembered how my mother had embraced him for his lack of home and family, how he'd later taken my hand in marriage. Every trace of our first meeting in the Underworld had been erased from my mind, yet I hadn't been able to stop staring at his beautiful, smiling face as he gazed upon me with such tenderness and love. Flower petals had drifted from the sky and caught in his loose brown curls, so different from the dusky shade he had once been. On our wedding night, I had burned with the desire to touch him, but he'd dragged the seduction out for months, wanting to earn my heart before making love to me.

Over the centuries, he'd always earned my love through patience and steadfastness, yet here I was allowing Death to toy with my emotions after a few blows to my pride. How could I ever doubt that Teddy was my only choice? There was no other option. Once again, I had failed.

"Don't touch me!" I shrieked as I disentangled myself from Death's embrace. "I'm not playing your little game. The moment Teddy remembers who I am, we are going home. Either take my help or leave it."

I stormed away from a dejected and utterly lost Death, but I couldn't afford to care about a man with selfish motives, even as my heart constricted. Not when the fate of my relationship with Teddy hung in the balance.

~

The first time I'd ventured beyond the palace on my own, I hadn't gone any further than the river basin, where I'd sobbed alongside the new souls who clung to their memories like a security blanket. Desperate to escape Death and, in some ways, myself, this time I ran beyond the river basin to hide behind a cluster of billowing, untamed bushes that offered the perfect escape. I crawled and hid inside, the cool shade scented with fresh soil and gnarly roots.

Wrapping my arms around my knees and drawing them to my chest, I released my pent-up sorrow and frustration, utterly convinced that I was alone.

Except I wasn't.

The backside of a cool hand caressed my cheek, startling me from my woes. A young man with pale skin and dark red hair clad entirely in leaves, almost the spitting image of a grown-up Peter Pan, regarded me with fascination in his gooseberry eyes. A smattering of freckles dotted the bridge of his nose, but the smooth planes of his elvish face possessed no other beauty marks. The young man seemed ethereal. Not quite human.

The space inside the bushes was wide enough to accommodate us both as he sat on his haunches with his forearms resting on his knees.

The stranger flashed me a crooked grin that promised nothing, but mischief compared to Teddy's sweet, wry ones.

"Why the long face, beautiful?"

"None of your business," I snapped, unlike my usual friendly self. "I doubt you would understand."

He cocked his head and thoughtfully mulled over my words.

"Try me," he shrugged with cool nonchalance. "I'm a wood nymph. I have all the time in the world." He lifted his chin slightly as he studied me through narrowed eyes. "But you're not dead, are you? You're different."

I hated that I stuck out like a sore thumb. I was tired of being treated as though I was special when that was the complete opposite of how I felt.

"Sometimes I wish I was dead," I muttered darkly, turning my face away from him.

The young man snorted. "That's the most ridiculous thing I've ever heard."

"More ridiculous than someone who lacks the patience, maturity, and insight to resist temptation in favor of true love?" I couldn't resist divulging.

Comprehension dawned on his unearthly face.

"You must be the young mortal everyone's talking about," he flashed me a devilish look.

This was news to me. Who knew the rumor mill in the Underworld was so active?

"I want to go home," my chin wobbled as a fresh wave of tears stung my eyes and nose. "I want the old Teddy back, the one who remembers me. The one who loves me."

The young man shifted closer and laid a reassuring hand on my back. "I'll pretend to understand everything you're talking about if you agree to follow me into the forest for a surprise, I guarantee will cheer you up."

His words startled me.

"Follow you into the forest?" I echoed. "I'm not going anywhere with you. My mother taught me many things about stranger danger and following a man into a dark forest was high on her priority list."

"Ironic that you're calling *me* strange when I happen to think the same about you," he quipped before extending his hand. "Come on. There's a glade not far from here where we dance and make music. I promise I won't bite."

Chasing away my tears, I studied him for a long moment. The ripe gooseberry eyes were bright and full of whimsy. The smooth, elegantly sloped planes of his face were open, honest, and trustworthy. I realized I could either wallow in self-pity inside a bush or follow a stranger into the depths of the forest, the promise of revelry thick between Us.

Against my better judgement, I accepted his hand and crawled out of the bush after him. The young man towered over me, an impressive structure of lean, sinewy limbs that reminded me of a more athletic version of Teddy. Our definition of exercise back home was competing against each other at *Dance Dance Revolution* at the local arcade. Tall, thick trunks sprouted into leafy growth that created a canopy overhead, casting the mossy green path below in a peaceful sort of gloom. Vines hung from the branches overhead like ropes and wound around the pale trunks like lights on a Christmas tree. Thick, billowing ferns fringed the path that wound deep into the forest, leading us to some unknown destination.

We hadn't traveled long before the young man parted a cluster of leaves, revealing a bright sward filled with an explosion of colorful flowers that glowed with an ethereal splendor, the lively strains of music soaring high as the revelers basked in the light cast by an assortment of colorful lanterns strung overhead. Like the pale man standing beside me, both male and female dancers wore leaves strung with colorful beads, their perfectly symmetrical features not quite human. The women wore their long hair in loose, rippling waves that made my heart prick with entry.

The moment they noticed us hovering on the outskirts of the glade, the dancers beckoned like sirens, making it impossible not to join them. I loved to dance, something I hadn't enjoyed since entering the Underworld. Until now I had believed such happiness remained elusive in such a grim place.

The mysterious young man tugged on my arm, and I trailed after him like a lost, wide-eyed child. The musicians performed on a raised platform. Some of the instruments were recognizable, like the harp, fiddle, and drum. Other instruments were decidedly more otherworldly, created from blades of grass and dew drops. To my amusement, the party vaguely recalled a New Age family reunion where, at any moment, that one crazy uncle would break out the Ayahuasca.

Outstretched hands reached for my purple gown and dark hair as they embraced me with barely-disguised fascination and, within the span of seconds, I represented another link in their chain as we danced in spiraling circles and zig-zagging weaves that made my head spin. The chain broke off into swapping pairs as I moved down the line, the steady beat of the dum stirring spikes of adrenaline in my blood. I danced with everyone on the sward at a frenetic pace, sweat pooling between my breasts and on my lower back.

A tall, broad-shouldered man with leaves in his long black hair grinned impishly as he planted his large hands on my waist and spun me around in circles, making my unbound curls soar like coiled snakes.

"We have a newcomer!" A woman shouted over the din, the crowd parting as a figure stumbled through the underbrush onto the sward.

I would've recognized that shoulder-length brown hair and tall, lean frame anywhere, not to mention the smoky green eyes that searched the throng for me.

Teddy.

Had he followed me here? The guitar I'd abandoned that day in the garden was slung on his back like he had come prepared. Except... the very existence of the party seemed to rattle him. As his eyes swept over a sea of unfamiliar faces, he looked lost and disoriented, until his eyes settled on my face.

He didn't immediately notice me as his eyes scanned the crowd, but I saw him do a subtle double-take that softened my choked heart.

"Do you know that man?" My black-haired companion asked in a thick-accented voice as Teddy pushed his way through the crowd.

Willowy wood nymphs with glossy, leaf-strewn hair formed a semi-circle around my best friend, their graceful hands caressing his tunic and fluffy curls. I gritted my teeth as jealousy stabbed deep in my gut. Unable to answer my dance partner's question, I marched forward and slapped away all the thirsty hoes mauling my boyfriend like a horde of pesky flies.

"Get back!" I hissed, glowering at every fey woman who dared touch my man. Some of them looked angry, others wounded. "He's here for me, not you."

The moment the words left my mouth, I whirled around to face him with a hopeful look. "You *are* here for me, right?"

"So it would seem," he offered his usual dry humor, though his wide mouth twisted in an uncertain smile.

The light that touched his eyes quickly dimmed, replaced by an eager, way look. The music had stopped. The revelers flocked around us like gossip-mongers ready for the latest juicy bit.

"I've been thinking a lot about our conversation the other day," he sheepishly rubbed the back of his neck. "I've noticed you leaving the palace. I decided to follow you because... well, I think we need to talk."

My heart plummeted. "Do you think we could dance first? Carpe diem, as they say?"

Teddy blinked in obvious confusion. "I don't know what that means, but actually... I think we need to talk right now." He glanced around at all the hopeful faces surrounding us. "I don't remember how to dance, but you could always show me afterward."

Would there even be an afterward? The whole we-need-to-talk business sounded rather ominous. I nodded quietly and followed him to the gloomy outskirts of the glade where the cool air caressed my overheated skin. We sat beside each other on a fallen tree trunk, though Teddy maintained a comfortable distance. I would've preferred his thigh flush against mine, but beggars can't be choosers.

Teddy's mere presence reawakened the angst in my heart. I'd experienced these small, yet powerful twinges of pain while reading young adult romance novels late into the night, but I only welcomed the heartache in other stories.

Not my own.

Before he could even so much as blink, I launched into a well-deserved apology.

"I'm really sorry for the way I acted the other day," I touched my breast. "It's just... I've always had you to rely on. You're the mature, patient, sensible one. Now that you're counting on me, I don't know what to do. I want you to feel and think the same way about me, though that expectation isn't fair. We hardly ever fight. I don't want this situation to tear us apart."

Teddy listened carefully, a thoughtful look on his face. Long after I'd finished, he quietly mulled over my words, his normally wry mouth serious and eyes hooded, making it impossible to know what he thought or felt. The revelers had begun to dance once more, the beguiling music creeping through the branches.

At long last, those murky green eyes pierced mine. "I'm starting to remember certain things," he revealed. "Not much. More like small flashes of light whenever I close my eyes. I remember the most when I play," he reached for the guitar slung on his back and gently strummed the instrument. "Sometimes I sit for hours and pick through familiar melodies that are attached to deep reservoirs of meaning I can't make sense of, like learning how to walk without knowing what it means to walk." A curtain of hair obscured his face as he ducked his head. "And sometimes I dream about you."

Oh my God, my heart skipped a beat. *Is this really happening?*

Hope and excitement surged through me, emotions I struggled to conceal as I shifted closer to him on the smooth trunk.

"Oh? My voice cracked. "What happens in these dreams?"

Teddy remained hunched over the guitar. "About us driving around in my pick-up truck at night. See, I remember that much!" He exclaimed with a shy smile. "We're singing as we listen to music on the radio, until one particular song comes on that makes you go wild."

These weren't simply dreams, but actual memories of our life back home.

"What happens next?" I urged, sliding closer to him.

"I park somewhere and watch as you climb out of the truck," he went on in a hushed voice. "The headlights illuminate your body as the wind rustles your hair and dress, the red one with the row of buttons in front. The music blares as you dance, and I want to join you but I know I'm running out of time. So I watch, entranced, as the wind picks up your dress, flashing a glimpse of your thighs. The sight fills me with so much longing that I'm incapable of speech or rational thought. All I can hear is a voice repeating the same message over and over."

I leaned forward; spell bound.

"What does the voice say?" I whispered.

Teddy paused as though mustering the courage to share a private memory.

"Small town witch gonna mess me up," he said grimly. "I remember having the distinct impression that the small-town witch was you."

My heart plummeted, but I also had the strange urge to laugh. Either that or smack my forehead.

"Oh, Teddy," I sighed. "That's a lyric from one of our favorite songs, "Small Town Witch". We used to listen to it all the time. Do you honestly think I'm a witch?"

"Not in a bad way," he shifted uncomfortably on the fallen tree. "I don't know how to explain it, but it's like..." Turning to face me, he illustrated with his hands. "We're from a small town, you're like a witch with your special powers, and... I can't keep myself from you, as though you've cast a spell on me. In a strange sense, you *have* messed me up. For good, I think."

I had no clue what to say. I was torn between sobbing and laughing uncontrollably. The way he'd uttered the confession with such tenderness, as though he expected me to spurn him at any moment, tore my heart to shreds. Teddy touched my shoulder, his fingers grazing my bare skin.

"You know what I think?" He mused aloud. "I shouldn't have stayed in the truck. I should have danced with you and savored every moment of my time spent with you."

To my shock and delight, he jumped to his feet and offered me one of his large hands for me to take, like some unconventional prince from a fairy-tale.

"May I have this dance?" He flashed me a barely contained smile that made my bones ache with the intensity of my love for him.

Grinning like a fool, I accepted his gallant gesture and allowed him to guide me back to the sward. The revelers ceased dancing long enough to applaud our return. They swallowed us into the throng as if they knew our struggle and sensed our readiness to defy the forces that threatened to tear us apart.

The colorful lanterns overhead bathed the sward in turquoise, magenta, rose pink, and canary yellow, the music's sweet serenade heightening the emotions that welled in my heart as I gazed into Teddy's eyes. As promised, I taught him how to dance. At first, his movements were clumsy, and he stepped on my bare toes more than once, but he quickly found the rhythm. Before long we circled and swayed, parted and met. Heat simmered between our palms as the promise of a second chance blossomed like spring after a hard frost.

Teddy gazed upon my upturned face with his heart in his eyes, and I returned his open affection with equal tenderness and sincerity. I never wanted to forget the way he looked at me. To think he might love me without knowing what it meant to love would carry me through those hopeless moments when I couldn't see the lighthouse on the seashore. Our dream-like bubble didn't last forever as the music picked up its tempo, but nothing could disrupt the tentative bond we had formed. We clasped hands as the revelers formed a circular chain and, for the first time, Teddy and I laughed together like old times.

We broke away from the chain of dancers and pranced around the glade like playful children, our smiles bright and laughter deafening. We'd barely scratched the surface of sorting through our problems, but the meaning behind his confession was clear.

Teddy refused to warm the bench. He was tired of waiting for the axe to fall.

The worst had already happened, except for losing the will to fight.

Later on, I urged Teddy onto the platform so the revelers could watch him play the guitar. He remembered more than I had expected, playing a range of songs that tugged on beloved memories. Growing up, Teddy had played for me all the time, but he'd always avoided eye contact as he sang. Now he seemed unable to tear his gaze from mine as his distinctive voice echoed around the sward. After speaking with the other band members, he managed to convince them to play a surreal, otherworldly rendition of "Who Is She?" by Monster, one of his obscure favorites.

Oh who is she?/ A misty memory/ A haunting face/ Is she a lost embrace?

Teddy's voice was light, raspy, and cracked occasionally, which made a shiver travel up my spine. His vibrato fluttered like a bird's wings, delicate and airy without detracting from his masculine timbre. I stood at the front of the throng, utterly hypnotized, as though Teddy sang for me alone.

For the first time, I realized Teddy wasn't the only one who had been messed up for good.

Once Upon A Dream

The revelers, or at least the fey women, threatened to overwhelm Teddy as he hopped off the platform clutching his guitar. The crowd threatened to swallow me, as well. In the next instant, however, my lover's sweaty body was pressed against mine, one strong hand planted firmly on the small of my back. Wisps of hair curled around his face, his tunic clinging to his lanky frame, the musky scent of his body filling my lower belly with heat. The urge to bury my nose in his hair where the scent was strongest was overpowering.

The wood nymphs who had resided in the Underworld for so long that they'd become the stuff of legends themselves pulsed around us, but Teddy steered me through the crowd until we were safely out of reach.

"Why are we leaving?" I asked, though I wasn't complaining. While the revelers seemed benign, something about their overzealous nature unnerved me. "I don't think I'm ready to go back to the palace."

"Sorry for tearing you away," he flashed me an apologetic half-smile. "I'm not ready to go back, either, but I need to be alone with you."

Need.

Such a powerful world. Teddy *needed* food, oxygen, and sleep… but did he truly need me? Removing his hand from the small of my back, he walked close enough that our hands brushed as they swayed. The mossy carpet muffled

the sound of our footfalls and heightened the awkward silence. It dawned on me as Teddy veered off the path and pulled back the curtain of a willow tree that he knew exactly where he was going, even if only by instinct.

"Come on," his eyes twinkled in the gloom. "I want to show you something."

Tentatively, I stepped over the mossy threshold, the breath freezing in my lungs as the fringe of vines, leaves, and fragrant blossoms glowed with thousands of tiny beams of light that swirled like moving stars. Strangely enough, a wood swing, the same kind in my backyard that always gave me slivers, hung from one of the tall branches. Beyond the fringe of vines, a crystal-clear pool glowed unnaturally bright. The water flowed around several large boulders, though I realized upon closer examination that the boulders were, in fact, ancient remains of a marble statue of Death.

The familiar handsome face was submerged halfway, his fearsome scowl only partially visible. Something light tickled my brain, like a stray hair that teased my nose, as a memory washed over me. I whirled to face my companion and found that he watched me expectantly.

"We've been here before," I gasped.

Teddy arched a quizzical brow. "I thought you remembered everything."

"Memory doesn't work like that," I said as my eyes drank in our surroundings. "It isn't possible to remember everything as clearly as it happened. Sometimes memories are clearer than crystal. Other times they are mere shadows of what they once were. Sometimes they're completely forgotten, only to be remembered at the most random moments. Assuming we're dealing with a single lifetime, that is."

"I don't remember much," Teddy rubbed the back of his neck, "but I remember pushing you on this swing." He touched the frayed rope that supported the small piece of wood. "Would you like me to push you for old time's sake?"

The hem of my purple gown dragged on the lush carpet of wildflowers as I perched on the slab of wood that was older than time itself. Teddy grabbed the frayed rope and pulled me back like a slingshot, and I shrieked as the swing arced forward, my bare toes leaving the ground. The swing groaned under my weight as I glanced over my shoulder and caught Teddy's delighted smile. I hadn't been on a swing in ages and, physically, I felt like I had outgrown the pastime. My body no longer seemed to fit the tight space, but that didn't stop me from pumping my legs, some reckless part of me daring to climb higher and higher.

Well, until the rope snapped and I collapsed on the ground in an unceremonious heap.

I landed on my backside, my tailbone smarting from the impact. Tears of embarrassment pricked my eyes, in spite of the laughter at my own expense. Teddy was crouched beside me in a heartbeat.

"Are you okay?" His brow furrowed in concern as his hands ghosted over me, assessing the damage. "Are you in

pain? I'm so stupid for suggesting that I push you on that swing. The damn thing looked ancient."

"Don't worry," I giggled, my cheeks flushed and hair wild. "I'd rather create new memories with you than relive the old ones. I have to admit that was an epic fail." My words failed to reassure Teddy, his touch continuously skating over my bare skin, searching for scrapes or bruises.

An idea struck me. "You know what?" I winced. "I am feeling pretty sore."

"Where?" He demanded. "Let me see."

I rolled over onto my stomach and rubbed my backside through the purple gown. I wasn't wearing underwear and the whisper of fabric, combined with the anticipation of his own, made me shiver.

"My ass is really smarting," I adopted the most innocent voice I could muster. "Could you massage it for me?"

Teddy paused, utterly speechless. The sleeves of my gown slipped down my shoulders as I glanced expectantly over at him, my tailbone protesting for real as I kicked my legs back and forth in a coquettish fashion.

"Aren't you going to help me?" I batted my eyelashes.

"Of course," Teddy sprang to life and crouched beside me. Tentatively, his hands cupped my bottom and froze. "How does that feel?"

"Could you give me a massage?" I squirmed in obvious dissatisfaction. "My body needs your touch."

Maybe my efforts to seduce him were a little ham-fisted, but he needed a push in the right direction. I didn't want him to think I was a tease, that I behaved like this with every man. That was the last thing I wanted. Maybe that's why Teddy hadn't initially trusted me. Perhaps he'd assumed he wasn't special in my eyes because I spent time with Death. To my surprise, Teddy straddled my legs and kneaded my bottom with both hands, his touches firm, slow, and deliberate. The fabric of my gown caressed my smooth skin as he massaged my supple flesh. A low moan escaped my throat as his thumb traced the cleft of my backside.

"Is that better?" Teddy breathed huskily in my ear.

"Oh, you have no idea," I sighed blissfully, the intoxicating scent of spring clouding my judgement, "but I think I would prefer your skin touching mine." I bunched up the skirt around my waist before he could argue, grinning wickedly to myself as his soft moan fell on my ears. "Is that better?"

Teddy's hands were immediately on my bare skin, except his touch was more tender, heated, and exploratory than before. He cupped my bottom, the heat of his palms searing my skin as he savored the weight of each rounded cheek. Carefully, he traced my cleft. My core ached with arousal, but this moment was about rediscovery, not sex.

Teddy and I had shared more than a lifetime's worth of experiences, but the threat of separation had always

tethered us to our past because we'd always believed that was the extent of what we could call our own. After an entire childhood of waiting, we were finally free to challenge everything that stood between our love and freedom.

To my surprise, Teddy ducked his head and kissed my bare skin, his touch quickly growing feverish.

"I'm going to fight for you," he panted harshly as he nuzzled my cheek. "I don't think I can live without you. I don't have to know you *here*," he touched his temple, "because I already know you by heart."

I rolled over onto my back and stared at him with glittering eyes, only half-aware of the slight widening of his eyes as the small thatch of hair between my thighs came into view. "Do you trust me?"

"What do you mean?" Teddy asked warily.

"Do you trust that, no matter how hard Death tries to sabotage our bond, I will always choose you?" My eyes bore into his. "Do you realize that I only behave seductively around you because I desire you? I reserve that for you alone."

Teddy hovered on the verge of speech, making anger flicker in my breast.

"What's holding you back?" I demanded. "Trust is a choice. Have I ever given you a reason not to trust me?"

"It's not that I don't trust you," He raked a hand through his hair and sighed despondently. "For as long as I remember knowing you, only the lack of faith in my own desirability has made me doubt you."

I propped up on my elbows, keenly aware that the lower half of my body was still on display. "What do you mean?"

"From the moment I laid eyes on you, I found you painfully beautiful," he said. "Even now my entire body hurts just looking at you. The moment you first spoke to me, I realized your outward beauty came from within. Not only are you kind and thoughtful, I truly believe that you'd do anything to help me remember my past. But…"

My heart thudded in my chest as I resisted the urge to shake him.

"What's holding you back?" I whispered.

Teddy dropped his gaz.

"Every time I see you with Lord Death, a part of me withers," he murmured. "I can't explain why. It's like watching something precious being wrenched from my grasp and, no matter how hard I struggle, I'm bound to end up alone and forgotten. When you declared your love for me, I couldn't fathom why you had chosen *me*."

His words made my heart ache.

"Why wouldn't I be in love with you?" I caressed his cheek.

My heart fluttered as he pressed my palm flat against his cheek, as though terrified I might slip away. "Because you don't know your own heart. I've seen the way you glow in Lord Death's presence. I've seen your flushed complexion. The only reason you might choose me is because you're comfortable with our history. That you don't know any differently because you've been with me for so long."

The thought churned my stomach.

"I know you don't remember much, but have you ever been attracted to another woman?" I asked. "Haven't you ever noticed that someone other than me was beautiful? What about the fey dancers who fawned over you? Didn't that make you feel special?"

Teddy shifted uncomfortably. "Sort of."

"There's no shame in finding someone else attractive," I shook my head. "We're only human."

Teddy looked as though he wanted to argue.

"Yes, but whatever appreciation I might've felt for their looks was nothing compared to my love for you," he blurted.

Our eyes widened the moment we realized what he'd said.

Love?

Without a second thought, I grabbed the front of his tunic and yanked him close. My eyes fluttered closed as my lips captured his in a softly passionate kiss that left us

ragged and breathless. I wrenched myself away from him and touched my tingling mouth.

"Exactly," I grinned impishly as his eyes slowly cracked open, his lips parted. "Death might make me feel desired, that doesn't diminish my love for you. I vow here and now to make you feel so loved that I will leave no doubt in your mind of how cherished you are." I grabbed his hand, jerking him out of his daze as I dragged him to his feet. "Come on, Teddy! Let's take a dip in the water before we face the dragon waiting for us back at the palace."

I could tell from his sleepy look that he longed for more kisses, but we splashed in the cool water fully-clothed. We stayed in the shallow end since Teddy didn't remember how to swim, and I admired the way his tunic and leggings clung to his body. I noticed the way he eyed my sopping wet dress. The promise of blistering exploration hung in the air, but our laughter remained as innocent as those summers spent on the banks of our favorite river. Death's marble head watched disapprovingly as we created new memories that could never be taken from us.

When our fingers turned into prunes, Teddy gave me a piggy-back ride on our trek back to the palace, my cheek pressed flat against his back as we lapsed into a comfortable silence.

"It doesn't make sense to me, but I *am* in love with you," Teddy's voice vibrated through my chest. "I hope you know that."

"It makes perfect sense," I murmured sleepily. "I couldn't resist loving you for all those years I didn't remember you."

Legendary Lovers

The days bled into each other as Teddy and I slowly rediscovered our love. We were inseparable. Using my velvet coverlet, we created a hammock in the courtyard so we could nestle in each other's arms as we swayed. When I told him stories about our clandestine meetings in the Den of Beasts, he insisted on paying the bat-like iguanas a visit.

Teddy rolled on the mosaic floor with laughter as the creatures streamed after me with their leathery wings and snapping jaws, apparently as fond of me as before. The gargoyles snapped at the hem of my gown, and I tangled myself in knots trying to escape them. Teddy grabbed the ringleader of the pack, and the wretched thing licked his face with one long, forked tongue.

"Traitor," I huffed, blowing a stray lock of hair from my eyes.

Teddy rolled the gargoyle onto its spiny back and rubbed its soft underbelly. The others clamored for his attention.

As I flopped down on the decorative pillows beside him, I added, "You know what they remind me of? Geese."

"Geese?" Teddy flinched, a tell-tale sign that an elusive image flashed through his mind.

Cradling the gargoyle like a baby, he folded his lean body into a comfortable sitting position beside me. I tentatively grabbed a leathery creature and copied Teddy's methods of seduction, but I only ended up with a few scratches on my face. Dropping the gargoyle nestled in his arms, Teddy immediately cupped my face in his large hands and examined my wound. It moved and humbled me that he was able to care so deeply and freely about a woman he only vaguely remembered. He tore a strip off the hem of his tunic, something I found oddly sexy, to staunch the blood.

The reckless gargoyle that had flailed in my arms had the decency to look abashed. Needless to say, we never visited the Den of Beasts again. As we nestled in our hammock that night, tangled in one another's embrace, I told him about the geese that congregated by the river back home, how we grew up feeding them seeds and breadcrumbs, and how the overzealous geese sometimes flapped their wings as they chased after us. I told him about our fishing trips using poles of our own making, how he'd bravely volunteered to gut my fish because I was too squeamish. Ultimately, he hadn't been able to because he'd come to the conclusion that killing even the smallest creature was unnatural - at least to him.

I regaled him with stories of his ability to transform scraps of metal into beautiful objects, like the jeweled bangles he'd once given to me for Christmas. Not wanting to confuse or overwhelm him, I chose not to include the times over our many lifetimes how he'd bestowed gifts upon me. Memory was a strange, fickle thing; I wasn't capable of remembering everything at once, but sometimes a thought or conversation sparked something in my mind. Despite my efforts to hold back, he insisted on knowing everything.   "What were our past lives like?" He asked as I cradled his head against my chest.

"We always grew up in the same village, town, or city," I whispered, my eyes glazing over with thought. "We met at different points in our lives, but we always clicked, as though we immediately knew each other. I always lived alone with my mom, except for those rare occasions she died prematurely from illness or plague. Sometimes we were surrounded by family, other times we were alone. You always seemed to have older siblings that couldn't be more different from you."

"Do I have siblings now?" Teddy's head shifted on my chest as he glanced up at me. "What is my family back home like?"

"Well," I began, "you have three older brothers: Brandon, Lucas, and Trevor. You're the youngest and most sweet-tempered, whereas your brothers... well, they enjoy wrestling and hockey, while you're artistic, gentle, and intellectual."

"Do we get along?" He pressed.

"For the most part," I shrugged. How could I explain that his older brothers had often mocked his stammer and flushed his anxiety medication down the toilet as a practical joke? How could I avoid painting them in a negative light when they had often tormented him as the youngest sibling that didn't measure up to their standard of masculinity? "You're the only son that works full-time at the auto shop fixing cars. In your spare time, you drop by the shop and watch me sing show tunes to the plants." I closed my eyes. "Sometimes grease smears your face and hands, and I can smell the sweat staining your shirt. It's the most arousing combination of smells."

Whenever I brought up feelings of longing or desire for him, hoping it might nudge him in the right direction, he shied away from the conversation, as though overwhelmed and more than a little confused. Part of me wanted to push harder, but I remembered how patient he had always been with me.

Maybe a little too patient, a huffy voice whispered in my head. *Sometimes all a girl wants is to be thrown down on a bed and ravaged.*

Ignoring these thoughts, I taught Teddy how to play hide-and-seek, one of our childhood favorites. More than once I caught him spying on me when he was supposed to be counting, which I found hilariously sneaky. Teddy loved searching for me, and I was very skilled at hiding. Each time he found my hiding spot, I ran through the palace's arched corridors and covered walkways, screaming riotously until he rounded a corner and captured me.

I hadn't seen Death since that morning in the garden, but sometimes I saw a shadow lurking in a corner or slowly moving across an ornately carved wall. I often sensed him before I saw a flicker of red from my periphery. Teddy and I explored the palace through our games, until one day we found life-sized chess pieces on a checkered floor. Growing up, Teddy had belonged to our high school's chess club and struggled to teach me for years. Unable to remember the

rules or the significance of the pieces, I taught him how to play tic-tac-toe with them instead, part of me waiting for Teddy to correct me as I imagined the look of horror on his face upon realizing my disgrace.

The knights wielded actual swords, and I slid one from the statue's grasp, astonished by how heavy it was as it clattered to the floor. Teddy reached for his own, and I watched how elegantly he wielded the sword, as though it weighed nothing. A flash of recognition passed over his face like a fleeting shadow, and I found myself holding my breath. The flex of his biceps stained the sleeves of his tunic as he rotated the hilt, slashing the blade through the air in a smooth figure-eight.

"Why does this feel so natural?" Teddy mused aloud as the blade bisected his face, transforming him from the underdog boy-next-door to a dashing knight. "Like the sword is an extension of my arm."

"Because it is," I stepped forward, dragging my own sword behind me. "You're an even better swordsman than Death. The only thing you sometimes lack is faith in yourself."

Before registering what I was doing, I hauled my sword over my head and struck, though Teddy's blade clashed with my own as he expertly blocked the blow. Rotating his wrist, he twirled the sword before slashing across my midriff, a blow I narrowly missed.

"Careful!" I shrieked as my heart lodged itself in my throat. Teddy's shoulders rounded as heat suffused his cheeks. "Sorry."

My blade swiped the air in a silent challenge, and he advanced on me with slow, precise strokes that sent me reeling backward. I managed to block every one of his blows, a line of sweat pearling on my brow as adrenaline surged through my veins.

"Not bad," Teddy praised rather breathlessly, his cheeks flushed and eyes eerily bright.

The excitement of rediscovery was palpable. Even if Teddy couldn't remember his life from before, the skills flowed naturally through his blood. The clang of our swords filled the air, accompanied by our playful banter.

"I never thought I'd be lucky enough to have such a beautiful woman as my opponent," he grinned wickedly, displaying a confidence that seemed uncharacteristic of him.

I darted around the towering chess pieces, using flight to my advantage. I couldn't match him blow-for-blow, so I figured I could throw in an element of tag to the mix.

"Were you expecting a competent man?" I raised a haughty chin, thinking of Catherine Zeta-Jones from *The Mask of Zorro*.

Teddy offered a lazy shrug. "Whatever I expected, it wasn't you."

Was he actually trying to *flirt* with me? For the first time since wielding a sword, he seemed unsure of himself, as though he'd forgotten how to speak to me. The struggle to quantify the meaning of his words without the proper references was clearly a struggle.

"How dare you!" I exclaimed indignantly, fighting back a grin. "I was born with a sword in my hand. My father, the most dangerous man in the province, taught me."

"I doubt he's more dangerous than I, based on your skills," he quipped before grabbing my wrist and pushing me up against a large chess piece, his breathing rough. "I could teach you in exchange for something I've longed for since the moment I first saw you."

If Death had spoken these words, they would've made him seem arrogant, entitled, and self-assured, but not Teddy. The shy innocence that fueled his words made the hopeful;

earnest quality of his tone thicken our exchange with a charged sexual tension.

Tossing back my hair, I stared up at him through hooded eyes. "Name your price."

"A kiss," he half-whispered.

Unable to tear my wide eyes from his unblinking gaze, I focused on the fringe of dark eyelashes that contrasted sharply with his jade irises. I watched his face inch closer, until his nose tenderly brushed my own. Lightly, he kissed my parted lips, a mere taste that barely quenched my thirst. His lips were so soft and tasted so sweet - sweeter than strawberries, peaches, and watermelon combined. My eyes fluttered open as he drew away.

I wanted more.

Disappointed, I admitted under the guise of the role I'd adopted, "That hardly seems like a satisfactory payment for your services."

Teddy looked somewhat crest fallen. "Did you not enjoy the kiss?"

"Of *course,* I did," I emphasized my words, "but don't you want more?"

Teddy dropped his sword, though he barely moved a muscle. He towered over me in all his lithe elegance. His jade eyes devoured me through a haze of longing.

"Of course, I want more," he said in a strangled voice. "I just…"

"It's okay," I stroked the crook of his neck. "You're safe with me. You can tell me anything."

Teddy rubbed the back of his neck with his free hand, seeming to wilt at the prospect of his confession.

"I don't know how," he said at last. "It's not like picking up a sword or a guitar. Every morning when I wake up, the warmth and softness of your body fills me with the incredible urge to do… something. Some urges make sense, like touching and kissing, whereas others leave me baffled. And the worst part?" He laughed humorlessly. "I'm terrified of failure, of somehow displeasing you, so I repress everything that threatens to broach the surface, for I'm not capable of taking the lead. I never wanted you to know this, but now I see no other way around it."

Teddy stepped away from me, breaking our intense closeness. I watched him retreat within himself, my eagerness crushed against that familiar guard. Like Teddy, however, I would never give up.

"Do you know how attractive your vulnerability is?" I lowered my own sword as I stepped forward. "Once upon a time, I told you that I was upset over my perceived lack of choices, something that wounded you deeply. For as long as I can remember, I was the oblivious one, unaware of who I was and what had come before. Now I have the opportunity to teach you. Do you know how valuable a gift that is?"

Teddy watched me with a wary sort of curiosity. "What are you suggesting?"

"I'm going to teach you," I shrugged with an impish grin.

He perked like a dog that had caught a whiff of a rabbit. "When?"

"It'll be a surprise," I gave him an exaggerated wink. "Prepare yourself, Kershaw. I'm going to blow your mind."

~

Wielding the upper hand in our physical relationship solidified my status as a shameless, unabashed tease.

Sadly, I didn't immediately devour him the way he half-expected. I noticed the way he braced himself whenever I drew near. And the best part? I allowed him to think the worst with the promise of brushing my lips against his

before abruptly drawing away. No matter what I did, the spell I cast only intensified.

I plied him with fruit and chaste caresses, watching his eyelids droop. Teddy repaid my light, seductive teasing with open adoration. One dusky evening, he plucked a flower from the garden and tucked it behind my ear as my fingers tip-toed up his chest. I saw that look of panic flash across his face as I drew near. I hadn't reenacted scenes from *Moulin Rouge!* for his pleasure like I'd promised, but I was sort of living the plot of a soap opera in a strange sense.

The way Teddy gazed at me with such bright-eyed wonder made me second-guess myself, though. Was I approaching him the wrong way by leading with my sexuality? To be honest, I didn't know any other way, since we had the friendship part down. Teddy was the heart of this relationship, not me. But that didn't mean I shouldn't try.

"Teddy?" I studied his profile as he gazed up at the stars.

"Yeah?" He murmured softly.

"Let's get out of here," I grabbed his hand.

"Where?" He stumbled as he trailed after me through the cool garden.

My eyes sparkled with mischief. "Oh, somewhere private where we can, you know, *talk*."

Over the past few weeks, we'd befriended a few of the inconsolable souls that dwelled in the river basin, and I had reenacted a few of their favorite movies, *Mrs. Doubtfire* being the most sought-after performance. The souls that hadn't lost their memory had rolled on the grass in fits of uncontrollable laughter as I screamed and whacked my blazing prosthetic breasts with an imaginary spatula. Making a cup of English tea without frosting concealing my true identity didn't pack the same comedic punch as Robin Williams' performance, however. A few familiar faces glimpsed us and waved, but thankfully they didn't disturb our privacy as we found a secluded spot beneath a tall cluster of trees. The untamed bushes enclosing the area were overflowing with hot pink hibiscus flowers.

Teddy lay sprawled beside me, his torso propped up on one elbow as he stared down at me with unfathomable eyes.

"I know you want to touch me," I murmured as I worked my fingernails in slow circles on his scalp.

Teddy swallowed hard. "I-I don't know how, but I want to so badly that I can think of nothing else."

"Trust your instincts," I coaxed in a breathless voice. "Trust me. I'll tell you if I don't like something."

Slowly, he nodded and the hand on my waist moved upward to firmly mold my breast. For the span of several heartbeats, he did nothing else. My back arched as he found my nipple, my soft whispers of encouragement inviting him to play. Teddy gauged my reactions with avid curiosity as

he experimented with squeezing my nipple, until my sharp cry of pain made his thumb circle my areola through the thin fabric to soothe my body's protest. The hyper-awareness that came with the sensation almost made the sharp pinch worth it.

A hollow ache filled my breast as his hand slithered further up my chest to trace the clasp holding one section of my gown together.

"I want to see you," he moaned as he dug his fingernails into my flesh and raked them across the fabric that pooled in loose, sumptuous waves in the valley of my breasts.

"Don't worry about that right now," I stretched my arms overhead like a kitten basking in a perfect patch of sunlight. "Touch me everywhere. Feel every part of me."

Unexpectedly, Teddy pinned my wrists overhead as he rolled on top of me, all sharp edges and lean, hard muscle compared to my soft, yielding body. I whimpered softly into his mouth as he captured my lips in an all-consuming kiss, more heated and demanding than what had come before. The way he buried his hands in my hair and dragged his lips down my throat made me feel like the most desirable woman in the world, and I made sure he heard my pants and moans to leave no doubt in his mind.

Just as I was beginning to fall in love with this new, exploratory version of Teddy, he shocked me beyond reason by devouring my breast through the muslin of my gown, soaking the thin fabric with his lapping tongue. My back arched instinctively, thrusting my nipple further into his mouth. Between the shock of his death and the loss of his memory, I felt as though I'd lived without his touch for ages. Knowing that he acted on a deeply primal urge with no tangible idea of what he was doing made me ache from a strange blend of pleasure and pain. All of those familiar pangs filled my lower belly, triggering a surge of need that stretched from my breasts to my core.

Teddy's hair trailed down my body as he covered every last inch of clothed flesh, his potent overflow of lust bathing my soul without compromising the reverence of his touch. The moment he reached my bare feet, his teeth flashed in the semi-darkness as he nipped at my toes. A warm, dry breeze rustled his hair and teased my wet nipples, making me shiver in delight.

"You're making this game very difficult by not baring yourself to me," he said.

The way his heated gaze raked over my body convinced me to take matters a step further, even if only a little.

"Here, I'll give you a sneak peek," I flashed him a teasing grin as I slowly bunched up my skirt, revealing my smooth, bronzed skin one painful inch at a time. I crooked my finger in a silent invitation. "Come here."

Teddy obeyed and stretched out beside me in the grass with wide, devouring eyes. I grabbed his wrist and spread my legs far enough that a faint, heady musk perfumed the air. Writhing in anticipation, my body jolted rapturously when his fingers discovered my slick, ripe folds, the scent of my arousal growing stronger with the contact. Teddy sucked in a shuddering breath, moved beyond speech and perhaps rational thought. He immediately spread his fingers wide in a gentle, though firm exploration of my pussy.

The light, undeniably reverent touch made me cling to him that much tighter, the trembling of my thighs the only tell-tale sign of my pleasure. All I could do was stare up at the velvety expanse of stars suffused with peach, saffron, and cobalt, the sky akin to an artist's palette, more brilliant than anything I had seen back home. His slick fingers eventually brushed my clit, and I clutched fistfuls of the long grass as I choked out, "There."

"Where?" He immediately sought my gaze, not quite aware of the breakthrough he'd just made.

"Do you feel that small nub at the crest of my sex?" I grabbed his hand long enough to move his fingers over that painfully sensitive spot. I whimpered, the act of guiding him through my own pleasure strangely intimate and real, and I saw comprehension dawn as his fingers ghosted over my clit once more.

"What do I do now?" He asked in a strangled voice, the crease of his brow making him look lost and uncertain.

"Circle *very* slowly," I said calmly, "and keep circling it with infinite gentleness, no matter how loud I whimper or cry."

My instructions only raised more questions in his mind, though he kept them to himself as he concentrated on circling that small, tight nub. My eyes fluttered closed as he gazed upon my face, my fingers tangling in the hair at the nape of his neck. The sensation was indescribable, like the euphoria that came from scratching an itch that had bothered me for days. No matter how often my hips bucked in near spasmodic pleasure, no matter how hard I begged his fingers to circle harder and faster, he maintained a steady pace, his expression more serious than I had ever seen.

The calloused pads of his fingers made me come harder and longer than I had ever been able to on my own. Tremulous bliss crashed over me like thunder, too swept away to notice Teddy's intense, almost feral gaze. When I came back to myself many throbbing moments later, I heard the low rasp of Teddy's voice first.

"That was incredible." he breathed, completely thunder struck.

"What?" My eyes snapped open. "I haven't even touched you."

"That day I woke up not being able to remember anything," he mused softly, "and I was so lost and terrified because I didn't know who or where I was." For a moment, he paused and stroked my face. "And then I saw you, as though I'd been found. Korey, you've been my light in an otherwise dark tunnel. Something deep within urges me to run to you, and I'm beyond grateful that I continue to listen to that instinct. No matter how hard or confusing this

journey has been, in spite of our arguments and misunderstandings, I knew you would help me find my way. Seeing you come undone like that because of *me*? I could die happily from that experience alone."

"We're not done yet, Sparky," I teased, though my heart threatened to burst from his declaration. "We have a lot more ground to cover."

"Now?" His eyebrows rose meaningfully.

"I can't tell you," I shook my head, pretending to lock my mouth and throw away an imaginary key. "It's a secret."

Teddy collapsed beside me and groaned loudly. "You really are a small-town witch, aren't you?"

Desire

The evening of Death's small gathering, the dressmaker presented a sumptuous gown she had designed for me. Crimson silk flowed over her arms like a ruby river dappled with starlight. Cordelia tugged a white shift with billowing sleeves over my head before I was stuffed into the red confection that practically boiled over with heat. There were small, precise tears in the sleeves festooned with ribbon that Cordelia used to draw the shift through, creating white puffs along the length of my arm that made me look like Venetian royalty. The empire-waisted gown featured a brocade bodice covered in gold swirls that laced tightly to enhance the ruffled frill framing my cleavage.

The waterfall of fabric parted in front to create a train that would make any young woman feel like a princess. On trembling legs, I followed Cordelia down the long maze of corridors to the Great Hall where a flurry of activity awaited me. A gaggle of women chartered animatedly in the vast chamber, the torchlight and opulent candelabras casting a flickering play of light and shadow on the stone walls. The undead version of *The Bachelor* welcomed twelve contestants clad in gold silk, mossy green, and deep plum, some with winter pale flesh as unspoiled as fresh snow and a smattering of dark-skinned women whose visage reflected the undertones of the dusky sky. I was the only one who wore red, and I stood out like a sore thumb as I joined their ranks.

The women inspected me curiously, apparently sizing me up as potential competition.

Esme sat at a long table near the end where Death's empty throne awaited his lily-white ass. I hadn't seen her in ages, though Teddy had mentioned sometimes bumping into her as she roamed the palace like a lost soul. As for me, I never saw her and Death never talked about her, though I couldn't help noticing the dark shadows that rimmed her eyes and the wanes of her cheeks. Even as forlorn as she seemed, Esme remained unnaturally beautiful. A sharp pang of guilt lingered because I understood how precarious her role in Death's life was and, while I had tried pushing him in her direction, I suspected there was too much pain there to be resolved.

A man cleared his throat behind me, and I whirled around to face the newcomer, only to gasp at the astounding transformation. Teddy froze as I drank in the sight of him. Clad in a velvet royal blue doublet layered with swirling gold filigree, he struck a rather imposing figure with his broad shoulders and height, the Shakespearean hosiery clinging to his lean, shapely legs like a second skin. One leg matched the royal blue doublet, while the other's pale cousin made an appealing contrast that drew my attention to the codpiece secured with black silk ribbon. His normally tangled hair had been tamed into the very picture of smooth elegance that fell around his boyish face in fashionable waves. The undead contestants immediately flocked around him, seemingly unable to resist the lure of fresh meat.

"Where are you from?" One caressed his velvet garb, whispering close to his ear.

"I've never seen you before," another said, touching his chest.

Jealousy flared to life in my breast. I was on the verge of parting the group of women like the Red Sea (hey, I could grow flowers without seeds, water, or sunshine and save people from the brink of death, so why not?), but Teddy's voice halted me dead in my tracks.

"Sorry, ladies," he couldn't resist flashing them a winning smile, the bastard, "but I'm saving myself for the most beautiful girl in the room."

The contestants searched among their ranks, perplexed, until he parted the throng like a hot knife through butter and confidently wrapped his arm around my waist. The women opened their mouths in angry protest, but Death sauntered into the chamber as if on cue and murmured in rich, dulcet tones, "No need to fight over a mortal when there's plenty of me to go around."

The faint quirk of Death's full lips and the subtle arch of his brow was enough to distract them and, as they scrambled to fawn over him like rabid fangirls, Teddy's arm tightened around my waist. Meanwhile, Esme looked even more desolate than she had before. I studied Death's smug face as he exchanged kisses with every woman, wondering why he entertained such vapid creatures rather than rekindle his lost romance with Esme. Did his ego require that much stroking, or was it so bruised that he compensated for the loss?

Before I could answer my own question, Death turned those liquid gold eyes on me. "Of course, I can't forget Lady Koreyna," he stalked forward, knocking Teddy aside, and kissed me full on the lips.

I frantically pounded on his chest and bit down hard on his bottom lip, which made him wrench away from me with a soft hiss. He touched his now swollen lip and arched an inky black brow.

"Who knew little Korey liked it rough?" He grinned wickedly around his thumb. "Now every time I feel the swell of my bottom lip, I'll think of you."

Teddy inserted himself between us, nearly boiling over with rage.

"Don't you dare touch her!" He snarled. "If I had a sword, I'd run you through to add a spark of interest to your fake little party."

"How could you possibly kill me when I'm neither dead nor alive?" Death mocked, though he shrugged. "But I'd like to see you try. I'm sure Korey would love nothing more than to cradle her lover's broken body when I am through with you."

Sensing danger, I stepped forward.

"Come on, Teddy," I grabbed his shoulder. "We're leaving."

"Ah, ah, ah," Death clucked. "That wasn't part of our deal. The more you resist, the longer you will remain here with me. Now, come, you'll be sitting beside me tonight."

"What about Teddy?" I protested. "I have a place for him at the other end of the table," he swept an elegant hand.

I wanted to resist Death's commands. I had hoped spending the party with Teddy would be, dare I say, fun. I'd imagined us whispering among ourselves as we mocked Death's attempts at flirting.

Teddy watched me from the other end of the table as Death gestured for me to take the seat directly across from Esme. The witch refused to meet my gaze. The evening only grew more tense. With a snap of his fingers, dusky blue shades filed into the chamber bearing platters of food. The smell that swirled around the room was heavenly.

Spinach pie with flaky, golden-brown crust sizzled from the heat and salted butter. Freshly baked bread that released clouds of steam when torn open. Salted pork that gleamed a healthy pink in the torchlight and endless racks of lamb. Candied apples dusted with nutmeg and cinnamon. The mingled scents of garlic and onion made my mouth water, but I refused to partake of the meal as pomegranate wine flowed freely.

I occasionally checked to make sure Teddy remained as stoic and unrelenting as possible. Prior to Death's little social gathering, I'd explained the importance of not eating otherworldly food in terms his normal self would've understood. Copying straight from the plot of *Pan's Labyrinth*, I'd explained that a pale, skeletal man with a bloody mouth and eyeballs in his hands would eat him if he even went so far as to lick his plate clean. The lie had worked like a charm.

Despite his fears, Teddy's eyes glittered with temptation, his lips parted in thinly-veiled lust, and I could hardly blame him since he'd lived on a steady diet of fruit since joining me in the palace. My stomach twisted in knots, but I remained focused on my goal, even as Death offered samples from his own plate, hoping to add insult to injury by spoon-feeding me in an inappropriate display of intimacy. Esme merely pushed the food around on her plate, hardly taking a bite. Teddy frequently stole glances down the length of the table at me, even as women clamored for his attention.

Halfway through the meal, Death snapped his fingers once more and a bevy of shackled, scantily-clad shades danced to a percussive beat, their long chains clinking as they undulated and swayed their hips. The two musicians sat cross-legged on the ground with their drum and flute. Teddy stared, stony-faced, at the dancers, a detail that didn't escape Death's notice.

"Theodoros, it's impolite to stare at barely clothed women in the presence of your one true love," he mocked.

A muscle in Teddy's clenched jaw twitched.

"I'm not staring," he countered. "I'm horrified that you would exploit those who have suffered for your own entertainment."

"How noble of you," Death taunted. "Would you like to share your own personal history? Oh, that's right. You don't remember."

The undead contestants tittered as Teddy bowed his head in shame, but neither Esme nor I cracked even the faintest of smiles.

"That's enough!" My voice rose above the din, stern and reprimanding.

"Oh, but I'm sure they'd love a good story," Death reclined lazily on his throne. "You see, Lady Koreyna fell in love with a shade that had once taken his life, and cycled through endless lifetimes with him as opposed to spending an eternity with yours truly."

The undead cooed in a way that made Death's eyes glint with satisfaction.

"That's not the whole story," I interjected. "As charming as Death might have initially seemed, Lady Koreyna quickly learned of how cruel and selfish her captor was. The fact that he kicks people when they're down is evidence enough."

Death's nostrils flared.

"At least I'm not a shameless tease who makes nothing more than false promises," he snapped.

Everyone gasped as I tossed my goblet of wine in his shocked face, to which Esme grabbed her own and splashed him with another wave of dark red liquid. The undead immediately pushed away from the table and mopped his face as he coughed and sputtered. Esme flashed me a quick smile and jerked her head, as if to say, "Get out of here."

"Come on, Teddy," I grabbed his hand and dragged him away from the humiliating scene.

In a shadowed corridor lined with suits of armor, he twirled me into his arms and tightly embraced me.

"Thank you," he murmured between kisses to the crown of my head.

"For what?" I feigned ignorance, my chest still burning with anger.

"I have a feeling that you've always protected me," he said. "Like a guardian angel."

My eyes snapped upward to meet his gaze, and the knowing twinkle there made me beam.

"What did you remember?" I nearly shook him.

Teddy laughed and sandwiched my hands between his.

"The shackled women stirred my memory of our first conversation, as well as Death's revelation that I once belonged to him." He paused for a moment, hesitating. "And I remember meeting you a thousand times over, how you guarded and protected me, and now I'm kicking myself for ever doubting that you loved me. And," he added with bright-eyed enthusiasm, "I remember what guardian angels are. Now I don't have to play Charades."

Overjoyed, I swept him into a tight embrace.

"Oh my God!" I squealed, squeezing him. "Do you know what this means?" "What?" He laughed and squeezed me back.

"We can go home because you passed the test!" I exclaimed brightly. "We need to confront Death as soon as possible. We need to - ."

Teddy silenced me with a kiss, his lips firm and insistent. Backing me up against the wall, he cupped my face, his lips gently tugging on mine as he tenderly kissed the corner of my mouth. When he pulled away, his eyes were bright with yearning.

"Come to my bedchamber as soon as you undress," he stroked my face. "I want you more than I've ever wanted anything in my life. No more excuses. No more teasing. I'll be waiting."

Teddy kissed me one last time before stalking down the corridor, tall and purposeful.

Now *that* was a way to seduce a woman.

~

I crept out of my bedchamber, the train of my nightgown whispering on the marble floor as I moved like a shadow to Teddy's quarters. I clutched the dark shawl draped around my shoulders as I knocked on the ornate door. A splash resounded within the chamber and, a moment later, the heavy door creaked open. A sliver of Flora's porcelain mask appeared. As Cordelia tended to my needs, she served Teddy. I wondered if this arrangement was strange for the female shades, considering he'd once belonged to their ranks. Did they resent him?

"My lady," she dropped into a curtsy. "How may I serve you? I have just poured the young lord's bath."

My hopeful expression fell.

A bath?

The thought of another woman bathing Teddy rankled me, even though he'd wasted plenty of opportunities to hook up with the female shades when he was one of them. In many ways, they treated him like an irritating younger brother. Still, no woman was going to lay a finger on my man.

"Exactly," I forced a confident smile. "I'm relieving you of your duties for now. I will take over from here."

"But, my lady - ."

I pushed open the door and swept inside. "I insist."

Teddy's bedchamber was similar to mine, except the sky-blue tapestries that decorated the walls and the gold four-poster bed that came with a matching coverlet, a white gauze canopy enclosed around the exquisite furnishing, was a sharp contrast to my fiery red. Teddy leaned against the wall wearing a thin robe that flared at the collar, teasing a glimpse of his smooth chest. The dark eyebrows that overshadowed his green eyes rose as I entered the room, a lovely heat suffusing his cheeks. Flora curtsied again before ducking out of the room, but I paid her no mind.

Anticipation coiled in my lower belly as I imagined him slipping off the robe and dipping his limbs into the steaming water.

I arched an expectant brow, though a flirtatious smile twisted my lips. "Aren't you going to undress for me?"

The breath hitched in his throat as he pushed off from the ornate wall. My shawl whispered to the floor as he tugged on the sash around his tapered waist and slipped off the robe without meeting my gaze, allowing the flimsy material to pool around his bare feet. For the first time since making love in the cave bordering The Forbidden Lands, my eyes roamed Teddy's naked body. The lean, well-defined chest. The taut, flat abdomen. The subtle flare of his ribcage that tapered into an elegantly curved waist. The definition of his pelvis made my pulse quicken.

Ignoring the cock that stood at half-mast, I watched him cross the room in several long strides, his sac gently swaying with each step. He clumsily splashed into the copper tub, treating me to a swoon-worthy view of his small, pert backside. His long arms braced the edge of the tub as he awaited my touch with shallow, uneven breaths. I grabbed a bar of lavender soap from the nearby tray, lathered my hands, and smoothed my palms down the length of his arms, dropping to my knees behind him. My sudsy hands gilded easily over bare skin as I committed the curve of muscle and sinew to memory.

As I splashed water and soap on his shoulders, I brushed his dark curtain of hair aside and kissed his nape. Teddy's knuckles turned white as his grip on the tub tightened, though he didn't utter a sound. I imagined his eyes screwed shut and his breath caught in his chest, one furtive glance over his shoulder proving I wasn't entirely wrong. My teeth worried his earlobe and my tongue traced the shell of his ear as he leaned into my touch, a soft moan escaping his throat.

Encouraged, my arm snaked around his torso, my fingers 'accidentally' brushing his pink nipple.

"You like that, don't you?" I kissed the shell of his ear, a well-known sensitive spot for him. "You like to pretend you're sweet and innocent, don't you? But I know how much you enjoyed stroking my pussy the other night." I flicked his nipple again. "Who knew the quintessential boy-next-door loved foreplay with the thrill of being caught. Sex in the forest.

Sex on the beach. You name it. You're a filthy boy, Teddy Kershaw."

I had no experience with dirty talk, but I was determined to try. If I could verbally walk him through the act of making love, hopefully I could ease his anxiety. The pad of my index finger circled his nipple, another sensitive spot, until a much-needed pinch became necessary. Water splashed over the lip of the tub, soaking the front of my nightgown. The clinging fabric outlined my full breasts, the transparency leaving very little to the imagination.

"What are you doing to me?" He whimpered, his body's undulating movements disturbing the water's surface.

"I'm showing you how to make love," I kissed the juncture of his earlobe and jaw before marking the sensitive spot with my teeth.

A small yelp escaped him, but I licked the pain away as I wrapped both arms around his waist and lathered his body

with soap. Most often in romance novels, the heroine falls in love with the alpha male type, the one that takes charge in the bedroom, not the shy, sweet, sensitive underdog. By all accounts, I should be in love with Death. Teddy losing his memory should be a tragedy, but I'd come to realize through courting him that I enjoyed playing the aggressor in our relationship.

Traveling through the Underworld with no way of protecting myself aside from my magic had made me feel powerless but learning to please him made me come alive. Based on the Hades and Persephone myth, my captor and I should complement each other perfectly. Instead, I found my complement in Teddy. In some ways, our friendship didn't make sense because we were so different, but we managed to bring out the best in each other. In the end, that was all that mattered.

My hands wandered every last inch of his body, except for his cock. Each time my hands glided down the length of his body, his muscles tensed as though bracing himself for the desired contact, a barely perceptible sigh of disappointment slackening his body when I avoided his throbbing length. I knew I was a shameless tease, but I wanted to see how far I could push him before he cracked. I *wanted* him to pounce me. I *wanted* him to lose control. Teddy was sweet, mild, and soft-spoken, but I *loved* slowly torturing him until he came apart in my hands. There was something so incredibly sexy about a reserved man losing control over the woman he loved.

And so I massaged his scalp with expert fingers and carefully rinsed his hair with steaming water that poured down his back in rivulets, and I watched as his lips parted in a silent moan as his eyes fluttered closed. Once I finished washing his hair, I rounded the copper tub and leaned over the edge as the water splashed the front of my nightgown. The linen clung to my enogrged nippls, and I watched as Teddy's pupils swallowed the jade irises. He reached out and traced my sensitive areolas though the sheer fabric, and his shy touch made my stomach lurch. The raw power of eliciting such emotion in another human being surged through me as I filled a pitcher and poured the waterfall down my front.

Teddy watched through a haze of lust as I sauntered over to the large bed, the clinging fabric exaggerating the sway of my hips, and spread Nicole Kidman-style on the blue coverlet - ready, willing, and trembling from head-to-toe.

Never in my life had I acted so boldly. Making sure he watched my every move; I allowed my legs to fall open in both an invitation and a silent challenge.

"What are you going to do now that I'm soaking wet for you?" I purred like a wanton sex goddess, despite the frantic pounding of my heart.

My eyes flickered to the decorative sword mounted on the wall, similar to the one I'd used to defy Death. I writhed on the bed and clutched the front of my wet nightgown, as though aching to tear it off. Teddy's eyelids drooped in quiet longing, practically crawling out of his skin with need. "Are you going to cut this damn thing open or rip it off with your bare hands?" When he simply stared, slack jawed, I trailed my fingers down the length of my body and reached for the hem of my nightgown. "Or should I touch myself while you watch?"

A powerful wave of forbidden desire surged through me at the mere suggestion. Showing him I meant business, I squeezed my breasts and writhed on the bed, my chest rising and falling as I panted like every femme fatale I had ever seen in a movie. I watched through hooded eyes as he slowly emerged from the copper tub. The water sluiced down his glistening body, making me all-too aware of the pounding heat between my thighs as I struggled against the restrictive confines of my nightgown. Wanting him so badly that it physically hurt filled me with the sweetest misery, and I wondered if he felt the same.

I wanted more than his body, though. I wanted his sweet, shy half-smiles and sly looks. I wanted his tender, adoring gaze. I wanted his explosive laughter and the soft rasp of his voice. I wanted our inside jokes and playful arguments. I wanted everything he had to offer, but I didn't know how to make him fully remember. I tasted the mounting desperation of our kisses. What if he came to and realized he wasn't capable of trusting me, that jealousy would rule his perception of me forever? All I wanted was to make him feel desired, so I crooked my finger and admired the sway of his velvety sac as he removed the jewel-encrusted sword from its sheath.

Water pooled around his feet, tiny rivulets tracing paths down his pale body, as a glimmer of recognition flashed in his eyes. I bolted upright on the bed with hope fluttering in my chest, but the moment passed like a shadow. I found myself pressed against the soft mattress as he carefully slid the blade inside my bodice. The sword tore easily through the damp fabric, the metal clattering on the marble floor as he proceeded to make small tears all the way down to my hem, until I lay vulnerable and prone beneath him. The act of tearing open my nightgown in such a barely controlled manner was so deeply erotic that it transcended everything I'd ever read in old-fashioned bodice-rippers about swashbuckling pirates laying claim to their women.

Teddy crouched near my feet for a long moment and stared up the length of my body, his warm, sultry breath tickling my toes. Slowly, ever so slowly, he trailed succulent kisses up my body as he unwrapped me like a present, licking, nuzzling, and grazing his teeth up my legs, until he exposed the small thatch of hair between my thighs. Hypnotized, he massaged the feminine curve of my stomach, an area of my body I was self-conscious about, but he molded the extra flesh like play dough, reverent and curious all at once. I sighed, whimpered, and trembled in delight as he worshipped every last inch of my body, but whatever pleasure I had experienced was nothing compared to him discovering my breasts.

> The way his eyes widened when he saw them… the way he kissed them. The way he looked at and touched my body made me feel like the most beautiful woman in the world,

like I was the only one that mattered. Teddy kissed my breasts the way he ravaged my mouth. He devoured my nipples with a sweep of his tongue and grazed their peaks with his teeth, sucking and laving until they were red and glossy. He molded my flesh with the firm insistence of his strong lips. Knowing he'd forgotten how to pleasure a woman made every caress raw, sensual, and deeply moving, his actions stemming from a place of instinct.

"Why are you so beautiful?" He panted against my breast, trembling and bleary-eyed. "How could you possibly want *me*?"

At this point, Teddy's insecurity was more of a challenge to prove my love than a gut-wrenching betrayal. Instead of dampening my arousal, his doubts only stoked my desire, perhaps because his ache for reassurance made me feel needed.

"Let me show you," I shrugged out of the tattered remains of my nightgown and forced him to roll over onto his back.

My hair tumbled around my shoulders as he pressed quick, exuberant kisses to my lips, and I allowed my loose curls to trail his body as I kissed down the length of him to his weeping cock. Small drops of pre-cum leaked from the divet, and I hungrily licked them away, enjoying his salty, musky taste. A sharp cry of surprised pleasure escaped his throat.

God, I loved how unguarded his reactions were, as though he was incapable of holding anything back.

Teddy arched his lower back off the bed and screwed his eyes shut, his damp hair a tangled fan on the pillow, as I licked and sucked until he snarled his fingers in my hair in a desperate plea for me to stop.

"I need…" Teddy's chest heaved with each sharp, asthmatic pant. "I need…"

"Don't worry," I crawled up his body and straddled his hips, "I know exactly what you need."

My inner walls stretched to accommodate his length as I lowered myself onto him. I couldn't resist grinning triumphantly when his eyes rolled back and as I undulated my hips in a slow, serpentine fashion. The feel of his cock stroking my tight, wet heat made my toes curl as a heaviness settled in my breasts.

"I love the way my pussy feels wrapped around your cock," I blushed red-hot with my use of these spicy sentence enhancers, unsure if I was using them effectively.

Teddy grunted an unintelligible response as his hips bucked against mine, the slap of our flesh renting the air, but he somehow managed: "What… does… it… feel… like… for… you?" He convulsed beneath me. "Tell… me."

"I feel whole again," I whispered in his ear as I nuzzled my cheek against his. Teddy sat up and wrapped his lean, powerful arms around me as I circled my hips in some semblance of a sultry lap dance. "To be honest, I was terrified you would no longer want me."

Teddy's thumb smeared the lone tear winding a path down my cheek as he urged my hips to stop with his free hand. I wanted to grind my hips in silent protest, the sensation too powerful to ignore, but I obeyed.

"While I don't remember everything from our past," he panted breathlessly, "I don't think a world exists where I don't love you."

Hearing that declaration on his lips lifted a heavy weight from my chest I hadn't known was there. For the first time since entering the Underworld, hope filled my heart until it overflowed. An untimely sob wracked my body. Embarrassed, I sought refuge behind my hands, but Teddy gently uncovered my face. Cupping my cheeks, he captured my mouth in the sweetest, gentlest kiss I had ever tasted.

Leave it to him to transform my filthy sexcapade into something far more meaningful. The kiss intensified, sending a bolt of electricity straight to my core, as he lifted me in his arms and rolled me onto my back without once breaking eye contact.

"It doesn't matter if I remember the past," he moaned as he slowly rolled his hips against mine, bracing my thigh as I wrapped one leg around his waist. "All that matters is the here and now. Korey, I don't ever want to be parted from you, not even in death. I will fight to keep you. You are my purpose, my reason for living."

"Teddy," I gasped as I curled my fingers in his tangled hair. "I love you so much."

Resting his sweaty forehead against mine, he panted as his thrusts roughened. "And you are my heart, my world, my *everything*."

Our lips met, only to be torn apart seconds later as pleasure rocketed through every part of my body. The sight of my head tossed back, my expression contorted from the sheer bliss of our union, made Teddy fall to pieces in my arms. Briefly, I wondered what sex must feel like to someone with no memory of the past. If him grabbing me thirty minutes later for round two was any indicator, I'd say it was pretty mind-blowing.

~

"Once we're back home, I can teach you how to drive, how to use an oven, how to bake chocolate chip cookies," I mused aloud in the aftermath of our lovemaking.

Teddy's head rose and fell with my breathing, and I absently stroked his hair as I made plans for our future.

"Your family will be heart-broken when they learn that you have no memory of them," I prattled on, "but we'll explain that you hit your head on a rock. Everyone will have to simply hope for the best."

Teddy lifted his head from my chest and studied my face for a long moment, his eyes searching.

"What's wrong?" I sat up in bed.

Alarm bells rang in my head as he touched my face, his brow furrowed deeply. After a moment, he stroked the hair back from my face as his piercing stare softened into a look of pure adoration.

"I know your face," he murmured slowly, making my heart stop. "It's haunted my dreams for centuries."

"Are you messing with me?" I shoved his chest.

"We're neighbors, aren't we?" His eyes shone bright as though a lightbulb glowed from within. "We met in second-grade. You saved me from Conrad and his gang. I remember the first time I saw you. You were missing a front tooth and scrunched up your nose when you didn't like something. I thought you were an angel."

My eyes frantically searched his serene expression. "Is that all you remember?"

"Well," Teddy shrugged, "I know that you're a little shit for trying to brainwash me into thinking *Moulin Rouge!* was my favorite movie."

The dead-pan delivery was achingly familiar. I searched his face and found vestiges of that guarded quality he'd always possessed, and I could tell he clung to its security now, for every line of his face betrayed his intense vulnerability.

"Teddy," I whispered as tears streamed down my face. "You're back."

A look of guilt flashed across his face as he rubbed the back of his neck.

"I can't believe I ever doubted you," he laughed humorlessly, not quite meeting my gaze. "Have you ever

loved someone so much and waited for so long to be with them that it blinds you to reason? I wasn't lying before. You *are* my world, Korey. I've spent so many years convincing you to see me as more than a friend that I never gave you the chance to fight for me." Tears dripped from the tip of his nose. "You actually sacrificed your life for me." At last, his bloodshot eyes met my own. "You really love me, don't you? And I was too blind to see it. I was too - ."

"Hey," I wound my arms around his neck and cradled his head to my chest. "Don't beat yourself up. I'm grateful you gave me the opportunity to prove my love. This should be a happy moment."

"I know," his voice wobbled, "but I feel like I've failed you. How could I ever doubt you?"

"Teddy," I cupped his tear-stained face and kissed his forehead and eyelids. "The past is gone. All we have is the present. All that matters is our love for each other. Time will heal all other wounds."

He leaned forward and kissed me full on the lips.

"I love you, Korey," he whispered breathlessly as he pushed me back onto the bed, every movement purposeful. "God, I love you so much."

As he settled his weight on top of me, I realized how hard he was. I tasted relief, passion, guilt, and affection on his tongue as he ravaged my mouth. The weight of our shared history welled between us as deep, abiding love and arousal became one.

Unlike before, Teddy frantically consumed me as though making up for lost time, our tears mingling with our soft, whispered moans. We kissed long and hard as his body slowly moved in tandem with mine, each stroke powerfully languid.

"I love you, Teddy," I murmured against the shell of his ear as he ravaged the crook of my neck.

He emerged red-faced and panting before he claimed my mouth in a searing kiss.

"Say it again," he demanded as he thrust into me.

"I love you, Teddy," I tangled my fingers in his hair.

"Again," he growled as his thrusts grew more erratic.

I said those three little words over and over again, until pleasure transformed my voice into a high-kenning cry that pushed him over the edge. We poured our hearts and souls into each other, reliving within the span of seconds everything we had shared, and, in that moment, we truly became one.

Beautiful Crime

The next morning, Teddy and I walked hand-in-hand to Death's throne room, where the god himself lounged on his throne. I'd sensed Flora's surprise the moment she discovered me tangled in the sheets beside Teddy, but there was no shock in Death's amber eyes as he quietly brooded, as though he'd foreseen the impending confrontation.

"Have courage," I whispered, squeezing Teddy's hand as we steadily approached the dais, a gesture he returned with equal reassurance.

"To what do I owe this pleasure?" Death smiled thinly, a deep reservoir of bitter resentment boiling within him.

"We've come to request that you relinquish your hold on us, for Teddy has passed the test you gave him," my voice wavered as I spoke, and I covertly wiped my sweaty palm on my modest gown.

Death arched a dubious brow. "Has his memory been restored?"

"Yes," I lifted my chin. "He remembers *everything*."

For one, imperceptible moment, Death froze.

"Is that so?" He mused in that familiar detached manner. "Well, he is free to leave as soon as he wishes. As for you… I've decided to keep you for myself."

"*What?*" Teddy and I shouted in unison.

Death shot us both an annoyed look.

"Do you really think I would have forgotten your betrayal so easily?" His fingernails dug into the arms of his throne as he leaned forward. "Do you honestly think I care about your supposed love? No," he shook his head. "Not after enduring centuries of Esme's hollow commitment as she pursued the mortal who had forsaken her. You see, he drank from the river, preferring oblivion over her love and, no matter how hard she struggled to restore his memory, he clung to his ignorance like a child. Meanwhile, I waited with bated breath for the day she would love me. That's right, Korey. My love for her was pitiful and weak. I allowed her to break me when no other woman had. By the time she came to her senses, I was long gone, completely out of reach. I vowed that no other woman would make a fool of Lord Death, but then *you* came along. I will not allow you to make a fool of me again, so your life is sufficient payment for your callousness."

I opened my mouth to speak, but Teddy pushed me behind him as he drew out his sword with an ominous hiss of the blade.

"You're going to release her," he warned in a low voice, "or I will make you look even more foolish for losing to a pathetic, spineless mortal like me. Isn't that how you've described me in the past? How does it feel to have created such a worthy opponent from mere scraps?"

Death eyed Teddy dangerously.

"So it's true," he smirked. "Your memories *have* been restored. I recognize that familiar loathing in your eyes. I never thought it possible for a mortal to regain his power so quickly. Not even Esme's great love can boast of such success. What's your secret?" He tilted his head to one side. "Were you simply tired of trailing after Korey like a lovesick puppy? But you've always done that, haven't you?"

Heat suffused Teddy's cheeks.

"It isn't hard when you truly love someone, when that person is your entire world, and you would do anything to come back to them," he murmured quietly, not rising to Death's bait. "I sense your pain. Your loss. Don't make yourself the villain of your own story because you are intent on escaping defeat. I'm sorry for taking her from you, for turning your dreams to dust, but enough is enough. The game is over. Now it's time for Korey and I to go home."

Death's upper lip curled as his features contorted from some unreadable emotion. Some mixture of rage and grief, I assumed.

"How dare you sympathize with my plight, you insolent boy! Your cheap words have fallen on deaf ears."

"Maybe I understand more than you think," Teddy sheathed his sword. "Once upon a time, I thought I loved a young woman that crushed my soul. Her betrayal gutted me. I never thought I would move on or find happiness, especially as a shade, but Korey was proof that my story wasn't over. If Korey walks away from you today, I don't

believe yours is, either. You just have to let go and trust that everything is going to be okay."

A play of different emotions flickered across Death's face. Desolation, grief, resentment, and pure, unadulterated fury. Within seconds, he was on his sandaled feet and had drawn his dagger as he descended the steps of the dais. Without a second thought, I blocked Teddy's body with my own, not giving either man a second to register my actions. The dagger pierced my gut and tore through the other side as Death thrust with every ounce of strength he possessed. I choked on a gasp as blood rushed up my esophagus. The pain was so blinding in its intensity that my body immediately went numb as I slumped forward.

"NO!" A ragged cry tore from Teddy's throat as Death instinctively unsheathed his blade from my stomach.

Death's bloodless lips trembled in a wordless plea as he stared at the blood-stained metal. Warm blood gushed from my mouth, staining my lips a ruby red. Teddy cradled my body as he eased us onto the marble floor, my limbs as limp as a rag doll's Tears streamed down his splotchy face as he rocked me back and forth, those salty tears dappling my face like stars.

I couldn't speak.

I could scarcely breathe.

All I heard was the violent sobs that wracked Teddy's body and the clatter of Death's blade as he staggered, looking stricken. My memory served up images of Teddy

cradling my frail body at the end of each lifetime as he sealed the bittersweet victory of his lifelong mission, but my life wasn't supposed to end like this. Not so young and without the promise of another life cycle at our fingertips.

This was our official good-bye.

We had run out of chances to make things right.

"We were so close," my best friend repeated in that desperately broken voice. "We were so close..."

"I-I love you, Teddy," I managed in a halting voice.

"Don't say that!" He touched my face, my hair, my slackened jaw, and drooping eyelids. "I'm going to take care of you, like I always have. You're going to live, Korey."

"No," I shook my head, already accepting defeat.

I wanted to say that he no longer had to worry about me, that he could go on without me, but I wasn't selfless enough to let him go. The very thought of another woman being able to touch, kiss, and talk for hours about everything and nothing... the pain was worse than the dagger in my gut, worse than blood-stained lips and ruptured organs.

I *wanted* to live.

I wasn't ready to die, and the sheer unfairness of the situation made me weep.

"You're not leaving me," Teddy shook me. "I'll follow you into the dark. I'll follow you anywhere if you promise to wait for me."

I reached blindly for his face and clumsily stroked his cheek, and I savored the warmth of his palm as he covered my hand with his own.

"Don't… don't worry about me," the words tore from my lungs, releasing another wave of tears. "I'll be here. I promise. I…"

"No!" Teddy cried as my hand fell away from his face. Burying his nose in the crook of my neck, he rocked me until I was fast asleep. "I love you, Korey. I love you too damn much."

The rest, as they say, was history.

Bodyache

My spirit didn't hover over my body and the scene of my untimely death the way others with near-death experiences had described.

Instead, I dreamt that I was a child once more playing outside on a bright, winter day with Teddy. We created snow angels and rolled around until we were cold enough to beg for hot chocolate from the neighbors. That day was the fullest day I'd ever lived because I was present in the moment. So often children long to grow up and see themselves fulfilling whatever dream that played in their minds as they drifted off to sleep, only to long for the simplicity of their childhood once they're fully grown.

Not that day.

Not that small snapshot of time.

It was strange to realize that I never once foresaw the end of my story. I never imagined how Teddy and I had lived hundreds of lifetimes together. That we were meant to be. As it turned out, however, death was capable of keeping us apart. Just not in the way I had expected.

After what seemed like an eternity, I regained consciousness - first, through my sense of touch. My body rested on a light, airy cloud that mirrored how I was feeling on the inside. I was naked beneath a downy coverlet that both chilled and warmed my bare skin. The air was thin and cool as it passed through my chapped nostrils, and I barely suppressed a shiver as my limbs slowly stirred on what I

now realized was a feather mattress. My mind was like the surface of a still pond, calm on the surface as a million different thoughts struggled to break through the haze.

Slowly, my eyes cracked open, my vision blurry as I blinked once, twice, three times. My eyes focused on a white, ornately carved baseboard with intricate vines spiraling upward. In fact, the entire room was white, resembling some abandoned cathedral with its vaulted ceilings and stained-glass windows, except… the white, cobalt, and winter blue panes of glass depicted a queen ruling amidst clouds and an endless backdrop of glittering stars. The stone, too, wasn't exactly as it seemed, more like crystallized glass or ice.

Well, that would certainly explain the chill.

Not even the fire roaring in the hearth could warm this vast space, its presence more for decoration than for practical use.

"Did you sleep well, young Korey?" A rich voice, softer than a sleepy exhale, caressed my eardrums and I turned my attention to the most beautiful woman I had ever seen.

The woman's blonde curls were piled high on top of her head, secured with ornate, jewel-encrusted bands that made her twinkle in the white light. She wore an Elizabethan gown with a wide, voluminous skirt, puffy sleeves, and a white frill around the collar that emphasized her regal bearing. Strands of pearls wound around her neck and jewels glittered on her long, delicate fingers. I studied the design on her icy blue gown, gold filigree threaded with

pearls that looked more opulent and splendid than anything I could ever imagine. This woman looked like a fairy godmother come to life and, the moment the thought crossed my mind, I remembered being impaled on Death's blade.

"Am I... dead?" I croaked.

The woman's mouth crooked. "Not quite. We saved you before your soul could pass through the Underworld, so in a sense you currently exist in a state of limbo." Her laughter tinkled as she waved a regal hand. "We have longed to meet you for centuries, and I'm sure you have more than a few questions."

"Who are you?" I clutched the coverlet to my breasts.

"The celestial beings, of course," her eyes twinkled like glass shards in flickering candlelight. "Many centuries ago, your mother enlisted our help to rescue you from the Underworld. We did not expect Theodoros, a mere shade, to accompany you, but we decided to include him in the fabric of your tale once we recognized his pure love and devotion."

I sat back and considered her words. While I had always been grateful for Teddy's presence in my life, it seemed cruel to rope him into a situation like mine.

"More like you played games with him," I amended. "And me."

The celestial being tilted her head to one side and studied me with curious eyes. She possessed the same air of detachment that Death often expressed, yet I found her particular brand less unsettling. In many ways, her manner of speech represented the element of air, light and curious with a decidedly flighty nature.

"How so?" Her delicate brow furrowed. "We bound him to you so he could always find you. We ensured that you could never venture far without causing him severe discomfort. Now that you're able to remember your past lives, would you honestly trade your memories for oblivion?"

The souls who resided in the river basin had faced the same dilemma with only a single lifetime under their belts. If I never saw Teddy again, would I spend the remainder of my existence dwelling on what I couldn't have or drink from the river?

"Why go through the trouble of erasing my memory, binding our souls, and treating my virginity as a prize to be won if I was only meant to die?" My voice rose in accusation. The celestial being seemed unperturbed, as though she'd expected this reaction. "Why give me special powers that only attract plague and suffering because of Death's narrow-minded pursuit? Do you realize how many lives were wasted in this ridiculous game?"

The woman's eyes darkened as she considered my words.

"You were never meant to die, but Death's lapse of judgement when he plunged his dagger into your gut was always meant to be. Death and Theodoros were tested so they could grow and change for the better," her whispery voice echoed in the vast space.

Finally, I was being given the answers to every question I'd longed to ask. I had an idea of what Teddy had been forced to learn, but what about Death? Was he capable of growth and change?

"What do you mean?" I asked.

"Both Theodoros and Death once suffered the tragedy of loving, or at least, wanting someone who couldn't love them in return," she began serenely. "While Esme eventually came to desire the ruler of the Underworld, her timing was off. In an act of rebellion, she nearly destroyed his entire kingdom out of sheer desperation to rekindle his love, so he banished her. Meanwhile, Theodoros married a young woman he had coveted for many years, a person who had overlooked him in favor of a trusted friend. Both committed atrocities, one in taking his own life and one taking the life of another, but these mistakes converged with you at its epicenter. Blinded by desperation and heartache, Death only saw you as a prize to be won, whereas Theodoros saw you as a second chance at a life he had forsaken. Some might call your mother overprotective, but she only guarded you because she understood how wicked men could be. From the moment Theodoros' life was restored, your mother knew he was the son-in-law she had long since craved. We also recognized his value. Initially, restoring his life was a simple reward for his bravery in escorting you home, but he made it plain that he wished to marry you. That he loved you. And so we bargained with him because we saw his wounded

heart and lack of faith in his own worth. At the same time, Death clamored for your return, so we bargained with him, as well."

Most of this information I already knew, but it was reassuring to hear it directly from the source.

"But my virginity?" I interjected. "Both Teddy and Death believed that I would belong to them if they claimed me first, thus eliminating my choices."

I expected her to look abashed, but instead her eyes twinkled with silent mirth.

"Oh, the choice was always yours," her mouth twisted wickedly. "That tiny detail was my own form of trickery. Men often suffer under the delusion that a woman belongs to them once they lay physical claim, an idea that is preposterous. Both

Death and Theodoros needed an incentive to fight for you, which was the possibility of losing you to the other."

Accepting this answer for its surface meaning was a tough pill to swallow.

"Teddy experienced intense anxiety and heartache because of your deception," I pointed out. "And what if I had been raped?"

The celestial being's expression flattened. "I hardly think Theodoros would have done such a thing."

"I'm not talking about him," I huffed impatiently. "I'm talking about Death." Comprehension dawned on her delicate features.

"Ah, yes," she mused. "The indulgent one you nicknamed Decadence. I doubt he would have forced you. The point of the test was to reveal each man's true character. While Death may not have coerced you, he certainly would have used his means of seductive trickery, the only way he knows how. As for Theodoros," she flashed me a meaningful look, "he had the advantage of arranged marriage for many centuries, but he only took your virginity when he was absolutely certain that you loved him in return. Unwilling to accept anything less, he patiently stoked the flames of your courtship, no matter how often you initiated intimacy. As the world evolved, it became harder and harder for him to express his love, requiring higher levels of patience and dedication than before. This lifetime has been especially tough for poor Theodoros. The moment news of your magic became widespread, he knew it was only a matter of time until Death came for you. Yes, I am quite convinced that he has redeemed himself and earned your eternal love."

"What about me?" I shrugged. "Where did I fit into this equation? How was I tested?"

Delighted surprise lit the celestial being's face, as though she hadn't expected me to ask.

"There was nothing for you to prove, my child," she smiled warmly. "All that was required of you was to have courage, embrace your womanhood, and grow deeper in love with Theodoros. We expected very little of you, but we were impressed with your strength and the power of your

love. Not once were you obligated to teach Theodoros how to be human again, yet you filled his days with familiar creature comforts. Instead of grieving the loss of his memory, you embraced the new beginning with zest, charm, and an extra dose of naughty teasing, I might add."

The celestial being's light teasing made me blush. Most of the time, I'd had no clue what I was doing or if I was making the right decision.

"Who exactly are you?" I craned my head with narrowed eyes. "I had never heard of the celestial beings until I was abducted. Are you some sort of god?" I searched around me. "Is this heaven?"

"Not exactly," she smiled ruefully. "The celestial beings are merely storytellers who weave the thread of each mortal's life into a rich tapestry."

She had revealed enough to make me crave more.

"Were Teddy and I fated to be together?" I asked.

"Fate, chance, coincidence," she said airily. "Call it whatever you like."

She was giving me the freedom to decide, and I knew deep in my heart that Teddy and I were meant to be. If that was the case, what was I doing here?

"What happens now?" I ventured warily.

"What would you like to have happen?" She tilted her blonde head to one side. "Would you prefer to remain

here in our realm, or would you like to return home as though none of this had ever happened?"

The answer seemed obvious, but I picked at my cuticles in quiet uncertainty.

"What will become of Death if I return home?" I couldn't resist wondering aloud.

"Taking your life through violence was a necessary means, for nothing else would have shocked him from his tirade," she explained. "Death is a misunderstood creature who has endured an eternity of loneliness. Don't fret, my child, for his story is continuing to unfold in unexpected ways. You'll see."

Now that I knew Death wouldn't come for me, the way forward was clear.

"I want to go home," I said in a small, wavering voice.

I'd been utterly lost since accepting Death's hand in pursuit of my best friend. The celestial being slipped a magic wand tipped with a shimmering star from her sleeve.

"Very well," sparks showered from the star as she waved the wand over my head. "Be free, my child. I wish you luck on your new journey. May you live a long, happy life."

The moment the star touched the crown of my head, a vacuum sucked me out into space. I found myself tumbling through the air before I landed flat on my back on the banks

of a familiar river. The landing should have killed me, but instead I heard Teddy's frantic voice.

"Korey?" He shook me violently. "Oh God. Korey, wake up!"

The first thing I noticed, aside from the trembling of my body, was that his stammer hadn't returned. We were no longer bound. As if waking from a deep sleep, my eyes fluttered open as I gasped for air. My body ached. My head throbbed.

But I was *alive*.

Teddy threw his arms around me as I sat up and drank in our surroundings. The chasm that had opened upon Death's command had been sealed. The once gray, overcast sky now shone gold and periwinkle blue. The river babbled as it weaved a path through the forest. The air reeked of fresh soil, dew drops, and pine.

"Teddy," I pulled away from him so I could study his face. "Was that all a dream?"

Dried blood caked the side of his face from the gash on his forehead. Tears streamed down his face as he touched me everywhere - my face, my hair, and my red floral dress. He looked at me as though I were the dearest person in the world. I couldn't resist returning his adoring gaze and tentatively touching his wound. He flinched, but he never once tore his eyes from my face.

"More like a nightmare," he choked on a sob as he caressed my cheek. "Oh, Korey. I almost thought I lost you. I was prepared to follow you. I begged Death to take my life, but he refused."

I gently covered his mouth with my fingers and shushed him. "I'm so incredibly relieved that we're home, so I don't want to think about Death now. We need to take you to the hospital. I'm worried you might have a concussion."

Teddy leaned on me for support as I wrapped one of his lanky arms around my neck and hauled him to his feet. As we left the banks of the river, the back of my neck prickled with awareness. Glancing over my shoulder, I caught sight of a dark figure leaning against a tree, his garb modern and sophisticated, his black hair swept back from his face.

Death's amber gaze met mine, holding me in suspense for a long moment before his full mouth crooked in a weak half-smile, his eyes deeply mournful. I watched as he moved behind the tree trunk and disappeared. Somehow, I knew that was the last time I would ever see Death, a thought that brought equal measures of relief and sorrow. In many ways, he had tortured me with his cruelty, but I remembered the way his presence had often intoxicated me.

As I cradled Teddy's weight, I doubted the celestial beings hadn't sought to test the strength of my love. I could breathe easier now knowing that Teddy and I were free.

Forever Young

The sky shone a brilliant blue as we stumbled our way through the forest. Teddy and I stared heavenward, unable to tear our eyes away from the sun and white, billowing clouds. The air was perfumed with the scent of pine trees, sweet mountain rain, and wildflowers. Never again would the dry, acrid smell of brimstone fill my lungs. We hardly spoke as we made our trek, too blinded by the beauty of our world to speak.

Eventually, we made it back to Pebble's Creek, and I ignored the gasps of passerby as we made a beeline for the small hospital at the far end of town. Once inside the lobby, Lena, a young woman who had never concealed her infatuation for Teddy, gasped and clutched her chest.

"What on earth happened?" Her round blue eyes fixed on his pale face.

In the past, I had always teased my best friend over Lena's obvious adoration and attempts at flirting, but now something feral growled in my chest, making me want to bare my teeth like a wild animal. I sucked in a deep breath to maintain my cool.

"We were standing on the edge of the small cliff that overlooks the river when he fell headfirst on some sharp rocks," I explained coolly. "He's awake and seems aware of his surroundings, but I'm afraid he might have a concussion. He needs to be seen right away."

"Of course," she said in that irritatingly sweet voice as she handed me a clipboard. "Please fill out his information first."

I grabbed a sunflower pen and began filling out the paperwork, surprising myself with how much I already knew. Lena eyed the way Teddy leaned on me with his head on my shoulder, a subtle look of distaste curling her upper lip.

"You know," she began primly, "you two might consider finding another pastime. The river is far from the hospital and, to be honest, seems a little childish."

"Where else are we going to have dirty, unapologetic sex?" I couldn't resist wiping the smirk off of her face with my shameless rebuttal.

Teddy snorted softly, lifted his head, and planted a kiss on my cheek. "I love you, Korey."

I stroked his hair as he rested his head on my shoulder. "I love you too, pickle."

Lena bristled as I handed the clipboard back to her.

"Please take a seat," she said coldly. "We'll call him back shortly."

~

Hardly anyone was in the lobby, so Teddy's name was called quickly. The nurse pushed him in a wheelchair so I no longer had to support his weight, but to be honest, I missed his warmth and faint musk that was a heady blend of

sweat and morning dew. The laceration on his forehead required seven stitches, and the doctor was careful to probe his head for further injury.

Teddy changed into a hospital gown, and I squeezed his big toe for support while he received a CAT scan. The nurse and doctor watched our interactions carefully, for they had known us since we were children. Everyone in town knew we were inseparable best friends.

"I always knew the two of you would someday end up together," the doctor eyed me sagely. "It was only a matter of time."

"Are we invited to the wedding?" The nurse jokingly added, making me blush.

Had our budding romance been obvious to everyone, except me?

While Teddy waited for the results of the CAT scan, I excused myself to call his parents and my own mother. His parents hadn't worried at all because they'd assumed we were together. My mother, on the other hand, raced to the hospital to wrap me in a tight embrace.

"Oh, Korey," she stroked my hair as she clutched me to her. "I was so worried about you two. The bastard finally came, didn't he? How did you escape?"

I pulled away from her to search her face. "You knew?"

"Oh, honey," she stroked my hair again, "I've always known. I've been there every step of the way. Who do you think was responsible for guarding you? Someone had to beat back the tidal wave of boys."

My brow furrowed. "Even Teddy?"

"In my opinion, Teddy is the only one that has ever deserved you," she sighed, "but that relationship needed to evolve naturally so you were ready for the challenges presented to you when you-know-who popped back into the picture." Her hands ghosted down the length of my arms as she studied me appraisingly. "And I see you put up a pretty good fight."

"It's over," I said, a weight lifting off my chest as I spoke the words. "Death will never come knocking on my door again. Not until it's my time to pass on. The cycle has been broken. And you know what? I think I'm ready to finish the final chapter of my story with the love of my life and my memories intact."

My mother wrapped her arms around me and rocked me like a child. "That's all I've ever wanted for you."

~

I loved watching Teddy's family fawn over him. While his mother cradled his wounded head to her breast, his three older brothers who were equally as tall but twice as thick, nearly crushed him as they each hugged him in turn. Teddy had endured many lifetimes of feeling like the black sheep of his own family, and I hoped he realized how loved he was and that perhaps being the black sheep wasn't such a bad thing, after all. I visited Teddy everyday as he recovered at home, and his older brothers teased me endlessly for tending to his wound.

"Korey, you're going to spoil him if you keep babying him," they offered me a cheeky wink as I rubbed ointment on Teddy's stitches. "Pretty soon he'll be ringing a bell for you to wait on him hand and foot."

"You're just jealous that you're not in his shoes," I retorted with equal sass. "I've seen you with a cold before. I seem to remember your girlfriends rubbing your head as you sniffled like the big, tough men that you are."

When Teddy's family wasn't around, he caressed and fondled me like an old man in a nursing home who couldn't resist the young nurse assigned to him.

"Stop!" I swatted his hands. "You're recovering."

"But I feel fine," he complained before wrapping his arms around my waist and dragging me onto his lap. "I need you."

I collapsed on his lap and wrapped my arms around his neck. "What does your family say about your stammer?"

"They assume hitting my head on a rock cured me," he shrugged with a wry grin. "Since that's a more likely explanation than the truth, I simply nod like the shy, quiet boy I've always been."

My eyes dropped as I mustered the courage to ask something that had bothered me since returning from the Underworld.

"I have a question," I began tentatively. Teddy merely stroked my cheek and waited for me to continue. "If you were absolutely convinced I was going to choose Death over you, why was it so simple for you to make that decision to trust me? I don't feel like I did much to convince you otherwise."

"You didn't do anything?" He echoed, as though he'd tasted something foul. "You were willing to sacrifice your life for me not once, but twice. Once I knew that, regardless of whether or not I remembered our history, I was convinced. But there's so much more. When I was at your mercy, you never took advantage of me, except for trying to hoodwink me into believing *Moulin Rouge!* is a good movie. And, to be honest, I only ever said I disliked it because watching a saucy movie like that with you sitting beside me only exacerbated my longing. Now that you know how I truly feel, I haven't forgotten your offer to reenact scenes for me. I don't think I ever truly doubted you, but myself. Death made me feel like less of a man, and I knew he had the power to seduce you. It also helped that I found you completely irresistible during those weeks I couldn't remember a thing. Like I once told Death, loving you is easy - even when everything else is hard."

I captured his lips in a sweet, rather heated kiss that made him whimper softly. I relished the softness of his lips as we each sucked in a long, deep breath. When we parted, he looked as dazed as I felt. His throat worked as he swallowed hard.

"Now I have a question for you," he said as he moved me off his lap. My breath hitched in my throat as he slipped off the bed and knelt before me. "Korey," he reached inside his back pocket and withdrew a simple gold band engraved with flowers, "I can't wait anymore. This ring has burned a hole in my pocket for years. Will you… will you marry me? Let's get out of here. Like now. I don't want to waste time on wedding plans. I've daydreamed about this forever, and I've always imagined us eloping to some remote place. Please, I can't live a second more without you."

The silent plea in his eyes broke my heart.

"Of course, I want to marry you," I cupped his cheek, "but I don't want to elope. I want to marry in front of our friends and family, the people who have watched our love story unfold from the beginning and wear the clothes we wore the night of the spring festival. You know, my red dress and your flannel shirt. Imagine flowers exploding overhead as we stand together at the makeshift altar. Imagine marrying by the river, a place that has seen us through all of our adventures. Imagine us driving out of town in your pick-up truck with cans dragging behind us and confetti falling from the sky. Doesn't that sound magical?"

Teddy's eyes glazed over, deep in thought.

"Now that you put it that way..." One corner of his mouth curled in a half-smile. "Let's do it."

"Tomorrow?" My eyebrows traveled up my forehead.

"Why not today?" He suggested with a shrug. "I mean, why not?"

~

And that is how Theodore Kershaw and Koreyna Sakis decided to marry.

Running hand-in-hand throughout Pebble's Creek, they spread the news of their impending ceremony by word of mouth. The news spread like wildfire. The town ventured through the forest late that afternoon to gather around the riverbank where the pair had once made their vows under entirely different circumstances. A beaming Teddy wore his ratty t-shirt, long-sleeved flannel button-down, and jeans, whereas Korey wore the red dress he had secretly loved for years with flowers in her wild mane of hair.

The town watched as the pair recited their vows and exchanged rings, a gold band for Korey and one made of twine for Teddy. The sky that day was a brilliant blue without a single cloud in the sky, the scent of pine in the air. Once their union had been sealed with a kiss, Korey sent fireworks exploding in a shower of silky petals overhead, making the crowd erupt in rapturous applause. Korey stole a glance at her new husband, doing a double-take as rose petals rained upon his head, reminding her of the first time they had married upon returning to her village.

Nothing held them back as they ran like children through the forest and climbed inside his pick-up truck.

Korey glanced out her window as he turned the ignition and caught sight of her mother, the one person aside from Teddy that had protected her. She blew her a kiss and, to her delight, her mother caught it.

"Don't worry," she shouted over the rev of the engine. "I'll come home."

"Get out of here," her mother jerked her head with a small smile. "I haven't had a date in centuries. Do you honestly think I'm that worried?"

Hand-in-hand, the newlyweds drove away from Pebble's Creek without a backward glance, unaware of what their lives held in store for them.

Teddy and Korey became the stuff of legends in the Underworld. The story told the tale of a young man who died and was reborn, and the childhood sweetheart that brought him back from the depths. And anyone involved knew all-too well that this description barely scratched the surface of the young couple's journey. For instance, the story didn't take into account the life they actually lived. How the pair traveled all over the world and provided relief for third-world countries still inflicted with plague. Eventually, they settled down in Pebble's Creek and co-owned a business. How Korey gave birth to their first and only child, a baby boy with green eyes and a thick growth of dark, curly hair.

River, they named him.

The story didn't account for how they grew old together, how Teddy died in her arms, and was buried by the river they had played beside as children. How Korey sat beside her husband's grave as she prepared for her own death. At the end of all things, Death, the villain of Korey's tale, embraced her spirit as she left her body and carried her across the midnight sky to the Underworld. The world below flashed images from Korey's life. She saw baby River nestled in her arms. She saw herself spreading life throughout the darkest corners of the world.

"Look at how much life you've lived," Death whispered in her ear, his voice no more than a gust of wind. "I regret ever wanting to take that from you."

Death carried her soul to The Land of Eternal Spring where the wood nymphs danced on the sward, the crowd parting to reveal a familiar figure clad in a worn flannel shirt. Those familiar jade eyes twinkled through his mop of dark hair, and Korey ran into his outstretched arms so he could pick her up and twirl her around in circles. The crowd cheered as they sealed their reunion with a kiss, the taste sweeter than it had ever been.

Korey had forsaken a life of immortality in favor of a normal existence, but the legends, in a way, kept them forever young.

THE END

Printed in Great Britain
by Amazon